UNDEAD
WITH
BENEFITS

Also by Jeff Hart

Eat, Brains, Love

UNDEAD

WITH

BENEFITS

JEFF HART

HARPER TEEN
An Imprint of HarperCollinsPublishers

JAKE

MY FIRST WEEK AS A ZOMBIE ENDED WHEN A DARK-haired psychic collapsed into my arms, blood curling out of her nose, her eyes wide and pleading with me. Behind us: a farmhouse where a horde of Iowan zombies were still snacking on recently massacred government agents. Around us: tall grass and the unconscious bodies of our friends, courtesy of some psychic mojo I couldn't even begin to understand. In front of us: the future, the great unknown, and probably a lot of walking.

"We need you to help us. To help me," Cass said,

all groggy. "Promise not to eat Tom. Promise, promise, promise . . ."

"Okay, I promise."

After that, Cass passed out and I was alone. In the middle of nowhere.

Well, Jake. What now?

The Most Perfect Day of My Life began in a grain silo, just after sunrise, somewhere in western Illinois.

I'm using the word *life* very loosely here, since I guess some people might argue that I'm not technically alive in the strictest sense. Sometimes my heart stops beating, my brain is reduced to animal functions, and my flesh rots. Most of the time, I'm totally normal, though. The living dead living it up.

So let's define *life* as the span beginning with my glorious birth, proceeding on through learning to poo alone and going to school and playing video games—all that uneventful, normal stuff culminating in my unfortunate contraction of a zombie STD. Since then I've teamed up with Amanda Blake (superhot, also a zombie) on a cross-country trip to find a cure for zombitis (not the technical term), which might be hidden away somewhere in Iowa. We've eaten some people, evaded government hit squads, had a few run-ins with other zombies of questionable sanity and friendliness, and met a teenage psychic who'd apparently been tracking us across the country. It's been a crazy week. That's *living*—it can feel lopsided sometimes, weighted toward the big moments. Anyway, I plan to keep doing it for a while, hopefully until my peaceful death from old age mourned by a grateful nation.

Or, more likely, in the not-so-distant future with a bullet to the medulla oblongata. The most hilarious-sounding part of the brain to get shot in!

But to christen this day—a Wednesday, maybe, it's getting hard to keep track—with being the Most Perfect Day of My Life, well, that doesn't leave a whole lot of room for improvement. I suppose that's partly because I've never been a guy who thinks much about his future, and partly because there's a good chance I might get killed pretty soon. Let's just call it Jake Stephens's Awesome Day, The Best So Far, With Strong Potential To Be The Best Ever, Or Definitely In The Top Five Because You Never Know. Jake Day, for short.

Jake Day starts in a grain silo.

Oh, also, I should point out that just because Jake Day begins with sex, it's not *all* about sex. Jake Day is about feeling just a little closer to normal in that lull period between horrible things happening. Everyone should have a Jake Day. Only with their own name inserted in place of mine. Or you can keep the "Jake" as tribute to me, the inventor of the concept.

I think part of having a really amazing day, like Jake Day, is being able to take a breath and actually realize how good things are in the moment. Jake Day is all about that feeling of rightness with the world. If someone told me to go to my happy place—if I were, for instance, being tortured by a zombie warlord—it's to Jake Day that I would retreat.

Jake Day is about feelings and stuff.

Feelings improved by the availability of sex, sure, but still. I'm talking about a higher state of emotional contentment here. And sex.

I'd been trudging along carrying both Amanda (did I mention she's my girlfriend?) and Cass (who was still passed out from the omega-level psychic bitchslap she'd delivered to Amanda), for what felt like hours—it was only forty-five minutes, but whatever—and the grain silo was the first structure with walls I'd come across. Also, when I say that I carried both girls, what I mean is that I'd carry Amanda a few yards, set her down, drag Cass a few yards, set her down, etc. At one point I might have tried tying them together with my shoelaces and pulling them through the fields like that, but apparently I'm not very good with knots and my feet kept slipping out of my sneakers.

The silo wasn't locked. I shoved Amanda's limp body inside. Then I propped Cass in a sitting position next to the door.

"You'll be our lookout, okay?" I said, my voice sounding extra loud at night in all that empty farmland.

Her head lolled to the side.

Kind of a dick move, I guess. She could've been eaten by coyotes and I would've felt bad about that. But I figured that if anyone came looking to do silo stuff (what do people do in silos, anyway?), them panicking over Cass's lifeless-looking body would give me some warning. I also worried that Amanda might wake up hungry, and wanted to keep some distance between the two girls.

"We'll be right inside," I told Cass, even though she was knocked out.

Before I'd been expelled (I assume) from Ronald Reagan High School for eating my classmates, my buddy Adam had tried convincing me to join the Agriculture Club. You'd visit a farm and milk cows for a gym credit. I didn't sign up because I didn't believe the New Jersey school system had the right to free labor from students, forcing us to pick cabbage for The Man, and also because I'm lazy. My buddy Adam did sign up, though, as part of some scheme to start growing his own pot in a shadowy patch of earth behind an abandoned barn. I think that was bullshit and he was just overcompensating for preferring horseback riding to rope climbing, but I ate him before the first harvest came in, so I'll never know for sure.

Anyway, point is, I'd never been inside a grain silo before. It was sort of like being in a hollowed-out rocket. The floor was covered in a layer of what looked like corn kernels that were ankle-deep at the room's sunken center.

Stacked against the walls were piles of burlap sacks and assorted pointy farming things. I pulled Amanda toward the center of the room and collapsed with her smack in the middle of all those kernels. I let out a groan of relief. The kernels were surprisingly supportive and comfortable against my sore body. I felt a little like the Scrooge McDuck of popcorn.

Overhead, metal beams crisscrossed at ten-foot intervals, leading up to an opening in the ceiling. I watched the night sky slowly lighten and listened to Amanda's steady breathing. Maybe I slept a little, although I was still pretty keyed up from everything that'd happened back at the farmhouse. The Necrotic Control Division had tracked us down and captured Amanda, with the help of an enslaved and feral version of her zombie ex-boyfriend Chazz. He got killed (boohoo), along with a whole bunch of NCD peeps, when a mob of bloodthirsty Iowan zombies led by a tomahawk-wielding nut job named Red Bear crashed the party. I guess at some point during the whole massacre thing Cass decided to quit the NCD and throw her lot in with us, which seemed to me like a real risky maneuver, but then I'm not exactly in a position to be questioning other people's bad decisions. Anyway, she promised to get us into Iowa, so I promised not to eat her friend Tom.

Big night.

As we sat there, I worried that whatever superpsionic

hex Cass inflicted on Amanda might've turned her into a vegetable. But only a little. Sure, I just met her hours ago, but Cass didn't strike me as the mind-wiping type. Even if her and Amanda had sorta gotten off on the wrong foot.

The sky was a bruised shade of purple when Amanda finally moaned and opened her eyes. The kernels shifted around us. At first there was a flash of panic on her face, but then she saw me and a shaky smile took shape.

"I'm alive," she observed.

"You are."

"We made it." She paused. "We did make it, right? Where are we?"

"A silo. What do you remember?"

She sifted a hand through the grains pensively. That hand ended up on my shoulder.

"I remember charging that guy. I—I was going to eat him. Then, um, I don't really know how to explain it. It was like when you turn off a TV and there's that one little dot left in the middle. That was me. My whole world was that little dot and then . . . blip. Gone."

"Huh," I replied. "Sounds kinda awesome, actually. Trippy."

"I thought I'd been shot in the head, Jake."

"Nah. The psychic girl did some kind of telepathic limit-break thing and knocked everyone out," I explained. "Probably didn't work on me because my brain's so huge."

Amanda stared at me, her eyes wide and watery, and I

realized maybe she wasn't quite ready for joking around. I brushed some hair out of her face because it seemed like a thing to do, to show her that her beautiful head and soft hair were still totally intact.

"We made it," I said. "We're fine."

Amanda grabbed my hand and entwined her fingers with mine. She was quiet for a moment. Outside, birds were starting to chirp.

"So, you said you loved me back there," she said, eventually. "And I'm realizing now I never said it back."

"Yeah," I replied. "It's, uh, no big thing. Just baring my soul and shit, that's all."

Amanda smirked at me and squeezed my hand. "I do, though. Love you back."

"Okay, cool."

"Cool," she repeated, deadpan. "Here I was feeling guilty and you say *cool* to me."

"Awesome?"

She stared at me.

"Stupendous?"

"Just shut up already," she said, and rolled toward me through the grain.

And that's where it happened, with a million pieces of unpopped popcorn as silent witnesses. The way I remember it, actually, some of the kernels did explode into fluffy popcorn blossoms, born from the heat of our lovemaking. Or not. But it was still different from all the sex I'd had before, serious and intense, each of us locked in on the other's eyes. There was this hey-we-almost-just-died desperation to it, like we might never get another chance, so we better make the most of this grain silo.

Let Jake Day commence!

Afterward, we walked outside, and Cass was still knocked out right where I left her. Amanda glanced at her, but didn't say anything. She was distracted by the horses. There were two of them, grazing right in front of the silo. In the dawn light, I realized they were a boy and a girl, or a mare and a steed or whatever. The mare was a tawny blonde and the steed dark brown. They didn't seem afraid of us at all.

My stomach growled.

Amanda looked at me. "Hungry?"

I nodded, still watching the horses. "How does that expression go? I'm so hungry I could . . . ?"

So, we ate them. I guess if Cass had woken up right at that moment, she would've been pretty freaked, what with the two of us all covered in horse guts, the flesh around our mouths that congealed gray it turns when we eat. Maybe it was because we'd just seen each other naked, but Amanda wasn't even all self-conscious like she gets sometimes while devouring living flesh. Except for all the anguished whinnying, it was a pretty beautiful moment.

JAKE DAY!

We started walking later that morning. The miles of wide-open farmland didn't seem as intimidating in daylight as they had the night before. It was slowgoing, mostly because I was carrying Cass over my shoulder. Amanda didn't offer to take a turn, not that I really expected her to.

Eventually, we found a creek and decided to try following it toward civilization.

"This is how the pioneers did it," I told Amanda. "They found water and it led them to Thanksgiving."

"Uh-huh," Amanda replied. She nodded toward Cass. "Should we try dunking her?"

"Come on, Amanda. Don't be mean."

"I don't mean, like, waterboarding her. Maybe if we splash her face, she'll wake up and do some actual walking."

I set Cass down at the edge of the creek and gently splashed some water on her face. She didn't move. Some of the dried blood around her nose and mouth floated away in crusty little islands. I looked at Amanda and shrugged.

"Maybe we should wash up too," I suggested. "We look like we just escaped from a Rob Zombie movie."

Amanda looked down at herself. Both of us were pretty covered in gore, some darkened and stiff from the night before, and some fresh from the horses.

"Yikes," she said. "You've got a point."

We washed up as best we could in the creek. It would've gone better if we'd actually had soap, but at least we managed to downgrade from total blood-soaked horror show to mildly filthy teens with suspiciously stained clothes. The sun was out and the creek water was surprisingly warm and refreshing. Something in me unclenched at that point. Even though I knew it wasn't logically true, it felt like we were finally out of danger. Amanda must have felt the same because soon we were splashing each other and laughing like dumb little kids.

We didn't even notice the fisherman approaching until he was just twenty yards away.

"Good morning!" he shouted, causing both me and Amanda to jump.

He was a middle-aged guy in a floppy khaki hat and those big rubber wading boots.

"Rough night?" he asked us, smiling. He'd noticed Cass passed out on the bank and must've figured we were just coming off a night of farmland partying. But then he noticed the pinkish tint to the water flowing toward him, took a closer look at our appearance, and his face fell. "Uh," he added, suddenly nervous.

"Real rough night," Amanda replied, grinning and stepping toward him. "You wouldn't believe it."

The fisherman took a step back. "I suppose I wouldn't."

"Say, mister," I began, a folksy twang in my voice,

because we were in the Midwest now. "You wouldn't happen to know which way the road is, would ya?"

The fisherman pointed with his rod in the direction we'd been headed.

Amanda turned to me. "You were right. Such a good pioneer."

I grinned at her, then stepped out of the creek and picked up Cass. "Much obliged," I said to the fisherman, and started toward the road. He hopped onto the creek's opposite bank as we passed, not wanting to be near us. Amanda lingered a few steps behind me, staring him down.

"You should forget you saw us," Amanda told the fisherman, her voice so sweet you could almost ignore the menacing, unspoken *or else*.

About a mile farther on, we started hearing car noises from the highway. The creek eventually burbled its way into a little park and picnic area—wooden tables, a swing set, a hillside overlooking where the creek fed into a larger river. It was the kind of place teenagers in the '50s drove out to for secret groping sessions. Only a beat-up maroon sedan was parked there now. It probably belonged to the fisherman.

Amanda opened the unlocked driver-side door, reached her hand behind the sun visor, and came away with a set of keys.

"Lucky break," she said. "Probably karma for not eating that guy."

"Karma shmarma," I replied, setting Cass on the ground so I could stretch out my arms. "This is the Midwest! Where people trust their neighbors enough to leave their keys in the car. Where strangers politely greet innocent if blood-covered zombies while out for a mid-morning fishing trip. I *love* the Midwest!"

Amanda went to the back of the car and opened the trunk. Inside was a picnic basket, which she immediately tossed aside, and a blanket, which she spread out across the trunk's grease-stained floor.

"Not bad," she said. "Plenty of legroom."

"Um, why can't we just use the backseat?" I asked, my mind wandering back to our glorious encounter at the silo.

Amanda narrowed her eyes at me. "Not for us. For *her.*"

I looked at Cass, pale and slumped against the side of the car.

"You want to put her in the trunk."

"Yes."

"That seems mean."

Amanda checked her reasons off on her fingers. "We're fugitives and she looks dead. We kind of kid-napped her. She'll be safer locked in there if one of us suddenly needs to eat."

"But . . ." I looked again at Cass, mentally urging her to wake up. A bug landed on her face. "That's where we usually keep, you know, *our food.*"

"It's not like that," Amanda replied. "It's for everyone's safety."

I sighed. "Okay, but we have to check on her, like, every hour."

"I'm sure she'll kick the backseat when she wakes up," Amanda countered, then put up her hands when I gave her a stern look. "All right, all right. Every hour or so."

Together, we lifted Cass into the trunk. I tried to set her down gently, but Amanda dropped her ankles before I let go of her armpits, so there might've been some clunking around.

With that done, Amanda turned on the radio and pulled me into the backseat for twenty minutes of making out.

JAKE DAYYYYYY!

"Fuckin' guys shooting nets at us," I said, feeling what I'd call hyperwistful, thinking about last night's scene at the farmhouse. It was like remembering clips from a really over-the-top action movie as seen through a strobe light while hopped up on one of those direct-to-the-heart adrenaline shots. "That literally happened to us. It figuratively blows my mind."

"I know, right?" Amanda replied. She was sitting in the passenger seat, rubbing my leg, because we still couldn't keep our hands off each other. We couldn't stop moving. "That guy with the hatchet?"

"Red Bear!"

"Who is *like* that?" she exclaimed. "Seriously, who does that? Who buys a hatchet?"

"Bananas. Bananas times one thousand."

We were only driving through some small town in western Illinois, but a powerful rush had come over me. Everything we'd gone through, plus the lack of sleep, plus hooking up with Amanda this morning—goddamn, I felt invincible. By the way she gripped my leg and how wide her eyes were as she scanned the passing storefronts, I could tell Amanda felt the same.

"There we go!" she yelled, pointing at the department store that anchored what was otherwise a completely vacant shopping plaza. I swerved into the empty parking lot and slammed the brakes, parking across two spaces because no painted line could contain me. I felt like a bank robber.

We barged into the store, startling the college-aged dude who stood behind the only open register. There was some horrible Michael Bolton soft rock on the store's sound system, but it was otherwise library-quiet.

"Shall we shop?" I asked Amanda, my voice echoing off the linoleum tiles.

"Hell yes," she replied as she snatched a pair of sunglasses off a nearby stand and shoved them on.

We were still wearing our creek-washed gore ensemble—well, I was anyway. Amanda pulled off her shirt as she walked toward the nearby women's department and tossed it aside. She took her time picking out a replacement, settling eventually on a blue-and-white, striped, sleeveless thing.

The cashier was staring at her—I had been too, of course, but I stopped before he did. When I started toward him, I noticed him gulp and glance toward the phone next to his register. He was trying hard to look at me without actually looking at me, like he didn't want to make eye contact. He was scared. I felt kinda bad about that, briefly. But at least we weren't going to eat him, right?

"Hey, dude," I said as I arrived at his register. "Can I get some shopping bags?"

"Su-sure," he replied. When he bent down to get them, I yanked the cord out of the back of his phone. Just in case.

"Don't make a big deal out of this, but we're not paying for any of this shit," I explained. "We've been victimized by the government."

"Okay, man. C-cool."

Amanda tackled me from behind, kissing my neck and ear, cackling as I stumbled into a table of impulse-buy cuff links and earrings. I grabbed her shoulders and kissed her hard. Distantly, I heard the cashier shudder. Who knows what he thought—likely that he was about to be murdered by a pair of horny psychos—a feeling I guess I could understand. We looked the part.

"Did you tell him to give us all the cash too?" Amanda asked me once we were finished kissing.

"Not yet," I said.

She spun toward the cashier and screamed, "Put the money in the bag, motherfucker!"

Jake Day involves some crime, okay?

After the store, it was at least half an hour of frenzied driving before our laughter subsided. We had a stolen car and stolen clothes, and a psychic who had promised to help us get into Iowa, where there was supposedly some kind of zombie cure. Granted, she was unconscious in our trunk, but still. We were in love. Life was good.

As the sun set, it started to feel like I was coming down. Amanda leaned her head against my shoulder drowsily. We passed a highway ramp toward Des Moines that was blocked by huge, orange detour signs. Neither of us mentioned it, but a few miles later Amanda spoke up.

"So, what now?"

I knew Amanda wanted to talk about our future undead-related plans, but I wasn't ready for that yet. Except for occasional breaks to make sure Cass didn't suffocate in the trunk, I didn't want to think about going to Iowa. I wanted to keep living in the incredibly consequence-free moment.

"I don't know," I replied. "We've got some cash. Motel room?"

"No, I meant . . ." Amanda looked up at me and must've read my reluctance, because she trailed off. "Yeah," she said after a moment, kissing my cheek. "That sounds perfect."

And it was perfect. Because it was Jake Day. All the heavy stuff didn't matter so much. We hadn't eaten all our friends, we weren't fugitives pursued by a shadowy government agency, and we weren't going to have to snack on something with a heartbeat sooner rather than later. Things were easy. Somewhere in Iowa, there was a cure waiting and we were going to find it. I mean, whenever we got around to it. Piece of cake.

Then Cass woke up and everything started to change.

CASS

COPING WITH TELEPATHY. THAT'S WHAT THE GOVERN-
ment called the special class crammed into the training
schedule for us psychic recruits. Not Your Mind Is Magical 101 or something equally positive. *Coping.* Because
our powers aren't meant to be enjoyed; they're meant to
be managed and endured. The class was three hours long
and met six times total, which is literally one-fourth of
the class time devoted to the Necrotic Control Division's
Headshot Techniques and Logistics course. Thinking
back, I'm not sure if the class was so short because the

government didn't know all that much about psychics, or because they didn't want *us* to know all that much about ourselves.

Our instructor devoted one whole session to nosebleeds. The prevailing wisdom was to recognize that the sight of blood meant you were going too hard. Also, always keep a pack of tissues handy.

There wasn't any time spent on blowing beyond your previously understood psychic boundaries by simultaneously knocking out two people at once. None of the pamphlets addressed what to do upon waking up in the trunk of a car driven by zombies, with no idea how long you've been unconscious for. And of course our instructors never discussed going AWOL from an organization you'd once had faith in because . . . because why? Sudden objections to living-on-undead brutality? Loneliness? A stupid schoolgirl crush? As I lay there, curled up and trying to figure out what I'd done and where I was going, the car pulled over. Two doors opened. Slammed closed. Keys jingled, clinked in the lock. Sunlight poured in and I had to shield my eyes.

"Oh, look," said Amanda. "Sleeping Boring awakens."

That's how I—a government-trained psychic—found myself standing on the side of a deserted country road with the two zombies I'd spent the last week of my life tracking across the country.

And one of them in particular looked less than happy to see me.

"All right, Magellan," Amanda said, one hand on her hip and the other pointing on the map to an empty spot of country on the southern border of Iowa. "We're here. Where's this secret entrance?"

Still clad in my bloodstained NCD jumpsuit, my hair matted and crunchy with sweat, I glanced between the freshly showered Jake and Amanda and felt the keen urge to dive back into the trunk.

"Guide us," Jake said, and my heart cooed like a little dove I wished I could've crushed the life out of. After all that time in his head, I was kind of thrilled to be talking to him in person. Except that was stupid. He didn't know me. I mean, they'd been keeping me in *the trunk*. I'd gotten myself into a dangerous mess, and I didn't know how to get out of it.

"We have no idea what we're doing," Jake continued.

That made three of us.

I accepted the road atlas from Amanda and pretended to study it while trying to mentally compose myself. Even through the haze of my telepathic hangover, the bloodbath at the farmhouse was painfully fresh in my memory, like a bad dream I couldn't shake. In exchange for saving me from the wild Iowan zombies *and* the corrupt Necrotic Control Division, who I'd learned had sinister plans of their own, I promised Jake that I'd escort him and his murderous girlfriend into Iowa. He'd kept his end of the bargain. Now, five minutes awake and out of the trunk, it was time to keep mine.

"Well?" Amanda prodded, dramatically holding her nose in the air away from me.

"Sorry," I replied. "I need a second here."

"The little Xs are roadblocks we already drove by," Jake offered, and pointed helpfully at the map.

"Oh, okay," I said, like I knew what I was talking about.

Unfortunately, I didn't know the first thing about Iowa.

As of last week, I hadn't even known for sure the place was quarantined. I'd heard rumors around Washington, but was never told anything official. I didn't know how big the zone was or what kind of security we'd face. I certainly didn't know how to get us in there.

"Hypothetically," I started, testing the waters, "what if the route into Iowa I know about isn't, um, open anymore? Or if I can't exactly remember the way?"

They both stared at me. Amanda clenched and unclenched her fists.

"I dunno," Jake said, shrugging. "Guess we'll figure something else out."

"Hypothetically," Amanda added, mimicking me, "we'd have to figure something else out to do with you too. For instance? Face eating."

"Jesus, Amanda," Jake groaned, rolling his eyes. "She's kidding."

I swallowed hard. It occurred to me then that maybe my decision to roll with the fugitive zombies wasn't my wisest. I'd badly wanted to bail on the NCD after my boss, Alastaire, revealed himself to be a zombie-enslaving psychopath, and most of my squad got killed. Going on the run seemed like a decent plan when I was desperate and shell-shocked. I guess I hadn't considered the high probability of getting eaten. Of course, I'd had other reasons for bailing on the NCD, primarily my totally inappropriate psychic crush on the undead guy who, for reasons that I now realized were totally naive, I didn't think would let anything bad happen to me. Depressed, alone, not being around people my own age for about a year, and living in other people's heads—yeah, Cass, sure, you're a good judge of character.

I rolled up the road atlas and clutched it.

"I need some time to figure out the best way in," I explained. The more I talked, the more unsteady I felt; my knees wobbled like string cheese, and a colony of floaters soared across my vision. "And I think I need some rest."

"You've been sleeping for days," Amanda countered.

"Rest outside of a trunk," I insisted.

"So picky." Amanda snorted.

I ignored her and appealed directly to Jake. "I'm not

one hundred percent. And I'm starving. Do you guys have any food?"

He glanced sheepishly at the car. I noticed a large cardboard box in the backseat. While I watched, something small and furry tried to scramble over the edge but couldn't navigate the flap and fell backward.

"Uh, probably not the kind you'd want to eat," he answered.

"So we have to feed her now?" Amanda muttered.

A pickup truck rumbled down the road, the driver slowing to gawk at us as he passed. I waved my hand up and down my filthy ensemble.

"I need new clothes too," I said. "Also, we probably shouldn't just be out in the open like this. We're fugitives, right?"

"We?" Amanda sneered.

"You think the NCD won't be looking for me after I bailed on them?" I asked, cocking my head at her. "Plus, after that mess at the farmhouse, they'll be looking even harder for you guys. We're not safe until we get into Iowa, and I need to pull myself together before we even think about sneaking in there."

Jake and Amanda exchanged a look. I noticed Amanda's cavalier attitude briefly slip. I didn't know for sure the NCD would be looking for me, especially with most of my squad dead and Alastaire hopefully bled out in a field somewhere. Without me to track them, though,

24

Jake and Amanda were likely as safe as they'd been since turning undead. Still, it seemed like a good lie.

"She makes some good points," Jake said.

Amanda sighed. "All right, but we're rolling down the windows."

Jake grinned at me. "Welcome to the Maroon Marauder! That's what we're calling the car."

"No we're not," Amanda said over her shoulder, already ducking into the passenger side.

Jake moved the cardboard box of furry things into the trunk and we got on the road. In the backseat, I tried to ignore all the plaintive squeaking coming from the trunk. I suppressed a shudder. That could've been me back there.

I was probably being a little too ambitious when I decided that, out of the two bags' worth of gas-station food Jake bought for me, I was going to eat the microwave burrito first. The cravings of the recently comatose are inexplicable, I guess. After that last bite of chewy tortilla shell and gooey, processed meat, I immediately felt sorry for myself.

Then I felt carsick.

Amanda didn't want me puking in the backseat or anywhere in her field of vision, so we cut the day's drive short. They bought two rooms for us at a seedy motel just off the highway in western Wisconsin. I didn't want to know where they'd gotten the money for the food and the rooms; I just wanted to get someplace dark and with better air circulation than a trunk so I could get rid of this throbbing headache and maybe, if my brain pains allowed it, come up with a plan.

I drew the blinds in my room and stretched out on the lumpy motel bed. It felt amazing; my bones and muscles seemed to gradually uncrinkle, like how a dried sponge expands when you pour water on it.

I must have dozed off. I woke up when someone knocked on my door. Still half-asleep, I expected to find Tom standing outside with orange juice and donuts. Instead, it was Amanda with a bag of clothes from a nearby outlet mall. My heart sank—those days of NCD-managed TLC were over—but I kept my face stony for Amanda.

"Here," she said, handing me the bag. She didn't wait for a thank-you, immediately breezing off to the room next door, where Jake waited for her. I was actually glad she kept it short and bitchy; she'd eaten Harlene, and a pile of clothes that ranged purposefully from boring-as-heck to straight-up dorky wasn't going to make up for that.

At least they were clean. I did appreciate that.

I spent the rest of the day poring over Jake's road atlas. It looked to me like the highways in western Iowa terminated before Iowa City and Cedar Rapids. I made a line in the road atlas, connecting the roadblocks, estimating where this mythical zombie barricade would be. It encompassed most of the state's eastern area. There were fewer towns in northern Iowa along the Minnesota border, and more hardly trafficked rural routes. That seemed like a good place to try slipping through. They couldn't have locked down every road into the state, right?

"Gotta start somewhere," I said to myself. My headache had started to clear and I could feel that familiar tickle of the astral plane out there, beckoning to me.

I wondered what Jake might be thinking.

No. None of that. No spying at all, in fact.

I tried not to listen to Jake and Amanda's muffled conversations through the wall. I think they were getting drunk. I also tried not to overthink my decision to stick with the zombies. I owed Jake and had nowhere else to go. Simple as that.

It was a long, lonely night.

And by midafternoon the next day, we were going nowhere fast.

"Well?" Amanda asked, catching my eyes in the rearview. She drove while Jake napped in the passenger seat.

"Keep going until you see the exit for route fifteen," I answered, studying the road atlas that was open in my lap. "We'll try that one."

"Try," repeated Amanda dryly.

27

"Well, at least we're in Iowa," I said defensively.

"Iowa wasn't the deal," she replied. "*Infected* Iowa: that's what we want. And anyway, I think we crossed the border back into Minnesota."

We'd spent all day hopscotching across the Minnesota-Iowa border. I had made a lot of fresh *X*s in the road atlas and was steadily running out of northern routes to try. At least we knew that the NCD quarantine didn't extend across the Iowa border in a perfectly straight line, although that seemed like a pretty trivial detail. More important was the frightening scope of the NCD's operation.

Some of the highways led into detours that just kept on in a circle, always more phantom roadwork to keep you doubling back toward Minnesota. Others ended in roadblocks formed by government standard-issue black SUVs. We were always too cautious to approach those, but I didn't need binoculars to recognize the NCD jumpsuits turning away cars. We hadn't seen anyone get through.

It was the biggest Containment job I'd ever seen. How they'd been able to make such a massive space disappear without anyone asking questions made my skin crawl.

I used to think playing psychic spin doctor for the NCD made sense—we wouldn't want to start a panic after just a few isolated zombie attacks—but if we'd lost an entire state? That should be on the news, the president doing that whole somber "My Fellow Americans . . ." thing.

Five minutes of uncomfortable silence later, the familiar orange detour signs started to pop up. Amanda disgustedly shook her head and stepped on the gas. I added a fresh *X* to the road atlas.

"Have you even been to Iowa?" she asked me.

"Not personally, but they briefed us on emergency access points. We just have to keep looking," I replied, trying to make this lie sound official. Then, for some reason, I kept talking. "I'm from California, originally."

"Who asked?" she snapped, and turned on the radio.

I went back to studying the road atlas, not sure why I'd bothered to share a detail about myself. I guess I expected more talking on my cross-country drives, but then maybe I'd seen too many '80s road-trip movies. There'd been only one conversational highlight so far, which at least proved life among the undead didn't have to be constantly miserable.

It just required Amanda not be around.

We'd stopped at a gas station that morning and I'd decided to stock up on provisions while I had the chance. I had the sinking feeling that microwaved convenience food was going to be my primary diet for as long as I stuck with the zombies. Lucky for me, this minimart had a better selection than most—single-serving boxes of cereal! white-cheddar popcorn!—so I was really loading up.

I noticed that Jake was wandering the aisles behind

me. He must've come in to pay for the gas. I stopped to watch him run his fingers longingly across a package of beef jerky. He let out a deep sigh that I interpreted as profoundly sad.

"Um, you all right?" I asked, stepping closer with my armload of people food.

"Huh?" I'd startled him out of some daydream. "Yeah, I'm cool. Just sorta jealous of all your options here."

"Oh," I replied hesitantly. "Yeah, gas-station burritos are really enviable."

Jake looked at me seriously. "They are."

I guess when you're used to eating small, furry animals to stave off human-sized hunger pains, you'll take anything. I tried to think of something that might make him feel better.

"Well, I'm a little jealous that you get to eat, uh . . ."

"Guinea pigs?"

"I'm jealous of the guinea pigs," I said quickly.

Jake grinned. "You're a bad liar."

"Where did you even get so many?" I asked, thinking about the huge cardboard box that occupied my former residence in the trunk.

"Pet stores," he replied, like that should've been obvious. "Actually, if you see one while we're driving, let us know. You can never have too many."

"Okay, sure." I paused, not wanting the conversation to end, but flailing for something to say. "Why guinea pigs anyway?"

"Cost-effective. And they're surprisingly dense, like, meatwise." I could tell Jake wanted to change the subject. He grabbed a package of Oreos from a shelf and looked at them longingly. "If I were you, I'd get these."

"Um, I'm more of an oatmeal-raisin girl."

Jake narrowed his eyes at me. "Oatmeal raisin? Ugh, you're ruining the vicarious eating experience here."

"Vicarious eating?"

"Yeah." He sheepishly rubbed the stubble growing in around his mohawk. "Yesterday I was watching you eat that pepperoni Hot Pocket and it was, like, I don't know, a spiritual experience. Is that weird?"

"Yes," I said, laughing. I was secretly aghast that Jake had watched me eat a Hot Pocket that I'd probably barfed up soon after, but also flattered. I think I might've blushed. "But I, um—I don't mind if you watch me eat," I added quickly. Then mentally smacked myself.

Where's a conversation supposed to go after that? Right into an awkward silence. Jake put the Oreos back and picked up a package of oatmeal raisin. He raised a dubious eyebrow at me.

"Ready?"

"As I'll ever be!" I chirped enthusiastically. Apparently, all that time focusing on psychic connections had rendered my social skills totally cornball.

Jake smiled at me, like he didn't notice or didn't care what a dork I was being. We paid and returned to the car. I made sure to angle myself so he could see me in the rearview while I ate my cookies. I couldn't really tell if he was watching me or not, and eventually he started snoring. He'd been asleep ever since.

I brushed some crumbs off the road atlas. What was I doing here?

I watched as a glimmer of drool formed in the corner of Jake's mouth and tried to figure out why I liked him. As if there weren't other, uninfected fish in the sea. As if I couldn't do better than cute-but-decomposing. He was cuter before he let Amanda shave that mohawk onto his head too. I should've gotten over this infatuation by now. Maybe I'd been lonelier than I thought in my eighteen months with the NCD. Maybe it was some kind of psychic sympathy—he was my age, his thoughts fun to spy on, and I needed a friend. Who knows? I could plant a feeling or thought in someone else's mind, but I couldn't explain exactly why Jake had taken root so firmly in my own.

I'd been staying out of his head, though. No more telepathic eavesdropping, not since we'd been together. I thought Tom would be proud of me for that. Actually, he'd probably lecture me for sticking with them and tell me how I was responsible for all the people they'd eat now and in the future. I kept telling myself that I owed Jake. I was suddenly a deeply honorable person. These two might be mass murderers, but I made a promise that I'd help them get into Iowa and find the cure. Now that

I'd disowned the NCD, I needed a new cause. Maybe that could be assisting disenfranchised zombies. I could take applications and personal essays, choosing the undead candidates who tried the hardest not to eat people.

I didn't want to admit to myself that maybe I was hanging around because I hoped something might happen with Jake and me, even if I couldn't imagine how that would work.

Anyway, I told myself, I hadn't actually helped Jake and Amanda yet. Not really. I was just a passenger. There was still time to get over my weird crush and do something moral and upstanding. I just needed a little more time.

And that's when the trooper's siren first blared.

At first, I thought it was a sound effect in one of the club remixes Amanda stole from the most recent gas station. Then I noticed the flashing blue-and-reds behind us. Jake jumped awake, wiping his face with both hands and staring around wide-eyed.

"Oh crap," he said as he glanced past me, out the back window. "How fast were you going?"

"Sixty-five, I swear," Amanda replied. "I don't know what this pig's deal is, but . . . oh."

"What?"

She tapped her finger on the speedometer, which still hovered at sixty-five even though we'd pulled over to the shoulder. "It's stuck."

"And you're just noticing this now?"

"I steal the cars. I don't, like, inspect them." Amanda looked over her shoulder at me. "Shouldn't you have seen this coming?"

"I'm not clairvoyant," I told her.

"So you say."

"Oh, c'mon, Amanda," Jake interrupted before I could reply. "Give it a rest."

We all turned to watch the trooper approach in the rearview. He was a well-built middle-aged guy with that swagger you see on a lot of cops, plus the big aviator sunglasses and a toothpick tucked in the corner of his mouth. He already had his book of citations out, flipping the cover open and closed, like he couldn't wait to get started.

"Looks like a dick," Jake and I said in unison. We stared at each other in surprise for a moment, and I mumbled, "Jinx," but he'd already turned back to Amanda.

"What're we going to do?" he asked. "We have, I don't know, a lot of criminality happening here."

"Don't spaz out," she replied, and pulled the front of her tank top a half inch lower. "I get out of these all the time."

The trooper wore a chunky class ring on his middle finger, with a big amethyst stone that I thought might crack the driver-side window with the way he knocked against it. Amanda obediently rolled it down and the cop took a step back, sucking his toothpick and eyeballing the three of us, his thumbs jammed through his belt loops.

"License and registration," he said, overenunciating every syllable so it sounded more like *lie-cents and reggie-stray-shin*. However you pronounced them, we didn't have either.

I'd never been pulled over before, on account of my enlisting with a covert government organization before my road test. My few interactions with local cops over the last year had involved me flashing an NCD credential and them looking seriously bewildered. All that is why it only gradually dawned on me that we—three fugitives in a stolen car with no paperwork and a trunk filled with small animals—were in a bit of a jam.

"Oh my god," Amanda bubbled, a sudden girly lilt in her voice, like she'd just jumped out of this cop's birthday cake. "I'm so sorry, officer, but my car is totally broken."

She tapped the speedometer and the trooper leaned his head in to check it out. As he did, Amanda subtly arched her back and leaned toward the window. I rolled my eyes. Next to her, Jake kept his fingers tightly laced across his belly. He stared straight ahead, wide-eyed and stiff, which I put down to the innate panic of stoners when faced with badges.

"Uh-huh," the cop said, having seen enough. He leaned out of the car and dully repeated, "License and registration."

"Aw, don't be that way," Amanda replied, and I

couldn't tell if that was really disappointment in her voice from her first attempt at sex kittening getting rebuffed, or just another helpless-bimbo put-on for the cop. She was good at this, I'll admit. "I'll get the car fixed right away, I promise. I'm really, really sorry for wasting your time, officer."

The trooper pushed his aviators up his nose with his middle finger and stared at Amanda, his upper lip twitching like he wanted to snarl. "You think you're the first piece of jailbait to try flouncing her way out of a citation, sister?"

"Oh, I'm eighteen, if that's what you're worried about," Amanda purred back without missing a beat.

Honestly, I'd been trying to be good about not invading people's psychic safe zones and about resting my powers after how hard I pushed myself getting us away from the Farmhouse, but I couldn't help it. I peeked at the uppermost layer of the trooper's psyche, wanting to see if Amanda was making any progress. Our incorruptible trooper was remembering the five-day sexual-harassment class he'd had to take after his *last* on-duty incident involving a buxom bimbo. And he was thinking how nice it'd be to get to pepper spray the kind of uppity, um, let's say *lady* that'd gotten him in so much trouble in the first place.

Like the suddenly much creepier agro-trooper had said, we weren't flouncing our way out of this one.

"I'm gonna start a countdown to ten, Miss Thing," the cop was saying when I broke psychic contact. "And if I'm not holding some papers when I'm finished, you're gonna get to see my nasty side."

Before Amanda could respond, Jake's stomach let out a thunderous rumble. I'd thought he was just nervous, but now I noticed that his skin had definitely lost some of its healthy glow.

"The hell," said the trooper, leaning away from the window.

Amanda gawked at Jake, the trooper momentarily forgotten. "Seriously? Right now?"

He shrugged helplessly. "I guess I didn't have a big enough breakfast."

The trooper pushed his sunglasses up his face, staring at Jake's unnatural pallor. "You all right, son?"

"Maybe you should get out of here, before you see *our* nasty side," Amanda warned the trooper, the sexpot act totally dropped.

It didn't look like the trooper was going to budge. He was weirded out, but I don't think he grasped that he was in grave danger of being digested. I decided to give him a psychic shove. It was just like working Containment for the NCD—we made sure witnesses believed our zombie cover stories by nudging their brains in the right direction. Here, I just amped up the flight portion of the fight-or-flight instinct anyone with a dangerous job quickly learned to trust. Later, it's unlikely the trooper would've been able to properly explain why he backed away from our car and then sped off down the highway—only that he had the sudden, intractable urge to get as far away from those three strange kids as humanly possible.

"Okay," the trooper said, backing slowly away. "Just drive carefully, please."

That left me as the only human in the area of one hungry zombie.

Jake stared at me, his breathing ragged and hoarse, his skin ashen.

"Don't look at me like that," I said.

"I'm—I'm not," he stammered, then practically flung himself out of the car, headed for the trunk.

"Make sure you eat enough this time," Amanda shouted after him. She watched the trooper's car disappear around a bend. "Still got it," she said to herself. She tossed her hair, dyed black with patches of blonde throughout. "I thought losing the blonde would be a major handicap. I'm sure you know what I mean."

I had more on my mind than standing up to Amanda for brunettes everywhere. My voice drowned out the panicked chittering of the guinea pig Jake had plucked from the trunk. "If he'd turned zombie just now, would you have . . . ?"

Amanda met my eyes in the rearview. "Protected

you?" She flashed me a wild smile. "Gosh, I don't know! Would've been interesting!"

My hands shook. I looked away.

After a few minutes, Jake returned looking normal again. He let out a big sigh of relief and smiled at Amanda.

"Sorry," he said. "Guess I got stressed there."

"It's cool." She plucked a piece of fur off his shirt. "All better?"

Jake nodded, then looked at me. It was the same disbelieving look he'd shot me when the trooper had first driven away.

"You did something, didn't you?"

"Um, what do you mean?"

"Like, you brainwashed that dude."

I shook my head. "Not exactly. I just, you know, nudged him toward wanting to go."

Amanda turned around too, and now both zombies were sizing me up.

"Seriously?" she asked. "You did that?"

Jake laughed at her. "Did you really think you convinced him with the power of boobs? Dude, it was like the start of a porno where instead of sex there's just a ton of Tasering."

Amanda gave Jake a dirty look and then turned away, starting the car.

"That was cool of you," Jake said to me, smiling. "Just

don't brainwash us. Okay?"

"I won't, I promise," I replied, with a solemn tone that made it sound like I was making some major pledge. Jake was only joking around with me, but I took it seriously. I was going to stay out of his mind for good.

Even if every time Amanda said something mean to me or did something casually intimate like pick a piece of dead animal fur off Jake's shirt, I thought to myself . . . *I could make him like me.*

That wasn't me. I really, really didn't want that to be me. But I could do it, if I wanted to.

Amanda still hadn't pulled back onto the road. She caught my eyes in the rearview again, a bit of mischief glittering there.

"So . . . ," she said, "what other tricks can you do?"

JAKE

IF YOU EVER MAKE FRIENDS WITH A GOVERNMENT-trained psychic, I highly recommend getting them to steal awesome stuff for you. It's the best.

The nearest place to test out psychic shoplifting was the sleepy burg of Pipestone, Minnesota. It was named for the local Native Americans' tradition of turning the area's magic rocks into pipes that allowed communication with the spirit world when you smoked from them. I read that in a brochure.

A town literally named for getting stoned. How could I resist?

Unfortunately, Pipestone turned out to be a buzz-kill. And not just because there wasn't a giant sandstone bong rising up from the horizon.

"This place is like a diorama," Amanda said.

"No kidding," I replied. "Do you think we might see a real-life tumbleweed?"

I'd never been to a place like this before, where it seemed like you could stand at one end of Main Street and see clear through to the other side of town. I'd never been to a place where Main Street was synonymous with Only Street. It was flat, the buildings no higher than two stories, the main road wide enough for a dozen covered wagons to pass side by side. Hell, we were in a place where it wouldn't be strange to see a covered wagon in the first place. Everything was so weirdly spread out. I suddenly missed the clutter of New Jersey.

There were a few people on the sidewalks and all of them turned their heads to watch us drive by. I think some of them even ducked into buildings and closed their windows, like when the bandit gang rides into town in one of those old westerns.

"Is there something off about this place or is it just me?" Amanda asked.

"It feels kind of like a ghost town that people forgot to leave," I said.

Amanda parked our car outside the Pipestone Trading Post and Gift Shop, an actual log cabin with signs advertising local crafts and hiking supplies. Apparently there was a big, rocky quarry and waterfall nearby, presumably where the ancestors of this town once mined for magic rocks before they died of boredom.

I turned around to look at Cass. She'd been pretty quiet since working her psychic mojo on that cop, although I'm sure Amanda replying to her every word with nuclear-level sarcasm didn't exactly encourage conversation attempts. She smiled weakly at me.

"So how does this work?" I asked her.

"Um . . ." Cass thought about my question. I could tell it wasn't so much that she hadn't worked out an answer, but that she wasn't totally convinced she wanted to tell me. "We'll go in and you'll take whatever you want up to the register. When the cashier asks you for money, just say . . ." Her voice dipped suddenly into spaced-out surfer territory. "Uh, hey, dude, I just, like, gave you a hundred, man."

I squinted at her. "Is that how I talk?"

"Yeah, actually," Amanda put in.

Cass smiled a little. I realized it was the first time her and Amanda had come close to agreeing on something.

"Just try to sound confident," Cass continued. "I'll handle the rest."

"Sweet," I said, clapping my hands. "Mutant-powers time!"

"What if it doesn't work?" Amanda asked.

Cass shrugged. "What do you guys normally do when you need something?"

"Steal it and run away," Amanda answered.

"Like badass outlaws," I added.

"If it doesn't work, do that."

Amanda shook her head. "I'll keep the car running."

"One last question," I said, stopping Cass before she could get out of the car. "Should we be worried that you might suddenly go all Dark Phoenix?"

Cass stared at me blankly. "I . . . don't know what that means."

"Just ignore him," Amanda said, rolling her eyes. "It's probably about comic books."

Inside, the first item to catch my attention was the grizzly bear. It was stuffed and mounted, up on its hind legs, flailing its paws and roaring. A price tag dangled from one of its claws. I raised my eyebrows hopefully at Cass.

"Um, let's maybe start smaller?" she replied.

Besides us and the bear, the only other creature in the store was the withered old man hunched behind the cash register. He looked like the type who'd have a banjo close at hand and probably had a ton of stories about "the Japs." He sucked on some hard candy judgmentally, watching as I inspected a rack of hand-carved stone Native American pipes.

"Sup," I said to him.

He wrinkled his forehead at me in response. "You aren't from around here," he observed.

"Nah. I'm from back east," I replied casually, remembering my sophomore-year community service at the old folks' home and how much they liked hearing a young person talk. "Just passing through."

"That's wise," said the old man. "You won't want to linger."

He turned away from me, busying himself with something behind the register. Cass had sidled up next to me.

"I feel like we're in the beginning of a horror movie," she whispered.

"I know," I whispered back. "When does the guy with the leather mask burst out of the back room with a chain saw?"

She shuddered, but grinned at me.

I picked out one of the cooler medium-sized pipes. The thing looked like a hybrid between a flute and a crowbar, and was decorated with beaded leather tassels and what I assumed to be authentic American eagle feathers. I held the pipe up for Cass to inspect.

"This good?"

She shrugged. "I don't know. It's your, uh, paraphernalia."

I snorted. "Paraphernalia. Who calls it that?"

Cass looked a little embarrassed. "Sorry. I've never actually done that," she said, waving at the pipe.

"Oh man!" I exclaimed. "We've gotta smo—"

"Decorative use only," barked the old man, interrupting.

I examined the pipe again. "Psh," I muttered. "We'll see about that."

On my way to the register, I also grabbed a black cowboy hat off a rack. It wasn't exactly Johnny Cash level—the material seemed more like cheap felt than whatever actual cowboy hats are made out of (cowhide? I dunno), but it looked badass. And I was a zombie outlaw now, so why not?

This was the point where I'd usually just strut out the door, brazen stealing having become our style over the last couple days. Instead, I glanced over my shoulder at Cass. She was biting her lip but gave me an encouraging nod.

I set the items on the counter in front of the old man. He sighed, like I was disturbing him.

"Let's call it fifty dollars," he grumbled.

I looked him in the eyes, trying to really amp up the incredulity. "Dude, I just gave you sixty bucks. Where's my change?"

For just a second, there was annoyance and disbelief on the old man's face. But then it was like something passed through his field of vision: his eyes momentarily lost focus and his pupils got all big. He shook his head once, sharply, like he'd just dozed off, and then opened the cash register. He handed me ten bucks.

"My mistake," he muttered, rubbing the back of his head. "Thank you for your patronage, son. Be careful out there."

I managed to play it cool until we were outside the store. Then I turned to Cass, wide-eyed and grinning. "Dude, I can't believe you can do that! It's amazing!"

"Dude," she repeated, deadpan, her hand dropping away from her face. She'd been pinching the bridge of her nose. "Yeah. I guess it's pretty cool."

"Did it actually work?" Amanda asked. She'd gotten out of the car and was peering at a bulletin board posted outside the trading post.

I pushed my cowboy hat down on my head and tipped the brim toward her. "What does it look like?"

"Like maybe I should be in charge of making our shopping list, so we end up with more than goofy hats and bongs."

"It was just a test run! Now that we know the psychic credit card—no offense, Cass—is working, we can get serious about our supplies." I paused. "What do you even pack for breaking into a government quarantine zone?"

"I've got some ideas," Amanda replied. She started back toward the car, but first jerked her thumb at the bulletin board. "Maybe that explains why this place is so creepy."

I took a closer look at the board. It was absolutely covered with MISSING notices. Almost all of them were teenagers and almost all of their disappearances had taken place within the last six months. But the one thing every flier had in common? Every missing face was last seen somewhere in Iowa.

"How is this not national news?" I exclaimed, glancing over at Cass. "You NCD people must have hella good PR dudes."

Cass didn't look all that interested in the bulletin board. She still lingered on the sidewalk in front of the shop, a distant look on her whiter-than-usual face. I thought about how she'd fainted after using her psychic hoodoo back in Illinois and worried she might be about to pass out or something. As soon as I took a step toward her, she snapped out of it.

"Everything okay?"

"Yeah," she replied, keeping her voice quiet, probably so Amanda wouldn't overhear. "I'd just never done that before."

I squinted at her. "What're you talking about? I've known you for like three days and I've already seen you straight knock people out with brainpower."

"No, what I mean—I've never done it like *that* before. For personal gain, you know? Breaking the law."

"Ah," I replied sagely, catching on. "With great power comes great responsibility."

"Spider-Man. I know that one," Cass said, smiling a little.

"So," I started tentatively, turning the pipe over in my hands, a symbol of our ill-gotten telepathic gains. "Is this going to be weird for you? Because we can just steal shit the old-fashioned way. You don't have to help if this, like, violates the psychic code or something. I get it."

"There's no code," Cass replied, staring down at her feet. "It's nothing like that. I just—" She sighed and looked up at me. "I kinda liked it, okay? Does that make me a bad person?"

I tried not to laugh. This girl had messed with just one old man's brain and was now asking me—a guy who'd literally messed, as in, smeared on my face, more than a couple brains—my thoughts on morality.

"I'm probably not the best person to ask," I answered honestly. "If it's any consolation, pretty sure you're the least criminal person in the car. And doing it this way is less public for us, less rampagey, you know? Safer for humanity."

Cass snorted. "Very heartening. Thanks."

"No problem," I said, and then, without really thinking about it, I tossed her my black hat. She caught it against her chest. "Welcome to outlaw life."

"Outlaw life," Cass scoffed. "Let's hope I don't end up on a wanted poster."

"Or one of those," I said, pointing toward the bulletin board.

Amanda honked the horn impatiently. As soon as

I'd climbed into the car, she pinned me with one of her dagger-sharp glares.

"What was that about?" Amanda hissed, jerking her chin toward Cass. Our conflicted psychic was studying the bulletin board now, turning the black hat over in her hands. After a moment, she resolutely plopped the hat on her head.

I stifled a laugh, realizing only then what a goofy wardrobe choice the cowboy hat was.

"Just a pep talk," I said to Amanda. She kept staring at me. "What? She's not as used to the lifestyle as we are."

"What lifestyle is that, exactly?"

"You know, the criminal lifestyle."

"Criminal *undead*," Amanda stressed. "And no, she wouldn't be used to it because she's not one of us. Stop romanticizing things with stupid hats."

"I don't—that doesn't even make sense," I replied, flustered, not sure how or why we were fighting. "What's wrong with you?"

Amanda shook her head. "God, you're oblivious, Stephens."

"Really? I hadn't noticed."

"Durp durp," Amanda replied, rolling her eyes. "You're so funny. Everything's a joke."

Cass climbed back in the car and Amanda peeled out of our parking spot. I looked over at Amanda, wanting to ask her what I was being oblivious about, but also knowing she wouldn't want to talk about it in front of Cass. So maybe I wasn't that oblivious after all.

"What're we stealing next?" Cass asked from the backseat.

I thumbed through the marked-up road atlas. "GPS, for starters."

"Don't think this gets you off the hook for Iowa, Coyote Ugly," Amanda said, eyeballing Cass in the rearview.

Cass self-consciously touched the brim of her hat. She put on a good front, but I could tell Amanda was getting to her. It was like being back at RRHS, watching Amanda grind down the new girl until any in-crowd aspirations were undermined by shame-eating and that wild-eyed shakiness usually reserved for movie POWs fresh out of Vietnam. I thought we ditched this side of her back in New Jersey. I didn't like it.

I was about to say something when I noticed the blood.

"Look at that," I said, pointing toward a billboard at the entrance ramp for the thruway. The ad was for Kope Brothers Pharmaceuticals, some Iowa company that promised "a healthier tomorrow" for the happy family it depicted lounging in hammocks. I'd seen a lot of these ads out on the highways—that wasn't the eye-catching part. On this particular billboard, every family member was literally defaced by jagged skulls, and scrawled over the billboard's bottom half was a giant CUM 2 DEAD

MOINES, all in a very dark shade of crimson.

"They've been here," Amanda said. "Those Iowa freaks."

"All those missing kids," I added, connecting the dots.

"I hope that's paint," Cass said from the backseat.

"Me too," I replied.

It definitely wasn't paint.

CASS

WE DROVE TO OMAHA BECAUSE THE CITY NESTLED right up against Iowa's western border and yet hadn't been swept into the quarantine zone. Also, Jake and Amanda figured that a bigger city would provide better opportunities for psychic-assisted shoplifting.

They were right.

We hit an electronics store first. Picked up a GPS and a Nintendo 3DS that Jake explained he couldn't live without. After he came back to the car with video games instead of something remotely useful, Amanda decided she wouldn't sit out any more shopping trips. So that pretty much ruined my day. And not just because I'd had fun wandering the store with Jake, listening to him ramblingly explain why some game called Metal Gear Solid should've been called Metal Gear Flaccid, thinking about that moment with the cowboy hat and how he'd totally been flirting with me, and ignoring my inner Tom warning me not to mistake kindness for romance.

It ruined my day because the psychic stuff was easier with Amanda.

We hit a camping-supply store for a tent and sleeping bags, a shoe store for boots and sneakers, and every pet store we could find in the GPS. Which meant I'd taken an active hand in Nebraska's guinea-pig holocaust, so I wasn't feeling good about that. At every one of those stores, when Amanda approached the dude/guy/lecher behind the register and sweetly explained that she'd already paid, it was incredibly easy for me to slip into their minds and make them believe.

Because they wanted to believe the hot girl. These sad retail boners hung on her every word.

It made me want to die.

The worst one was our last stop of the day, a coffee shop a few blocks from our hotel. We spread out around a table in the back; Jake busy with some game where an elf in green spandex shot sword lightning at little trolls, Amanda scanning the room like a bird of prey, and me trying to enjoy the spiced ginger coffee and homemade Milano-style cookie I'd bought with some stolen money. The cookie was amazing, actually; it made me feel just slightly less gloomy, and the sugar helped the achy brain I'd been dealing with.

There were a few young people sitting at tables, artsy guys mostly, sipping coffee and working on their laptops. When one of them put his computer away and stood up, Amanda jabbed me in the ribs with her elbow.

"Go time," she said.

"Ow," I replied.

"Never say *go time* again," snickered Jake, without looking up.

"Shut it," Amanda shot back, already on her feet.

With Amanda leading the way, we cut off Laptop Guy before he made it to the door. He was short—shorter than Amanda, actually—wearing some baggy jeans, sandals, and a coffee-flecked T-shirt. His immediate reaction with Amanda standing in his way was to try straightening his unkempt brown hair.

"Hey," Amanda said, all demure sweetness, pointing at his laptop bag. "I think you grabbed my computer by accident."

In the time it took Amanda to speak, I'd slipped gently up against Tim's mind. That was his name, by the way. I knew that now. There was a dull ache behind my sinuses—maybe I'd pulled this trick too many times today—but I pushed ahead anyway.

"Uh," Tim said to Amanda.

Why is she talking to me is this my laptop wow she's hot I'm so stupid just an accident where's my laptop, Tim's mind said to me.

Just an accident was the phrase I plucked out of Tim's stream of consciousness and pushed forward.

"Shoot, sorry, it was an accident," Tim said, handing over his laptop bag to Amanda. "I have the exact same one . . . at home?"

Yes, Tim. At home.

"It's totally cool," Amanda said, smiling. "I do klutzy stuff like that all the time."

"Say, maybe I could buy you a coffee to apologize," Tim said hopefully.

"That's okay," Amanda replied, gesturing at our table. "I'm here with my boyfriend."

Tim looked momentarily crestfallen but then, remembering something, reached into his back pocket and pulled out a flier. He thrust it at Amanda and she plucked it from his hand with two fingers, avoiding the part he'd sweated on.

"If you're not doing anything tomorrow, you should come by the demonstration," Tim said as he backed toward the door. "I'll be running the drum circle. Well, as much as one can run a drum circle." He chuckled awkwardly.

"Awesome!" Amanda declared with faux enthusiasm. "Except I have a noise allergy to bongos, soooo . . ."

I'm sure Amanda forgot about Tim the moment he was out the door. Poor guy was just a means to an end. Meanwhile, Tim would go home, gradually come to the realization that he'd given his laptop away, and live the rest of his life with the humiliation of that time in a coffee shop when he'd been grifted by a bimbo and then stupidly asked her out. It didn't seem fair.

"You're good at that," I said quietly to Amanda, my gaze tracking across the coffee shop to Jake. "Conning nerds."

"Huh?" Amanda replied, distracted by Tim's flier. "Are you talking?"

She breezed back to our table before I could respond. Jake watched her coming with a grin, making grabby baby hands at the laptop. I sighed and followed.

"It's like Christmas!" Jake exclaimed, yanking the laptop out of its bag. "I hope you asked that dude about the graphics card."

"No, dork, I did not." Amanda thrust the flier at him. "Look at this."

Jake hardly glanced at the flier. He shrugged. "Cool. A drum circle."

"Can I see?" I asked, tired of being out of the loop.

Jake handed me the flier. The thing was cluttered with images, like the people who made it couldn't decide which activist iconography they liked the best. There was the Guy Fawkes mask, a bunch of faceless soldiers marching in lockstep, and a headshot of the president with his eyes blacked out. Also, for some reason, a ton of lightning bolts. Sandwiched between all the clip art: *CITIZENS DEMAND ANSWERS TO SECRET GOVERNMENT AGGRESSION IN IOWA! TRANSPARENCY! NONVIOLENCE! DRUM CIRCLE! NOON @ CITY HALL.*

A few weeks ago, what I held in my hand would've been unthinkable. Protestors marching in a major city, asking questions to which the answer was, *Uh, zombies . . . ?* A public-relations nightmare for the Necrotic Control Division.

"Containment isn't working," I breathed, realizing only then that Amanda and Jake were both staring at me.

"Containment?" Jake asked.

"Is that some kind of gestapo term?" added Amanda.

"We're not the—I mean, they're not that . . ." I sighed and pushed my hands through my hair, frustrated with myself. My first reaction had been to defend the NCD. "Yeah, it's an NCD thing."

"What does it mean?" Jake asked.

Both zombies were looking at me with obvious curiosity. Feeling awkward and more than a little ashamed by my association with an organization so easily compared to evil secret police, I scanned the coffee shop for an out. It didn't seem like the best place to leak government secrets.

"We should get out of here," I suggested. "Laptop Guy might realize we scammed him and come back."

Amanda frowned at me, but Jake nodded.

"Good call. We gotta keep a low profile," he said. "You're a natural at the fugitive lifestyle."

"Thanks," I replied.

"But I still want to hear more about your life as a secret agent," he added with a disarming smile. "Let's debrief."

I spent plenty of nights in three-star hotels like Omaha Suites during my time with the NCD. My squad would rest up after a successful day of zombie hunting in the starchy beds, and Harlene would lead briefings in the musty conference rooms over freshly microwaved continental breakfasts.

We never used the pools.

All the lights were off except for the ones built into the rectangular pool's underwater walls; they bathed the whole room in a soothing, aqua-tinged glow. The pool's filter buzzed, a gentle ripple passed through the water, and shadows twisted across the stucco ceiling.

"*Cannonball!*" Jake screamed, the slapping of his bare feet across the rubber deck a sort of drumroll before he flung himself into the air, curled up, and plunged into the deep end.

According to hotel policy, there wasn't supposed to be any pool usage after 10:00 p.m. Even though it was well after midnight when we wandered down from our rooms, we didn't let any bold-font warnings about drowning get in our way. I'd felt a strange sense of accomplishment while watching Amanda and Jake jimmy open the pool's security door. I was one of the black hats now. The rules no longer applied. Debriefings didn't have to be boring anymore.

Amanda and I both took a step back from the pool to avoid Jake's splashing. She bent down to open the twelve-pack of spiked cherry soda they'd discovered on a trip to a nearby liquor store and presumably shoplifted without my assistance.

"Don't let him splash that," Amanda warned, glancing up at me and the stolen laptop I held protectively in my arms.

I looked over to where Jake was lazily backstroking. "Why'd he want me to bring this anyway?"

She shrugged. "He wants to show you something. But he's also ADD and wanted to go swimming."

I stepped around a pile of neon foam noodles and set the laptop down on a deck chair a safe distance from Jake's splash zone. When I turned back around, Amanda had stripped down to a black T-shirt and underwear and was swimming her way over to Jake. I watched him watch her, the way he puffed out his skinny chest a little more as she approached, and my stomach turned over.

I rolled up the legs of my jeans and kicked off my shoes. I sat down on the edge and dipped my feet in, trying to ignore the playful way Jake and Amanda were circling each other in the deep end.

The water was warm and for a moment I felt soothed enough to close my eyes and try to forget my status as awkward third wheel. I took in a deep breath through my nose, sucking in that hotel-pool smell of industrial-strength chlorine and damp feet, then sighed it out.

I'd never really gotten into drinking. The government was cool with emancipating psychic teenagers and using them to combat zombies, but they drew a hard line at underage boozing. Anyway, now seemed like a pretty good time to start. I reached over and grabbed one of the sweating glass bottles, twisted off the top, and took a swig. It tasted just like cherry cola except with an undercurrent of cough syrup. Not great.

Before I realized what I was doing, I'd chugged half the bottle.

"Whoa, easy there," Jake said, laughing as he swam over.

A head rush fizzed through me, and it briefly occurred to me to worry how alcohol might interact with psychic powers. Then, I burped.

"Sorry," I said, covering my mouth.

"You don't want to swim?" Jake asked, ignoring my belch and any of the other rookie-drinker signs I'm sure I was giving off.

I looked past him to where Amanda tread water a few feet away, watching us, the lower half of her face submerged, reminding me of an alligator.

"No, I don't have—" I realized not having a swimsuit was a pretty stupid excuse considering they were in their underwear. "No thanks," I finished lamely.

"You're missing out," Jake replied, and lifted himself over the pool's edge to grab a couple bottles, his pale buttcrack flashing as he stretched. I snorted, then felt myself blushing, glad for the low lighting. Amanda cleared her throat.

"So," she began as she swam closer, "are you ever going to tell us about this Containment thing?"

"Yeah!" Jake jumped in, his enthusiasm echoing. "Tell us about the scary government."

I took another quick swig from my bottle as I tried to decide just how much to tell them.

"Containment is the part of NCD that makes up cover stories for zombie attacks," I explained.

"Like us being school shooters," Amanda said, accepting a drink from Jake.

"Yeah. Like that." I peered down at my toes, wiggling them in the water.

"Back up, though," Jake said, pointing his bottle at

me. "How do you even get to be a psychic?"

"Did any scientist guys ever come to your school and give you tests where they asked you to predict shapes and stuff? They probably said it was for an anthropological study or something."

"I think I skipped that day," Amanda said.

"Ugh, most boring assembly ever," Jake groaned, then stared at me. "Wait, so those guys were for real?"

"Yeah," I said, picking at my bottle's label. "I passed their test."

"And they just took you out of school?" Amanda asked.

"Yeah."

"Wow, that's demented," Amanda said. Her voice had softened a bit, although it could've just been the alcohol.

Jake floated his bottle cap toward the pool's filter. "Okay, so, why do they want to keep the zombie plague a secret?"

"So they can enslave us," Amanda declared.

"No, I think the cover-up started just so people wouldn't freak, and then it got out of hand," I explained patiently. I'd given this some thought over the last couple days while trying to piece together what I knew about Iowa. "The whole enslavement thing was just a pet project of one high-ranking weirdo."

"The guy with the bow tie," Amanda said.

I nodded. "Alastaire. Anyway, if people are starting to

protest, it means the NCD is losing control."

"Cool, man. Conspiracy over!" Jake slapped the water excitedly, looking around at us. "That's a good thing, right?"

"What happens when they finally do lose control?" Amanda asked, way more serious than Jake. "Could it all go public?"

"I don't know," I replied. "I wasn't exactly in those meetings. My last mission was chasing you guys. Not superhigh on the totem pole."

"Hey," Jake said, smirking. "We're important."

"Well, yeah, as far as Initial Necrotization goes, you guys killed the most people. Like, ever."

I don't know why I said it. It wasn't meant to be a dig or anything like that. It was just a statement of facts; brazenly public high-casualty necrotizations were a top priority for us. It didn't occur to me that mentioning the RRHS massacre might kill the almost-amicable mood that'd been developing.

Amanda drained the rest of her drink and let it drift away. Then she dunked her head under the water. Meanwhile, Jake blinked at me like I'd just peed in the pool.

"New—new record," he joked weakly.

Amanda resurfaced abruptly, close to the edge. I flinched when she flipped her wet hair back, but she didn't even look in my direction.

"I'm going back to the room," she said.

"Amanda . . ." Jake swam toward her, but she hopped out of the pool before he could reach her. Both of us watched her go.

"Hey," I began lamely. "I'm sorry, I didn't—"

"Don't worry about it," Jake replied quickly. He climbed out of the pool and wrapped a towel around his waist. "We don't like to talk about it. Uh, obviously."

"I know you didn't mean to hurt anyone," I said gently, thinking about all that time I'd spent in Jake's head. I'd felt his guilt firsthand, knew how painful it could be, and hadn't meant to go dredging it up. As he walked by me, I resisted an inappropriate urge to touch his hand. And an equally inappropriate urge to touch his mind. In a weird way, I missed being in there.

"It's cool," he said hurriedly, desperate to get off the subject. He sat down in a deck chair and opened up the laptop. "Do you know why we're trying to get into Iowa? It's not just because it's the land of undead freedom. We heard it's pretty shitty, actually."

"You think there's a cure," I answered. Back at the farmhouse, Amanda talking up the cure to Chazz was what freed my mind from Alastaire's psychic assault. Just the mention of it had been enough to make my old boss flip out.

Jake waved me over. "We have proof."

He'd logged in to the hotel's Wi-Fi and pulled up a grainy YouTube video. I watched it over his shoulder, trying to pay attention to the video instead of the chlorine smell on Jake's ear and neck. The screen was filled with the pockmarked face of an old man with wild, silver hair, like Einstein crossed with a lion. He was in a basement, I think, somewhere dark and dingy. He looked like the crazy old guy in horror movies who warns kids not to reopen the murder camp.

"Some guy calling himself the Lord of Des Moines posted this," Jake explained. "I think he's the head zombie in Iowa and he's holding this old dude hostage."

"Head zombie," I muttered, disbelieving. "There's a head zombie?"

"Just watch," Jake said, and pressed PLAY.

The old man on the screen came to life, all twitchy and erratic sounding, like he was barely keeping it together. I had to huddle close to the laptop to hear him, my face right next to Jake's.

"This is the Grandfather and this may be my last transmission. I remain stranded in Des Moines with no possibility of escape. If this is truly the end, there are two things you must know: First, the undead of Iowa grow bold and restless. It won't be long until they do something . . . uh-uh-uh . . ."

The video started to skip, like a DJ scratching a record. I glanced over at Jake, his eyebrows wrinkled in confusion.

"Uh-uh-AWESOME!" said a suddenly autotuned

version of the Grandfather. Then a digital rainbow wiped across the screen, replacing the grim old man with a trio of French bulldogs riding skateboards. Some cheeseball C'mere Eyes song—"Wild Young Thangs," I think, not that I ever listen to them—blared on the soundtrack.

Jake slapped the laptop closed.

"Uh, someone edited that," he said. "There weren't supposed to be bulldogs."

"I figured."

"Even though that was pretty cool—how did they get *three* of them to skateboard at once?" He shook his head, trying to stay on topic. "Maybe your, um, Containment people got to it. To hide the truth, distract us dumb people with puppies, you know?"

"You think they've got people discrediting zombie rumors by turning them into internet memes?" I asked, skeptical at first, but the more I thought about it . . . "Actually, that does sound like something they'd do."

"Anyway," Jake said, "before the bulldogs got edited in, the Grandfather dude said something about how he cured the undead. And then a bunch of zombies jumped him, so maybe he didn't do such a bang-up job. But the important part is—there's *a cure*."

"But why haven't the zombies or the NCD or that old Grandfather guy actually used it yet?"

"Because we haven't rescued him. Duh."

I smiled and nodded, trying to look enthusiastic,

because Jake looked so hopeful talking about it. But I didn't like his chances—our chances, I guess—of succeeding where a massive government organization had failed. He must've picked up my skepticism because he immediately put on his serious face, which I think took a real, concerted effort on his part. I wanted to hug him.

"Look, I know it's, like, a crazy longshot suicide-mission thing. But what I'm trying to explain is . . . we want to do better. You bring up our school all casual, but we think about that all the time. We've gotta live with it. If we can find this cure in Iowa, though—which is, like, seriously the only thing we can think of to do—if we find it and cure an apocalyptic plague, that sort of balances things out, right? It doesn't bring back our friends or anything, but it saves humanity. So maybe we could be pardoned or something."

"The outlaw hero," I said. "You're like Han Solo."

"Well, that's about the coolest thing anyone's ever said about me," he replied.

"It was a good speech. You earned it."

I smiled at him. I felt like we were having a moment. Then he closed the laptop and stood up.

"All right, I'm gonna catch up with Amanda," he said, glancing toward the door. "Now that I've, like, told you all my hopes and dreams."

"Um, okay," I replied, feeling my smile fade, then trying not to let it show, and ending up with a huge, crazy grin. Jake didn't seem to notice.

"Hopefully tomorrow you can actually get us into Iowa," he continued thoughtfully, lingering, like we were making plans to hang out and catch a movie. "Then we'll all make good. Us for, you know . . ." He made a chomp-chomp motion with his hand. "And you for helping the NCD kill however many undead-afflicted Americans."

I hung around the pool for a while after Jake left, watching blue ringlets fight with shadows across the ceiling.

I don't think Jake had meant to make me feel like crap, but he had. First, for getting his hopes up about Iowa, a promise that I had absolutely no way of keeping. And second, for pointing out that he and Amanda weren't the only ones with dead bodies on their conscience.

"I shouldn't be here," I said, talking to myself. I didn't just mean in the pool after midnight—I meant Omaha, on the run with some zombies, all of it. I wished that I'd flunked that psychic-aptitude test, that I'd never been pulled out of high school, that I had my safe and boring life back, where the most morally objectionable thing I had to deal with was a fourth refill on an endless pasta bowl at the cheesy Italian restaurant I used to work at.

Harlene was going to put it all back to normal for me. Before Amanda killed her.

I found myself out of the pool and padding down the hallway, wet feet leaving dark prints on the faded carpet. I crossed the lobby, the night clerk sparing me just a glance before going back to her romance novel. I was headed for the pay phone.

It wasn't that late in San Diego yet. My mom would still be up. I would tell her everything—and then I'd tell her I was coming home. I'd duck out of here before the zombies woke up and spend the rest of my life trying really hard not to check in on Jake.

She answered on the fourth ring. I could hear the TV in the background.

"Hello?" My mom. My wonderful mom. Just hearing her voice was enough to bring back sensations of home— the smell of the beach from the patio, the burbling of her fancy coffee brewing in the kitchen, the perfect body divot in the long section of our couch. It had been so long since I'd been home.

"Mom," I said, choking up a little. "It's me."

"Carrie?" she asked, confused.

She thought I was my sister. "No, Mom, it's me. Cassandra. How—how are you?"

"Oh, dear." She still sounded confused. "I'm sorry. I don't—could you hold on a moment?"

"What—Mom?" The phone jostled around and I could hear my mom talking to someone. I didn't understand— she'd sounded distant, like I was a stranger calling in the middle of the night. It didn't make sense.

And then a man cleared his throat. A yawn, like he'd been woken up.

"Cassandra," he said, his voice smooth, familiar, skin-crawly. "I'd been hoping you'd call."

I hung up the phone, hard, like it'd electrified me. I was rooted in place, an acidic cola-flavored bubble rising in my esophagus.

I could picture him there. Drinking coffee my mom presented to him in a mug and saucer, sitting with his feet up in the same recliner where my dad used to read the paper, straightening his bow tie in the same bathroom mirror where Carrie had taught me how to best conceal pimples.

Alastaire was in my house.

JAKE

HEAVY SHIT, MAN. JUST HEAVY SHIT ALL THE TIME. Eating people/rodents, new psychic friends reminding you of your personal death toll, government conspiracies, zombie road gangs, crazy old men with possible zombie cures.

A lot going on.

I'd developed an appreciation for the normal moments, you know? Those little pockets of time when nothing stupid was happening, when the universe was like, *Shh, dude, take a breath for a second and don't think about how lame I am.*

For instance, Amanda stood in the open bathroom door, steam rolling out from behind her. She was wearing a red polka-dot bra and matching underwear. I'm not sure when she'd stolen those, but it was really cool that she'd hidden them from me. Keep the whole air-of-mystery thing going. If I were a cartoon character, I'd have exaggeratedly wiped the steam off my oversized glasses, then rolled my tongue up and shoved it back in my mouth.

Instead I just stared.

She'd been showering when I got back to the room, so I'd stretched out on the lumpy hotel bed and killed time with a public-access show about monster trucks. My shirt was half off. Because I'd been scratching my belly.

I realize I'm not exactly keeping up in the sexy department, okay?

"I cannot believe you're my girlfriend," I said, thinking out loud.

Yeah, I went there. *Girlfriend.* Alert the Facebook community—it's time for a status change! Resurrect all the friends I ate two weeks ago so that I can sprint past them getting high fives before tearing through one of those paper banners pep-rally style—it's got CONGRATULATIONS ON ALL THAT BOOTY, JAKE painted on it—and then I bust out my most epic dance moves (sprinkler, so much sprinkler) while the marching band knocks out a rendition of Marvin Gaye's "Let's Get It On." And one of those male cheerleader guys does backflips in the background.

It's cool. No big deal.

"I can't believe it either," Amanda said, smirking at me.

I sat up a little bit. "So, before—when you took off. Do you want to, uh, talk about that?"

"Not particularly."

"All right, cool," I said, nodding, accustomed to the Amanda Blake method of bottling up feelings. "But you're okay?"

"Don't I look okay?"

"Obviously, you *look* better than okay," I replied. "But I mean in the emotional sense. Like, is your inner Amanda wearing her happy underwear?"

"Oh my god, you're corny." She sighed, awkwardly adjusting one of her bra straps. "She just bugs me, all right? I don't trust her."

I waved this off. It'd only been a few days and I already felt like I'd had this conversation about Cass a billion times.

"She's totally harmless," I said. "I mean, except for the omega-level psychic powers, but I don't think she'd use those against us."

"Not against *you*, maybe."

"What's that supposed to mean?"

"Dude, she's totally crushing on you," Amanda said, hitting me with a level stare, like I was an idiot. "Little psychic stalker."

"What?" I snorted. "No, she's not. Wait—really?"

"And you encourage it!" Amanda exclaimed, hands on her hips. *"Oh, Cass, aren't you going to swim with us? Wanna see my butt?"*

"Jeez, we were *in a pool*. Is it so wrong to wonder if she might want to swim?"

"You gave her a fucking hat."

"I was just being nice!" I scuffed a hand through my hair, thinking back to my conversations with Cass. Trying to remember what, exactly? Her making eyes at me or something? They were all just normal, PG, nothing-to-see-here chats. Maybe I was in my boxers before. Big deal. "You're being crazy."

"I'm a girl, stupid. I have a sixth sense for these things. No psychic powers necessary."

I pointed at her, grinning, because my realization was profoundly amazing, perhaps the hugest affirmation of the Jake Stephens charm in recorded history.

"You're jealous," I declared.

"Ha! Unlikely."

"Then, like, territorial," I revised. "Possessive!"

"Get over yourself," Amanda replied, rolling her eyes. "It just needed pointing out because you're so freaking oblivious."

"You keep saying that—"

"I'm in my underwear here, Jake," she said. "Before that, I was showering for like ninety minutes. Waiting for you."

"Waiting for—" I gulped. "I thought you might be, uh, fetal-ball shower-crying or something."

"Yeah, no." She shook her head, glancing at the screen. "And I find you out here watching . . . monster trucks?"

"They're kinda awesome."

"Jake." She sighed. "You suck at sexy banter."

"Is that what we're doing? I thought we were arguing."

"We're transitioning."

"Oh, okay." I cleared my throat, going for a deeper register. I picked up the remote. "Check me out, baby. I'm about to hit the power button on these monster trucks. And then I'm gonna turn the volume up. On this macking we're about to do."

Amanda fought back a smile.

"That'll do," she said.

Two things about what happened next:

1) That bra had a front clasp. Seriously, the best.

2) It was kinda perfect, although maybe we were just getting good at it. But it also had that melancholy end-of-vacation vibe, as if we both somehow knew this might be our last chance to hook up for a while. No three-star hotels in Iowa. Just zombies and weirdness.

Enjoy the quiet moments, right? Even if they're not quiet in the literal sense.

* * *

A small, angry voice woke me up later that night. It was an authority voice, the kind you hear on bitter, middle-aged dudes like my uncle Joe who think they know everything and are always lecturing you at Thanksgiving dinner about the right to bear arms. I opened one eye into a slit, not wanting to give away my position in case our room was being invaded by a well-regulated militia of Uncle Joes.

It was Amanda, watching a clip from Fox News on our laptop. Some old fuckface with a waterfall-sized comb-over and a chin like a deflating hot-air balloon was hollering right into the camera. Scrolling and flashing text graphics that said things like *escalating violence*, *red alert*, and *declining morals to blame* surrounded his bloated face.

"—want to talk about moral decay in this country, you need look no further than New Jersey," the anchor ranted. "You've got this rat, this idiot, Kyle Blake, taking this cockamamie story about his sister—the school shooter, and her little coward accomplice—he takes this story about her to some newspapers that used to have integrity, that used to know the meaning of journalism, but are now just glorified tabloids, liberal rags—"

A black-and-white picture of Amanda's brother, Kyle, appeared in the corner of the screen. He looked grim and beaten up—literally, his left eye swollen closed. I realized it was a mug shot.

"And I'm not even going to glorify this nitwit's

story with a recap. He doesn't deserve it. This toad is basically—those kids' bodies, they aren't even cold in the ground—and he's running his mouth, trying to snatch up some spotlight. These bleeding hearts talking about the first amendment, talking to me about freedom of speech—well, it's not free, and this bottom-feeder is going to find that out. You ask me, they should sit him down right next to his sister when it comes time for the needle to get passed around—"

Amanda stabbed the PAUSE key. She had other tabs open in the browser, all stories about her brother and his crazy conspiracy theories, stories about his arrest for "agitation," all stuff we'd missed being on the road the last few days. All stuff that was sort of our fault.

Amanda touched her brother's face on the screen. I figured I should probably stop pretending to be asleep and propped myself up on an elbow. She didn't look over at me. Maybe she was too pissed off to move.

"How much did you see?" she asked through gritted teeth.

"Too much," I replied. "Like, enough to give me brain damage. I'm sorry about your brother."

She slapped the laptop closed and tossed it to the end of the bed. "I want this to be over, Jake. I want it to be over so bad."

"I know," I replied. "Me too."

"Do you?" she asked sharply. "Because sometimes it

seems like you're just having fun. Like this is some road-trip vacation or whatever."

I didn't say anything back. She was right—sometimes I was like that. Maybe too often, I don't know. Maybe I stretched Jake Day and similar moments of awesomeness too far. But the alternative, thinking about the horrible shit that was happening, like, every second? I'd go nuts.

After a minute, Amanda pushed her forehead into my chest. I lay back with her curled up against me, slowly stroking her hair.

"I'm sorry," she said quietly.

"It's okay."

Before I could say anything else, a big chunk of her hair came loose in my hand, a rotten piece of scalp dangling from the roots.

"Oh shoot," I said. "You're—"

Amanda snapped into a sitting position and grabbed the hair away from me. She looked mortified in more ways than one. Even in the dim light, I could see her skin had turned that congealed gray. Her eyes glistened with tears. She leapt off the bed, away from me.

"Goddamn it, I thought I could hold it off," she said, covering her face and running for the bathroom.

"Not like I haven't seen it before," I replied. "It's okay."

"Stop saying that," she snapped, her words slurring a little. She stopped in the bathroom doorway to shake the chunk of scalp and hair at me. "Nothing about this is okay, Jake!"

"Okay, okay," I said, trying to calm her down, not realizing that I was okaying totally on reflex. "Shit."

Amanda let loose a frustrated zombie sound, then slammed and locked the bathroom door. I climbed out of bed and tried the doorknob, making sure she was locked inside.

"I'm going to get you something from the car," I called through the door. "Stay in there, all right? No rampaging."

She thumped something against the door in reply—maybe her hand, maybe her forehead—and then let out a throaty, sorrowful moan. Could be she'd already gone full zombie, but I didn't think so. That was thirty percent undead hunger and seventy percent human sadness locked behind that bathroom door.

I yanked on some clothes and hustled out of our room. The hallway was quiet. No guests poked their heads out, curious about the monster sounds from down the hall, so we had luck and good soundproofing on our side. The elevator doors hissed open a half second after I thumbed the button.

"Whoa!" I shouted, surprised, as I crashed into Cass getting off the elevator.

She looked stunned to see me. Or maybe just stunned in general, actually. She wobbled backward into the elevator, which, granting that I'm concealing a lot of muscle mass under this unassuming frame of mine, still seemed like an overreaction, like she was already woozy. I hadn't bumped her that hard. I instinctively touched her arm to steady her, and she gratefully clasped her free hand over mine, sighing.

That's when I noticed she had a wad of tissues stuffed up against her nose, bloodstained, and was a friendly ghost shade of pale.

"Jeez, what happened to you?"

"Nothing," Cass replied, all nasally and distant. "Fine."

"Um, really?" I still hadn't taken my hand off her arm. "Because you look all messed up, Cass."

"Nope. All good," she replied, almost like she was wasted. I wondered how much of that twelve-pack she'd plowed through downstairs. To illustrate how all good she was, Cass made an expansive gesture with her tissue-holding hand, inadvertently flicking some blood onto the elevator wall.

The elevator doors buzzed and tried to close. Cass jumped at the loud noise and at the same time some clarity returned to her eyes. She looked from me to the blood she'd splattered on the wall, her eyes widening in embarrassment.

"Oh no," she said. "I just did that."

"It's okay," I replied, cringing at another use of what

was apparently my phrase of the night. "It's not even the grossest thing I've seen in the last ten minutes."

"Oh good," Cass said, still a little loopy. "I'm gonna go now."

Cass dropped her hand off mine and I let go of her arm. We did an awkward little spin-dance in the elevator, trading places. She peered down the hall like she was trying to figure out where to go next. I hit the button for the lobby, but held the doors open for another second.

"Hey, I just have to go down and get something real quick. Should I, like, check on you? Are you going to barf?"

Cass shook her head. A couple strands of hair ended up hanging suspended from her blood-sticky nostril.

"No," she said quickly. "Just bed now. See you in the morning."

"Are you su—?"

She cut me off. "I can get you in tomorrow, Jake. Into Iowa. For sure."

"Yeah, that's the plan," I replied.

"No, no, I was lying before, but now I can do it for real. Promise." She smiled at me. There was a little blood in her teeth. "Good night, cute boy."

"Uh, good night."

I let the elevator doors close.

So much for the quiet moments.

CASS

THE SOUND OF AN AIR HORN GOING OFF RIGHT AGAINST my ear woke me up, blaring and sharp, so loud it made my teeth grit. My eyes felt welded shut, so I blindly waved my hands around, trying to ward off the noise the same way I would a swarm of hornets. The cacophony stopped for two seconds of sweet, merciful silence, and then resumed, pummeling my head with sharp, jangly noise.

It was the bedside phone ringing.

I managed to crack my eyes open. My room was dark, the curtains drawn, and yet what little light made it through stabbed my retinas like hot pokers, digging into my brain, all the way to the base of my skull. Huge black floaters sailed across my vision. I felt like I might faint, but fought it back. Tried to focus.

I backhanded the phone off the hook. Managed to pick it up with both trembling hands. I had to work some moisture into my mouth, tasting blood and sandpaper.

"What," I managed to gurgle into the phone.

"THIS IS THE FRONT DESK. CHECKOUT WAS OVER AN HOUR AGO."

I held the phone away from my ear and sobbed. "Please stop yelling."

"WE NEED TO CLEAN THE ROOM."

"Ten minutes," I croaked. I wasn't going anywhere in ten minutes. I just needed the loudspeaker on the phone to shut up.

I dropped the phone and took a deep breath. I glanced back at my pillow, unsurprised to find it dark with dried blood. I groaned as I swung my legs out of bed. Everything felt brittle, like my body was made of dry twigs that might crumble apart from a strong gust of hotel air-conditioning. Except for my head—that was swollen like I'd snorted wet cement. I couldn't stand just yet, was afraid I might collapse under the weight of this headache.

I needed Tom. He should've been there, with an orange juice at the ready, checking me for brain-hemorrhage symptoms.

No. I was on my own. And I had to get moving.

After about five minutes of gently massaging circles into my temples, I managed to get my legs under me. I stumbled toward the bathroom, noticing on my way that a note had been slipped under my door. I detoured with some effort and snatched it up.

Hey, Cass—We'll be waiting downstairs when you wake up. Or maybe at that protest. Hope you're not dead in there! Your friend, Jake Stephens

Jake. I bumped into him last night, didn't I? Things got majorly foggy after what happened in the hotel lobby. I didn't even remember coming to bed, although I was proud that in my delirium I'd remembered to put out the do-not-disturb sign and chain the door.

I made it to the bathroom and turned the shower up to extrahot. As the room filled with steam, I braced myself on the sink and stared at my reflection in the mirror. Pale, face crusty with dried blood, eyes practically swallowed up by dark circles.

This is what Alastaire did to me.

Two minutes after I'd hung it up, the pay phone in the hotel lobby started to ring. I'd spent those two minutes staring at it and willing myself to wake up from what had to be a nightmare.

On the fourth ring, the night clerk clicked her tongue at me, annoyed. "I'm assuming it's for you, sweetheart."

I took a deep breath and picked up the phone. I could still hear the living-room TV on the other end of the line. My living room. I didn't say anything—couldn't—and after a moment of waiting, probably enjoying the sound of my shaky breathing, Alastaire sighed.

"Come on, Cassandra. Let's get the histrionics out of the way."

The words came in a flood then, like the sound of his voice had punctured my hatred reservoir. I cupped my free hand around the receiver so the night clerk wouldn't hear every forcefully hissed syllable.

"What the *hell* are you doing there? What did you do to my mom? You sick freak, you should've bled to death when you had the chance."

Alastaire didn't lose his cool. "To answer your first question, I'm convalescing. As you're aware, I lost more than a little blood back at that farmhouse."

I remembered Amanda's zombie ex-boyfriend Chazz chewing through Alastaire's arm. I'd set that in motion. I won't lie—it wasn't weighing very heavily on my conscience.

"What did you do to my mom?" I repeated. "Did you hurt her?"

"Of course not. She's very sweet," Alastaire replied, sounding almost affronted. "It was all in the emancipation agreement she signed when you joined the NCD. In cases where an asset—that's you—violates her confidentiality pledge or becomes otherwise problematic, a certain amount of psychic damage control is allowable."

"There's no way that's in there."

"No one ever reads the fine print."

"You—you made her forget me?" I kept my voice down, but wanted to scream. My grip on the phone was white-knuckle tight. "You *erased* me?"

"Temporarily," Alastaire replied dismissively. "I needed to get your attention. I have a mission for you."

I scoffed. "You are bonkers, crazy-pants nuts if you think I'd do anything for you."

"My dear, I'm holding your mother hostage. We can skip the bravado phase. You'll do what I ask."

I didn't reply. Alastaire was right. If he'd told me to march back to NCD headquarters right then and there, I would have.

"In regards to methods of communication, this talking-on-the-phone business is quite primitive for people like us," Alastaire said, totally changing gears on me. "I've looked for you on the astral plane, but you're so closed off. I couldn't make contact."

"That's probably because you're a mind rapist," I replied. I actually didn't have any idea what he was talking about—communicating on the astral plane. From his smug tone of voice, I think Alastaire sensed my ignorance. He was still trying to be my psychic mentor and it grossed me out.

"I want you to reach out to my mind, the same way you would track a zombie," he said, patiently lecturing.

"Just like with a zombie, huh? When I find you, will someone shoot you in the face for me?"

He ignored me. "It shouldn't be difficult. Our minds have been in contact before, and you know where my physical body is located. Picture it. Feel me there. Reach out to me like—"

"Shut up, shut up. You're going to make me barf." I glanced over at the desk attendant. She wasn't the nosy type and had already gone back to reading her novel. Still holding the phone for show, I sat down on a nearby bench, closed my eyes, and slipped onto the astral plane.

The shower helped loosen up the vise clamped to my brain. The migraine wasn't going anywhere, but it'd at least subsided to the point where I could turn my head without sailing into a bout of vertigo.

I put on some fresh clothes and dumped yesterday's in the trash. Between that and the pillows, housekeeping was going to be really weirded out. Oh well.

I plucked a bottle of water from the mini fridge and pressed it to my forehead. Then I crossed to the window and pushed open the curtains, the sunlight stinging my eyes. At least it was tolerable now, unlike when I first woke up.

The sidewalks on both sides of the street were jam-packed with people marching, waving signs, and chanting. They looked young mostly, but there were a few older folks sprinkled in. The police were out in force, try-ing to make sure the marchers didn't spill into the street, although traffic had nonetheless slowed to a crawl. Now that I was close to the window, I could make out the rhythmic hum of their raised voices. "WE WANT THE TRUTH! FREE IOWA NOW!"

I wasn't looking forward to going out there. Kudos on your sense of civic responsibility, guys. Way to ask our screwed-up government the tough questions. But could we maybe keep the chants down to a whisper? Not like anyone in Washington was going to listen anyway.

I grabbed my things, which pretty much amounted to a few changes of clothes stuffed into a shopping bag and a cowboy hat, steeled myself, and left the room. I ducked my head under the frosty glare from the annoyed maid waiting outside and made it to the elevator.

Something had happened here last night. A hazy memory I somehow knew I should be embarrassed about. I'd talked with Jake. Oh god, did I call him cute? To his face?

They were waiting for me in the lobby. Amanda stood by the front window, watching the protesters stream past. Jake was sprawled out on one of the couches, face hidden behind a newspaper. The headline read: GRIZZLY BEAR BLAMED FOR 13 DEAD IN SALT LAKE GROCERY STORE. That one had the stink of NCD cover-up all over it. The incidents were really piling up.

"Hey," I said, standing in front of Jake, hands in my pockets. He lowered the paper and smiled at me, although his eyes widened a fraction at the sight of my face. Obviously, I'd washed off all the blood, but there wasn't anything to be done about the dark circles and general paleness.

"You're up," he said cheerfully. "We were getting worried."

Amanda turned away from the window to look at me. "Wow. You look shittier than usual."

"Thanks," I replied, ready to brush off this typical Amanda greeting. But then I noticed a puffiness to her face, her eyes a little red-rimmed, and my headache-induced grumpiness reared up. "So do you, actually. What were you crying about? Did the hotel not have the right conditioner?"

Amanda stared at me, openmouthed, but couldn't muster a comeback. She just huffed and turned back to the window. I frowned; winning a round with her didn't feel as good as I thought it would.

"Another fun-filled day with the super best friends," sighed Jake. He squinted at me, lowering his voice a fraction. "So, how's the hangover?"

"Bad headache. Nothing I can't handle."

From the table next to him, Jake picked up a blueberry muffin wrapped in a napkin, handing it to me. "You missed the continental breakfast," he said.

"Thanks," I replied, sitting down next to him.

Jake jerked a thumb toward Amanda. "She got it for you. I was, um, running an errand."

"He was buying pot from some protester," Amanda explained. Jake did a little fist pump and grinned at me.

"Oh. Well. Priorities." I picked a sugary piece of crust from the muffin top. "Thanks, Amanda."

Amanda shrugged in response, turning back around. "Is all this—?" She waved a hand at my face. "Did you really go to town on those drinks? Or is it because of the psychic stuff yesterday?"

"Something like that," I said evasively.

"Wow, so it really wipes you out," Amanda said, sitting down on an adjacent couch. "Bummer."

Jake looked between us with his eyebrows raised encouragingly, like we'd had a major breakthrough talking to each other with this much civility.

"It's just a bad headache, really," I continued. "I'll be fine."

"Cool," Amanda replied, with an amount of sincerity I think was probably painful to produce.

"And there's a plan now, right?" Jake jumped in,

looking at me expectantly. I must've told him something along those lines last night, and he must've broached the subject with Amanda. "You figured out a way into Iowa."

"Yep. That's right," I said, and stuffed a chunk of muffin in my mouth to buy myself a few seconds. "I can get you over the border today."

"What're you going to do after?" Jake asked, the thought clearly just occurring to him. "You can't come with us, right? Not if it's as bad as they say. You'll be, uh—"

"A meal," Amanda finished.

"I think I'll just go home," I said quickly.

Amanda seemed satisfied, but not Jake. He squinted at me, like he could tell something was up. Before he could ask, Amanda spoke up.

"So what is this plan you suddenly decided to come up with? There is a plan, right? Not just more driving around."

There *was* a plan. It just wasn't *my* plan.

On the astral plane, I imagine myself as the wind. It's like I'm gusting through a city at night, and all the lit windows are minds. Some of them are open—likely because I've come in contact with that mind before—but most of them are closed. I could force my way through the cracks of those closed minds if I wanted to, but that might involve breaking the window, so I don't try. I stick to the minds I know or the minds I'm tracking. I've done this a hundred times.

A hundred times and I've never felt one of those minds suck me in, like a dark cavern on the horizon, a vacuum.

Not until Alastaire.

Suddenly, I stood in my living room in San Diego. All the details were right: the retro shag carpet that my mom loved so much, the creepy plaster gnome next to the television, the working fireplace that no one had ever bothered to light. It had all the sensations of home, but I felt like I'd just become aware of a dream. It felt unreal around the edges, like if I focused too hard, I might snap awake.

Not to mention, Alastaire was sitting on my couch. Right in the spot where I used to curl up for after-school naps. He was dressed in one of his slick suits, bow tie and everything.

"What is this?" I asked, looking around. "How is this possible?"

"This is the intersection of our minds, Cassandra," Alastaire said, again adopting the whole patient-teacher tone, mansplaining his butt off. "A shared dreamspace, you might call it. Very few psychics are capable of projection at this level. You should be very proud."

I wandered around the room, forgetting for a moment how skeeved out I was and just basking in this psychic approximation of home.

"Why here?" I asked.

"It's easier if the place is familiar to us both," he replied. "Stops our minds from quibbling over the details."

I stopped in front of our cluttered mantelpiece. My mom hadn't been able to decide which photos of my dad to display after he died, so instead she tried breaking the pictures-per-square-inch record. As I looked over the photos, the ones of me and my dad started to shift and twist, like someone had smudged an inky thumb over my dad's face. I stared, transfixed, as the images slowly took shape again, my dad's likeness replaced by Alastaire. There he was, grinning, wearing a bow tie, hands on my tiny shoulders as he taught me how to ride a bike.

"Major quibble!" I shouted, taking a startled step back. "I am so definitely quibbling, you creepy douche!"

"Ah, I'm sorry," Alastaire said, and I was surprised by the embarrassment in his voice. "Sometimes the id can be difficult to control in here."

I turned to face him. "Is that how you see yourself? Like a father figure or something?"

"Never mind that," he snapped. "We have more important matters to discuss."

"Because you are *not* a father figure to me," I continued, ignoring him. "You're like the creepy stranger in the van looking for his lost puppy that my actual dad used to warn me about. You're like—"

A sharp cracking sound from behind made me jump. One of the picture frames had shattered.

"Are you quite done?" Alastaire asked.

"Quite," I repeated. My words were a little shakier than I'd have liked; he still scared me. "What do you want from me, Al?"

"The incident at the farmhouse was not exactly the highlight of my career," Alastaire began, almost like this was a debriefing. "I lost an entire unit of NCD soldiers, including a field commander and a high-level psychic. Not to mention my Pavlov device proved less than satisfactory in its first field test."

I snorted, relishing the fact that I'd caused his grotesque zombie-controlling device to malfunction. "My bad."

"Yes. Your bad, indeed," he said, nodding in agreement. He paused for a moment to wiggle the fingers on his right hand, looking down at them longingly. "You know, they had to amputate this arm, Cassandra."

"Uh-huh," I said, ignoring the tiny pang of guilt I felt for causing this evil jerk to get maimed. "And then did they fire you?"

"No," Alastaire replied. "But my star has fallen quite a bit within the NCD. So much so that I've been reduced to this. . . ." He waved his hand disgustedly at my living room.

"Feel free to leave at any time," I said.

He shook his head. "Actually, I believe this humbling experience was in order. I'd gotten ahead of myself, you see. Controlling the undead is still a possibility, Cassandra, but not while their plague spreads across our country unchecked. Something must be done to ebb the tide of chaos or else all our scientific advancements will be for naught. Don't you agree?"

I folded my arms. "It's hard for me to agree with anything you say, ever. Don't take it personally."

"There is a man stranded in Des Moines who I believe has created a cure for the undead," Alastaire continued, undeterred.

"The Grandfather."

"Ah." Alastaire smirked. "So you've seen his little videos. His real name is Doctor Nelson Fair. He didn't start all this 'Grandfather' business until his mind broke."

"So he's nuts?" I asked, feeling a mounting sense of dread about this whole Iowa expedition.

"Indeed. Even so, I have reason to believe he's been successful with his experiments. Once upon a time, during the first years of this plague, when cases were few and far between, we worked together. Since then, I believe he found employment with a company called Kope Brothers Pharmaceuticals."

I remembered the defaced Kope Brothers billboard we'd seen when leaving Pipestone. "I've heard of them."

"I always found Doctor Fair's research . . . shall we say, distasteful? Apparently, the private sector does not share my reservations."

"You? This Grandfather guy skeeved out *you*?"

"No matter what you might think, I am not a monster." Alastaire leaned forward, studying me. "Speaking of, are you still hanging around that zombie boy? Nurturing your doomed little romance?"

His question caught me off guard. It wouldn't have surprised me if Jake's picture suddenly appeared on the mantelpiece. I wondered if astral projections could blush.

"What does that matter?" I asked, going for sharp, but honestly worried what he might want from Jake.

"It's a stroke of good luck," Alastaire said, nodding approvingly. "You'll need the boy to get close. Doctor Fair appears to be a prisoner of war, so to speak."

I snorted, shaking my head. "Jeez, relying on me and my zombie friends. You sure the NCD didn't fire you? Why don't you just send in the marines or something?"

"I've already tried that."

That raised my eyebrow. "Um, what?"

"A highly trained black-ops team parachuted into Des Moines two weeks ago with the intention of extracting Doctor Fair and his cure." Alastaire paused dramatically. "They didn't make it out. And they weren't the first team sent in."

"So, you're telling me I'm a better bet than black ops now?"

"I believe an undead agent working in concert with the NCD would be better positioned to acquire this cure from an overrun city in the grip of a zombie warlord, yes," Alastaire replied dryly. "Perhaps, if my field tests hadn't been disrupted, a zombie with my Pavlov device could have been sent in. Instead, I'll be relying on you to do the mind controlling the old-fashioned way."

I tried not to let my disgust register. I'd sworn off any kind of mind control where Jake was concerned, but Alastaire didn't need to know that, not while he was holding my mom hostage.

"How did you geniuses let it get so bad?" I asked. "I mean, a whole state . . ."

Alastaire frowned, like I'd offended him. "The Kope Brothers were subcontracted to develop an undead vaccine. Doing so entailed a certain amount of human testing. When that got out of hand, beginning with a massive incident in Des Moines, it was in everyone's best interest to cover it up until the issue could be resolved. Reputations were on the line, and so forth."

I shook my head in disbelief. "But it hasn't been resolved."

"No, it has only gotten worse," Alastaire replied. "Which has necessitated further cover-ups, larger quarantines, bigger subcontracts. It wasn't until Kope's headquarters finally went dark that the NCD's policy went from isolation to intervention."

"Man," I said. "You guys all freaking suck. Seriously."

"Some of us more than others," he said casually. "With subtler options having failed, there are those within the government who believe the next step to our undead epidemic is a military one. Soon, the full might of the United States military will descend on Iowa. You see, there's no need to cure that which is rendered extinct. No one will be spared, not even Doctor Fair. The risk of further infection is too great. I'm using what little pull I have left to delay this militaristic inevitability. However, you'll want to be quick about our work."

I stared at him. Basically, he was offhandedly describing an entire state worth of people—undead or otherwise—getting murdered.

"You—you're serious?"

"Barbaric, I know," he replied. "And too little, too late, if you ask me. Certainly not the course of action I'd have recommended, but then, one of my subordinates saw fit *to have a zombie chew off my arm.*"

And suddenly, Alastaire was right in front of me. He didn't move like normal; he didn't have to, not on the astral plane. His hand was under my chin, jerking my face upward, so I had to look right into his eyes, burning with an anger he'd been keeping at bay. I was distantly aware of a warm sensation on my face—a geyser of a nosebleed for my physical body.

"This is your mission, child. I've arranged for an operative to meet you at the border. He'll get you past the NCD. Use your new zombie friends to find the doctor. Do whatever you have to do. Acquire the cure. Rip it out of his goddamn mind if you have to. Bring it to me. Or else, I'll let you watch through my eyes as I butcher your mother. And she'll never even know why."

I tried to look away, but his dark eyes held me. The living room was getting smaller and smaller around us, the walls closing in.

"Okay," I gasped. "I'll do it."

"Good," he said, and let my chin slip. "Then our business is concluded."

"A friend of mine will meet us near the Deadzone," I told Jake and Amanda in the hotel lobby, still picking at my muffin. "He'll get us past the NCD presence and you'll be free to do whatever on the other side."

"A friend of yours?" Amanda asked. Even Jake looked a little skeptical.

"An, uh, NCD person," I explained, wishing my head wasn't throbbing so I could coat these half truths with some psychic sugar. Even though I'd promised not to mess with their heads, circumstances had changed.

"No way," said Amanda, shaking her head. "Total setup."

Jake sighed, standing up for me, just like I knew he would. "Jeez, Amanda. Why would she go through the trouble? She could've busted us anytime she wanted."

Amanda fixed Jake with a searching look. Even though I'd never been in there, I knew how her mind worked; she was looking for angles, figuring out motivations, calculating how to work people. Jake smiled at her—a mellow, carefree smile, like we were debating what to see at the movies—and she relented.

"Fine," she muttered.

"We trust you," Jake said, flipping that easy smile in my direction. My stomach turned over.

He shouldn't have.

JAKE

THE CROWD ON THE SIDEWALK PARTED JUST ENOUGH to let me nose our car out of the parking lot and into the street. A couple of hippie girls in swishy, patchwork dresses and FREE IOWA tank tops sprayed Silly String onto our windshield. I waved at them and hit the windshield wipers.

"I don't even get it," I said. "Are they, like, pro-zombies? Or against? What're they protesting?"

Amanda eyeballed a shirtless punk-rock dude with suspenders and a huge anarchy symbol shaved into his head. He stomped along the edge of the barricade, practically daring the cops to mess with him.

"Deodorant," Amanda observed and flipped on the air-conditioning. "That's what they're protesting."

"No, seriously."

A harried cop waved me into a line of traffic that was going nowhere slow. The street was one-way, and that way went in the opposite direction of the marchers. We were traveling upstream against a lot of angry and colorful fish, but the cops at least had mostly confined them to the sidewalks. I just needed to find somewhere to turn off.

"They don't even know why they're out here," Amanda said dismissively. "Someone handed them a flier and they're all, like, oh, cool, a chance to break out my devil sticks."

I scanned the crowd, but didn't see any devil sticks. A solemn bunch of middle-aged people walked past, linked arm in arm, all of them holding pictures of missing children.

"You think they'd still be out here if they knew about us? Not *us* specifically. I mean the whole people-eating-people thing. Would they march for that? For zombie rights?" I was rambling. The traffic jam plus the exhausted condition of my two lady friends had me feeling the need to make conversation. And, honestly, all the chanting had me sort of amped up.

"If they knew the truth, they'd probably be shooting at us. Or locked away like . . ." Amanda trailed off, getting self-conscious. I don't think she wanted Cass knowing about her brother. She didn't get much sleep last night, even after I fed her some guinea pigs through the cracked bathroom door. She stayed up until dawn looking for more news about Kyle. None of it was good.

Cass, who, from the look of her, totally rivaled Amanda in the up-all-night department, spoke up from the backseat, where she was stretched out with an arm draped across her face.

"It's the not knowing that they're protesting," she said. "They're mad because they've been kept in the dark. I'd be angry too."

"Yeah! Let's get angry!" I hollered, honking the horn. "Down with government! Up with people!"

Some of the protesters right outside our car cheered. They waved at me, encouraging me to get out of our car and join them. If I hadn't been on my way to a top-secret world-saving mission that would totally knock all their sandals off, I would have.

"Oh my god," Cass moaned. "If you honk that horn again, you'll be cleaning up my exploded brains."

"Mmm," I said, smirking. "Brains."

"Not funny," she replied.

"That's your fault, though," Amanda said to Cass, having been chewing this over for a few seconds. "They're in the dark because of you guys."

"Yep," Cass answered simply. "You're right."

We inched a little farther down the block, closing in on an intersection where we could hopefully turn off from the protest. Something odd caught my eye in the rearview. A strange ripple passed through the crowd behind us. It was like at a concert, where you could be packed in shoulder-to-shoulder rocking out, but then that one drunk guy starts peeing and the audience reacts like a singular organism, shifting and isolating for the good of all.

"Something's up," I said. Amanda looked first at me, frowning, and then out the back window. Cass sat up, shielding her eyes.

From back toward the hotel, a skinny, shirtless guy with a yellow peace sign painted on his chest sprinted by our car. His hip slammed hard into the side mirror and he didn't even slow down.

"Keep driving," Amanda said.

"Good advice," I replied.

Traffic wasn't moving. I rolled as close as I could to the bumper of the car in front of me. A cop walked down the yellow line, headed in the direction we'd come from. He was talking all serious into the little radio on his shirt, one hand on his holstered gun.

"I can't tell what's happening," Cass said. There was definitely a commotion behind us, people jostling for position, spreading into the road.

"Maybe it's just a fight," I said hopefully. "Like, *I'll show you who believes in the first amendment more*, and shit just gets wild."

"Green light!" Amanda shouted.

I honked at the car in front of us. He sped up, we cruised into the intersection, and that's when the dam broke.

All at once the protest flipped and now the entire crowd was streaming in our direction. Screaming and running, shoving one another, stepping on backs. The terrified faces brought back half-remembered red-tinged memories of that first fateful day in the cafeteria. I saw the cop who'd walked past us get dumped on his ass, shouldered out of the way by some panicked college kids. And then, farther back, I'm pretty sure I saw a severed arm fly into the air.

"This is bad," Amanda said.

"Crowds," I said. "I really hate crowds."

I swung us hard into the left turn. People sprinted frantically through the intersection, so I had to pump the brakes. I really didn't want to add vehicular manslaughter to my list of crimes if I didn't have to.

"Get us out of here." Amanda was trying really hard to stay calm.

"Trying," I said.

A guy who didn't look much older than me slammed

right into the side of our car. His T-shirt was all shred-ded and bloody, making Che Guevara's face look slightly more badass. I could see a mouth-shaped laceration on his shoulder. He slapped his hands against our windows, smearing blood on them, then tried the backseat door. Cass recoiled, but not before jamming down the lock.

"Some bitch back there is eating people!" he screamed. "You gotta help me! Let me in!"

"No, uh, no room," I shouted through the window.

A gunshot rang out above the screaming. One second Che Guevara was jogging next to our car, and the next he was crumpled on the ground missing the side of his head.

"Oh my god," Cass gasped.

The panicked crowd shifted then, now running away from a businessman in the crosswalk holding a pistol. He swung it in a wild arc, screaming, "YOU'RE BITTEN," before aiming at the backs of a young couple trying to get away.

"Fuck it," I said, and gunned it.

There was enough space for me to drive around the businessman, but I didn't bother. He didn't see me com-ing. The car wasn't going fast enough to knock him up in the air, so instead he went under. It was like going over a really crunchy speed bump. I glanced in the rearview mir-ror and briefly caught sight of him lying motionless in the road before he disappeared beneath another crowd surge.

Space opened up in front of us, so I floored it. We outraced the chaos, leaving behind sirens and screaming. I didn't take my foot off the gas until we were safely on the other side of town, away from it all, getting the hell out of Omaha.

I realized then that I was shaking. Amanda had her hand on my leg, steadying.

"I ran a guy over," I said matter-of-factly.

"He was shooting people," Amanda replied. "Innocent people."

I looked into the rearview. Cass's gaze was waiting for mine.

"You did the right thing," she said solemnly.

I breathed a sigh of relief. I know it's twisted, but it made me feel better that we were in unanimous agreement about my spur-of-the-moment decision to mow down a stranger.

"Just making sure I didn't, like, cross some ethical boundary just now."

"Psh." Amanda snorted.

"Let's try not to think about those," Cass said quietly.

"Someone must've turned," I said, taking a deep breath. "Just like what happened with us."

"I hope they're—" Amanda paused, biting her lip. "Shit, I don't know what I hope."

I tried to catch Cass's eyes again, but she'd closed them. She was rubbing circles into her temples.

"Isn't this just going to keep happening?" I asked. "How could the NCD ever stop this?"

"Oh, it seems like they're pretty much screwed." Cass shrugged. There was a world-weary grimness in her voice that I hadn't heard before. "I think we're all pretty much screwed, actually. Or am I the only one getting a distinct zombie-apocalypse vibe from the last few days?"

Amanda blinked and said nothing. She squeezed my leg and I put my hand on top of hers, squeezing back. I think we'd both always assumed that once we straightened out our personal undead thing, there'd be a world to go back to.

"I love your optimism," I said, and turned on the radio. "How about some music? Any requests?"

It took a while to find a station not reporting on the mayhem in downtown Omaha.

We didn't talk much on our way back onto the thruway. I found a mellow soft-rock station—not usually my thing, but I wanted something that couldn't possibly soundtrack an apocalypse. This dude jamming on his acoustic guitar singing about building a soapbox racer with his dad totally fit the bill. Some real everything-is-good-in-the-heartland John Denver bullshit. Living in a fantasy world, but whatever.

Amanda fiddled with my DS for a while, got bored, and ended up staring sullenly out the window. After punching some mysterious coordinates into the GPS, Cass stretched out across the entire backseat, sunk so low that I couldn't see her in the mirror anymore. I turned my head to check on her every few miles. She'd pulled out the black cowboy hat and pushed it over her eyes like she was sleeping, but I'd occasionally catch her mouthing words, arguing with herself. She was radiating some seriously confusing vibes, like something major had changed with her. I wanted to ask if she was all right, but didn't want to give Amanda the wrong idea. Because apparently being a well-behaved, polite, empathic young man in a car with two totally hormonal undead/mutant/post-human ladies was an invitation to do some wack-ass love-triangle like in one of those stupid romance books my sister used to read, where there'd always be two guys with eight-packs, flappy, open dress shirts, and were-wolf eyes lustily eyeing one bodice-ripped teenager with blushing virgin cheeks. Except in this metaphor, I guess I'm the one with the ripped dress.

Twenty minutes later, the big orange signs warning of an impending detour started popping up on the side of the highway. We'd passed into Iowa proper a while back and were headed east toward Prairie Rose State Park, where I pictured flowers blooming out of giant ears of corn. I sat up straighter and arranged my hands at ten and two, just in case this entailed some stunt driving.

"The GPS is pointing me toward the closed exit," I announced.

Cass sat up with a groan. "That's fine. Just drive around it."

We zipped by a sign that promised Des Moines in 120 miles. The dry British lady on the GPS told me to take the next exit. I could see it up ahead, barricaded by yellow barrels and one of those big, wooden crossbeams. I slowed down and coasted onto the shoulder, rumble strips rattling the undercarriage. It was a tight squeeze, and the side of the car scraped against the metal guard-rail, peeling off some paint.

And then we were through. Winding up an on-ramp and emerging on a new stretch of highway, no roadwork in sight.

"Well, that was easy," I said.

"Don't tell me the solution this entire time was *drive around*," Amanda complained.

"No." Cass shook her head. "Look out your window."

Amanda and I both turned our heads. I noticed coils of dark metal piled on the side of the road. There were dusty tracks on the highway from where they'd been recently dragged aside.

"What are those?" Amanda asked.

"Spike strips," Cass replied. "Maybe some other, worse stuff. They cleared the way for us."

That on-ramp had basically transported us into an

alternate dimension, one where we were the only people left on Earth. There weren't any other cars on the highway in either direction. I glided back and forth across the lanes before settling smack in the middle of the road.

Amanda turned to look at Cass. "Going to be pretty tough for you to hitchhike back," she said. "Good thing we got you those sneakers."

"I'll be fine," Cass replied, sounding tired. She'd taken off the black hat and stuffed it into the shopping bag with the rest of her things.

"It's very flat," I observed.

It took me a second to realize that it wasn't just the natural geography messing with my perception. The land we were passing through had been leveled—trees cut down to stumps, cornfields razed, highway signs dismantled.

"So they can see people coming," Cass explained.

The idea that someone up ahead was watching us through some military-grade telescope, maybe dialing in a drone strike at that very moment, made me drive considerably slower. We were driving toward a bunch of people trained to kill zombies. Whose idea was this? Because it abruptly struck me as a really god-awful one. I mean, the hotel we'd been staying at had a pool. We could have been lounging poolside right then.

"What is that?" Amanda asked, pointing toward a chrome band that'd appeared on the horizon.

"Grace and Summer mentioned a wall," I said, remembering what the mostly friendly undead lesbians had told us. "With, uh, guys on top shooting at them."

Grace and Summer also warned us to stay out of Iowa, but now didn't seem like the time to bring that up. We were kinda committed.

The wall stood at least twenty feet tall and stretched across the highway and into the fields. I couldn't tell what it was made out of—chrome, steel, some kind of shiny metal. At this distance, I could make out wisps of barbed wire along the top and some blocky protrusions that my inner *Call of Duty* master identified as gun turrets. I didn't see any men to operate them, though. I didn't see any signs of life at all.

"Pull over here." Cass spoke up. We were still a good two miles off.

I did as she said and we all sat in silence for a moment, contemplating the huge structure before us.

"So? What do we do now?" Amanda asked.

"Wait," Cass replied, squinting toward the horizon.

It was way too quiet out here. I could hear the guinea pigs rustling around in the trunk, conducting stupid guinea-pig business. I tried the radio, but every station was static.

"All right," I said, "songs with *wall* in the title. I'll start. 'Another Brick in the Wall.' Pink Floyd."

No one said anything.

"Okay, I took the easy one. 'Wall of Toddler Skeletons.' Severed Lung. It's a B-side."

"'Wonderwall,'" Cass said. "Oasis."

"Oh! Cass gets on the board first," I said way too enthusiastically.

Amanda sighed dramatically. "'Wall to Wall.' Chris Brown."

"Ugh," I replied. "Negative points."

Ignoring me, Amanda twisted around to stare at Cass. "I don't like this. What *the fuck* are we waiting for?"

"Him," Cass responded, all cool, pointing through the windshield.

We stared in the direction of the wall. A dark shape had detached from all the glinting silver and started careening toward us. Even at this distance, I could hear the guttural belching of a motorcycle.

"This *Easy Rider* guy is your friend?" I asked.

"Sort of," Cass answered, keeping up the whole tight-lipped secret-agent shtick she'd been pulling since the hotel lobby. She opened the back door and struggled out of the car, like her body was cramped up. "You guys should stay put."

"What if we don't want to?" Amanda snapped.

"Calm down," I whispered to her. "You're just nervous." She fixed me with an electric death stare and I decided to shut up.

Cass leaned back into the car. "If you don't, this guy

will probably blow your head off."

I hit the power locks.

The motorcycle guy came to a stop down the highway, a safe distance from us. The sun and that shiny-ass wall were behind him, so I couldn't pick too many details out of his burly shadow. His motorcycle was one of those low-slung chopper types with the high handlebars, and he was the kinda guy to ride it without a helmet while smoking a cigar. He straddled the bike and waited, staring in our direction.

"All right," Cass said, trying to sound like she wasn't nervous. "Be right back."

"Be careful," I said. Amanda said nothing, just stared at the motorcycle man, her body clenched like at any moment she could duck for cover under the dashboard or make a break for it.

"Oh, I almost forgot." Cass stopped outside my window. "You guys need to pretend to be my zombie slaves. Okay, bye."

I rolled up the window so Cass wouldn't have to hear Amanda screaming at her.

CASS

HE SMELLED. THAT WAS THE FIRST THING I NOTICED. AS I walked toward him along the highway shoulder, his stink came bounding out to meet me. It wasn't like forgot-deodorant-on-a-hot-day smell either. He smelled how I imagined cavemen probably smelled—the unsuccessful ones who got eaten by dinosaurs because their stench gave them away.

He sat astride his motorcycle and smoked a cigar. He was big—tall and wide—but stretch marks and saggy skin pockets gave the impression he used to be bigger. It looked like he'd spent the last few months foraging for food on a deserted island, and the experience had left him sunburned, sinewy, and filthy all over. He had two guns slung over his shoulders—a long rifle with a scope, and a sawed-off shotgun. His belt had to be some kind of special-order survivalist thing because it had more than a dozen compartments and pockets, many of them bulging with what was probably ammunition, totally compromising the theory that belts should hold up one's pants. His hair was prematurely gray, long, pulled back in a greasy ponytail. He wore a leather vest with no shirt, ripped and bloodstained jeans, and surprisingly clean running shoes.

I stopped in front of his motorcycle. He pushed a pair of mirror aviators down his nose and gave me a skeptical look. Then he wet his chapped lips, snorted like something funny had occurred to him, and put the glasses back on. He didn't say anything and it didn't seem like he had any intention to do so anytime soon.

As far as hard-ass mercenary types went, this guy reminded me a little of Jamison, the heavy hitter in my old NCD squad. Except with Jamison I could always tell there was an off switch, that he used to be a regular person before getting swept up in the zombie-killer lifestyle. I didn't detect any of that muted humanity from this guy. He looked like he was born mean, probably stubbed out cigarettes on his mom during breast-feeding.

I wished I'd worn my black hat. I was afraid it'd make me look silly—which it did—but I could've used some of its power. It felt like I was entering a place where looking crazy would be an advantage.

"You're my guide?" I asked, breaking the prolonged silence. I tried to keep my voice from squeaking. "I'm Cass."

"Truncheon," he said, his voice scratchy, like emphysema wasn't far off.

I gave him a weird look, not sure if that was some password I was supposed to recognize.

"Like the club," he clarified. "It's what people call me."

"Oh." *Nice to meet you, Mr. Truncheon,* I thought, but didn't say. For some reason, I didn't think cute would play well with a guy nicknamed for a weapon.

Truncheon looked up at the sky, like he was trying to discern something from the position of the sun.

"You're late," he said at last. "I'd started to think I'd imagined the whole thing."

"Sorry. We had problems getting out of Omaha."

Truncheon didn't seem interested in my excuse. Now that we were past introductions, he seemed excited to talk to me. Like it'd been a while since he had a conversation.

"That bow-tied dweeb comes to me in a dream last night," Truncheon said. "You believe that? Haven't heard from him in months, figured maybe someone'd finally done the world a mercy and offed him. He tells me he needs me to pick up one of his operatives. Got some special mission he's on about. Tells me, if it's a success, he can clear up some . . . legal complications for me back in the real world, make it so I don't have to live in the Deadzone anymore."

I glanced toward the wall, surprised. "You *live* in there?"

He grinned at me with teeth like pads of butter. "Honey, I *like* it in there. I ain't trying to go back to the real world. I asked our mutual friend, 'What else ya got?'"

I folded my arms, wishing the government could come build a giant wall between me and this guy. A smell-canceling wall.

"What did he offer you?" I asked, regretting the dread in my voice. I needed to push that down and get tough. Today was going to be a messy day and I needed to be ready for it.

"A squad," he replied. "I used to be NCD, kid."

"You're joking."

Truncheon grinned, like he was glad not to be recognizable as a government man. "Still am, according to the paperwork. But no one pays me much attention except our mutual friend. He's a jumped-up prick, but he's got a real appreciation for the unorthodox."

"That's one way of putting it," I replied, thinking of

zombie slavery, my hostage mom, and trademarked bow ties. "Why do you want a team?"

"The jumpsuits and the bureaucracy they can cram up their asses, but I love me some NCD brainpower. He promised me autonomy and a new psychic." Truncheon shrugged. "Plus, it gets lonely in there."

My throat constricted. "A *new* psychic?"

"Yeah. My last one sorta broke."

I was pretty confident Alastaire was too attached to the idea of me as his psychic prodigy to ship me off to Truncheon's smelly postapocalyptic boarding school. Even so, I felt the growing urge to get as far away from this NCD lone wolf as possible, preferably to a place that sold lice shampoo. Truncheon wasn't even paying attention to me, though; he gazed over my shoulder toward the car.

"He said I could probably have the girl too," Truncheon said, referring to Amanda. "She looks fresh, unlike most of the rot on the other side of the wall. He said I'd be doing you a favor, taking her off your hands. Not sure what he meant by that, exactly. Cryptic jerk-off. All this is after the job is done, of course."

I glanced back at the car. I could see Jake and Amanda in silhouette, her making animated gestures and him slowly nodding. I swallowed a lump of revulsion before turning back to Truncheon. Tried to make my shrug as nonchalant as possible; I didn't want to give anything away—not my psychic powers and not my relationship to my zombie passengers.

"Whatever," I said. "Can we get on with it?"

"She nice to talk to?" Truncheon asked, running a hand over his crusty, bristled chin. "Companionable?"

I glanced back at the car again. It looked like Amanda was yelling now.

"Not particularly, no."

He shrugged. "Not that it matters. Your standards get real low on the other side."

I tried not to shudder, to keep my posture loose and detached, like I was ordering a pizza instead of brokering the rights to a pretty, young zombie with this gruesome survivalist in the shadow of a wall that shielded humanity from the country's one and only undead party zone. No big deal. I let my head loll around, insolent and bored. Truncheon frowned at me, then gazed down at himself like he'd only just realized his disgusting state.

"It's a different world on the other side," he said grimly. "You'll find that out soon enough."

"Cool story," I said. "Can we get on with this?"

Truncheon jabbed a thick finger in my direction. "You know, you remind me a lot of *him*. Same shitty attitude about polite conversation. Same judgmental psychic eyes."

"What? I'm not a psy—" Without some telepathic nudging, the lie sounded feeble. A bark of laughter from

Truncheon cut me off before I could even finish it.

"I was only guessing, sweetheart," he sneered, and tapped his temple. "We don't all need magic powers. Some of us are just keen observers of the human condition."

"Guess that's why you choose to live with the zombies," I replied, deadpan.

"Yep," Truncheon said. "Exactly right."

Truncheon reached around to the back of his motorcycle, where a burlap knapsack was strapped. He tossed it toward me. I made no move to catch it; the sack landed with a puff of dust at my feet.

"Stuff you'll need is in there," he explained.

I knelt down and checked the contents. Handcuffs and chains. Muzzles. A handheld version of the stun guns NCD agents had recently started carrying around. The ones I'd seen before had all been rifle sized; this one fit neatly in the palm of my hand. Turning it over, I noticed MANUFACTURED BY KOPE BROTHERS emblazoned on the grip. Like the Deadzone itself, the weapon was another gift from the NCD's favorite corporate benefactor.

I shoved the stun gun into the front of my jeans, hidden under my shirt. Truncheon watched me with one eyebrow suggestively raised.

"You know how to use that thing?"

I'd never actually fired one, but he didn't need to

know that. He already knew more than I was comfortable with. I nodded.

"Don't worry about me," I said. "What happens
next?"

Truncheon jerked his thumb toward the wall. "The
boys know I'm bringing you through. All the same, they
get jumpy. You just keep up appearances and let me do
the talking."

I shouldered the knapsack with some effort, the
chains inside clanking around. Keeping up appearances meant getting Jake and Amanda to put on those
chains—not exactly a conversation I was looking forward
to having. But what other choice did they have at this
point? I'd brought them too far. For that matter, what
other choice did I have?

"What's your plan once we're in the Deadzone?"
Truncheon asked. "You going with the soft touch or the
hard?"

"Soft," I answered quickly. "Definitely soft."

My plan was to ask Jake and Amanda really nicely
if they'd sneak into Des Moines and steal a zombie cure
for me. That's what they were trying to do anyway, right?
Alastaire favored playing the zombies until they'd gotten the cure and then ripping them off, but all that
Machiavellian crap hadn't worked out for anyone so far.
I'd decided to try honesty. We could share and my mom
wouldn't get killed. Everyone wins. Except for Amanda,

I guess, but we could work that out later, once the cure was in hand.

"Hard touch works better in there," Truncheon warned. "You'll learn that soon enough too."

I touched the stun gun hidden under my shirt. "You'll know if I change my mind."

My backup plan was to hold Amanda hostage and make Jake go into Des Moines alone. But that was only if things got desperate, if they refused to help me, which I just couldn't see Jake doing.

I definitely needed my black hat.

I turned away from Truncheon and headed back for our car.

"See you on the other side," he called after me.

The other side. It kind of felt like I'd already crossed over. Maybe I'd been naive to think I was doing good while I was with the NCD, but at least I'd had something resembling a code. Now I was in this murky, amoral territory populated by creatures like Alastaire and Truncheon. I was becoming one of them.

A fresh swell of psychic hangover broke across my brain. I'd been able to keep myself upright and functional during my conversation with Truncheon and was paying for it now. The reinvigorated headache sent a wave of nausea through me. I felt suddenly hot, like I could feel individual beams of heat reflecting off the wall behind me, and yet a cold sweat spread across my spine. The knapsack suddenly felt like it weighed a ton and that I was carrying it through quicksand. I was about to faint.

I need help.

And then Jake was there. Steadying me. He took the knapsack from me and slung it over his shoulder with a grunt. He led me back toward the car, one of his hands on my elbow, the other on the small of my back. A flash of memory came back to me—him holding me up outside the hotel elevator. I managed to put on a shaky smile.

"We have to stop meeting like this," I joked badly. *Good one, Cass.*

He looked nervous. This display of chivalry probably wasn't winning him any points with Amanda. I tried to zero in on her face, but everything beyond Jake was a blur.

"I heard you," Jake said to me, sounding dumbstruck.

"Huh?" It was hard to hear him over the thunderclap of my own heartbeat.

"I heard you inside my head," he said.

Psychic slippage. That's what my instructors had called it, when you couldn't keep your thoughts to yourself. It was an amateur mistake, something that I'd never had to deal with, being such a gifted prodigy of the telepathic arts. Until now, at least.

"Did—did you hear me think anything else?" I asked Jake cautiously.

"It was more like a feeling," he said as we paused

outside the car. I could sense Amanda watching us intently. "A guilty feeling."

I peered up at him, trying to get a read on his thoughts the old-fashioned way. What are the physical giveaways for when a guy knows you've just used his girl-friend as a down payment to a mercenary? That pretty soon you might double-cross him? I didn't see any in his sweet, confused face.

"Are we going to be okay?" Jake asked, opening the driver-side door so I could collapse into the front seat.

I couldn't answer honestly, so I just pretended not to have heard.

JAKE

"TRUNCHEON." I REPEATED THE NAME AGAIN, BECAUSE I just couldn't get over the total excess of badassery riding a motorcycle in front of us. "He's like a freaking video-game character."

Neither of the girls seemed interested. At this point, I was pretty used to my gaming references falling flat. Not my best opposite-sex material, granted, but I'd never before come across an actual human being that looked like a refugee from a Capcom shooting game as designed by Todd McFarlane. It demanded comment.

"Did you guys see he's wearing a utility belt? He's wearing a utility belt. It's probably where he keeps his power-ups."

"Okay, we get it," Amanda said, sitting beside me in the backseat. Our words were muffled thanks to the serial-biter muzzles we'd strapped into. "Maybe reflect on your new crush in silence."

"Don't cheapen this by making it sexual," I replied with mock offense. "There are guys like me who merely know the *Contra* code. And then there are dudes like my new best friend Truncheon who are living it."

Amanda sighed, the breath whistling through the air slits in the muzzle. "Do I even want to know what that is?"

"It's some retro shit," I explained. "Up, up, down, down—"

"No, I do not." Amanda answered her own question.

I fell silent. Amanda reached over and took my hand, gave it a squeeze, our chains clanking together. I looked over at her and could only really see her eyes above the muzzle, so it was hard to tell, but I think she was smiling at me. The banter helped, I think. It'd become a kind of coping mechanism for us, especially useful as we were slowly driven toward a giant wall manned by zombie killers.

I winked at her. She rolled her eyes at me.

"You look kind of hot in that muzzle," I whispered.

"Like a supervillain on her way to lady jail."

She stared at me. "Thanks, but I'm going to pretend you never said that."

"Me too," said Cass from the driver's seat.

Cass didn't have much to say once I'd gotten her back to the car—verbally or otherwise. She explained the plan was to take us through the wall like we were zombie slaves assigned to her, which Amanda and I had already put together, argued over, and settled on as not having a better option. So we ended up in chains (left those carefully unlocked, thank you very much) and muzzles, and Cass seemed relieved not to have to convince us. I think she passed out with her forehead against the steering wheel while we ate a couple guinea pigs and put on our slave costumes. She looked wiped out. Once we were on the road again and Cass was driving, I'd caught her drifting, the car sliding across lanes toward the median. I kicked the back of her seat and she came up alert, had been clinging to the wheel ever since. We were only going about fifteen miles per hour. Truncheon was up ahead setting the slow and totally nonthreatening pace.

We didn't talk any more about Cass's psychic distress call. She seemed embarrassed by it, so I tried not to let on how whispers-in-the-dark creepy it'd been to have an outside voice trample in on my thoughts. I also tried not to overanalyze the ball-shrinking, sizzling guilt feeling that'd raced through me, or how I'd felt something weirdly similar before but couldn't figure out exactly when. Nope. Let's just forget about all that.

As we closed in on the wall, I noticed some movement along the top. Those turrets I'd picked out before had operators now, shadowy figures aiming machine gun barrels at us. I swallowed hard and kept this detail to myself. Pretty soon we were close enough to the wall that we couldn't see the top anymore.

"Glad we didn't try to climb over," I said to Amanda, both of us staring at the wall.

"I bet you are," she said. I could hear her teasing smirk. The wall was sleek metal all the way up and across—smooth-plated titanium or adamantium or some experimental government alloy they didn't have a name for—there weren't any handholds anywhere. At some point, while Cass was talking to Truncheon, we'd debated scrapping this whole plan, going back to civilization, and finding a grappling-hook store. That idea had broken down when I told Amanda I'd never mastered the rope climb in gym class.

"My amazing core makes up for my average upper body," I told her.

"Uh-huh."

A gap opened up in the wall where it met the highway, loud hydraulics powering the metal plates apart. Flashing lights and a dull siren alerted everyone inside that they had visitors. Truncheon passed through first. We followed.

"Oh man," Amanda whispered. "So many."

"It's like a genocidal Ghostbuster convention," I whispered back.

Underneath the wall, in a cleared space that served as both parking garage and rec center, the NCD jumpsuits were everywhere. They sat on the hoods of Jeeps, cleaned their guns, and stared at us. They sat around picnic tables, ate buffalo wings, and stared at us. They paused from poring over tactical maps, hastily covered them up, and stared at us. They stopped highly competitive games of Ping-Pong and stared at us.

It was like one of those dreams where you show up for class in just your underwear and all your classmates have rifles with bayonets and start trying to stab out your brain.

"Try not to look, uh, emotional," said Cass through clenched teeth. "Look zombieish. And don't hold hands."

Reluctantly, I released my grip on Amanda. I kept my eyes straight ahead. Slumped my shoulders in the way of disaffected undead. Desperately held in a nervous fart.

One by one, the NCD guys went back to doing whatever they were doing. Up ahead, an older agent with a clipboard was exchanging words with Truncheon. The filthy mercenary didn't seem even a little intimidated by all the hardware surrounding us. I guess he'd done this before.

"Why are there so many?" whispered Amanda.

Cass didn't answer. It did seem like the agents were

massing here, like it shouldn't take this many dudes to keep a wall upright. But what did I know about secret military operations?

A young NCD guy who looked fresh out of boot camp, bright-eyed and buzz-cut, sauntered over to our car. He was staring at us zombies, grinning dumbly, like we were animals at the petting zoo and he'd just bought a quarter's worth of those bran feed pellets. He tapped on Cass's window and, after a moment's hesitation, she rolled it down.

"You got two of them things, huh?" he said conversationally. The agent rolled up his sleeve, displaying a bandage on his forearm for Cass's inspection. "I was supposed to get in on that program, get me a zombie of my own. They even put this damn nozzle thing on me. But I heard it didn't work, that the bigwig in charge got himself demo—"

"Agent, do you have orders to come talk to me?" Cass cut in coldly, a steel in her voice I hadn't heard before. She didn't let him reply. "Do you have orders to even *look* at me or my property?"

The agent's grin flickered, but I could tell he wasn't sure if she was serious or not. She was pretty little and hungover looking to be acting so hard, although I could see her eyes burning like hot coals in the rearview. I wouldn't have messed with her, personally.

"Hey, whoa there—"

She cut him off again. "I will use you for food and your squad leader won't even miss you. My zombie will crap you out and they'll call it a dishonorable discharge."

I laughed. Couldn't help it. Luckily, muzzled as I was, the laugh came out harsh and raspy, something a new recruit might mistake for zombie hunger. The agent flinched and backed away.

"Sorr—" he yelped, but Cass had already rolled up the window.

"You're a terrible Trojan horse," Amanda said to me.

"Not my fault! I didn't know she was going to make with the one-liners."

"You guys have got to stop talking," Cass said, looking deflated, like acting the part of the NCD hard case had sapped her even further.

"Sorry," I replied.

"Yeah," Amanda said, adding hesitantly. "Impressive bitchiness, though."

Meanwhile, Truncheon had finished talking with the clipboard guy. He revved his motorcycle way louder than necessary, showing off, a plume of black exhaust curling out of the tailpipe. He waved for us to follow him as the NCD guys stepped begrudgingly aside.

We drove through the NCD encampment and out the other side of the wall. As soon as the gate closed behind us, Amanda and I stripped off our chains, helping each other with the straps and buckles of the muzzles. We let it all pool in the footwells.

"Iowa," I said, feeling a brief flare of triumph. "We made it."

I turned to watch the wall recede behind us. Unlike the side facing nonquarantined America, the inside of the wall was covered in warning signs—DO NOT APPROACH, most prominently, but the one that stuck out for me was ALL TRESPASSERS PRESUMED HOSTILE CONTAMINANTS. That explained the husk of a station wagon we passed on the side of the road, riddled with bullet holes, a torn white flag with the spray-painted message UNINFECTED mounted on the roof. I couldn't see if there were any bodies inside because the windows were too spiderwebbed and broken for a clear view. But I bet they were there, cut down trying to escape. It was as if the NCD had left the car there as a warning to anyone else with ideas of rushing the wall.

"Fucked up," I said quietly.

"Massive, gaping understatement," replied Amanda, turning her head to stare at the wreck.

For the first few miles, the land on the Iowa side of the wall was cleared of any kind of cover, just like it'd been on the other side. Things changed once the wall disappeared from view. Trees started popping up again, fields of corn, road signs, houses, and farms. We were on a rural back road, cruising, and it was almost normal.

Except there weren't any people.

And then there was the smell. It fell somewhere on the spectrum between rotten meat and spoiled cheese that'd been sprayed with sweet-smelling perfume. It hit me whenever the wind picked up and got stuck inside my nostrils. The weird thing? I didn't really mind it so much. It was gross, yeah, but I had a tolerance for it. I noticed Cass wrinkling her nose, though, sucking in breaths through her mouth.

"That's what we smell like, isn't it?" I asked her.

"Uh," she replied, "not all the time. Not now. You guys smell fine now."

"Thanks for that," said Amanda.

Cass shrugged and pulled her shirt up over her nose and mouth.

As Truncheon led us east, deeper into Iowa, I started noticing the abandoned cars. Some of them were just parked on the side of the road like their owners had wandered off to get gas or otherwise decided to randomly take up walking. Others were straight-up crashed, some head-on into one another, some wrapped around trees, some flipped over like sad turtles. Still no people, though. I'd expected chaos like we'd gotten a taste of back in Omaha, not this eerie quiet. What was the point of building a wall around an abandoned state?

"This isn't so bad," I remarked after a few miles.

Amanda elbowed me. Pointed.

Oh yeah, so there was a dead guy hanging from a

tree. It wasn't totally clear whether he'd done it himself or if someone had strung him up. His head was swollen soft and purple above the noose, the body below withered, gray, and partially eaten. His feet were chewed off, toe bones brilliant white in the late afternoon sun. Whatever zombie had gone this-little-piggy on him hadn't been enterprising enough to climb up for the rest. A cardboard sign that read ISAIAH 26:19 was pinned to the corpse's ratty flannel shirt.

"Ugh, I stand corrected," I replied. "Either of you guys know the Bible?"

Both girls shook their heads. Cass looked pretty grim, focused on the road ahead.

"Bet it's something about the end of the world," Amanda said.

"Oh, you mean the guy swinging from a tree didn't pick out a happy quote?"

The corpses started appearing more frequently after that. Grisly sun-cooked lumps on the side of the road—or in the middle of the road, or hanging out of cars, or once smeared gruesomely across a truck's windshield—usually so torn up and rotten that they didn't really register as human bodies. Or maybe I was just getting desensitized to the whole thing. So far Iowa looked a lot like the suburbs on the day after Halloween, except instead of pumpkins smashed open everywhere, it was human heads.

I watched a crow take flight from within the hollowed space of a body's rib cage. The birds were the only sign of life we'd seen so far.

A few miles farther into the middle of nowhere, Truncheon pulled off the road and into the dusty parking lot of an abandoned gas station and auto shop. In normal times, this place would be like an oasis if you popped a tire out in the country. Now, it seemed ominous. The building looked like it'd been ransacked once (gas pumps hung limp off their hooks, windows shattered and boarded up) and then reassembled by some enterprising Mad Max type (barbed wire everywhere, armed bear traps cluttering the parking lot).

"Does he live here?" I asked as Truncheon hopped off his motorcycle and picked his way carefully toward the garage.

"Let's find out," Cass said, opening her door.

Truncheon heard the door open and spun toward us.

"Stay in the car!" he shouted, hands cupped around his mouth.

Chastened, Cass shut the door. We waited.

"Uh, can't we just drive away?" Amanda asked. "Do we still need this guy?"

"He knows the area," Cass said. "He'll get us to Des Moines."

From inside, Truncheon flung open one of the shop's garage doors. He parked his motorcycle inside and then drove out in a black conversion van.

"What's with the van?" I asked.

"Not sure," Cass replied, and I detected a bit of appre-hension in her voice. Maybe she hadn't discussed this part with our esteemed guide.

"Maybe his crotch just hurts," I offered.

"Maybe," Cass said.

Truncheon pulled up next to us, hopped out, and went into a stretch where he knuckled the small of his back and stuck out his belly.

"Gross," Amanda observed.

"Worst thing we've seen yet," Cass added.

Done curling his spine and thrusting his hips, Trun-cheon motioned for Cass to roll down her window. She complied reluctantly, letting a bunch of fresh odors into the car. In a place overrun with bad smells, Truncheon's BO conquered all. I'd never considered how badly action heroes must reek.

"Let me see that," Truncheon grunted, gesturing to our road atlas lying open on the passenger seat.

As Cass handed over the map, Truncheon's gaze turned toward me and Amanda. I couldn't really see his eyes through the mirrored aviators, but I got the feeling they lingered on Amanda more than me.

"All right, here's us," Truncheon began, turning back to Cass, and pointing to a spot on the map just west of Des Moines. Then he licked his thumb and pressed it onto the nearby city, creating a damp circle on the map. "Everything outside of this radius is anarchy. That's good. Anarchy ain't so bad in the country—lots of places for gals like you to run and hide. Inside the circle is where the zombies that haven't rotted out have organized, where the trouble is. Normally, I don't go poking around thereabouts unless absolutely necessary, but we got a mission, huh?"

I exchanged a look with Amanda. I thought we were the ones on a mission.

"So here's the lay of the land," Truncheon continued. "We take back roads, in case the Lord's got his people patrolling. They don't usually scavenge out here anyway. There's more fresh meat to be had farther east in Cedar Rapids."

"Why Cedar Rapids?" Cass asked.

"City only just got brought inside the wall a few weeks ago," Truncheon replied, like this detail was inconsequential. "Still plenty of uninfected holdouts there, waiting for the government to come chopper them to safety. Idiots don't realize who put up the wall in the first place."

"Dude," I muttered in disbelief. "That's cold."

Truncheon didn't even glance at me. "On the outskirts of Des Moines, your entourage here will take my van. Get in there and do whatever they're supposed to do. You and me will head to a safe house I've got nearby and wait shit out. You know how to play gin rummy?"

In response, Cass rolled up her window.

Truncheon stood in the road for a moment, his expression at first dumbfounded and then offended. After glaring at Cass for an uncomfortable thirty seconds, he finally got back on the road, signaling for us to follow.

"You're not really going to, like, hang out with this guy, are you?" I asked.

"I don't really have a choice," Cass replied, adding with quiet resolve, "I'm not playing any freaking cards, though."

Amanda leaned forward to look at Cass. "So, I appreciate the chauffeur thing and all, but what exactly did he mean about your *mission*?"

Cass forced a nervous laugh. "Oh yeah. About that."

Amanda glanced at me, like she wanted my diplomatic help. I could see the first sign of smoke from her temper flaring.

"Uh, is there something we need to talk about, Ca—?"

"Look out!" Amanda yelled.

Without warning, unless you count brake lights, Truncheon's van went into a skid. Startled, Cass slammed the brakes. We fishtailed for a second, but ended up on the shoulder, dust kicking up around us, inches from Truncheon's back bumper.

"The hell is he doing?" Amanda asked.

Cass shielded her eyes with one hand. "There's

something up ahead."

I hopped out to get a better look. Ahead of me, Truncheon had climbed into the front doorway of his van and set his sniper rifle up on the roof. He screwed a silencer into the barrel, but paused to glance at me.

"Want to see something cool?" he asked.

"Uh."

Amanda and Cass had gotten out of the car too, but they hung back, probably repulsed by Truncheon. I stood next to the rear of the van, squinting down the road.

"You see him?" Truncheon asked me conversationally as he peered through the scope.

I did. The zombie was about a half mile down the road and ambling in our direction. His movements were herky-jerky—one foot dragged uselessly behind him, head lolling from side to side on his shoulders. One of his hands was outstretched toward us.

"Is he waving?" I asked.

"Heh." Truncheon snorted, then blew the top of the zombie's head off with a silenced puff from his rifle.

"Whoa," I said, taking a step back.

"Got it in one." Truncheon shouldered his rifle and grinned proudly in my direction, but that look faded fast when Amanda started yelling at him.

"Asshole! You just *killed* that guy!" she shouted.

Truncheon hopped down from the van and pointed his rifle at Amanda.

"You need to stop yelling," he commanded. "There

could be more wandering around in the fields and we don't want to attract them. Me and your sweet little friend"—he glanced at Cass—"we aren't at the top of the food chain around here."

Amanda lowered her voice, but at the same time stepped forward, toward the rifle, letting Truncheon know she wasn't impressed. Her shoulders were square, chin titled up, going into ice-queen mode. Cass took a couple discreet steps away, toward me.

"That was a person," she seethed at Truncheon.

Truncheon barked a laugh, shaking his head incredulously. He looked at Cass. "What'd you bring with you? A couple peacenik zombie goody-goodies?" His gaze swung to me. "Don't you eat people?"

"We're trying to cut back," I said, speaking the nonchalant language of badass dudes everywhere. "But we've made exceptions before."

"Christ." Truncheon lowered his rifle and pointed down the road toward his kill. "That was a ghoul. How you kids'll end up if you don't manage a balanced diet. No person left. Ain't no coming back once you're like that. I saw one of those things chew through a family of five and not come back to life even a little bit."

"Uh"—I raised my hand—"why did you watch a family of five get eaten?"

"Beside the point," Truncheon replied.

I looked at Cass, who'd been watching this whole exchange nervously. "Didn't you get, like, character references before hiring this guy?"

"You cherry Deadzone tourists don't know a god-damn thing," Truncheon snapped, glaring at all of us. "Here's rule number one: see a ghoul, kill a ghoul. They're bad for the fucking ecosystem."

"Oh, so you're a conservationist?" I asked.

Amanda yawned. "All right, whatever. We're in. I didn't sign up for any secret missions. What're we still following Pigpen and his molester van for?" She snapped off a mocking salute at Truncheon and started for the car. "Let's bail."

"Good point," I agreed, and moved to follow her. "Smell ya later."

"Time for the hard touch?" I heard Truncheon grumble to Cass.

"Hey, wait—" Cass reached out to stop me. "We need to talk about something. I need a favor."

Amanda was already back at the car. "Hey," she yelled to Cass, "let's talk after we ditch the murderous smelly guy, all right?"

I shot a sidelong glance at Truncheon. He was watching this whole exchange with detached interest. It didn't seem like he was going to shoot us if we tried to leave, at least not right this second, so I turned to Cass.

"Favor, sure, whatever. But let's go first. You don't want to hang out with this dude, do you?"

"No, but—"

A loud metallic thud rang out and we all flinched

and went silent. I glanced toward the cornfields, worried ghouls or hatchet-wielding Des Moines zombies or pissed-off NCD agents eager to revoke our day pass were going to come charging out at us. But then the noise hit again—like someone stomping a piece of sheet metal—and I realized it was coming from the back of Truncheon's van.

We all turned in that direction. Something was trying to get out through the back doors. I inched closer to our car, and Cass followed me. Amanda and I exchanged a look.

Truncheon grunted, annoyed, and wrenched the door open.

Immediately, a guy's body came flying out from the van, like he'd been in the process of lining up another kick. He crashed right into Truncheon, which was pretty much like hitting a brick wall. Somehow, the guy managed to land on his feet in the road. He did a little shuffle-dance as he tried to figure out which direction to run. It was probably a tough call on account of his head being tied up under a burlap sack and his hands being cuffed in front of him.

Truncheon struck him hard in the face area with the butt of his rifle and the guy collapsed, knocked out.

"Uh, what is going on right now?" I asked Cass.

"This—" Cass hesitated. "I didn't know about this part."

With a put-upon sigh, Truncheon picked up the body

and dumped it back into the van. There were others back there too—three of them, not counting the escape artist—all sacked and handcuffed, and apparently more tightly secured to the van's metal benches.

Truncheon slammed the van closed and turned to us. We were all staring at him.

"What?" he asked.

Amanda pointed at the van. "Who are your friends?"

"Oh, them." Truncheon grinned at us. "They're for you guys. You want to get into Des Moines, right? Well, that psycho Lord in there is gonna be expecting tribute."

"Are they . . . ?" I trailed off, itching my mohawk. "You've got *people* back there?"

"Oh no," Cass said quietly, bracing herself against the car, like her knees had just gotten weak again. "I did not—"

Truncheon laughed at us. "What did you kids think? That you'd come to the Deadzone—where the undead outnumber the living, for shit's sake—and nobody'd get eaten? You like the taste of eggshell in your omelets or what?"

"Where did they come from?" Amanda asked suddenly. "Who are they?"

Truncheon shrugged, acting bored, but I could tell he was one of those dudes who liked to deliver speeches.

"The living are like currency around here," he answered. "You wonder about every penny you see lying on the sidewalk?"

Amanda and I exchanged a look. I guess we could've tolerated Truncheon's general skeeviness if it meant getting closer to the cure, but in the last five minutes he'd straight-up executed a fellow zombie and then revealed himself as an unapologetic human trafficker. I thought about Grace and Summer, the zombie couple we'd met back in Pennsylvania, and how they tried only to eat bad people. That was a slippery slope to get on, but Truncheon seemed like a pretty clear-cut case.

"I'd eat him," I said quietly.

"Unanimous," Amanda replied.

CASS

AT SOME POINT DURING OUR DRIVE THE SUN HAD GOT-
ten low, causing long, bent shadows to peel off from the
cornfield, dividing the road into alternating slats of
shade and dusky gold. The crickets were loud—I guess
the local undead hadn't gotten around to eating the
bugs—their chirping an incessant chorus that I only
really noticed when it suddenly stopped.

They knew there was a showdown brewing.

Or maybe I was just projecting my own rising sense of
dread onto the crickets, because they started right back

up again a heartbeat later, not the least bit interested in the life-threatening altercation going down on our little stretch of country road. Or who knows, maybe they were rapt and rubbing their little spiny cricket legs together in anticipation.

God, why was I thinking so much about the crickets? There's that cliché about time slowing down, but that wasn't the case here—things were happening. Moves were being made.

Amanda took a long step away from the door of our car and walked slowly to the side, her glare boring into Truncheon as she flanked him. Stalked him. I'd seen her do this before, when Tom caught up with us back in Michigan. She crouched low, made herself as small a target as possible.

Jake moved toward Truncheon's opposite flank. They wanted to make it hard for Truncheon to keep both zombies in his sights. Jake didn't quite have the predatory grace Amanda did; he took big, exaggerated tippy-toe steps, like someone trying to be sneaky in a cartoon. It would've made me laugh if this situation hadn't spiraled so rapidly out of control.

I stood rooted in place, feeling like an innocent bystander in one of those old-timey westerns.

"Is this a joke?" Truncheon asked, looking more amused than threatened. He hadn't even raised his rifle yet. In fact, he was leaning on it. He jerked his thumb over his shoulder, down the road. "Did you miss me wax that ghoul at two hundred yards? And you two are gonna what? Bum-rush me? You're confident in that strategy?"

Jake shot an uncertain glance over at Amanda, but she was too busy creeping up on Truncheon to notice.

"I shoot you first," Truncheon said, pointing at Amanda. "It'll be in the face, which is a goddamn crying shame, but easy come, easy go, I guess."

"Okay, hold on—" I said, finding my voice at last. I sounded small and squeaky.

"If you don't flinch or collapse into hysterics, and assuming you time it right, you'll close on me the second after I've blown the head off your fuck buddy," Truncheon continued, ignoring me and turning to Jake. "After that, unless you're some kinda secret Karate Kid, odds are I'll beat you to death."

Jake and Amanda had spread out on Truncheon about as far as they could without stepping into the cornfield. They both had wide angles on him, but they didn't look so eager to charge anymore.

"I like to do this thing after," Truncheon continued nonchalantly, "where I rip a zombie's head off and see how far I can punt it. I've got a measuring tape and everything."

"He's bluffing," Amanda said without her usual confidence.

"It's like amateur hour out here," Truncheon

grumbled, then glanced in my direction. "I'm losing patience with this bullshit, kid. You gonna get your pets in line or what?"

"What," I replied, and shot Truncheon in the groin with my stun gun.

If I'm being cool about it, which is how I intend to play it if I ever tell this story in a social situation, like if we're playing Never Have I Ever and someone says, "Shot somebody," I just pulled like a gunslinger and squeezed the trigger. Didn't even need to aim because I'm such a natural.

In reality, it was a lucky shot on pretty much every level. The stun gun caught on my shirt when I pulled it out, hitching it up, and screwing up any rudimentary aiming I might've done. But maybe that confused Truncheon—it must've looked like I was about to flash him—because he didn't duck, or raise his rifle, or do anything that even remotely lived up to all his badass talk. A sizzling blue arc of electricity flew from my fist and right into his nethers, which he managed to clutch only for a moment before all the spasming and mouth foaming took over and he fell to the ground.

Jake and Amanda both looked at me. I ran a hand through my hair, which felt tingly with static.

"Wow," Jake said, walking over with his hands up.

"Can we talk like people now?" I asked them. "Just for a second and then you can eat him if you want. Although

I'd definitely wash him first."

"How long have you had that thing?" Amanda asked, pointing at the stun gun. She'd uncoiled somewhat from her pounce-ready combat posture, but still looked tense.

"He gave it to me outside the wall," I replied.

"Can we shoot him again?" Jake asked, watching Truncheon convulse.

"And you were keeping it hidden from us why?" Amanda kept on, looking from the stun gun to my face and back. "In case we got out of hand and you needed to use it?"

"Jeez, dude," Jake cut in, sounding a little exasperated. "You know she just saved our bacon, right?"

"Saved my—" Amanda shook her head. "No. I don't have any bacon to save."

"It's an expression. The point is, Duke Douche 'Em over there was pretty convincing about how he'd have killed us. I mean, I was buying it."

"No, you're right," I said to Amanda, meeting her still slightly meat-hungry gaze and hoping like heck I wasn't misjudging this situation. "That is why I had it. As a precaution. You're scary. Does that offend you?"

Amanda stared at me, evaluating, and the crickets paused again. It was like she made some kind of mental calculation in that brief moment of silence. When the chirping resumed, Amanda shook her head once and walked toward Truncheon.

"Whatever. I don't even care," she said, sounding abruptly drained of all her killer energy. "We've got other shit to deal with."

"Thanks for shooting him instead of us," Jake said, standing next to me with his hands in his pockets.

I nodded. "You're welcome."

"Right in his little truncheon too," he said wonderingly. "Blistered the ol' billy club."

"Not on purpose."

"Sizzled the shillelagh."

I smirked at him. "Got a lot of these?"

"I'm running out," he replied, and paused. "Cooked the . . ."

"Cudgel," I finished.

"Nice."

Except for the occasional twitch, Truncheon's spasms had subsided. His body was clenched into an uncomfortable-looking C position, but the opposite of how you'd think. Standing over him, Amanda sniffed haughtily.

"You're lucky I'm not hungry," she told him. "And that there's not enough powdered sugar on the planet."

Amanda crouched down and tried to angle herself to catch Truncheon's gaze, but his eyeballs had rolled partly back in his head.

"Where are your keys, dick?"

Truncheon made a clicking tongue-stuck-in-throat sound. Amanda sighed and started going through his half million belt pouches.

"So," Jake said, turning to me. "You were trying to talk to me about something before. It seemed important."

I took a deep breath and recalled my plan to play this whole thing as honestly as possible. I'd been inside Jake's mind. I knew him. He'd do the right thing.

"Yeah, um, so," I said haltingly, not really sure how to start, and then opting for maximum blurting. "My old boss from the NCD is holding my mom hostage and he wants me to bring him the zombie cure or else he'll kill her."

Jake blinked at me. "Well, shit, between you and Amanda now I'm worried the NCD is dangling my family over a vat of lava or something."

I glanced at Amanda, still rifling through Truncheon's pockets, but totally listening. Jake caught my look and explained.

"Her brother is, like, a political prisoner or something," he said, lowering his voice a fraction. "He's a zombie truther, so they locked him up. What'd your mom do?"

I felt an unwelcome wave of sympathy for Amanda, we of the endangered loved ones.

"Nothing," I answered. "She didn't do anything. Doesn't even know why it's happening to her."

"Damn," Jake said, shaking his head. "Your people

are into some messed-up stuff."

"They aren't her people anymore," Amanda yelled over. When I looked in her direction, her gaze was softer than before. Maybe we'd finally found some tragic common ground. "You're done with them, right? This smelly bastard included."

"Right."

Jake waved his hand, like he didn't need to hear any more. "Cool, so we'll share the cure with you so you can save your mom. Unless you hate your mom."

"No, I definitely do not."

"Great! So, we'll share. Deal? Deal."

"If we ever find it," Amanda added, pausing her search to tick off caveats on her fingers. "If it exists at all. As long as there's enough. And assuming it's even something we can share."

Jake furrowed his brow. "Why wouldn't we be able to share it?"

Amanda shrugged. "What if it's a secret recipe or something?"

"We'll photocopy it," he replied. "Duh."

"Whatever. Found 'em." Amanda stood up holding Truncheon's keys. "I need, like, a bucket of hand sanitizer."

"He have anything cool in that belt?" Jake asked. "Smoke bombs? Batarangs?"

"He's got a pocket filled with teeth," Amanda replied.

"So . . . that's a no?" Jake frowned.

Amanda nudged Truncheon with her toe. "Help me move him out of the way."

Jake groaned dramatically, but eventually helped Amanda to drag Truncheon by his wrists and ankles and dump him a few yards away on the side of the road. I kept my stun gun pointed at him; I wasn't sure how long the shock would last and wouldn't have really minded having another shot at him. Shooting someone turned out to be kind of cathartic.

With Truncheon relocated, Amanda bent down and grabbed his rifle. She gave me a pointed look, like *now we're both packing*, and slung it over her shoulder. I guess we weren't going to be doing trust falls with each other anytime soon, but at least she wasn't actively screwing me over.

"I think we should chain him up," Jake suggested, eyeballing Truncheon. "That'd be some poetic justice, right?"

"You think we can fit him next to the guinea pigs?" Amanda replied.

Jake shrugged. "Probably."

I walked over to the van door. "Um, are we going to let these people out? Or at least take the sacks off their heads?"

While Jake retrieved some chains from our car, Amanda unlocked the van door. The guy that made a break for it was still unconscious on the floor, but the other captives greeted us with a synchronized barrage of gagged *mmmf-mmmf*s. I wondered how much they'd heard. Enough that we were being greeted as heroes. All of them were clad in filthy clothes, yellowed and crusty from sweat. The KO'd escape artist, another guy with a prodigious beer belly, and two women.

"We should probably make sure he's not dead," I said, and pulled the hood off the prisoner Truncheon had struck.

The guy had a bloody half-moon cut on his forehead from Truncheon's rifle butt, and my first thought upon seeing it was that it'd leave a scar and that he'd probably make it look good. He was preposterously handsome, the kind of country hunk you see tossing bales of hay in jean ads but don't think actually exists in the real world. His dark-blond hair was sweaty and matted from the hood, yet this cut-jaw dimple face made hostage hair look like lightly tousled bedhead.

I glanced over at Amanda. We'd both been staring at this guy for a moment longer than appropriate. "He's, um . . ."

"Alive," Amanda finished for me, fingering the strap of Truncheon's rifle.

Jake cleared his throat. He'd stopped behind us to check on the prisoner, his arms full of chains. I think Amanda and I both jumped.

"Okay, I'll say it," Jake said. "*Hello, nurse.* We found freakin' *High School Musical* over here."

I had the nonsensical urge to put the handsome captive's hood back on. I guess those NCD secrecy instincts die hard. I turned to the conscious prisoners still bound and gagged in the back, and lowered my voice.

"So, um, what are we going to do with them?" I asked.

Amanda bit her lip. "Yeah, I'm not sure how many humans I want to be responsible for out here. No offense."

"None taken," I replied. "We can't leave them like this, though."

"We can at least let them loose," Jake insisted, then raised his voice to address the prisoners. "You sack people aren't secretly murderous Wastelanders, are you? If there were, say, friendly zombies out here willing to set you free, you wouldn't reward them by trying to bash out their brains, would you?"

Two out of the three heads shook back and forth vehemently; the other just rolled listlessly side to side. Jake shrugged.

"Good enough for me! Let's ge—whoa!" Jake dropped his load of chains and shoved me into the back of the van, right on top of the good-looking prisoner, just before the grasping fingers of a little zombie girl would've wrapped around my leg.

She must've slunk out of the cornfield while we were talking. The girl couldn't have been more than eight when she necrotized—she was so little, wearing a cute, frilly dress covered in rust-colored bloodstains. Her hair was pulled into pigtails that had amazing staying power considering she'd likely been out here rotting for months. The same couldn't be said about her scalp; it'd split open where her hair parted, exposing a yellowed expanse of skull.

"This is really gross!" Jake shouted. He held the slavering zombie girl at bay with one hand on her forehead, a move he'd probably trotted out a few times with his younger sister. Zombie girl wasn't the least bit interested in him—she just kept staring at me and the van denizens with wide, watery eyes, clawing at the air with chubby purple fingers.

"Don't yell," I said, scrambling to my feet inside the van and trying not to step on Hunkalunk. "Truncheon said the noise could draw them."

"Oh, *now* you want to listen to Truncheon," Jake complained, but it seemed to give him an idea. He looked down the road to where we'd left Truncheon.

The burly survivalist looked more alert than he had a minute ago. He was trying to crawl into the cornfield, but his limbs, alternately droopy and twitchy, weren't cooperating. At the sound of his name, he lolled his head around to look at us.

Jake turned the zombie child in Truncheon's direction and pushed her off with a kick to the butt. Seeing an easier victim, the zombie shuffled off.

"Fu-fu-fu—" was all Truncheon could spit out in his condition. I think we all got the gist.

"Yeah," Jake said, "you were going to punt my head, so I'd say you've got this coming, dude."

"Hey, guys . . . ," Amanda said, pointing.

On the other side of the road, two more ghouls stumbled out of the cornfield. Man-sized ones this time, both clad in filthy denim overalls that hung loose from their decomposing bodies. The skin on their shoulders and the tops of their heads was black and peeling from weeks of sunburn. The broken shaft of a pitchfork jutted out of one's abdomen, the pointy end sticking out of his back. They staggered slowly toward the van, which must've looked like a human buffet with me and the prisoners back there.

"Maybe—uh, maybe we should get moving," I said, trying to sound mellow as I dragged Hunk Hostage away from the van doors.

"Probably a good idea," Jake said.

"I'll drive the van. You drive the car," Amanda said to Jake. She glanced at me. "You hide back here, I guess."

I wasn't going to argue. I handed Jake the car keys. Amanda ran to get the van started and Jake hustled over to the car. I reached out to slam the van door closed and that's when Truncheon screamed.

The little girl ghoul had collapsed across his legs

and was gnawing greedily at his jeans. Truncheon tried to kick her off, but he was still uncoordinated from the stun-gun blast, so it wasn't going well. I watched as the girl used her back teeth to tear off a strip of denim along with a sizable chunk of Truncheon's shin, tossed back her head, and gulped it down like a bird.

That moment of hesitation was all it took for Pitchfork Ghoul to close in on me. He got one yellow-nailed, three-fingered hand braced against the van doorway, and then his hairless and peeling head was snapping at me. I fell backward and kicked him in the chest. My foot actually hit square on the pitchfork handle, driving it farther through the zombie with a sound like slurping pasta.

"OOF!" It was a distinctly unghoul shout of pain.

I scrambled to my knees and stared out of the van.

"Oh crap!" I cried. "Sorry!"

Jake had come running back to help me; he'd wrapped his arms around the ghoul and tried to wrestle him away. And I'd inadvertently kicked a pitchfork into his stomach, creating an accidental zombie shish kebob or the world's most gruesome conga line.

"Uh, no worries," Jake said as he gritted his teeth and pushed on the zombie's shoulders, trying to pry himself loose from the pitchfork.

"Oh crap, oh crap," I repeated, torn between trying to help Jake and my screaming sense of self-preservation. There were more ghouls appearing from the cornfield now, staggering toward Truncheon's continued screams. Some of them broke off and ambled in our direction, arms outstretched.

"Jake?" I heard Amanda yell from the driver's seat. "What's going on back there?"

"Just—just go!" he yelled back. He wasn't having much luck budging the pitchfork. "Keep them safe! I'll meet you back at Truncheon's garage! I lo—gah!"

The other farmer-ghoul was close now. Jake managed to stick out his leg and trip him. He met my eyes, looking exasperated and a little scared.

I opened my mouth to say something. The only thing that came to mind was a swooning *my hero*. So, I didn't say anything.

"You should close that door," Jake said, trying to sound Zen, but his words were slurring. I noticed the skin on his neck was turning a swampy gray. "I'm, uh . . . we're all kinda hungry out here."

The van rumbled and we were pulling away. I found my words.

"Stay alive!" I shouted to Jake. "I'll find you! Whatever happens, I'll find you!"

Jake stared at me with fierce, hungry eyes. He tossed the ghoul away from him with new strength, the pitchfork's prongs tearing loose a coil of intestine. He started to chase us.

I yanked on the van door just as Amanda sped into a

bump. It flew back at me with more force than I'd anticipated, hit me square in the forehead, and knocked me off my feet.

My last thought before I lost consciousness was the realization that I'd just quoted the romantic part of *Last of the Mohicans* to Jake.

I'm such a loser.

JAKE

REALLY WISH THIS KIND OF THING WOULD QUIT HAPpening to me.

I glanced down at the three holes in my abdomen, quarter sized but torn jagged from the way I yanked out the pitchfork. Listen, if you're ever stabbed or impaled, the natural reaction is to tug that sharp something out of your soft body. Don't do it! Because you could pull something important loose. Like the wad of gray intestine that hung from my centermost puncture, looking like frosting being squeezed out of a pastry bag.

Mmm. Cake. Remember cake, Jake?

Cake Jake. Ha-ha. Rhymes.

What was I thinking about?

LET'S EAT SOME PEOPLE! WHOOP WHOOP WHOOP!

Oh, and I was running. I chased Truncheon's van like a dog that'd gotten off the leash. There were people in there. People in sacks.

INDIVIDUALLY WRAPPED! SINGLE SERVING!

Cass.

Cass was in there. I didn't want to eat her. I didn't want to eat any of them. That's what had gotten me the pitchfork in the guts, wasn't it? Being heroic. Being stupid.

I put on the brakes. It was hard. It was like going against my own instincts, like when you try to touch your own eyeball without blinking. My vision had that red hunger tinge to it and, once I'd managed to stop my feet, both my arms reached out toward the van of their own volition. My hands were that cold-oatmeal color.

I groaned as the van went around a bend, the sound gurgling and inhuman to my own ears. I had a brief vision of chasing the ice-cream truck as a kid, waving a crisp dollar bill, shouting to get the driver's attention—

AND YANKING HIM THROUGH THAT TINY TRUCK WINDOW AND BITING HIS FACE AND HIS LITTLE WHITE HAT OFF EAT

Nope. That's not how it went. He drove off and I didn't get any ice cream and I got a grip.

Get a grip, Jake.

I turned around and realized that pitchfork zombie had followed me down the road, albeit at his slower, baked-ghoul pace. He too watched the van disappear with a forlorn look on his rotten features. His empty eyes met mine and he let out a dry, frustrated belch.

Were we buddies now? I punched him in his stupid face, heard his brittle cheekbone crack, and watched him topple over. The pitchfork struck the pavement like a kickstand and propped him up there.

Well, that didn't solve anything.

LUNCH

Amanda would come back for me. Once they were safe and once she realized what happened, she'd come find me. She wouldn't let me become one of these ghouls. She wouldn't let me get sunburn on my exposed cranium. I just had to wait. Not give in to the zombie urges, not wander too far.

Oh shit. I'd staggered back down the road. Back toward—

LUNCHEON.

Truncheon. He'd never made it into the cornfield. He'd stopped screaming, but he was still alive. Breath whistled wetly out of his mouth. Pigtails had done a number on his right leg, stripping off the meat below the knee, and now she'd gone to work on the other leg, greedily gnawing a piece of calf muscle. One of the other zombies had fallen on him too, ripping open his abdomen, digging into the guts.

There were other ghouls closing in too. Drawn by the smell or the noise or whatever drives them.

Us. Drives *us*.

Oh god. I didn't want to become one of them. Lost, wandering, hungry forever.

THEN EAT

They'd already taken so much of him. I hoped there was enough left to straighten me out. I just needed enough so I could work some car keys. Get the guinea pigs. Find Amanda. Save humanity.

Just a little bit.

Too much to share.

I grabbed Pigtails, lifted her over my head, and flung her into the cornfield. The other ghoul glanced up and I kicked him across the face, sent him spinning into the road with a head that couldn't look straight anymore. The other approaching ghouls seemed to hesitate, watching me, moaning plaintively.

I'm the fucking alpha male.

ZOMBIE HOOOWWWWLLLL

And then I'd straddled Truncheon's chest, pinning his weakly flailing arms. Jammed my thumbs into his eye sockets.

Lift, slam.

Lift, slam.

Lift, slam.

BRAINS.

CASS

I DREAMED THAT I WAS BEING GENTLY CARRIED IN A pair of big, strong arms; my head nestled against pectoral muscles with the perfect firmness and support of one of those airplane neck pillows. I felt protected. Somehow, I thought, Jake had returned from his latest necrotization all ripped up and muscular. Everything was fixed—he was cured, my mom was saved, and he'd let Amanda down gently. He was carrying me somewhere safe, where we wouldn't be bothered, where we could finally get to know each other for real.

Pretty sure I was concussed.

I woke up on a cot, a musty-smelling sheet pulled over me. I tensed up, feeling disoriented. Once in a while it'd be nice if I could just fall asleep normally, instead of getting knocked out or pushing myself into a telepathy-induced stupor. I kept perfectly still, just in case something was nearby waiting to eat me.

To my left, on the other side of a flimsy partition, a man snored enthusiastically. Otherwise, the room was quiet.

If it was safe enough for some guy to be snoring, it was safe enough for me to climb out of bed.

The concrete floor was cool under my bare feet. Someone had taken my sneakers and socks off, and left them pushed under the edge of the cot. I slipped them back on carefully, still wary of making any noise.

I peeked around the partition to check out the snorer. He was a hefty, middle-aged dude with receding black hair that fled into a ponytail. Sleeping on his back, the guy's enormous belly raised up and down, those snores rumbling all the way from his diaphragm. I didn't recognize his face, but I remembered one of the van hostages carrying a major spare tire.

We'd made it . . . somewhere.

It was definitely underground; the walls were concrete with heavy wood support beams, and the space had that damp-basement feeling. It was pretty spacious for a cellar, though. There were other partitions farther into the room, separating a couple quieter sleepers. Candles flickered from built-in sconces, which I thought was kind of unusual for your average basement. After the eighteenth century we pretty much stopped designing rooms with torch positioning in mind, right? Even farther back, past the cots and partitions, I saw a wall entirely dedicated to canned goods and dry foods. And then, all the way at the back, a small chemical toilet with its own partition.

Well, I was going to have to hold it.

I guessed I was in a storm cellar. Or a bomb shelter. Or a really industrious combination.

"Psst."

I turned toward the noise. Seated on a stool at the far end of the room, next to the stairs and dead-bolted cast-iron door that I assumed led outside, was the male model we'd rescued from Truncheon. He'd gotten a bandage for the gash on his forehead and had also changed into a fresh T-shirt and jeans. If he had clean clothes that fit so well, this must be his place.

Also, it must've been him I deliriously remembered carrying me. I nervously shoved a strand of tangled hair behind my ear. I walked over and he set aside the dog-eared copy of *The Sun Also Rises* he'd been reading by flashlight.

"Hey," I whispered.

"Hey yourself," he replied, reaching out for a gentle handshake. "I'm Cody."

Of course. He looked like a Cody.

"Cass," I said.

"How's your head?" Cody asked, and reached out to brush my hair away from my forehead, softly pressing a bump I hadn't realized was there. He seemed totally comfortable doing this, like we hadn't just met. I didn't mind. "We were worried. You've been out for a while."

"I, um, yeah. I think I'm all right. What about you?"

He poked the bandage. "I've had worse, believe me."

Sure, I believed him. Cody had an aura about him like he couldn't possibly tell a lie, like the pledges he'd taken in Boy Scouts had set him on the straight and narrow for life. He reminded me—and I mean this in the most complimentary way possible—of a really handsome golden retriever. He seemed like the kind of person that'd be really good at small talk.

"Where are we?" I asked.

"Out in the country," Cody replied. "Best to stay out here. Less trouble lurking."

I didn't mention that all of Iowa seemed like country to me. Instead, I gestured to the wooden struts in the ceiling. "And this is like a bomb shelter?"

"Pretty much," Cody said. "Most of the houses around here have something for the tornadoes. Some people, like whoever owned this place, sprung for the whole nuke-resistant whoop-de-do. I used to think people like that were nuts, but now . . ."

I took another look around. I hadn't noticed the hazmat suits piled in one corner.

"I guess sometimes being paranoid pays off," I said. "You know the owner?"

"Naw, they're long gone," Cody said, gazing down at his hands. They were weathered and scarred, way too messed up for a guy barely older than me. "It was the closest safe house I could think of. Mandy drove us out here."

I blinked. *"Mandy?"*

"Sorry. Been told I've got a nickname problem. Your friend Amanda. She took off for a while, but now she's back."

I glanced back at the cots. "She's down here?"

Cody sheepishly rubbed the back of his neck. "The others were scared she might eat us, so they decided she had to sleep outside. Not exactly paying it forward, but I couldn't convince 'em otherwise."

From the steps I could see over the partitions, so I took a closer look at the cots. There was the pudgy, snoring guy, a skinny girl curled tightly into the fetal position and burrowed under her blankets, and a middle-aged lady I could tell was awake and secretly listening to us. They were who we'd blown up Alastaire and Truncheon's disturbing arrangement to rescue. I couldn't help feeling that the Save-Mom-Cure-Humanity project had suffered a setback because of these people.

It was the right thing to do, I reminded myself. After months working for the NCD, I needed to grab hold of every possible opportunity to do good.

But what about Jake? If Amanda hadn't found him, that meant he could still be out ghouling around, decomposing further every minute. And that was totally my fault. My instinct was to grope for him on the astral plane, but my brain still wasn't up for any psychic tricks.

"I mean, I was pretty sure she wasn't gonna eat us, you know, on account of her saving us just a few hours ago," Cody rambled on, "but I got outvoted. Feel pretty lousy about it, actually. She seems like a sweet girl."

"Sweet," I muttered in disbelief. In the short time I'd been unconscious, Amanda had managed to charm a hardened Iowa survivor with her boob voodoo. "You this open-minded about every zombie you meet?"

"Naw. I got good instincts for people, though," Cody replied, without a hint of irony.

"*Attractive* people," I clarified, not sure why I wanted to argue with this guy. I needed to get beyond this stupid high-school urge to compete with Amanda.

Cody didn't try to hide his abashed smile. "It's not like that," he replied lamely. "You know, my old girlfriend is a zombie. Ran into her a few weeks back. Hadn't seen her since summer vacation, figured she was dead for sure. But nope, there she was, looking like one of the homeless kids from Peter Pan. *She* didn't try to eat me, and Mandy saved us from Truncheon, so I figure the zombies ain't *all* bad. There are degrees, like with anything."

I didn't need psychic powers with this guy. He was a freaking open book. Part of me wondered how he'd been surviving out here, being so sweet and dumb.

"Yeah, they aren't all bad," I said, relenting. I sighed and stood up, dusting off the back of my pants. "I should go talk to her," I said.

Cody grimaced. "Right now?"

"You worried I'll disturb her beauty sleep?"

"Naw, it's not that," Cody replied with a sincerity that revealed a very loose grasp of sarcasm. "Around here, we human beings tend to stay inside after dark."

"I'll be fine," I said, patting around the waist of my jeans. "I have a . . ."

I *had* a gun. It was gone. Did I drop it in the van during my struggle with the zombies?

Cody knew what I was looking for. "Mandy took your piece. Said she'd keep it safe until you woke up."

I gritted my teeth. "Okay, now I'm definitely going out there."

"My pop taught me never to stand in the way of a lady with her mind made up," Cody said, his folksy chivalry making me cringe. He stood up and slid open a metal hatch installed at eye level in the steel door, peering through it. "Looks clear, but I'll keep a lookout all the same. You get into trouble, you come running, okay?"

"I'll be fine," I said, forcing a smile. I was more

worried about Amanda than any ghouls lurking around. "Thanks."

Cody lifted the hefty slab of wood that barred the door and set it aside. Before I could head out, he handed me a broom handle that had been propped up next to his stool.

"Take that," he said. "Aim for the eyes."

The end of the broom handle was carved into a deadly-looking point. For a moment, a fan-girl thrill went through me; I felt like a vampire slayer.

Outside, the sky was totally cloudless. The half moon lit the sprawling pasture and the nearby boarded-up house a washed-out gray, making everything seem flat and drained. It was disconcertingly quiet. If a ghoul was going to rush me, I'd definitely hear it coming.

Amanda had parked the Maroon Marauder just a few yards from the bomb shelter. She lay on its hood with her back resting against the windshield, one arm draped across her eyes, like a pinup girl from one of those grody hot-rod magazines. She stirred when I approached, hastily brushing the hollowed-out, furry husk of a guinea pig off the hood and into the grass.

"You're awake," she said, acting aloof as she looked me over. "Nice spear."

"Thanks," I replied, turning the weapon over in my hand in a way I hoped was vaguely menacing. "Cody gave it to me."

"Aw, isn't he sweet? Guy probably whittled it himself."

"Uh-huh. I see you already worked your magic on him."

Amanda raised an eyebrow. "What is *that* supposed to mean?"

"Just that he got all gooey talking about you." I shook my head, wanting to get off the topic. "Whatever. He probably has a zombie fetish."

"He's not the only one," Amanda said, and gave me a meaningful look.

Now it was my eyebrow shooting up. "What is *that* supposed to mean?" I parroted.

"Nothing. And anyway, I was just nice to him. It was no big thing." Amanda sat up, her detached attitude slipping. "What was I supposed to do? You guys, like, abandoned me with these *people*. I'm in this cracked-out dead state, Jake's gone, your dumb ass is knocked out yet again, and I've got four losers tied up and no clue what to do with them. So when the hillbilly hunk wakes up, I flirt a little and get him to bring us out here so I have a place to stash you while I look for Jake. It's called improvising."

"Okay, jeez, relax," I said, holding up my hands. "I guess I should be thanking you for not dumping me by the side of the road."

"I'm not a monster," Amanda hissed. "No matter what you might think."

The image of Harlene, the nicest lady and best NCD squad leader ever, bleeding to death from an Amanda bite wound popped into my head. That argued pretty strongly for monster, but I didn't bring it up. It was so hard to be civil with her, especially without Jake around to be our buffer. I wondered if she was having the same problem.

"Jake didn't show up at Truncheon's," Amanda said, thankfully shifting gears away from degrees of monstrosity. "I went back to where it all went down and he wasn't there either. I took the Marauder and left him some guinea pigs in the van, in case he shows up."

"Why didn't you stay out there?" I asked, trying not to sound too judgmental, even though I would've waited longer. "What if he shows up during the night?"

"Because you're here," she replied, like this should be obvious.

"So? I mean, I appreciate the concern but—"

Amanda cut me off with a sharp laugh. "Concern. Right." She shook her head in disbelief. "You track zombies, don't you?"

I knew where this was going. "Yeah, but—"

"So track *my* zombie," Amanda said, interrupting me again.

"It isn't so simple," I replied, tightening my grip on my improvised spear, not sure how this would play out. "He got hurt back there. . . ."

Amanda scooted across the hood toward me. "What do you mean *hurt*?"

"One of those ghouls had a pitchfork sticking out of

him. There was an accident and Jake, uh . . ." I waved my hand. "I think he lost control."

"Are you serious?" Amanda asked, eyes widening. She pushed both her hands through her hair and held them there. "So he could be wandering anywhere. Hungry, alone, stupid."

I nodded, feeling a stab of empathy as I watched Amanda's face scrunch up.

"I'm sorry," I said. "It was sort of my fault."

Amanda leapt forward. I hadn't been expecting it and didn't have a chance to even lift Cody's stake. She grabbed me hard by the shoulders, but I quickly realized she wasn't trying to eat me.

"You can find him, though, right?" Amanda asked, her eyes wide. "That's what you do."

"It doesn't work like that," I said gently. Amanda's expression darkened, but I continued anyway. "If he's a ghoul, his mind is dead. It makes him almost impossible to track. And right now my powers are fried, so I can't even tell if—"

She shoved me away.

"Forget it," she said bitterly. "It was stupid of me to even come back here. I'll find him myself."

"Hold on," I protested. "Just give me until morning to rest. I can try finding him on the astral plane then."

Amanda stood behind the open car door, staring at me. "Astral plane," she repeated.

"It sounds stupid when you say it out loud."

She shook her head. "So until then he's just out there decomposing or, like, eating his way through Iowa's last working day care. Or getting his head blown off by some wackjob like Truncheon. And this astral-plane thing might not even work. I get all that right?"

"Pretty much."

"Perfect."

I looked down at my sneakers, feeling overwhelmed but also trying to figure how to play this. If Jake really had gone ghoul—or worse—I was going to need Amanda. Without one of my zombie friends, there was no way for me to find and then smuggle this alleged cure out of Des Moines, which meant I could look forward to some telepathic snapshots of Alastaire murdering my mom. I wondered if I'd even have time to mourn before the army started napalming Iowa.

Yeah, I was starting to feel pretty much screwed.

"Please, Amanda," I said quietly, repulsed that it'd come to this. "I'll try to help. Just promise you won't bail on me."

She stared at me for a long couple of seconds, her face a blank mask, eyes chilly at best. Then, without another word, she climbed into the Marauder, started it up, and drove without headlights into the night.

I watched her brake lights until they disappeared.

JAKE

I CAME BACK TO LIFE SLOWLY.

The first things I became aware of were my feet, shuffling along across pavement all stupid, like my big toes had been magnetized.

Pick up your feet, dummy. You're staggering around like a—

Like a zombie. Duh.

I focused on walking like normal and, once I'd mastered that, my other functions started falling in line too. Breathing normal, eyes focused, walking with my arms at my sides instead of stretched in front of me. It was like coming down from a really outrageous high, that sudden sharpness of feeling yourself again.

Speaking of which, I checked my back pocket. The eighth I'd bought from that protester back in Omaha—he'd called it Husker Doolittle—was still intact. Whew. Everything else I owned might have been back in the car, including my sweet authentic peace pipe and the guinea pigs I'd need to eat sooner rather than later, but at least I'd managed to hold on to the first bud I'd been able to score since freaking New Jersey.

"So, I've got that going for me," I said out loud.

A six-pack of ghouls, all of them wearing hospital gowns, their decaying asses swinging around all sloppy and free, turned in unison to look at me. They'd been lurching down the sidewalk on the other side of the street. The cornfields I last remembered shambling through had given way to paved roads and buildings, a town or a city, hard to tell how big with all the streetlights out.

"Sup," I said, waving to the zombies. "Where are we?"

Their zombie sense must've told them I was inedible, because they groaned and turned away, shuffling off to whatever the ghoul nightlife was around here. A beautiful feeling of relief cascaded through me as I realized I wasn't one of them—I'd come back, puncture wounds healed, fresh as a graveyard daisy. Feeding off Truncheon had been enough.

For now. What was I going to do when I got hungry again?

I turned to watch the ghouls shamble off. They weren't doing so hot on the whole finding-food tip. The wind picked up, carrying an old fast-food wrapper from the mouth of an alley and sticking it to the bare ass of a ghoul. Mother Nature's way of taunting us abominations.

If the ache in my feet was any indication, I'd wandered far in my zombie state. I couldn't be sure if this was Des Moines or not. Wherever I'd ended up, it was a real dump. Broken shop windows, overturned cars, ghouls wandering everywhere—the complete set of collapsed-society clichés. I kept stepping in puddles that could've been anything from gasoline to blood. I'd never actually encountered gangrene, but that's how I interpreted the city's smell—like a moldy limb that needed lopping off.

It was dark, all the stars visible in the sky on account of the electricity being out. Hands on my hips, I stared up at the constellations, looking for the North Star. Not that I would've known what to do with it, if I found it. I'm not an astronaut.

I thought about Amanda. Except for the short time when she'd been captured by the NCD before I'd bravely rescued her like a boss, this was the first time in the last couple weeks that we'd been separated. Like, seriously separated. I don't want to come off as some emo boy who can't get to sleep unless he's sucking on a lock of his girlfriend's hair, but I missed her. If we'd had a normal relationship, like if we'd miraculously started dating back in Jersey when we were human, I probably would've relished the alone time after two weeks straight of being constantly on. (On my charm game, yo.) It was an opportunity to binge on comics and fart loud and free. But there wasn't anything fun to do in this godforsaken zombie wasteland, and I wasn't used to confronting this apocalyptic shit by myself. So yeah, I missed her.

"*Somewhere out there,*" I sang to the stars, "*beneath the pale moo—*"

A ghoul shouldered past me, interrupting. He stared at me, watery eyes uncomprehending.

"Fine," I said to him, sighing. "I'll bottle up these feelings."

Amanda would be looking for me. I'd told her to meet me back at Truncheon's motor garage/human-trafficking staging area because it seemed like a good idea at the time. Failing that, she'd know that I'd need to make it back to the car for food and probably check for me there. Both those landmarks—well, as much as an abandoned car near a cornfield could be a landmark in the Midwest—were in the same direction. Logic followed that I just needed to head that way.

Except I didn't know which way that was.

So I started walking.

My mind turned from Amanda to Cass. I had faith Amanda could take care of herself—she didn't have to worry about all these rail-thin shambling ghouls popping starvation-induced hard-ons for her. Cass, on the other hand . . . she and the people we'd rescued from Truncheon were literally fresh meat. Back at the van, she'd shouted something incredibly cheesy at me that I couldn't quite remember through the haze of zombie bloodlust, but it made me smile to think about. She was such a weirdo. I didn't want her to get eaten.

My mind wandered along with my feet, so I didn't even notice the music until I was almost right on top of it. It wasn't superloud, but I guess sound carried well when everyone was dead. Just ahead, a flashlight beam danced around from within a smashed-up Gamespot.

It seemed like a good idea not to rush out and introduce myself to someone brazenly scavenging the Deadzone. I pressed myself up against the wall and inched forward, putting my sneaking skills to good use.

I recognized the music. It was Anti-Bellum, this indie hard-core rapper who'd blown up on the blogs a few months ago with his concept album about Civil War battles. Pretty cool, actually.

Inching along, ninjalike, I failed to notice the ghoul on the sidewalk until I stepped in his guts and he started to screech. The poor guy had been cut in half and left leaning against the wall. The undead were literally litter.

"Sorry, sorry, sorry," I whispered, dancing away from the dark puddle of his intestines.

The music stopped. I cursed my novice-level stealth skills and ducked into the shadows of a doorway. I wished I had the forethought to pick up a weapon—there were all kinds of debris lying around, from boards with nails sticking out of them to loose femurs. I could've clubbed this guy and booked, but it was too late now. I decided on hiding.

I heard heavy boots crunching over broken glass and then a lanky shadow ducked through the smashed-in Gamestop entrance. I couldn't see much beyond the miniature sun of his flashlight, but his silhouette was tall and angular with a huge head, like a Martian scarecrow. He had a backpack on, and the hand not shining a light carried a small boom box. He swept the flashlight beam in both directions, just barely missing my doorway.

"Who's out there?" he rumbled, his voice gravelly and deep, like Christian Bale's corny interpretation of Batman. (I preferred Michael Keaton.) A couple ghouls across the street turned their heads at the noise, but didn't seem interested in rushing him. He was one of them. One of us, I mean. Like me.

Even so, I kept quiet.

"Motherfucker, I *heard* you," he growled impatiently. "Don't make me come looking."

He was only a few yards away from me, and my hiding

spot wasn't exactly Anne Frank level or anything. He'd find me without much trouble. Why piss him off?

I stepped out of the doorway and cleared my throat. He immediately swung the light into my eyes, blinding me.

"Ow, hey."

"Who is that?" he snarled.

"Uh, you don't know me."

"I know everyone. This is my city."

"Yeah, okay, Bruce Wayne," I replied, squinting and shielding my eyes. "You can go back to safeguarding the night or whatever. Just point me toward the highway that goes through the cornfield."

The flashlight beam shook. The guy let loose a self-deprecating, snort-filled laugh.

"Cool, I was going for a Dark Knight thing," he said, his voice now a couple octaves higher and less like a rock grinder. A normal voice. "Shit is murder on the vocal cords."

"Your flashlight is murder on my retinas," I replied.

"Oh, sorry."

He lowered the beam to my chest. I tried to blink away the huge lava islands floating across my vision.

"Hate to break it to you," he said, "but every highway in this stupid state goes through a cornfield."

"Great." I sighed.

"Where you trying to go?"

"Originally Des Moines, but I lost my girlfriend on the way, so now I'm just trying to get back to where we left our car."

"Well, the good news is, you made it to Des Moines," he said, and waved his flashlight around, illuminating the bloodstains and wrecked storefronts in brief splashes.

I kicked some loose rocks or maybe bones. I'd been worried this was Des Moines. It didn't look like a place hiding a zombie cure, or a zombie community, or much of anything at all. It looked like a shithole.

"Freaking paradise," I grumbled.

"It's what you make of it, man," the guy replied, sounding a little defensive. He cocked his head, thinking, and then sang a few lines of song at me. *"Keep pushin' 'til it's understood and these Badlands start treatin' us good. That's what your dude says, right?"*

The song was familiar, but I couldn't place it. "Uh?"

"Springsteen, man. Aren't you from Jersey?"

"How'd you know that?"

"Because you sound mad Jersey. I'm from Queens. East Coast represent!"

He shined his flashlight beam under his face. His features turned monstrous and exaggerated, but at least now I understood why I'd thought his head was so big. The guy had a huge, unkempt Afro. Otherwise, he looked pretty normal—couldn't have been more than twenty, black, a weird scar on his forehead that looked like puckered lips.

"Name's Reggie, by the way."

"Jake," I said, waving. "Nice to meet you. Thanks for quoting Springsteen instead of, like, trying to shoot me or something."

"The night is young," Reggie joked.

A curious ghoul wandered over and stood between us, like she wanted to get into our conversation. Reggie shoved her away and stepped in closer.

"Stupid things," he mumbled. "Anyway, I don't usually go for that blue-collar, old-white-dude shit, but Springsteen, he gets it. All his songs are about cars, loneliness, and ladies."

"My dad loves him," I said, trying to explain this willful gap in my musical knowledge. "So obviously, that makes him lame. Plus, being from Jersey and liking Springsteen is a total cliché."

"Yeah, true. You could be into him ironically, but that post-hipster guilty-pleasure shit is so played," Reggie replied. "Sincerity is underrated, man. Anyway, you should check him out."

"Uh, yeah, I'll put that on my to-do list," I said, feeling a wave of sad futility as this normal-seeming musical feeling-out was taking place in a blacked-out zombie wasteland. When was I ever going to have the chance to sit around listening to Springsteen? My life was kinda screwed right now.

As if sensing my sudden onset depression, Reggie put his hand on my shoulder.

"You want to hang out, Jake?" he asked. "Listen to some records? Maybe get something to eat? I just liberated a Sega Genesis if you're into that."

My mouth hung open. Reggie had just ticked off a list of my favorite things, all of which seemed impossible. There were no words capable of expressing the cruelty of his joke, so I just waved my arms.

He laughed again and slapped my shoulder. "Come on, man. I got a place up here."

"For real?"

He smirked. "Jake, it gets better."

I hesitated as Reggie started up the block. My experiences with Iowans so far were pretty much one hundred percent murderous. Reggie didn't seem like Red Bear and those others, though. He seemed chill, like the kind of dude I would've been friends with back home. I mean, he listened to indie rap and just looted a Gamestop. How could he not be one of the good guys?

I jogged after him.

We picked our way along the sidewalk and sometimes right down the middle of the street, Reggie leading the way with his flashlight. Each new block was just as gruesome as the last. I sort of missed when I'd been stumbling around in the near-dark. I'm not sure what

I'd expected of Des Moines—certainly not some hand-holding zombie utopia, not after meeting those psychos at the farmhouse—but I hadn't been ready for this nasty postapocalyptic hellscape either.

"How long have you been here?" I asked Reggie.

"Since the start," he replied. "I was here when things were normal, on the black-person exchange program."

"Um, Iowa had that?"

He laughed. He did that a lot, it seemed. Laughing was easy for him.

"I'm messing with you. I was going to school. Lucked out, actually. I think I was one of the first people to turn. That was like a year ago."

He'd been a zombie for a whole year, longer even than Grace and Summer. I grimaced. "So that means there's no . . ." I trailed off, not wanting to embarrass myself in front of this veteran zombie.

"No what?" He stopped and shined the flashlight at me.

I sighed, feeling stupid. "No cure. We came out here because we heard there was a cure."

"That's complicated," Reggie said, his voice not so easygoing anymore. "I mean, you ever hear that expression *the cure is worse than the disease*?"

I couldn't imagine that being true and didn't bother trying. All I cared about was confirmation that didn't end with a bulldog on a skateboard.

"So it's *real*? The cure?"

"Sure," Reggie replied, sounding disappointed by my enthusiasm. "It's real."

I fist-pumped in the darkness, hoping Reggie didn't see me. Sure, he'd sounded reluctant and sorta ominous about the cure, but I was choosing to ignore that. It existed! I was close!

We kept on walking. I stepped carefully around a gristle-covered rib cage and spinal column, shaking my head in disbelief.

"No offense, man, but I don't get why you'd live here."

"Oh, it's a mess down here, no doubt. We normally stick to the skywalks," Reggie replied, then shined his flashlight up, illuminating a glass-enclosed walkway built above the street, connecting two buildings. There were others just like it up ahead. "The ghouls haven't really figured out how to get up there, so it's not so annoying to walk around. We even cleaned up most of the severed limbs and arterial spray, despite most of the others not being big on chores and shit."

"The others . . ." I was thinking of Red Bear and the other bloodthirsty, leather-clad nut jobs I'd run into back at the farmhouse.

"The Sovereign Undead of Des Moines," Reggie answered, a bit of irony in his voice. "Almost two hundred at last count, I think. Plus a few thousand ghouls, but they're second-class citizens."

"Damn, that's a lot of zombies."

Reggie chuckled. "More show up every day. Like you."

"I'm, um, just passing through."

"Suit yourself," Reggie said, although I could tell he didn't really believe me. I decided to change the subject.

"So, you guys, like, elected this Lord guy I keep hearing about?" I thought back to what Red Bear had called him on the border. "Uh, Lord Wesley?"

"Heh." Reggie shook his head. "Elected? Nah. He just started talking and people started listening, I guess."

"Is he cool? I picture that Humungus dude in the hockey mask from *Mad Max*. Like, leather chaps with spikes and a slithery little gimp dude on a chain."

Reggie was laughing again. "Sorta, yeah. But don't worry, he's not so bad."

Reggie led me to the front door of a swank-looking apartment building. Unlike pretty much every other building I'd seen in Des Moines, the windows on this one were intact. Or newly installed, maybe. Reggie produced a set of keys to unlock the security door and I kept right on talking. I was excited. If I had a cell phone, I'd have already sent Amanda like a billion 911 texts. I'd met a friendly zombie! There was a cure! Everything was going to turn around! Hope you're alive!

"That's a relief," I said to Reggie. "I heard I'd need to ransom off some live humans just to get into the city."

Reggie led me past an empty elevator shaft to a flight of stairs. He glanced back at me with a crooked grin.

"What? You don't have any human meat to barter? I'm sorta regretting inviting you over."

"Dude, my inventory totally sucks right now." A thought occurred to me as we climbed the steps. "Except, I do have a bunch of pot."

Reggie stopped so suddenly that I almost bumped into his back. He peered down at me from the landing above, his eyes wide.

"Are you messing with me?" he asked, his voice low and Batmanlike again.

I pulled out my baggie of Husker Doolittle and dangled it in the flashlight beam. Reggie practically leapt down two steps and wrapped me in a powerful hug.

"Our meeting was destiny, Jake," he said, squeezing me. "You're my new best friend."

I laughed, struggling against his grip. "All right, all right, let me go."

It was a hike up five flights of stairs to Reggie's apartment. On the way, I noticed a trio of thick extension cords running along the edge of the steps. I'd been talking too much to notice it before, but now I could hear the distant rumbling of engines from the building's basement.

"Generators?" I asked.

"Yeah," Reggie replied as we reached his door, the extension cords disappearing underneath. "I gotta scavenge a lot of gasoline to keep this place running, but I think it's worth it."

Reggie unlocked the door and I stepped into paradise. It was a huge loft apartment, lit by strings of mismatched Christmas lights, with floor-to-ceiling windows looking out on the darkened city. It was a total rich-dude apartment, like something you'd see a stockbroker drinking martinis in, except Reggie had decorated it with all kinds of acid-trip black-light art and posters from Japanese ninja movies I'd never heard of. A plush, sprawling, U-shaped sectional couch dominated the living room, centered before an obscenely huge wall-mounted plasma TV. Hooked to the TV was pretty much every video-game system known to man, some that I didn't even recognize. DVDs, video games, records, and stacks of graphic novels overflowed from bookshelves and into carefully organized piles on the floor.

My knees felt weak.

"Dude," was all I could manage.

Reggie smirked. "As you can see, I've had a little bit of time on my hands. You like it?"

"It's the greatest thing I've ever seen in my life." I did a full 360, trying to take everything in, my hands on my head. "You all live like this?"

"Ha, no. Some of the others, they're more into that whole rough-and-tumble anarchy lifestyle. They mostly stay around the Ramada Tropics because it's got a pool.

Ramada *Tropics* in *Iowa*? You believe that shit? And dirty-ass water because none of them ever figured out how to work a filter or use chlorine." He shook his head. "Anyway, this is where I come to get away. My hideout."

"It's an amazing hideout," I replied, staring at his collection of video games and trying not to faint from the rush of blood to my nerd boner.

"Heads up," Reggie yelled, and tossed me a cold can of PBR from the fridge. He grabbed one for himself and then walked over to join me. He carried a tray with neatly arranged rows of dead-looking science mice. "You hungry? Want to try one of these?"

I squinted at the mice. They weren't dead, just unconscious, and coated in something dusty and orange.

"What the hell is that?" I asked.

"So"—Reggie set down the tray self-consciously—"I'm still working on this, but I've been trying to make the whole eating thing a little more, I dunno, palatable? Civilized? I drug these little dudes so they're not all squirming and pissing themselves when you start eating them, and then I roll them in taco seasoning for flavor."

"Wow," I said, staring in awe at Reggie. "I think you might be a genius."

We each ate a couple of the mice. As usual, the little creatures didn't quite satiate my hunger—even barely remembered, Truncheon's brains were the most satisfying meal I'd had in the last week—but I had to admit, these were better than normal critter snacks. Not getting my lips slashed by tiny claws was a nice change of pace, and the taco seasoning made the first bite taste almost like Doritos.

Afterward, Reggie put on a scratchy record, some trippy, cowbell-heavy '60s thing from a band called Strawberry Alarm Clock, and disappeared upstairs. I flopped down on the couch, feeling a little buzzed from the beer I'd chugged and whatever tranquilizers those mice were pumped full of. I felt more relaxed than I had in days, maybe since before that fateful day in the cafeteria. Through that haze of good feeling, a little guilt crept in—Amanda and Cass were out there somewhere, maybe looking for me, maybe in danger. And here I was reclining because holy shit this part of the couch had a built-in footstool. I'd gotten us closer to the cure, though, hadn't I? Hanging out with Reggie was technically, like, infiltrating the Iowa zombies.

Yeah, that's it.

Reggie returned, grinning and dusting off a sizable vaporizer that looked like a gumball machine or a retro robot. He held it up proudly.

"Tom Servo, out of retirement," he said. "We getting high or what?"

I hadn't smoked in weeks and that Husker Doolittle was not screwing around. It knocked me on my ass. Reggie fired up some imported shooter on his modded

Xbox called Bushido Machine Gun, but my fingers were numb and he was really good, shooting me with rocket-propelled katanas over and over. Eventually, we just settled into our separate areas of the couch, laughing about dumb stuff and talking.

Talking and talking.

Man, will I talk when I'm stoned. Like, more than usual. I'm pretty sure I told him everything—about the massacre at RRHS, my magical romance with Amanda, the weird little psychic we'd picked up and how I had a strange attachment to her, which is something I'd never even realized until that moment and man isn't weed just amazing?

"You sound like me," Reggie said. "I mean, the way you were before. Floundering, man."

"I wouldn't say floundering," I replied, too stoned to get defensive. "I was, uh, uniquely open to possibilities up to and including community college."

"I wasn't doing so hot before," Reggie said, countering my life story with his own. "I was sick all the time, ever since I was a kid. I had anemia."

"Like the eating disorder?"

Reggie laughed. "Nah, man, that's anorexia. My blood was all jacked up. All kinds of stuff would go wrong."

I laughed too, then felt bad. "Sorry."

"Hard to make a lot of friends when you're sick all

the time. Kids are shitty. You know how it goes," Reggie mused. "I came out here for school because it was far away."

I sank deeper into the couch, listening.

"I thought things would be different in college, but they weren't," he continued. "I had a scholarship for creative writing, but all my professors were dicks, man. They were like, why are you writing about spaceships, write about what you know, like the urban experience . . . and I was like, bitch, my parents were lawyers and sent me to college in Iowa, what am I gonna write about, drive-bys in our fuckin' Prius?"

"Word," I replied sagely, then started laughing at my own stupid voice. "Word!"

Reggie ignored me, on a roll now. "Then a ton of people here caught zombie and it was like a lawless war zone overnight." He fingered the weird scar on his forehead. "I'd seen every zombie movie, man, plus all those apocalypse movies. I played the shit out of every *Fallout*. I know my stuff. I was feeling better than ever. And, man, I'm *good* at it."

"Good at what?" I asked, furrowing my brow.

"Being a zombie," he answered, grinning at me. "You must be too. Two weeks old and already made it out here to the undead capital. With an NCD psychic hostage too. Goddamn."

"Uh, thanks, I guess," I replied, studying a really

interesting string of lights, timing my blinking with their breathing, or was it the other way around . . . ?

"Finally found something we're good at, man," Reggie mumbled, off in his own head now too. "It's the best feeling."

He was right, I realized. I did feel good. I hadn't made the connection back when Amanda yelled at me for not taking our journey seriously enough, but I did now.

Sometimes I really liked being a zombie.

CASS

I FELT DISCONNECTED.

I lay on my side in my bomb-shelter cot, the dusty-smelling sheet pulled up to my chin, a thin pillow squeezed against the side of my head to drown out the nearby snoring. I was in a state of fitful half sleep; every time I started to really drift off, the icy hand of my anxiety slithered up from the foot of the bed and tried to smother me.

I was alone out here. No NCD squad. No undead traveling companions. Just a dopey farm boy and some other equally scared zombie-apocalypse refugees.

No telepathy. I was truly on my own, even in my own head.

I didn't know when my powers would come back. I'd pushed too hard the other day with all the psychic shoplifting, and later Alastaire's astral-plane home invasion, and now I was paying for it. The migraine I'd been battling since yesterday morning had finally softened to a dull buzz, augmented by a steady throb from the bump on my forehead. But still the astral plane felt out of reach, like my brain's antenna was tuned to static.

I never realized how comforting the presence of other people's minds could be, especially out here where almost everything was dead.

My powers would return soon, I told myself. That's how it always worked; strain until the nosebleeds and then rest. Once they did, I could find Jake. Get the cure. Get safe.

I thought about my mom, at home with that freak Alastaire toying with her mind. It hurt to think about, but it also seemed far away—like the world outside Iowa, with electricity and laws and not as many decomposing cannibals, had frozen in time the second I crossed under that wall.

I guess I slept a little, my ramshackle brain producing ill-formed little quasidreams without any setting or plot, just the sensation of people being out of reach. Jake.

My mom. Harlene and Tom.

Birds started to chirp, their calls muffled by the shelter's depth. When I opened my eyes, the room was still dark and candlelit, but that dewy way-too-early morning dampness had also settled in. It would've been the time of garbage men and paperboys, if they all hadn't been eaten.

I figured I'd be the first one awake when I slipped out of bed, but Cody was somehow still astride his stool by the door. He had the slot open and was peering through it with a pair of binoculars. I crept up next to him.

"Is there something out there?" I whispered, not wanting to awaken the others unless it was absolutely time to start running and screaming.

Cody's back tensed; he hadn't heard me coming over the big guy's persistent snoring.

"Naw," he whispered back, lowering the binoculars and closing the hatch. "Just looking for warblers."

"Is that some kind of Deadzone lingo for *zombies*?"

"They're birds," Cody replied. I only now noticed the heavily written-in Audubon field guide in his lap. "When the power goes out, you find new hobbies."

I pinched the bridge of my nose, a little embarrassed. "Sorry. I'm slow this morning."

He sucked his teeth. "Also, you aren't in some *Deadzone*. You're in Iowa. Guthrie County, Iowa."

"Sorry," I repeated. He looked genuinely hurt, like I'd

just told him corn was the worst of all the grains. "I'm new here."

"It's cool," Cody said, and flashed me a smile. "Just gotta remember we ain't dead yet, you know?"

The springs from one of the cots whined as one of the sleepers rolled over. We were quiet for a moment. Cody wasn't so bad to talk to, I decided, and while I was stuck here without a plan, I should try learning as much about Iowa as I could.

"I just can't believe it's like this," I said. "I mean—how did it happen?"

"Shoot," Cody said. "I was hoping you knew. Like maybe they talk about us outside the wall."

"Most people don't even know this is happening, much less why," I replied gravely. "There's a whole conspiracy thing."

Cody's face fell. "Dang."

"We can take you back with us," I blurted without thinking. "We're just here to find something and then we're getting out."

The guy just looked so earnestly bummed, I couldn't help myself. Admittedly, without the cure or my deceased mercenary guide, I didn't know how I expected to get back through the wall. But Cody didn't need to know that.

Cody's smile was gentle and sad. "The others might take you up on that, but not me. I've been here from the beginning and I intend to see it through until it's fixed. This godforsaken plague can't last forever."

My return smile was shaky. Alastaire said there was going to be some scorched-earth military intervention here, which I don't think was the fix Cody had in mind.

"You're right," I said, not seeing any point in crushing his spirits. I took a seat on the steps next to him.

"Is that where Mandy took off to last night? To go look for your something or other?"

I winced. "Sort of."

"She coming back?" he asked, a little too eagerly for my taste.

"She better," I said, wanting to change the subject quick. "You've really been here since the beginning?"

"I'm *from* here," he replied, taking pride in it. "First time I saw one turn was at the YMCA they'd been evacuating people to. She used to be my bus driver."

"Jeez," I said, shaking my head, thinking about the map in NCD headquarters with the blinking lights for known incidents. None of this had ever been reported, at least not to agents on my level.

"One day, there was just a ton of them, eating people. The next day, there were even more. And then it just kept going." Cody paused, checking to make sure I was listening. "After the first couple weeks, when it became darn clear that help wasn't coming, my dad and I started looking for places like this. Places we could hide. Once we had a bunch of 'em mapped, we started picking up other survivors. We had a caravan thing going. Had to keep moving because the smart ones, like the one that runs Des Moines, they'd get wise to our hideouts."

I inclined my head toward the heavyset guy whose snoring had finally tapered off into a soon-to-wake gurgle. "Is that your dad?"

"Naw." Cody chuckled, and I realized just how ridiculous it was to think they could be related. "That's my boy Roy. Roy Boy." He grinned crookedly at the chance to use one of his nicknames. "He's pretty funny. Always talking about killing himself."

"Sounds hilarious."

"Eh"—Cody waved a hand—"he don't mean it. He's just a pessimist."

"Hard not to be, I guess," I said, thinking about what these Iowans had been through.

"Roy's a cameraman for Lucy," Cody explained, gesturing to the sleeping shape of the woman who'd been listening to us last night. "Or he was, before his gear got smashed. I call her Lucy Lane, like Superman's girlfriend, but she don't much like that."

"She's a reporter?" I asked.

Cody nodded. "They're from back east, out around Iowa City. That place didn't get put behind the wall until a few months back."

"So it's gotten bigger?" I asked, shaking my head.

"The, um, quarantined area?"

"Yup. Way Lucy tells it, there was a big outbreak out there and those government guys were more concerned with getting the wall extended than helping people."

Those government guys. I wondered if I knew any of them. Maybe we'd met at the NCD picnic last summer. The person responsible for condemning whole cities to death could have been strapped to me for the three-legged race.

"And then there's T." Cody was still introducing me to the sleeping people. He gestured to the last occupied cot. "She wandered into our camp a couple days before Truncheon grabbed us. She don't seem quite right, but that ain't so unusual around here."

As I looked at the huddled form in the farthest cot, something stirred in my mind. The first tickling of the astral plane. It dangled just out of reach, like when a word gets stuck on the tip of your tongue.

"And that's it," Cody finished. "That's all the living people I know."

I shot him a look. "Wait, seriously?"

I watched him look into the distance, running down a mental checklist.

"Yup. Well, except for you and Mandy. Pretty much everyone I knew from before is dead," he mused. "Or one of *them*."

I didn't know what to say. This wasn't like a pity

party; that everyone Cody knew was dead had become simply a statistic, like a home-run record, something that he thought was objectively impressive and interesting. I wanted to give him a hug, or a donut and milkshake, the stuff that cheered me up.

"You'll have to tell me your story sometime," Cody said, glancing sidelong at me. "We haven't had electricity here in months, so I'm bringing back this thing from social studies. The oral tradition."

"Yeah. Sometime," I said, not really feeling like opening up, even though I guess that's probably expected after someone tells you about the holocaust of their entire social network. "It's a pretty crazy story, tho—"

Something slammed against the outside of the metal door. I jumped off the steps and almost out of my skin.

Cody sighed and stood up. I don't think he'd even jumped. I'd startled him before, but zombies throwing themselves against doors he was used to. He opened the metal hatch nonchalantly.

"Just a ghoul," he said, peering out.

A guttural moan came from behind me and I whipped my head around, expecting to see a zombie closing in. It was just Roy, out of bed, shaking off sleep.

"Are we about to die?" he asked, his voice bringing to mind that suicidal donkey from Winnie the Pooh.

Cody laughed. "Naw, Roy. It's too early in the morning to die."

"Oh good," Roy replied halfheartedly.

Lucy had gotten out of bed too, and inched up behind Roy. She was probably in her thirties, curly dark hair, her skin light brown and covered with even lighter freckles. She looked spunky—you could tell she was a reporter, or at least something that required a certain amount of confidence. She caught me looking at her and flashed a tight smile, rolling her eyes at Roy.

The other girl—T, Cody had called her—stayed in bed.

"Everything all right?" Lucy asked.

"It's just the one," Cody answered. "He didn't bring any friends."

"Great," Lucy replied flippantly. "I'll get the coffee on."

"Can you please kill it already?" Roy complained.

Cody picked up the sharpened broom handle he'd armed me with the night before.

"It's probably going to smell," Cody warned me.

"I'm used to it," I replied.

Cody raised an eyebrow at me, then turned back to the slot in the door. I could see the yellowed eyes of the ghoul stupidly trying to shove his head through the tiny opening. Cody held his makeshift spear like a pool cue, patient, waiting for the ghoul to lurch into a position he liked. When he finally did, Cody thrust forward and the spear stabbed the ghoul between the eyes with a sloppy *thunk*. The ghoul collapsed and Cody pulled back the spear, now wet and sticky with blackened brain goo.

"That's that," he said.

"Roy always wanted a zombie alarm clock, didn't ya, Roy?" Lucy tittered from the small kitchen area.

"Ah, shut up," Roy grumbled, and sat down heavily on the edge of his bunk.

In the space he'd cleared, there stood T. She looked like a ghost from one of those creepy Japanese horror flicks, her lank reddish-brown hair streaked with gray and half covering her face.

I almost didn't recognize her.

She was skinnier than I remembered—way skinnier—and looked like she'd aged about a decade. We'd never really hung out a ton—we were on different teams and were always out on missions—but jeez. I'd never expected to run into my roommate from NCD headquarters in an outpost of human survivors in the middle of a cornfield crawling with undead ghouls.

"Tara?" I said, taking a step toward her. "It's Cass."

Tara cocked her head, staring at me like she couldn't quite place me. So I guess bunk beds didn't count for as much as I'd thought.

"Cass," she said, trying it out.

"You know each other?" Cody asked, mystified. I ignored him.

"What're you doing here?" I asked Tara.

"I . . ." She shook her head violently. "I don't remember.

I think I did something wrong. A lot of somethings."

"Something wro—?"

Without waiting for me to finish, Tara hopped forward and pulled me in close. Her breath smelled distinctly like cat food.

"He's watching us right now," she whispered in my ear. "You can't feel him because you're tired, but he's here. Daddy's always watching."

I swallowed. "Do you mean—?"

Tara touched her index finger to my lips. "He says for Truncheon, you're going to get a spanking."

With that, Tara let me loose, turned back, and faceplanted onto her cot. I stared at her, frozen in place.

Cody touched my arm. "What the heck did she say?"

I shook my head. "You wouldn't understand."

Maybe I shouldn't have been in such a rush to get back onto the astral plane. Alastaire was there, waiting, and according to the creepily childlike skeleton that used to be my NCD roommate, he wasn't too happy with me.

JAKE

I WOKE UP SPRAWLED ON REGGIE'S COUCH WITH A deathly case of cottonmouth. Daylight poured in through the windows, forcing me to shove my face between the cushions for merciful darkness. I remembered this time I slept over at my old (now dead) friend Henry Robinson's house and did this same head-burrowing routine, only to scrape my forehead on the dried-up carcass of the missing family lizard. That was traumatizing. Slowly, I lifted my head from the couch. I didn't know Reggie all that well and you never knew what kind of gross stuff could be hiding down in the crevices.

I sat up and worked some moisture into my mouth. In the light of day, the tranquilized magic of last night wearing off, I suddenly felt panicked to be separated from Amanda and Cass. I really needed to figure out my way back to them. What if they were in danger, out there by themselves? What if they'd been eaten? Or, well, what if one of them had eaten the other? And the noneaten one was all mad at me? It wasn't cool to just be in the wind like this.

But wouldn't it be the ultimate action-hero move to swoop in and save Amanda and Cass with armloads of zombie penicillin? I was so close!

Outside, some jerk leaned into his car horn. Okay, that was unusual. I didn't notice a lot of traffic out in Des Moines last night.

"Jake!" Reggie yelled from upstairs, where I assumed his bedroom was. "You up yet?"

I groaned and stood up, my hangover really kicking in without the couch to soothe it. The living room was empty except for me and the remnants of our two-man party: empty beer cans, stems, and records left haphazardly out of their dust jackets.

"Yeah, man," Reggie called down, hearing my painful moaning. "Ditto."

"What's with the honking?" I yelled back.

"That's our ride," Reggie yelled. "We're kinda late. Do

me a favor and go down there. Tell 'em I'll be out in a minute."

If I'd been less hungover or less distracted by fantasies of flinging handfuls of antidote pills from the back of a parade float while Amanda stood next to me in an evening gown doing that model hand wave, I might have asked some important follow-up questions. For instance: Who's driving us where, exactly? Or, what're we late for? Instead, I just stumbled to the door, accidentally kicking over a colony of beer cans on my way. I darted back inside the apartment for one second to grab a taco-mouse, and then I was ambling downstairs.

The honking stopped as soon as I pushed open Reggie's security door. A limousine idled on the curb, unlike any I'd ever seen. It was one of those big Hummer deals that you could probably fit a hot tub into. Attached to the front grill was a snowplow blade covered in darkened bloodstains. The roof was decorated with defaced Iowa state flags, and spikes that boasted a collection of severed heads. It was the heads that really got my attention, many of them badly rotten, the identifiable ones seemingly all older men with comb-overs. I stopped in my tracks, feeling like I might want to run back inside.

Someone popped up through the open moonroof.

"This guy . . . ," Red Bear said, pointing at me with his hatchet. Part of his mouth was carved out and permanently widened with little wooden sticks, giving the impression that he was smiling at me—but he definitely wasn't. He looked the same as when I'd first met him on that bloody night in the fields beyond the farmhouse—greasy, a phony Native American getup, blatantly psychotic. "Don't we know this guy, Cheyenne?"

Through the rolled-down driver-side window, the intense chick with bleached blonde dreadlocks I remembered Red Bear sucking face with sized me up.

"Farmhouse," Cheyenne answered, not all that interested.

"That's right!" Red Bear slapped the limo roof, startling me. "I thought maybe the NCD killed you, bro."

"Uh, nope," I said, glancing up and down the block for escape routes.

"Nope, nope, nope," mimicked Red Bear in a falsetto, as he clamored through the moonroof and jumped onto the sidewalk. "You just keep popping up, huh? Little popper."

"Little *pooper*," Cheyenne said, and stared hard at me while making a farting noise.

I stared back at these two zombie wackadoodles. Red Bear, sporting an arrangement of dried scalps on his belt, was dressed in a leather vest and pants, Cheyenne in a bikini top and a skirt made of probably-human hair. They were more along the lines of the freaks I'd expected from Des Moines. Reggie being cool and having an awesome apartment had lulled me into a false sense of security.

But wait, were he and Red Bear friends? Were they picking him up?

"So, um, you guys know Reggie, huh?" I said, making conversation, trying to feel out the situation.

Cheyenne snickered.

"Reggie?" Red Bear snapped. *"Reggie?"*

"Yeah, um, upstairs Reggie? He said he'd be right—"

Red Bear flung himself at me. He tackled me around the waist and we fell onto the sidewalk. Before I could think to punch him, he'd straddled my chest and pinned my arms. He held his hatchet under my chin.

"Reggie?" he screamed again, exerting the slightest pressure against my Adam's apple. "Your bitch ass doesn't know any Reggie."

"Dude," I whispered, afraid to move my throat too much. "I don't know why you're mad."

Cheyenne giggled. That just seemed to incense Red Bear more. I could see the muscles in his hatchet-wielding arm tightening up.

Behind us, the apartment building's door clattered open.

"Goddamn it, Red Bear," Reggie snapped, some of last night's put-on menace vibrating through his voice. Except, I realized, this time it wasn't a put-on. "Get off him."

Red Bear took his hatchet away from my neck, twisted my nipple hard with his free hand, and stood up. I rolled onto my side to face Reggie.

"Are you seriously friends with—?"

I trailed off when I got a look at Reggie's outfit. He didn't look normal anymore, not like he had the night before. He'd picked his Afro out so it was even bigger, donned a pair of shaded nuclear-scientist goggles, and draped himself in a sleeveless patchwork overcoat. He didn't wear any shirt under the coat, showing off the DTFU↑ tattoo on his gaunt chest. Tight leather pants and platform boots that increased his height by another few inches completed the ensemble. He looked like the boss from a fighting game.

He looked like one of *them*.

"Oh man," I said. "What the hell are you wearing?"

Reggie chuckled, but Red Bear took the opportunity to kick me in the ankle.

"Show some respect," Red Bear snarled. "That's Lord Wesley you're talking to. The Lord of fuckin' Des Moines."

CASS

IT WAS A BEAUTIFUL DAY. EVEN IN IOWA, OF ALL THE
states I'd been to the one that made the worst first
impression, there could still be beautiful days.

My mind was sharp. My powers were working again.

I reached out to Jake on the astral plane. I know, I
know—I'd sworn off psychic spying, but these were definitely extraordinary circumstances. Finding his mind
was easy, his psyche familiar and comfortable, the telepathic equivalent of an old T-shirt.

Like me, Jake had just woken up. He lounged on a

couch in a fancy-looking apartment that someone had tried very hard to convert into a nerdy clubhouse. I imagined a suited doorman standing next to a hand-painted NO GIRLS ALLOWED sign. What mattered here was that Jake was alive, in the nonghoul sense, and that he'd made it to Des Moines.

All that, and he felt optimistic. It came pouring through our psychic link like sunshine edging under the curtains. Jake felt like he was close. He was going to find the cure. Like, today.

I knew I could depend on him.

I jumped out quickly. I didn't want to push too hard too soon. And I could feel Alastaire out there, burning at the edge of my consciousness. He wanted to communicate with me, but I pushed him away, shut myself off from the astral plane.

As I climbed out of my cot, feeling cheered and rejuvenated, I caught a glimpse of Tara, still in her bunk and basically catatonic. Looking at her, the stockpile of optimism I'd siphoned from Jake took a hit. I worried that I was gazing into my own future as a burnt-out psychic vegetable. I hadn't been able to get any more information out of her and I refused to try making psychic contact. I was scared what I might find in there. Tara was like one of those gruesome antismoking ads where the people talked through harmonicas, except she was the malformed poster girl for everything that could go wrong as a psychic zombie hunter.

But otherwise, things were peachy!

Later, I stood outside the bomb shelter and let the late-morning sun bombard my face. In daylight, I could see that the shelter was built up against a large ranch-style house, the only structure in sight. Otherwise, it was just rolling fields of bright green grass that'd probably never been splattered by even a little brain.

Well, except for this morning.

Anyway, if there were any more zombies out here, we'd see them coming from miles off. It felt peaceful to be in the middle of nowhere, clutching a mug of terrible coffee made from those freeze-dried crystals and cooked over a hot plate. Now that it was just a matter of waiting for Jake to snag the cure, my life seemed suddenly manageable. Granted, I still had to survive in this zombie wasteland, but at least I had some hope to go with my coffee.

"Everyone's got an amazing story," Lucy was saying to me. "To be surviving in a place like this? Talk about tales of valor, you know?"

"Mhm," I replied.

Lucy crouched next to me in the shelter doorway, nursing her own mug of coffee and smoking a cigarette. I didn't really mind the company, although I got the impression Lucy'd already pitched her so-called Definitive Oral History of Undead America to the other survivors. I think she was buttering me up to ask for an interview. I wasn't paying much attention.

"I mean, a few months ago I was writing blog posts about farm equipment," Lucy kept on. "And then, last week, I escaped a horde of undead by jumping off a fire escape onto a moving van. That's gotta be worth a Pulitzer, right?"

"Gotta be," I replied.

I watched Cody and Roy walking through the field behind the house. They dragged the ghoul from this morning by the ankles, the idea to get him away from the shelter so he wouldn't stink up the place or possibly draw others. It was slowgoing; Roy kept losing his grip and taking dry-heave breaks.

"Take Stud out there," Lucy said, noticing the direction of my gaze. "Kid used to be some hotshot amateur race-car driver. His dad was a small-town sheriff. They refused to evacuate when it all went down. A father and son, fast cars and guns, saving yokels from the undead." Lucy shook her head in disbelief. "Can you imagine the bank I'll get for the movie rights alone?"

I snorted. These adults never ceased to amaze me. Everyone was trying to exploit the zombie apocalypse somehow. If it wasn't Alastaire and his zombie slaves, it was Lucy and her crack journalism. She didn't seem to realize how unlikely it was she'd even make it out of Iowa to talk to any kind of film producer.

Degrees of grossness, sure, but grossness.

Still, I was curious.

"What happened to his dad?" I asked.

Lucy looked pleased to gossip, although she lowered her voice in that respectful speaking-of-the-dead way.

"There used to be about twenty of us," she began, "but some of the others got it in their heads to make a break for the wall. Cody's dad, William, he tried to convince them to stay. To play it safe. He got outvoted. We all went because that's the kind of group we were. Lots of families, some kids. We stuck together."

I thought of the bullet-riddled cars we'd passed coming in, and braced myself for another tale of NCD cruelty. "Did they get shot crossing over?"

Lucy snorted. "Never even made it. One of the Lord's hunting parties caught us on the road. Only reason me and Roy are alive is because we picked the right car. Cody's like the Steve McQueen of Iowa."

"And his dad?"

Lucy shook her head. "He picked the wrong car."

"Jeez," I said quietly, because I'm not great in these one-on-one horror-story situations.

"Mhm," Lucy replied, stubbing out her cigarette and lighting a new one. "So what's *your* story, new girl?"

"No comment," I said, smirking. "Always wanted to say that."

"C'mon," Lucy persisted. "You're driving around the

boondocks with a zombie escort saving people from soldiers of fortune. And you're a baby!"

"I'm seventeen."

Lucy pointed her cigarette at me. "You don't have the bone structure to be from around here," she mused, "and you're way too young to be one of those government spooks."

I smiled and looked elsewhere.

"I gotta know your deal," she said. "It can be off the record. I prom—"

"You won't make it out of here alive."

Lucy and I both jumped.

Tara stood behind us, at the bottom of the shelter's steps. Her skinny frame swam in a hooded sweatshirt she'd probably borrowed from Cody, hair all sweaty and stuck to her face, staring at Lucy with big, penetrating eyes.

Lucy grumbled. She'd spilled her coffee when Tara popped up.

"Good morning, Scary," Lucy said. "Is that today's prophecy?"

Tara didn't reply. Her attention had transferred from Lucy to me; she stared, hands clasped behind her back, rocking back and forth on her heels. I tried to ignore her.

"You know, I don't think it was a coincidence you showed up at our camp just a couple days before Truncheon nabbed us," Lucy said to Tara, using a singsong voice normally reserved for talking to dogs or plants. "Maybe you're just pretending to be all retarded, hmm?"

"She's *not* retarded," I snapped, feeling a sudden rush of anger for this woman who thought she was such an authority on everything. I've been around zombies for eighteen months and you're trying to impress me with stories about jumping off fire escapes? Shut up.

Lucy didn't look chastened, more like delighted to have gotten a reaction out of me.

"Maybe we could talk about your relationship," she suggested casually. "I overheard that you know each other. . . ."

Before I could reply, Tara linked her arm through mine and rested her head on my shoulder.

"We *do* know each other," Tara said, like she'd just discovered this. "Let's go for a walk, Cass."

Still holding on to my arm—she was stronger than she looked, considering it looked like a strong gust of wind might disintegrate her—Tara led me away. Even though we'd been roommates back at NCD headquarters, Tara and I definitely weren't on the friendship level of strolling through a meadow arm in arm. We'd see each other for a day or two every couple months and were usually pretty tight-lipped—psychics aren't really comfortable around other psychics. The most detailed conversation I remembered us having was her insisting on bottom bunk because she had seniority.

"So you remember me?" I asked, once we were out of Lucy's eavesdropping radius.

"I remember you from a dream," Tara answered. "We shared a room. We were sisters."

I yanked my arm away from her. She peered up at me through her mangy hair, face screwed up and bewildered.

"You're mad," she said.

"I'm not," I replied. "I'm fine."

In truth, I didn't know what I was feeling. I wanted to empathize with Tara; I knew that's what a good person would do. She was like me and she'd been through something terrible and she'd come out of it changed for the worse. But when I looked at her, I couldn't help picturing a fried version of myself obliviously wandering the Deadzone.

I also remembered Truncheon's payment request; he'd wanted a new psychic sent to him. Because his last one was "broken."

"Were you working with Truncheon?" I asked, trying to figure out what went wrong, even though the obvious answer was *pretty much everything*. "Was he your squad leader?"

Tara answered with a big nod, like her head was loose on her shoulders.

"What were you doing for him?"

"We played a game," she said, pausing to furiously scratch the top of her head. "A scavenger hunt for people.

They always needed new bodies."

My fists balled up, nails digging into my palms. Truncheon had said humans were like currency in the Deadzone. The way I figured it, he'd been using Tara to track the uninfected instead of the undead. She'd find him survivors and they'd end up bound and gagged in his sicko van, headed for . . . well, definitely not somewhere safe.

"Did he trade them?" I asked, trying to keep my voice gentle despite how repulsed I felt. "To the zombies in Des Moines? Or . . . ?"

"The Brothers Kope," Tara answered, knuckling her forehead. "I couldn't."

That corporation again. If Lucy wanted a Pulitzer scoop, she should've been grilling Tara instead of me.

"You couldn't what?" I prodded.

"Cope," she replied, tapping her temple. "It'll happen to you too. Even Daddy's favorite won't be spared."

I wanted to slap her or shake her or both. But she was so childlike, so totally broken, it seemed cruel to keep pumping her for information. Even if she'd been party to some truly nasty stuff out here, I knew from experience that sometimes the NCD didn't leave you much choice.

Tara reached down and plucked a dandelion, holding it up to me.

"It's not so bad like this," she said, blowing off the fuzzies.

"Good to know," I snorted, falling silent.

Our directionless stroll had taken us across the pasture toward the road. Nearby, Cody and Roy had finished their ghoul dumping and were headed back to the shelter.

"He's got secrets," Tara said to me, staring at Cody. He waved at us.

"Who doesn't?" I replied, returning the wave.

"Sexy secrets," Tara mumbled.

Encouraged by my wave, Cody veered off to greet us, tipping an imaginary hat. That made Tara giggle. I had to keep reminding myself she was in her twenties.

"Morning, ladies," Cody said, smiling at us with perfect teeth. He'd sweated his way through spots on his white T-shirt, right around all the muscles. He glanced up at the sun. "Or is it afternoon?"

"Morning!" Tara exclaimed. "We're all in mourning."

Cody smiled brightly at Tara, like she wasn't weird at all. "Good wordplay, T."

I looked Cody over. Beyond the sweat he'd worked up dragging the ghoul away, he looked pretty drained in general. I hadn't noticed the dark circles under his eyes last night.

"You look exhausted," I said. "Did you even sleep?"

Cody waved this off. "Y'all needed rest more than me," he replied. "Even way out here, it's safest to have someone on guard."

"Someone else could've taken a shift," I continued, feeling suddenly protective of these misfits. "You don't have to do it all yourself."

"You know what's funny?" Cody asked, looking down and rubbing the back of his neck. "I used to yell at my dad for doing the same thing. Pushing himself. He used to tell me, *Cody, I'll sleep when I'm dead.*"

"Which will be soon," Tara chimed in, her gaze drifting toward the road.

"Goodness," said Cody, smiling easily at Tara, no offense taken at her soothsaying. "I better catch a nap, then."

We all turned at the sound of a car. The only access to this place came via a single road that you could see down for miles. I shielded my eyes from the sun, trying to make out the speeding car through the dust it kicked up.

"That's not Amanda," I said, barely finishing my sentence before Cody shoved me down into the grass. He yanked Tara down too, her spacey giggling totally inappropriate.

"Sorry," Cody said, apologizing for the manhandling. "We tend to hide from strangers around here."

It wasn't much of a hiding spot, the three of us on our bellies in the grass. I turned my head to look back at the bunker. Roy and Lucy had smartly hustled inside, but I could see the top of Lucy's head peeking out from the doorway.

The car came down the road slowly. As it got closer, I recognized the red-and-blue roof lights.

"Police car," I said. "That a good or bad sign?"

"Well, there ain't any more police, so . . ." Cody reached behind him, checking to make sure his broom-handle stake was still hooked through one of his belt loops.

The cruiser sported similar modifications as the freakish limo I'd glimpsed in Jake's mind. Metal studs in the shape of an anarchy symbol glinted on the doors and a decapitated pig's head made for a gruesome hood ornament.

"Definitely not a good sign," I said.

"It's one of the Lord's scavengers," Cody replied. "Just stay down. Maybe he missed us."

"Poor piggy," Tara added helpfully.

The cruiser creaked to a stop in the middle of the road, shouting distance from our spot in the grass. A rail-thin guy in his twenties with a shaved head climbed out. He was dressed in an acid-washed denim jacket and matching jeans, all ripped up and frayed, looking like the bad boy from an '80s romantic comedy. This Bender wannabe stared in our direction and cupped his hands over his mouth.

"Olly olly oxen free!" he hooted.

I glanced at Cody in time to see his brow knit in confusion.

"That means he saw us," I whispered.

"Shoot," Cody lamented.

He climbed back to his feet and I stood up too, because, solidarity. Tara stayed prone on the ground. A quick peek over my shoulder revealed Lucy and Roy weren't in any rush to show themselves either.

"Don't look back," Cody hissed. "You'll give them away."

Cody pulled his makeshift spear out from behind his back, doing so with a flourish definitely meant to intimidate. In response, anorexic Bender raised his hands defensively.

"Whoa, hoss!" he shouted over to us. "I don't want any trouble now."

"He's a liar," Cody whispered to me, I guess using those immaculate first-impression skills of his, or maybe reasoning that anyone driving around with a decomposing pig's head couldn't be trusted. To the zombie, he yelled, "What do you want?"

"Lord Wesley's got me looking for a couple young ladies," the zombie called. He glanced down at the palm of his hand, reading. "Amanda and Cass."

Cody shot me a look. My stomach turned over.

"I don't got a picture or nothing," the zombie continued, smirking. "Their friend's looking for 'em, though. We got a tight-knit community, right? We help each other."

Jake must've said something to his new friends in Des Moines and now they were out here looking for us. I couldn't decide whether that was a good thing or a bad thing. It would've worked out great for Amanda had she stuck around, but as a tasty human morsel I wasn't too keen on an escort into zombie central.

"You seen them?" the zombie pressed, shielding his eyes to stare at me. "Won't be any problems if you have. Everybody gets a pass today."

"You don't, uh, *want* to go with this guy, do you?" Cody asked me out of the side of his mouth.

"Um, no."

"Don't matter," Cody whispered. "Whether you go or not, I can tell this one'll be back to try eating the rest of us."

"You whisper a lot!" the zombie yelled cheerily. He pointed at us. "Those my girls? Don't make me come over there and check IDs."

I glanced down at Tara, who looked completely oblivious, gazing up at the clouds. I figured she'd be as safe stretched out in the field as anywhere else.

"So, you've got a plan, right?" I hissed through my teeth.

"Kill him," Cody replied, taking me by the upper arm.

"Oh. Easy enough."

"Follow my lead."

I didn't know how much help I'd be in the killing department, but I could follow just fine. We marched toward the road, Cody keeping me out in front of him. I pretended to struggle a little and Cody hovered the point of his stake by my neck. Cody outweighed the scrawny denim enthusiast by at least forty pounds and looked to be in much better shape, which meant it'd be a fair fight even if the zombie went into freshly turned feral mode.

The zombie didn't seem all that concerned we might try to fight, making no move for the nasty-looking bowie knife that hung from his hip as we approached. Instead, he unclipped a military-grade walkie-talkie from behind his back.

"Boss, I think I got one out here," he said into it, then looked at us. "Which one are you?"

"This is Cass," Cody told the zombie as we closed the distance, shaking me by the arm for emphasis. "You can have her. I don't want any problems."

"Sure, guy," the zombie replied absently, more interested in looking me up and down. "I'll treat you better than this redneck," he said to me, all suave. "You're worth a month's rations, baby."

"Wow," I said, rolling my eyes. "How many rodents is that?"

He snickered. "Nah, honey. We're talking the good stuff. The Lord's got this contraption where he deep-fries an ar—"

Before I could hear more about Des Moines's wonderful cuisine, the zombie's walkie-talkie came to life with a burst of static.

"You forgot to say *over*, stupid," a brusque voice

chided. "Where you at? *Over*."

He raised the walkie-talkie. "I'm—"

And that's when Cody lunged.

The walkie-talkie clattered to the ground. Cody drove the stake right into the zombie's open mouth, angled upward, trying to jam it straight up and into his brain.

He missed. The stake poked through the back of the zombie's neck, just at the base of his skull.

The zombie went pale, veins on his bald head pulsing with thick, black blood. His eyes went sharp and kill-crazy even as the rest of him took on that saggy, decomposed look. He bit down hard on the broom handle, and a couple yellowed teeth popped out of his mouth.

Unable to bite him, the zombie crashed into Cody. They fell to the ground, Cody on the bottom, still clutching the stake in front of him. The landing caused the stake to slide the rest of the way through, popping out the back of the zombie's neck. The fresh hole emitted a smell that combined bad breath with moldy spinal fluid.

Trying not to gag, I lunged forward, grabbing the blood-slick stake from where it'd fallen beside the wrestling pair.

Cody screamed.

I wasn't quick enough. The zombie had already sunk his teeth into Cody's cheek.

JAKE

"HERE COME SOME OF THOSE THEATRICS I WAS TELL-
ing you about," Reggie said to me, keeping his voice low
so the others wouldn't hear. "Just be cool."

I could barely hear him over the thumping bass of
Ludacris's seminal rap song "Move Bitch." The song
shook loose from Red Bear's ridiculous homemade
sound system—a boom box hooked to multiple speakers,
mounted by duct tape to a shopping cart, and powered
by a pair of car batteries.

"Let's do this!" screamed Red Bear, and pushed his

cart forward, knocking open the doors of the looted sporting-goods store we'd been sequestered within. He was greeted by a wild cheer from outside.

This mall was packed with zombies.

Cheyenne strutted after Red Bear, holding up a giant card with a menacing rendering of Reggie's face, like one of those boxing-match-ring girls. With her gone, it was just Reggie and me in the store, listening to Red Bear's beats and the fired-up crowd. I peeked my head outside, eyes widening.

"Damn," I said. "Iowans have way too much unprotected sex."

Reggie gave me a screwed-up look. "It's not like that, man. I need to explain some shit to you."

I opened my hands, ready for some enlightenment.

"Not right this second, obviously," Reggie said, waving to the door. "Go, man. I gotta come out last."

So I stepped out onto the mall's second-floor concourse, where the railings were lined with more than a hundred Deadzone zombies, partying it up. A puzzled ripple went through them as they caught sight of me—I didn't look much like them in my jeans and Chairman Meow Communist Kitty T-shirt. Someone lit a bottle rocket and it whistled past me before exploding in front of a cinnamon-bun kiosk.

I hustled to catch up with Red Bear and Cheyenne, trying to take everything in. Most of the zombies were the leather-heavy, overly pierced types I'd seen on the border. There were other cliques among them, though—some were dressed like British punk rockers, others like wood sprites or elves or some mythological crap with lots of twigs and tights, a few like urban graffiti kids with bandanas covering their mouths, and a couple even looked totally normal, like me. I got the feeling those were other recent arrivals, judging by how uncomfortable they seemed. I guess it took a little while to decide what costume you were going to wear here in the afterlife. Most of the zombies skewed young and angry, although I saw a few that were my parents' age, and one lady that had to be eighty years old, crowded in with the punks, her saggy boobs slipping out of a Sex Pistols crop top as she tried to jump up and down.

Yeah. Total freak show.

"LET THE GAMES BEGIN!"

I spun around as Reggie's voice boomed out of a megaphone. Last night, he'd been my new best friend. Today, he was the Lord of Des Moines.

In the limo, on the way to the mall, he'd still been Reggie. He'd come downstairs just in time to get Red Bear off me, then ushered me into the back of the limousine. Red Bear rode up front with Cheyenne, the two of them shouting giddily whenever the snowplow ran over a ghoul, which was often. Reggie and I had the huge backseat area all to ourselves—a stocked minibar, a flat screen, lots of buttons. I might've enjoyed myself more if I wasn't feeling tricked and a little panicked.

Watching me closely from the opposite end of the limo, Reggie hit a button on the ceiling and raised the privacy screen.

"Dude," I said immediately, in a way that singularly communicated my confusion.

"Sorry Red Bear jumped you," Reggie said. "He flies off the handle sometimes."

"Uh, yeah, I don't care about that tool," I replied. "Why didn't you tell me you're, like—?"

"America's first zombie warlord?" Reggie suggested, laughing. "I don't know, man. It never came up."

"It did come up," I insisted, remembering our walk to his apartment. "I was asking *you* about *you*."

"Oh yeah." He shrugged and looked out one of the tinted windows. "Guess I didn't feel like doing the whole undead-despot thing. It gets exhausting."

I stared at him, not sure where to begin. The limo bounced over something crunchy.

"So should I call you, like, *your lordship*?" I asked. "Lord Wesley?"

"Please don't."

"Where does the *Wesley* even come from?"

"Uh, it's my last name?" Reggie held out a hand, like a king waiting for his ring to be kissed. "Lord Reginald

Butler Wesley, Jr. I was trying to get *your grace* to catch on a few months back, but that was pushing it."

I snorted and looked out the window, still feeling misled.

"You know," Reggie began hesitantly, "I don't hang out with a lot of people."

"Wow, dude," I groaned. "I feel so honored."

"I didn't mean it like that," he replied. "I mean, everyone around here's gotten sorta intense."

"Uh, you call yourself the Lord of Des Moines," I reminded him.

"I told you I was good at the zombie thing, right? Well, I'm so good, other zombies drive me around in limos. I can't control my talents." He sighed. "I'm just trying to explain. . . . Sometimes I do normal stuff as a change of pace."

"A change of pace from *lording*? Shit, dude, you, like, conquered a city," I said, not sure whether to feel amazed or frightened. "I mean, it's a suckhole city, but still. How does that happen?"

Reggie chuckled and lightly touched the puckered scar on his forehead. "Come look at this."

I hesitated for a second, then scooted along the backseat until I was close enough to examine the purple knot of skin. Reggie poked it, moving around something still lodged underneath.

"Gross," I observed.

"This was right when everything started. I was running with some guys—Red Bear, for one—just trying to stay alive, find people to eat, that kinda shit. This was back when the fat local cops still thought they could make a difference."

I glanced out the window. In daylight, I could make out all the bullet holes and bloodstains on the buildings.

"One night," Reggie continued, "I got shot in the head. We'd all seen people go down from headshots, so we knew how it worked. My crew left me behind. But I survived."

"Obviously."

"I told you I'd been sick my whole life," Reggie went on. "Well, when I was in high school, my brain swelled and they cut a hole in my skull to give it space. Once I was better, they replaced the bone they'd taken out with a titanium plate."

Reggie knocked on his forehead. I didn't hear any metal noise, but I guess you wouldn't with all the skin and stuff. I shook my head in disbelief.

"You're like a half-ass Wolverine."

He smirked. "Anyway, when I showed back up, the others thought I'd walked away from a headshot, that I was unkillable or some ignorant shit. Legend spread." Reggie shrugged. "I let it. People started wanting to run with me and, like I said, I had some ideas. Turns out I'm like the Sun Tzu of postapocalyptic politics.

Pretty soon, the Lord was born."

Reggie took a deep breath and looked at me expectantly.

For the record, the nerd in me was totally carving a bronzed statue for Reggie to commemorate his achieving great power through fanboy tendencies. But the part of me trying to make responsible decisions with an eye toward a future that didn't involve eating people? That part was feeling pretty cheated. We'd come here because the Lord of Des Moines posted on a message board. Sure, maybe that wasn't the best source of information, but it was still disappointing to find out the whole thing was just some dork living out a fantasy. Amanda would've ripped his metal-plated head off.

"Well," I said, scooting back to my side of the limo, "it's a great supervillain origin story, I guess."

"Supervillain," Reggie repeated, frowning at the thought. "That *is* how it always goes, huh? The bitter loser gets extraordinary powers and tries to take over."

"Yeah, that's pretty much you," I said, then remembering this was a zombie warlord I was dealing with, quickly added, "No offense."

Reggie waved me off, looking more crestfallen than angry. I guess there wasn't a whole lot of time for self-reflection in the Deadzone, but it seemed like he was doing some now. We bumped along for a few minutes in silence.

"Boss, I think I got one out here," a tinny voice interrupted from inside Reggie's overcoat.

Reggie produced a heavy-duty commando-in-the-jungle walkie-talkie.

"I got some of my people searching for your friends," he explained. "The cool thing about running a dictatorship is that dudes go on errands for you."

"Um, you know one of them is human, right?" I said, leaning forward and wishing I'd kept my mouth shut last night. "Your guys better not hurt her."

"Come on, Jake," Reggie replied, frowning. "That'd be a dick move. And anyway, I've never met one of these psychics in person."

I leaned back, not sure whether to be glad Reggie was looking for Amanda and Cass or worried that the Lord of Des Moines was hunting them.

"You forgot to say *over*, stupid." Reggie spoke into the walkie-talkie, shaking his head. "Where you at? *Over*."

There was a burst of static in response, maybe a syllable, and then nothing. Reggie stared at the walkie-talkie for a few more seconds, his brow furrowed, then put it away.

"Some of these guys aren't so bright," he grumbled. "I could use a guy like you, actually. A normal guy."

I didn't reply.

"Look, man," Reggie finally continued, "if you're not into it, I get it. I'm a little burnt out on all this shit too.

Just—hang out for a little bit, all right? See what we're all about. Then, I'll hook you up with some Kope Juice, if you *really* want it."

"Uh . . . Kope Juice?" I asked, remembering the billboards we'd seen defaced on the way in.

"The cure, man."

"Oh. Rad." Playing it cool, trying not to kick my feet, thinking about how hard Amanda was going to make out with me.

"I'll be straight with you, though," Reggie said, smirking, "things might get a little bonkers. A little, uh, theatrical. Every despot knows, keeping the masses entertained is important."

He wasn't kidding.

"ARE YOU READY?" Lord Reggie's megaphone blared. The crowd screamed in response. "WELCOME TO THIS WEEK'S ROMERO RUN!"

I clung to a section of railing on the mall's second floor as the other zombies crowded in, trying to get a better view. I ended up squeezed in next to Red Bear, his jagged smile pointed in my direction.

"You're gonna love this, bro," he said.

I had my doubts.

On the first floor, a group of humans shifted like nervous cattle behind the lowered gate of a JCPenney. Farther down the concourse, a pack of zombies milled about anxiously. They were a dozen, mostly the leather-biker types, but they looked scrappier and hungrier than the ones up here, like they might go rotten at any moment. Two hadn't been able to keep it together and had already slipped into a state of near-ghoul decomposition. They had to be held in check by a buff zombie dressed all in red-white-and-blue spandex like an American Gladiator.

"*Dawn of the Dead* theme is my favorite," Red Bear said in my ear. "You seen that one?"

I nodded. I'd seen my fair share of zombie flicks. Anyway, it didn't take a film buff to figure out what was about to happen. At the opposite end of the concourse from the JCPenney, a finish line had been painted on the floor in front of a Bon-Ton. The humans were going to have to run for it.

"If you don't bring in enough food," Red Bear explained, giving me a meaningful look, "you'll end up down there with the other scrubs, dancing for your meals."

I gave him what I hoped was an icy look. He slapped me on the back.

"Don't worry, it's not so bad!" Red Bear yelled. "Sometimes I join in just for fun!"

Someone sounded an air horn. The punk-looking zombie manning Red Bear's sound system changed the track to the fight music from *Star Trek*. The crowd went apeshit.

"RELEASE THE HOUNDS," Reggie boomed.

Some zombies positioned above the JCPenney yanked a pair of ropes and the gate lifted with a metallic screech. The humans inched forward—huddled together in a tight formation, moving slowly. The crowd jeered. Someone chucked a water balloon filled with god knows what.

The American Gladiator released the ghouls he'd been holding back and they beelined right for the humans. The other zombies took it slower, flanking the group like wolves around sheep, but also apprehensive about something.

"Let's go!" Red Bear screamed, annoyed. "Get 'em, you little bitches!"

Their caution made sense when the first ghoul reached the humans—all thrashing arms and gnashing teeth—and a shirtless black dude in bloodstained cargo pants stepped forward to greet him.

Jamison. That was his name, right? The NCD hard case who'd shot me multiple times last week, who'd gotten captured back on the border, sort of because of me.

"Oh shit!" Red Bear yelled. "Watch out for the ringer!"

Jamison caught the ghoul under the armpits, lifted him, and slammed him viciously onto the tile floor. The ghoul hit so hard, his body bounced. Jamison stomped forward, his boot landing dead center in the ghoul's face, smashing his head like an overripe cantaloupe.

I cheered. Couldn't help it. I like an underdog. Red Bear looked at me sideways, but I wasn't the only one, even though the others were probably just cheering for the violence, or because now there was one less undead belly to compete with in Des Moines. What Truncheon had said about the ecosystem suddenly made a lot of sense.

"Stay tight! Stay together!" Jamison yelled at the other humans. There were only six of them total and none of them looked half as tough as him. Two women and three men, middle-aged and soft, all of them wearing KOPE BROTHERS COMPANY PICNIC 2009 T-shirts.

The second ghoul reached them. Jamison grabbed this one by the ears, twisted its head around with a crunching sound that carried above all the shouting, and tossed him disgustedly aside. He kept his eyes on the more aware zombies the entire time.

The remaining zombies were all spread out, some perched on top of kiosks, and others stretched out mockingly on benches. The American Gladiator stood in front of the mall's fountain, hopping from foot to foot, watching Jamison with a ferocious grin.

The humans inched forward, Jamison still in the lead. The others looked increasingly nervous as the distance between them and the zombies shortened. One of the old dudes had started to cry.

"They're gonna break," Red Bear said.

He was right. A water balloon sailed from out of the crowd and hit one of the middle-aged guys in the back of the head. He shrieked and, before Jamison could stop him, took off for the finish line.

Two zombies tackled him almost immediately and started tearing him apart.

"Stop!" Jamison yelled, not at the zombies, but at the humans. "Hold formation!"

For a second, I thought they might actually listen to him. But then one of the eating zombies tossed the severed hand of their comrade at them and the humans all took off, booking for the far end of the concourse.

The zombies on the second floor roared with approval. Red Bear elbowed me in delight.

"Sick," I said quietly.

I looked around for Reggie. He was farther down the railing, watching the action with his arms folded. He didn't notice me.

Jamison was the only human that didn't get tackled in those first manic thirty seconds. It didn't seem like any of the zombies were eager to tangle with him, more interested in the easy prey. If he'd gone for it right then, he probably could've made it to the safety of the Bon-Ton.

Instead, he tried to help a lady with a scrawny zombie wrapped spiderlike around her torso. That's when the American Gladiator barreled in. The freak in the spandex leotard squeezed Jamison in a bear hug from behind and bit down, hard, on the NCD agent's shoulder.

I thought that was it for him, but Jamison didn't go down easy. He smashed his head back into the zombie's face while trying to pry apart his grip. The American Gladiator was too strong, so Jamison shoved backward with all his weight, and the two of them went crashing through a bench. The zombie's grip loosened and Jamison rolled to the side.

The DJ queued up "Eye of the Tiger."

As Jamison got to his knees, the American Gladiator grabbed him and took another bite out of his upper arm. Jamison tried to shove the zombie's face away with one hand, groping through broken pieces of bench with his other. The zombie had really latched on, though, and Jamison crumpled backward with the American Gladiator on top, eating him alive. Jamison screamed, I'm not sure whether from frustration or pain, and slapped his hand against the zombie's ear.

The American Gladiator went limp.

He'd gotten hold of a nail from the bench. Jammed it straight through to the zombie's brain.

Jamison staggered to his feet, blood coursing down his shoulder. He looked around. All the other zombies were occupied, hunched over their humans. I saw his features go tight with rage and was sure he was going to charge back in, but he fought it back. Spit. And walked to the finish line. When the crowd cheered his arrival, he shot up a double bird. From above, some zombies lowered the Bon-Ton's gate, trapping Jamison inside.

"Hot damn," Red Bear exclaimed, "you know how long it's been since we had a returning champion? I am *definitely* playing next week!"

I realized the back of my shirt was soaked with sweat. My fingers tingled and there was a dull ache deep in the pit of my stomach. Like the zombies around me—writhing, screaming, light on deodorant—I gazed down at all the gore and my mouth watered. I was hungry, but in a way that felt dirty and weirdly illicit. I wanted to shove this feeling underneath my mattress and then set that mattress on fire. I felt ashamed having watched that.

The music cut off and a hush fell across the crowd. I looked down the railing and saw that Reggie had raised one hand in the air. Except for the feeding zombies down below, the mall was suddenly eerily quiet. He didn't even need to use the megaphone.

"That, bitches, was one of the greatest Romero Runs your Lord has ever seen! Those motherfuckers down there, they *earned* that meal! Ya dig?"

A cheer went up from the crowd. I glanced to my side and realized that Red Bear had slipped away.

"And that hard-ass human son of a bitch, he *earned* another week of fattening up and marinating in fear sauce! Ya dig?"

Another cheer, although somewhat less enthusiastic. I hoped that fear sauce was just a metaphor because it sounded gross.

"We've got a good thing going here," Reggie yelled, a growing tension in his voice. "And to keep it working right, all I ask is that you *earn*. That you *take* only what you *need*. This ain't breaking news, is it?"

A resounding *NO!* from the crowd, apparently well versed in the bylaws of Deadzone living. Some of the zombies around me had started to shift anxiously, as if something crazy was about to happen.

"DOUG TAYLOR!" Reggie screamed, spit flying off his lips as he pointed into the crowd. "GET YOUR ASS UP HERE!"

Doug Taylor was one of the middle-aged zombies. Nothing special about him. He was trying way too hard with all his leather gear when it looked like he'd be better suited to selling vacuum cleaners door-to-door. He tried to run when Reggie pointed him out, but Red Bear and Cheyenne had crept up on him. They grabbed him—screaming and thrashing—and dragged him over to Reggie.

"Uh . . . ," I said, glancing around for some clarification. No one nearby seemed interested in explaining to me what the deal was, or in making eye contact. Everyone was restless now, edging backward from Reggie.

"My friends!" Reggie shouted. "On multiple

occasions, Doug here has tried using American dollars—a currency we have no fucking use for!—to bribe extra rations from your fellow citizens! He has stolen! He has gone on unsanctioned hunts and not shared the spoils! He has been warned and he has not listened! YA DIG?"

This time the crowd booed and shouted curses at Doug. Red Bear and Cheyenne forced the poor guy, pleading and struggling, onto his knees before Reggie. With a flourish, Reggie removed a syringe from within his coat. The mere sight of the needle freaked some of the zombies out and they stumbled back.

I inched closer.

"Doug!" Reggie shouted, holding him by the chin. "We reject your kind! You are NOT one of us!"

And then I knew what was about to happen. I knew what was in that syringe. It was the very thing I was searching for.

Red Bear shoved Doug's head down so Reggie could jam the syringe into the base of his skull. An uncomfortable murmur went through the crowd as Reggie methodically pressed down the plunger. I realized that without really trying, I'd elbowed my way right to the front.

They let Doug go. He crumpled onto his face, cradling his head like he was afraid something might pop out of there. Hell, maybe the virus *was* going to explode right out of his brain and that's what Reggie had meant about the cure being complicated. Side effects include: explodey brain. Yeah, I'd call that a complication. Suddenly, I found myself wondering if the cure was really something I wanted after all. This did not look fun.

Everyone was quiet, a sort of reverent silence for Doug's whimpering. He twitched around on the ground, all clenched up, like he was trying to fold into himself. So, yeah, this part looked painful.

Then he stopped moving entirely. I noticed that his hands had turned that congealed-gray zombie color, but it wasn't quite the usual undead discoloration. His hands were a patchwork, spots of normal pink flesh separated by scabby mounds of dead gray. The same was true for an expanse of skin along his neck.

"Is that it?" a zombie behind me whispered.

That wasn't it.

Doug sprung onto his hands and knees and started to puke. He let loose a torrent of rotten-smelling chunks, the color and consistency of marshmallows that'd fallen into a campfire. He hacked and hacked until it didn't seem like anything else could possibly be hiding inside him and then he hacked some more. I covered my nose and mouth with my hand. Even some of the psycho-looking, hard-ass Iowa zombies crowded around me averted their eyes.

And then something changed, like a switch flipping. Doug rolled onto his back, panting, his bloodshot eyes staring up at the mall's skylight. Those splotches of dead, gray skin hadn't faded. He looked like an extra from a horror movie that hadn't finished getting into makeup.

But man, puke-covered and all, I wanted to eat him.

"Check the meat," Reggie said to Red Bear.

With casual grace, Red Bear unhooked his hatchet from his belt and swung it down at Doug. The guy was so out of it that he didn't even flinch when the blade opened a shallow cut on his shoulder. A cut that glistened wet and red, with no signs of turning moldy, zombie gray.

Doug was human. Alive. *Un*-undead.

"All good," Red Bear said.

Reggie's eyes landed right on me. For a moment, crazy as he looked in the Lord of Des Moines regalia, I caught a glimpse of the regular guy I'd hung out with last night. Maybe the Germans have a word for what I felt. Conflicted, for starters. In the middle of the Venn diagram between mystified, revolted, and hungry.

Reggie rolled his eyes and shrugged at me, like, *What can ya do?*

"LET'S EAT!" he screamed into the megaphone.

CASS

HIS BODY WAS SURPRISINGLY LIGHT. ROY LET GO OF THE armpits at the same time that I let go of the ankles, and he crumpled like a loose-limbed doll into the trunk of the police car.

"I used to have a jean jacket just like that," Roy said, peering down at the zombie. "The eighties were great."

"They always seemed like fun in the movies," I replied absently, staring down at the hole in the zombie's head, a blackened pit surrounded by flaps of dried, gray skin. "Cool music. No cell phones. Not so much cannibalism."

Gently, Roy eased me away from the trunk and closed it.

We stood on the side of the road and watched the sun dip steadily below the horizon. Out here, everything turned gold during the sunset. It was like living inside one of those whole-grain cereal commercials. It would've struck me as beautiful, except my gaze kept getting drawn back to the dried blood on the pavement.

"You haven't seen a lot of this kinda stuff, have you?" Roy asked, mopping sweat from his forehead with the sleeve of his shirt.

"I thought I had," I replied. "These last couple days have been on a whole new level of screwed up, though. And everyone's just so casual about it."

"You get used to it," Roy said resignedly. "You start to forget they're people."

"But they *are* people," I snapped. Zombie personhood was still a sore subject with me. The whole reason I'd left the NCD was because I'd recognized humanity in Jake. Humanity and, you know, other attractive qualities. Sure, I'd liked him, but it'd also seemed like the right thing to do. And yet, I hadn't really cared when Truncheon sniped that ghoul on the road, or when Cody did his staking. Did that make me a hypocrite? Or did morality just not apply in Iowa?

"I don't mean just the zombies," Roy said, chastened, peering over the crest of his belly to look at his feet.

"Everybody that dies. You see enough dismemberments, even of people you know, and it starts to get like . . . I don't know. Like the weather."

I blinked at him. Well, Cody *had* called him a pessimist. I guess this was his version of a pep talk. *You'll get desensitized eventually, Cass!* Great.

"Come on," I said, wanting to skip any further philosophical gems. "It's getting dark. Let's get this done."

I ducked into the cop car's driver-side window. The zombie's keys still dangled from the ignition, but I didn't use them. One ghoul had already stumbled through the fields and toward the bunker, drawn by the noise of today's fracas. Roy'd been forced to begrudgingly bash her head in with a shovel. We didn't want to draw any more attention, so I put the car in neutral and we started to push.

When Cody was pinned under the zombie, I hesitated. I'd never actually killed one before. The undead were lucky, in a way. They blacked out during their first kills and were driven by pure animal need. They came to with gory bits stuck under their fingernails and that emotional-hangover feeling of having done something bad, but they didn't have to live with all the mental pictures. They didn't have to *think* about it. In contrast, my first brain gouging was going down in the moment. You hear about those people spurred to heroic action who just ride through harrowing moments on instinct and adrenaline. Not me. My inner monologue was going over stuff like proper stake grips and which part of the skull was supposed to be the softest.

Of course, that hesitation almost cost me.

The zombie bit into Cody's cheek, but then must have sensed me standing there contemplating his demise, maybe even remembered via some guttering ember of rational thought that I was the one he'd come for, because he sprung away from Cody and lunged at me in a way that looked a lot like that worm-dance move.

I cried out and fell backward, scraping my palms on the asphalt. Dropped the stake. Not my finest moment, obviously.

Cody tangled his legs with the zombie's, preventing him from getting at me. They were both still on the ground, almost spooning, just a few feet from me. I kicked the stake in Cody's direction, and he snatched it up and plunged it into the back of the zombie's head.

The assisted zombie kill. That was way more my comfort zone. Even AWOL from the NCD, I still thought of myself as noncombat personnel.

Blood trickled down Cody's neck from the fresh ring of teeth indentations on his cheek. He took a deep breath, leaning against the lifeless zombie.

"Gosh," he said, smiling at me. "Close one."

* * *

"We aren't going to stay here another night, are we?"

Roy and I trudged backed into the bomb shelter just in time for Lucy's question. Her voice was an octave higher than it'd been earlier, that no-nonsense crack-reporter exterior crumbled. She'd been too busy meticulously applying disinfectant to Cody's bite wound to help Roy and me with the car; at the time I assumed she just wanted to get out of manual labor, but now I realized she was spooked. It really had been a close one.

"I don't see why not," Cody replied, and flashed her the same cavalier smile he'd trotted out for me after he killed the zombie. It lost some of its effect with one of his dimples hidden behind a bulky gauze pad, and he grimaced at the cheek usage. "Ow."

"Your dad's rule was to leave a place once they'd gotten a whiff of it," Lucy countered. "It's a good rule."

"He also had a rule about not traveling after dark," Roy put in, flopping down on a bunk.

Cody looked to me, his eyebrows raised imploringly. "Besides, we killed that zombie before he could give away our location. Right, Cass?"

I nodded, meeting Lucy's narrowed gaze. "Yeah. Cody even smashed his walkie-talkie. So they can't . . . what was it?"

"Triangulate us," Cody said proudly.

I didn't bother explaining that triangulation wasn't

really a thing with walkie-talkies—hey, I'd picked up some stuff during my G-woman days—or that it might've been beneficial for us to have an open channel into the Lord of Des Moines security network. All points I should've made back in the road when Cody was stomping the walkie, instead of mutely staring at his fresh disfigurement. Anyhow, like Cody, I didn't want to leave the bomb shelter. It seemed like the safest place to wait while Jake tracked down the cure. I'd gotten a glimpse of what being on the road in Iowa could be like, and it wasn't for me.

"Besides," Cody continued, trying to sound all blasé. "We need to wait for Cass's friend to get back."

I suddenly began reconsidering my position on staying put.

"Oh, I get it," Lucy said dryly, picking up on Cody's smitten tone just like I had. She turned to Roy, pointing at me. "Aren't you at all concerned that the freaking Lord of Des Moines himself sent a goon out here to find her?"

Roy bunched his shoulders, staring at the floor. "Eh, she's all right, Lucy."

Lucy faced me. "I'm sorry, but we don't know anything about you or your perky zombie friend that's currently off doing god knows what."

"Well," I replied, "we saved you from getting sold as zombie food. For starters."

Lucy snorted. "You know how many times in the last

month Roy or Cody has saved my ass or vice versa? That's just what we do around here. So thanks a bunch for saving me *yesterday*, girl, but I'm worried about you getting me killed *tomorrow*. You've got this aura of craziness about you that I just know is going to screw us."

I frowned. Did I really have an aura of craziness? I mean, my recent life decisions didn't exactly scream *I've-got-my-crap-together!* but I'd hoped to not exude chaos.

"She's not being literal." Tara spoke up from her spot on the back bunk, where she sat cross-legged, eating canned peaches with her fingers. "She can't actually see your aura. Your aura's just peachy, Cassandra."

Oh well, that was a relief. According to my burnt-out fellow psychic, I was totally fine.

"This one too," Lucy added, jerking her thumb at Tara while appealing to Cody. "Both of them. They just scream trouble, Cody."

"Humans stick together," Cody replied firmly. "That was another of Dad's rules."

"Yeah, but—"

Lucy cut herself off at the sound of a car driving up. For a moment everyone froze, totally silent, except for Tara slurping down a peach.

Closest to the door, I slowly pulled open the hatch and peeked outside. Cody jumped up from his spot on the bunk with a groan and crowded in next to me.

"Another patrol?" he asked.

"Nope," I said, recognizing the Maroon Marauder. "It's Amanda."

Cody immediately began slicking down his cowlicks.

"Great," Lucy muttered. "More trouble."

Ignoring her, I pulled open the bunker door and stepped outside, Cody right on my heels.

Amanda first pulled into the driveway, then drifted across the grass in our direction. The car wobbled slightly, like her grip was loose on the wheel, and creaked to a stop just a few yards from us. Cody stood up straighter and maybe puffed out his chest a little, self-consciously touching the bandage on his face.

"Hey there, Amanda," he said, sounding more country than ever as he greeted her through the open driver-side window.

Amanda's head lolled as she looked at him, her eyes half-lidded. "Hey . . . you."

It'd taken her less than a day to forget his name. Typical. And right back to the whole sex-kitten act too.

"Glad to see you back," Cody kept on cheerily. "Everything turn out okay?"

As I looked her over, I realized Amanda wasn't trying to make gross succubus eyes at Cody. She was actually exhausted and having trouble keeping her eyes open. Her hair was as unkempt as I'd ever seen it, that preposterous glisten she somehow maintained even on the road faded to a greasy sheen. She had something stuck on her chin—a tuft of guinea-pig fur.

"Hush now," Amanda said to Cody half-deliriously, pointing at me. "I need to talk to my friend Astral Pain."

"Flirt later," I muttered, elbowing Cody aside. "Give us some space."

Cody stepped back a few feet, his hands shoved into his pockets. He looked like he didn't know what to make of this situation; was he scoring points here or not?

"Sorry," he said to me, then craned his neck to look at Amanda. "I just wanted to say thank you again. For yesterday."

Recognition flickered in Amanda's eyes. Maybe she was remembering her role as zombie heroine.

"It was no big deal, handsome," she replied, totally on autopilot, but it made Cody beam on his way to the bunker. Finally, she focused on me. "What happened to his face?"

"Zombie bite," I replied.

"Oh. Shame."

"You've got something here. . . ." I brushed my own face in demonstration.

She sneered at me like I'd made her a sloppy eater, but eventually pawed awkwardly at the area around her mouth, missing on the first couple attempts.

"Gone?"

I nodded. "So, can I ask what the hell happened to you?"

"I can't find him," Amanda moaned dramatically. "I've been checking all these smelly-ass ghouls for mohawks and he's just nowhere. He's *gone*."

"Jeez," I replied, shaking my head. "Have you been doing that since last night?"

Amanda nodded and when that nod finished, her forehead rested against the steering wheel. She'd been hunting for Jake for eighteen hours straight and looked completely drained as a result. I knew Jake's whereabouts were like my biggest piece of leverage and I hadn't forgotten how miserable Amanda made me on a regular basis, but still I felt a swelling of sympathy.

"He's fine," I told her. "He's alive. Nonghoul. He's fine."

Amanda turned her head to look at me. Her forehead, scrunched in confusion, had an ugly red indentation from the wheel.

"Then why didn't he come?" she asked me, hurt. "I kept checking the garage. Why didn't he come?"

My mouth hung open. Was I supposed to cover for Jake here? Tell Amanda that he'd gotten into Des Moines and was close to the cure? Or that he'd been playing video games and getting stoned while she drove around searching for him? I mean, I'd felt some tenderness before, but I wasn't ready to be playing relationship counselor between the meanest girl in America and the zombie I inappropriately desired.

"I thought it'd be different," Amanda murmured as

my silence stretched on. "Dating a nerd, you know? But even they stand you up and let you down."

"He didn't—" I started a sentence I had no idea how to finish, but Amanda saved me the trouble by starting to snore.

JAKE

THROUGH THE WINDOWS IN THE SECOND-FLOOR FOOD court, I gazed at the Ramada Tropics, where Reggie said most of the Iowan undead population had decided to stay. In the fading sunset, I could see lights beginning to blink on in some of the rooms.

After a moment, I realized those blinking lights were actually flaming pieces of furniture being shoved out of windows.

There was no shortage of nice things to wreck here in Des Moines. It made me kind of sad to think about someone getting cured, coming back from zombie-life, and finding all their stuff spray-painted and burnt up.

"Hi, Wallflower," Cheyenne slurred as she sidled up next to me, her hand slithering through the crook of my elbow. "Are you lonely?"

I glanced over my shoulder to where the party was petering out in the food court. Some dumb-ass zombies were trying to surf on fast-food trays down a straightaway slickened with oil spilled from a deep fryer. Clinging to my arm, Cheyenne looked all kinds of wasted.

"How could I be lonely?" I asked, making a half-hearted joke of my discomfort. "This is the craziest party I've ever been to."

"Drink this and I'll like you better," she said, and tried to hand me a bottle that wasn't liquor but something yanked right out of a medicine cabinet, the skull-and-crossbones sticker only half-ripped off. When I shook my head—because even I have limits—she shoved me hard, flipped her dreadlocks, and staggered away.

I breathed a sigh of relief and went looking for a new place to hide out. I had some major emotions I was trying to get a grip on.

I'd eaten some of Doug.

His time as a restored human being lasted approximately thirty seconds. The zombies—us, we—fell upon him, ripped him apart. I justified this because I'd been feeling hungry and if I'd gone ghoul, who could say if any of these Iowan nut jobs would've brought me back. Also, Doug had totally eaten people in his time as a zombie, so it was like the circle of life.

The only parts left of Doug were the disfigured gray ones, the dead flesh that Reggie's injection didn't slosh off. So, yeah, the cure kind of sucked. Painful, pukey, and with the possibility of lingering zombie scars.

I sighed. Amanda wasn't going to like that.

The zombies here had a short memory. Doug wasn't even digested before the party broke out. There were zombies everywhere—looting, getting drunk, hooking up. I'd tried to stick close to Reggie, but it was too much. He was constantly surrounded by a throng of zombies that wanted to hobnob with the Lord of Des Moines. For a while I watched from the sidelines as he held court— talking people up and throwing back shots, with Red Bear nearby to scare off any zombie that lingered too long or said the wrong thing. I got bored with that scene after a while and started exploring the mall. That was a couple hours ago. The food court had been peaceful until the grease surfers and Cheyenne showed up.

I was officially the loser looking for a quiet place to hide at a party.

I felt kind of lame for not wanting to socialize with these zombies, but I wasn't yet at a point where I drank poison and set fires for fun. I wasn't ready to embrace the zombie anarchist lifestyle. I was feeling some residual guilt about the Doug eating. Hell, I hadn't even wanted this mohawk—that'd been all Amanda's idea.

I was a total poseur.

Eventually, I found myself in an empty Bath and Body Works. In my previous life I would've avoided a store like that at all costs, but I guess awkward social scenes and zombie apocalypses will make you take refuge in some pretty strange places.

I tried to pick out some girly lotion or body spray or fragrance cannon or whatever the hell that Amanda might like, but I didn't even know where to begin. I ended up just spraying a bunch into the air, trying to find the one that was most her, and possibly permanently damaging my sense of smell with all that berry-dolce-sangria intensity. My eyes stung like crazy.

"What kinda fruity shit is this?"

Red Bear leaned in the doorway sending his most disdainful sneer my way, although the way his face was cut, I'm not sure how many different expressions the dude was capable of. Embarrassed, I hurriedly stuffed the most recent perfume experiment into my back pocket.

"Uh, cherry blossom," I said. "What's up?"

"The Lord requests your presence," Red Bear recited. I could tell he didn't understand why Reggie wanted to hang out with me. It was the same look I'd gotten last summer when I crashed one of Chazz Slade's keg parties. *Who invited you?*

"Great," I said.

The party had mostly broken up, although there were still a few pockets of zombies up to no good. I guess most of them had gone off to swim in their dirty hotel pool or scavenge for living flesh or whatever zombies do to blow off steam after a busy day at the blood sport.

Red Bear led me to an exit that connected to the sky-walk on the far side of the mall. He didn't say a word the entire time, which I appreciated.

In the glass enclosure, lit by the dusky remains of the day, Reggie waited for me. He wasn't dressed in his Lord of Des Moines regalia anymore, but instead in a leather jacket, Stephen King Rules T-shirt, and jeans. The casual despot. He grinned when he saw me.

"Have a good time?" he asked.

"Uh." I glanced from Reggie to Red Bear, not sure what to say and not wanting to get tackled again, or worse. "Sure. It was a rager."

Reggie's grin turned sympathetic. "You get used to it, man, I swear. Plus, uh, you happened to be here on one of our wilder days. Sometimes we just have bands play or normal shit like that."

"How many Cradle of Filth cover bands you got?" I asked. "Like a billion?"

Reggie chuckled. "Maybe you want to be my Minister of Arts and Culture, huh?"

"Whoa, hold up," Red Bear interrupted. "We have titles now?"

"It was a joke," Reggie replied, looking suddenly annoyed Red Bear was still hanging around. "You can go, *Gene*. I've gotta talk to Jake."

Red Bear—aka Gene—cocked his head, his Adam's apple bobbing rapidly. He looked wounded and also like he wanted to hatchet my face, but he didn't do anything, just stalked back inside the mall.

"All right," Reggie said, clapping his hands, "after all that, you still want the cure?"

I was prepared for this question. It's pretty much all I'd been thinking about while wandering the mall. Maybe the cure wasn't all we'd hoped it would be, but Amanda and Cass still needed it. I wasn't going to pass it up.

"Yeah," I answered. "I want the cure."

"You get that it can fuck you up, right?" Reggie asked, surprised. "It knocks the infection out in a hurry and sometimes your regular immune system doesn't come back on in time. You end up looking part-rotted."

"Uh-huh." I nodded. "And then someone eats you. I know the risks."

"Dude." Reggie frowned at me, still disbelieving. "You might want to check that judgmental shit. I'm trying to do you a solid here."

"Sorry," I replied halfheartedly, looking out through the glass wall of the skywalk to the darkened street below.

"Nah. No you're not," Reggie replied. "That's why I like you, Jake. You're real."

"Uh, thanks."

"Anyway," Reggie said awkwardly, reaching into his overcoat. "Here you go."

And just like that he tossed me two injectors, exactly the same as the one he'd plunged into Doug. Luckily, they were capped, because I fumbled them on the catch. One of them dropped to the floor of the skywalk and I nearly cried out in panic, but it was fine.

Two perfectly good syringes of zombie cure, right in my suddenly sweaty and shaky hands.

I'd done it. We'd be cured. Amanda and I could be normal again.

"Keep those hidden," Reggie said, noticing that I'd frozen while lovingly gazing upon my prize. "They freak people out."

Carefully, I slid the syringes into my back pocket along with Amanda's perfume. In terms of side effects, Kope Juice made those boner-pill commercials with their endless lists of life-threatening possibilities look like children's aspirin. Still, horrible pain and permanent disfigurement aside, taking the cure seemed like a solid alternative to a life of cannibalism. Well, probably. Anyway, Amanda and I had traveled halfway across the country for this. I couldn't help feeling a sense of triumph. I tried to play it cool in front of Reggie, though.

"Thanks," I said in my macho-man voice. "It means a lot, dude."

"Just so you know, I think you're an idiot to take

these. The world is all about people eating each other, now more than ever, and you're choosing to be on the wrong side of that dynamic."

"Eh," I replied. "BFD."

Reggie chuckled. "Man, I'm not done trying to convince you not to take those. But I thought after today you might need a gesture to prove that I'm not a total heartless psycho."

"You know that's not a thing normal people have to prove to each other."

"We aren't normal people, Jake," Reggie replied, then slung his arm around my shoulders and started walking me down the skywalk. "So, you can go running back to your friends and life as a boring, edible, scab-covered human tomorrow, right? Tonight, we play *Street Fighter*."

It was hard to keep the giddy grin off my face. I started to walk with Reggie, figuring I could give him one more night of nerding out—the dude seemed lonely and he'd basically just saved my life. A few steps down the skywalk, I stopped in my tracks.

Friends. He'd said *friends*.

"Shit," I said, tapping my back pocket. "I need one more of these."

Reggie cocked his head at me. "Oh, right. For the little NCD psychic you're hooked up with."

"Um, ex-NCD. Yeah."

"Here's the thing," Reggie explained, all silky and

reasonable sounding as he stamped out my good vibes. "For a fellow zombie like yourself and your zombie girl-friend, who I'm sure is also cool, I'm like a humanitarian. You want the cure? I don't recommend that shit, but it's yours. You're my people, you know? But for some little secret agent with magic powers? Well, damn, Jake, I've never met one of those before. She's trespassing in my territory, man. Least she could do is come by and say what up."

I tried to imagine Cass walking down the streets below with all those loose ghouls, or hanging around the mall with the packs of bloodthirsty cosplayers. It didn't end well.

"I don't think that's gonna happen," I told him.

"Oh well," he said nonchalantly, resuming his walk with his arm around me. "I've got Kope Juice to spare for your psychic, Jake. She's just gotta come get it."

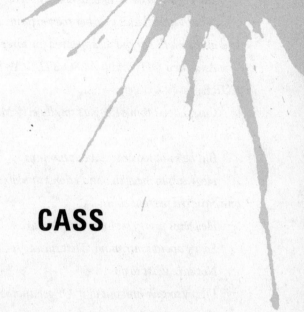

CASS

UM, CASS? ARE YOU OUT THERE IN PSYCHIC LAND
listening?

Is this how it works?

This is stupid.

It's like praying.

My fingers are on my temples FYI. If that helps.

*Amanda is going to be so psyched! She is going to make out
with you so hard!*

Not you, Cass. Sorry. Me. Off topic.

He wants you to come here, Cass. To Des Moines.

I'm stoned. Probably not helping.

Sun's almost up. What time is it in your part of Iowa?

I'm wasted. And beat.

She's going to be all like, ohhh, my hero!

What I'll do first is give her the perfume. Like, this is all they had at the mall. Sorry I disappeared for three days.

And then OH WAIT ALSO THIS AWESOME ZOMBIE CURE.

Cass, I don't think Reggie's totally evil. Maybe on the sinister side.

But he's not too crazy about humans.

He wants to meet you and I don't think his intentions are like one hundred percent chill.

He seems pretty set on it. For the cure.

Sorry about your mom. That sucks.

Not sure what to do.

I'll try to talk him out of it. Or get another vial of the stuff. I'll try.

Okay, you're not listening.

Amanda is going to be PUMPED.

I'm definitely going to do that perfume bit.

It's going to be great.

I snapped awake or, more honestly, leapt out of Jake's totally scattered and deeply discouraging mind. I didn't even have time to consider what I'd learned—that he'd acquired the cure, but not enough; that he was devoting the same amount of brainpower to his reunion with Amanda as he was to helping me save my mom—because something seriously weird was going down in the physical world.

Tara had crawled into bed with me. Her feet were freezing and pressed against my legs. Her stale breath gusted against the side of my face. For a moment, I remembered creeping into bed with my big sister as a kid and felt oddly comforted by the physical contact.

"That's right," Tara whispered. "We're basically sisters."

That killed it. I recoiled, both physically and mentally.

"This is not okay," I hissed, trying to put some space between us in the tiny cot.

"Daddy wants to talk with you," she replied, unperturbed by my obvious discomfort. "He wants you to stop being stubborn."

I glared at her, angry at the multiple violations of personal space happening here, until I noticed the thin tendril of blood snaking down from her nose.

"Maybe you should stop talking to him too," I whispered. "It's hurting you."

Tara shook her head and snuffed her nose. "Can't. It's my job."

"You should quit. I did."

And look how well that's working out, I stopped myself from adding.

Tara ignored me, her eyes glazed over. "He wants me to tell you that they're coming."

I swallowed. "Who?"

"The men with guns," she replied. "They'll be here tomorrow. He says you're running out of time."

With that, Tara slipped out of my cot and returned to her own. I lay there with my arms across my chest, trying to process everything. Jake didn't have enough of this so-called Kope Juice. He didn't have an angle on getting more that didn't involve me marching into zombie-controlled Des Moines and having coffee with a fanboy despot who probably wanted to eat my brains to try assuming my powers or some fantasy crap. And time before Iowa—already a festering hellhole—became a bloody, bombed-out war zone was running out.

Obviously, I couldn't go back to sleep.

I stood up, stretched, and stepped outside my partition. The faintest hint of gray light squeezed under the crack of the shelter's door. It was early, yeah, but I was going to need every minute to come up with some kind of plan.

Lucy was stationed next to the bunker's door, sitting on the stool I expected Cody to be occupying. She raised her eyebrows, surprised to see me up, and yawned into the back of her hand. Her other hand rested comfortably on the stock of the rifle I'd given her last night. She'd chilled out considerably on the whole "trouble" thing after I'd armed her.

Oh, right. While she was sleeping, I'd liberated the weaponry from Amanda. I'd given Truncheon's rifle to

Cody's group and stashed my stun gun under my pillow. Remembering it, I slipped back behind my partition to shove the weapon into the back of my pants. If I had to throw myself on the mercy of a zombie warlord, at least I'd be armed with a slightly stronger-than-normal Taser.

"You're up early," Lucy said to me as I approached. Everyone else was still in bed—Roy snoring, Cody curled into a surprisingly tight fetal position, Tara probably practicing creepy faces under her blankets.

"Lot to do," I said, slipping past Lucy to quietly open the door's hatch. The Maroon Marauder was still out there, although the windshield was too dew-covered to see if Amanda was awake.

"Lot to do," Lucy repeated, deadpan. "In the zombie wasteland. You serious?"

"Anything I can help with?"

It was Cody, sitting up in the cot nearest the door. It looked as if that missed sleep had finally caught up with him; his hair was all mussed, his temples wet with sweat, and he looked a little peaked.

"Um . . ." I did a mental run-through of the ramshackle plan I hadn't even realized I'd been forming. "Not right this second."

Cody started to reply, but hiccupped instead. His eyes widened in embarrassment and he put a hand on his stomach.

"Yup, well, let me know," he said quickly. "I think I ate something bad. I'm gonna rest awhile longer."

"It could be internal bleeding," Lucy put in, a little of yesterday's panic back in her voice. "Maybe you're hurt worse than you know."

"Jeez, Lucy, don't say that," Cody muttered, rolling over on his side.

Before I could address the superinteresting digestive problems of my favorite Iowan survivors, I heard the Marauder's door open outside. I peeked through the hatch and watched Amanda first stretch her legs and then start methodically brushing out her hair.

"Okay, guys, be right back," I told Lucy and Cody, then unbarred the door and stepped out into the cool morning air.

I'd figured one thing out for sure. I wasn't going to freaking Des Moines.

Amanda tossed the brush back in the car when she saw me coming. The vulnerability I'd seen from her last night was wiped away; a night's sleep had apparently restored her reservoir of iciness. We stood facing each other. She was giving off an angry vibe, so I went for the opposite, cool and deadpan.

"Sleep well?" I asked, a little surprised by my own tone. It was harsh.

She snorted. "You took my guns."

"Yeah, it's fairer this way," I explained with faux diplomacy. "You get to eat people and basically come back from the dead. So, we get the guns in case someone needs to shoot you."

"Whatever," she said after a moment. "It's way too early in the morning for this."

"What're you still doing here?" I asked her.

I was angry too, I realized. Or desperate. Maybe a little scared. Some nasty soup of those emotions portioned just right to make a boiling sensation bubble through me. In the moment, I tried to self-analyze why I felt this sudden uptick in animosity. Impending doom for my mom, me, and everyone else seemed like a good place to start. Also, maybe an overcorrection on the sympathy I'd felt for Amanda last night. Or maybe the nagging knowledge that she didn't understand Jake like I did, but got to sit around dramatically pining while he shopped for freaking perfume and totally failed to get me the cure.

So, yeah. Add a splash of jealousy to the mix too. I'm not proud of it.

"I'm waiting for you," Amanda answered me like this was obvious, like she was bored. "Do your whole astral-plane thing and let's go find Jake."

"Why would I do that?" I asked, crossing my arms.

Amanda squinted at me. "I don't understand your question. Like, what the fuck else are you going to do?"

"Have you considered that maybe he met someone else while he was lost out there?" I asked her. "A zombie with better taste in music?"

A shadow passed across Amanda's face. "Um, what're you saying?"

And just like that, my plan crystalized. Divide and conquer, like one of those mean girls from high school.

"He ditched you," I told Amanda. "He met someone else and ditched you. Well, both of us. But mostly you."

"Bullshit," she said, and took a step toward me.

"It's true," I replied. "I was in his head *all* the time. You know how often he wished he'd gotten stuck with one of the less-shallow girls from your high school? Which, I guess would've been pretty much any of them? Like, every day."

"Shut up."

"This new girl gets his references. She's a nerd like him and he doesn't have to explain everything to her. It was a total meet-cute." I shrugged. "He screwed us over. Just like Chazz, right?"

Amanda didn't reply. She took another step toward me.

"Anyway," I continued, "I'm pretty over hanging with zombies after this. So you should probably bail before I have my friends inside shoot you."

Amanda fixed me with a slow, predatory smile.

"You know how I know you're lying?" she asked.

"Just go away, Amanda."

"Because you're standing here like normal, dicking around, instead of bawling your eyes out and making a mixtape or something."

My face scrunched up. "What is *that* supposed to mean?"

"If he dumped me for some slutty hipster zombie, then he basically dumped you too."

I scoffed. "Um, he's your boyfriend. Er, was."

"Oh please. You're *into* him. I saw it when he first dragged your frumpy ass into that farmhouse. You *loved* it. That was like a dream come true for you." Amanda cocked her head at me, something occurring to her. "You really do spend a ton of time in his head, don't you?"

I tried to keep my composure, but I must've flinched. I took a step back.

"I mean, only when I was tracking him . . ." I said, feeling somehow weakened by her pompous smile.

"You love it in there," she replied, practically grinning. "I get it now. You're like some creepy psychic stalker. Don't worry, perv. Your secret's safe with me."

That smile. Like she'd figured me out, like she pitied me. I tried to keep my eyes from filling with tears, but it always happened when I felt humiliated.

"So what?" Amanda continued, studying me. "Why're you bullshitting so hard, huh? Did he already make it into Des Moines? Did he find the cure?"

I recovered myself and took a step toward Amanda, jabbing a finger into her chest. That surprised her.

"That's all you really care about, isn't it? The *cure*."

Amanda rolled her eyes. "Come *on*. Is this your new angle?"

I kept going. "I always wondered why you stuck with him in the first place. To have someone carry you out of trouble, like on that first day? So you wouldn't have to do all the driving? Was it temporary? Just until another, better-looking, stronger zombie came along? You seemed pretty broken up about Chazz. He was a real missed opportunity, huh?"

"You're embarrassing yourself."

Without even trying, I plucked a memory from the front of her mind.

"Or was it because of your low self-esteem?" I asked. "You need him to tell you you're pretty when you go all corpsey and your hair falls out, right?"

She shoved me away from her. I'd struck a nerve.

"You don't know shit," she hissed. "We're in love."

"Aww! In love!" I laughed at her. "You didn't even know he existed two weeks ago! I probably know him better than you do."

"Yeah, because you're a freak," Amanda sneered. "A stalker."

I stepped back into her face. "I know you too. You'll throw him away when you're done with him."

"Fuck off, Cass."

"You've been chewing people up and spitting them out *way* longer than you've been a zombie, you conceited bitch."

That did it.

Amanda grabbed me around the throat and I didn't even notice, too busy basking in the joyous feeling of punching her right in the face. She reeled backward, still holding me, and I fell into the grass on top of her. I hit her again, this time in the side of the head, and realized this was probably a terrible idea because she was so much stronger than me and, you know, ate people.

She rolled us over, still holding me around the neck with one hand. I felt the stun gun jab into my lower back. Yep. Should've used that. Her nose was bleeding, but she still looked pretty fresh. In control. Straddling me, she cocked her fist back.

"Tell me where he is before things get worse for you," she said.

A gunshot rang out.

Amanda's grip slackened as we both turned our heads toward the shelter. I expected to see Lucy standing there, having fired off a warning shot, but instead there was Tara, sprinting in our direction. She wasn't armed. At first, I thought she was coming to help me fight off Amanda, her scream like a battle cry.

Then the zombie tackled Tara from behind and bit down hard on the back of her neck. The screaming stopped.

JAKE

IT WAS NOON. OR PROBABLY AFTER, AFTER NOON. IT
felt like a Saturday and I guess it actually could've been.
Weird that a side effect of becoming undead was a total
loss of basic calendar skills. Anyway, it was one of those
lazy, quiet days where it seemed like everything could
wait.

I used to have a lot of those. Before.

So maybe I'd backslid a little bit since coming to Des
Moines.

I sat on Reggie's impossibly comfortable couch and

turned the two injectors of Kope Juice over in my hands. I wished they'd glow or something. Fizz and bubble like the test tubes in a mad scientist's laboratory. But no, they looked as badass as the insulin shots my grandma squeezed into her side flab after Sunday dinner.

I should go find Amanda.

First, I should talk to Reggie. Try to finagle a third injector for Cass. Maybe I'd have to cat-burgle one from wherever he stashed the meds.

Was I up for cat burgling?

Was I up for getting off this couch?

A random memory from a couple years ago hit me. It'd been around Christmastime and I was chilling in the basement playing some shooter when my dad came clamoring down the steps. This was a really unusual occurrence because it was like 1:00 a.m., and my dad was not in the habit of watching me play video games. He didn't actively take a stand against the time I spent achievement whoring and leaderboard grinding, but I could always tell he was sorta pissed I'd quit, well, everything extracurricular. He never came right out and said anything about it, except this one time he stuck a column from some old movie critic to the fridge that went on and on about how video games could never be art. No duh, dude, but you can't shoot space terrorists in a painting, now, can you?

Anyway, Dad came all staggering downstairs and I

remembered that his office holiday party had been that night, so he was totally bombed. I'd had my own first drink just a couple weeks earlier, stolen from his liquor cabinet, in fact, so I was a recently anointed expert on what wasted behavior looked like.

Those were the days, man. Raiding parental liquor storage with Henry and Adam, not a care in the world. Is it weird to feel nostalgic for sixteen when you're eighteen? I'm going to say no, but only if you've been shot multiple times by a shotgun, stabbed with a pitchfork, and eaten a bunch of people during those two middle years. Simpler times and shit.

Anyway, my dad stood behind the couch, swaying and breathing heavy—kinda zombielike, although that's not a metaphor that would've occurred to me at the time. I didn't pause my game or anything. I figured he'd drift away eventually.

"Son," he declared, slurring a little, "one day you're gonna wake up and realize the best years of your life have passed by and you didn't even realize it."

"Okay, Dad," I replied, my token response for all sentimental fatherly advice. "Whatever you say."

"Keep your frickin' eyes open is what I'm saying," he continued, ruffling my hair like he used to when I was little. "Have the good sense to notice when that time comes along and enjoy it."

"I am enjoying it," I said, waving my controller at the TV screen.

"Oh good Christ, not this," he replied, appalled I could confuse an Xbox all-nighter for these mythological best years of my life. "It'll be way better than killing pretend things in the basement. Trust me."

Well, I'd graduated to killing real things, so there's that.

I wondered what Dad would make of my whole voyage across the country. I mean, outside the gray area of mass murderer. There wasn't anything lazy or underachieving about the way I'd evaded our corrupt government and found a cure for zombification.

And yet, here I was with my ass planted on the couch again.

Before I could properly psych myself up, heavy footfalls started clanging up the fire escape. I quickly hid my vials of Kope Juice in a bandana I'd borrowed from Reggie, stashing them under the couch with Amanda's body spray.

Red Bear appeared outside the window. He paused, peeking in, his gaze inventorying all the treasures Reggie had amassed, his face sagging with that look of profound longing usually reserved for dogs that have to sleep outside. He noticed me and started, like I'd caught him at something. He hastily tapped the window with his hatchet, acting as if all along he'd been trying to get my attention.

"He wants us on the roof!" Red Bear yelled, his words muffled by the glass.

I looked up. I'd figured Reggie was still lazing around in his room, but apparently I was the only one being a total bum.

"What for?" I yelled back.

Red Bear pressed his whole face up against the glass, leaving behind a greasy imprint. "Meeting of the Small Council," he said, then resumed his trek to the roof.

All right. The roof. At least it'd get me off the couch.

Out Reggie's front door, up one flight of stairs, through a metal door propped open by a loose brick, and there was all of Des Moines spread out before me. On a sunny day like this, from up high, the city didn't look so bad. I mean, if you really squinted it looked like the citizens had endured a rash of spontaneous combustions with bloody spray patterns and singe marks everywhere. But from up here without scrutinizing too hard? Not so bad. The roaming ghouls could've been people on their way to work!

I was relieved to find Reggie dressed like a normal person again—jeans, T-shirt, flip-flops—no leather or goggles or kill trophies. He smiled as I emerged from the building and waved me over to the center of the roof. Red Bear stood nearby, scratching himself with the butt end of his hatchet.

"Dude, you gotta see this," he said as I joined them, pointing up to the sky. "It's some George Orwell shit."

Craning my neck, at first all I saw were clouds. But

then it moved, zipping across the sky, leaving behind a squiggly contrail. It looked like a floating trash can. I gasped.

"UFO!" I shouted. "Zombies, psychics . . . aliens. It all makes sense!"

Red Bear made a farting noise.

Reggie laughed. "Nah. That's a drone. Sent by our pals in the NCD, probably." He paused thoughtfully. "Aliens would make sense, though, you're right. Like some human-experimentation shit that got out of hand."

"That's stupid," Red Bear grumbled.

"Man, shut up, Gene. You don't know shit about sci-fi," Reggie replied.

"Um." I surprised myself by being the one to stay on topic. "Do you guys get a lot of drones? Is this, like, normal? Is there going to be an air strike?"

"They don't have the balls," Red Bear hissed.

"Haven't seen one in a while," Reggie answered casually. "Last time was right before the paratroopers."

I blinked at him. "Paratroopers?"

Reggie shrugged. "Yeah, they keep trying that shit. They don't realize it's like doing a food drop. Like zombies can't look up or something."

"Should I get . . . *the thing*?" Red Bear asked, staring eagerly at the drone.

"Nah," Reggie replied, after considering for a moment. "It'd be a waste. You know they gotta be up to something, though. We should probably check in down-town, make sure everything's cool."

Red Bear nodded and unstrapped a walkie-talkie from his belt. He stepped away to confer with whoever was on the other end.

"What's downtown?" I asked Reggie.

He grinned at me. "The beating heart of our republic, my man. It's what those NCD doofuses want to steal. The reason we've been allowed to flourish, because they're too afraid to blow it up."

My look must've been totally blank. Reggie grabbed me by the shoulders.

"Jake, I'll loan you a tie," he said, trying to be serious but finding it hard not to smile at his own goofiness. "We're going to corporate America."

CASS

THERE WASN'T ANY PRACTICAL REASON TO DO THE death imprint. I hadn't needed to do one since New Jersey, when I'd first started tracking Jake, and I didn't *need* to do this one either.

I wanted to.

I was pretty used to corpses in all shapes and sizes and very used to their sad, dead brains. Plunking down in the grass next to Tara's body, I felt an uncomfortable nostalgia, like an arsonist catching a whiff of gasoline. Telepathically jump-starting the synapses of the recently deceased to scrounge around for zombie identification clues—once upon a time that was my whole life.

I should've stayed in California with my mom. But I wanted something else. I wanted new and exciting and interesting.

Where'd that get me?

Sitting in the green grass, the sun big and shiny like it should've been wearing shades and grinning at dancing raisins, birds chirping carelessly, and me focused on the mangled body of my former roommate. Tara'd been bitten once, a chunk taken out of the back of her neck, enough to kill her. I hoped it was quick.

I hadn't been very kind to her. She'd frightened me. Partly because she was a messenger for the person I hated most in this world and partly because she seemed like a cautionary tale for the psychic lifestyle. Was my mind going to break, just like hers had?

Was it already breaking?

I wanted to get a look into that fractured place, see if I could learn anything. See what I had to look forward to.

How lucky for me that he hadn't gotten around to eating Tara's brain. The others back in the shelter weren't so lucky. He'd practically torn their heads clear off to get at the insides. Whatever. I hardly knew them. It wasn't any worse than seeing my whole squad picked off back in Michigan. They were just another crime scene, a couple more half-remembered faces to look back on one day when I thumbed through the mental yearbook of my formative years. Look at all the dead people!

Roy was right. It did get easier.

Maybe I'd actually like it in Tara's brain. Maybe psychic breakdown was preferable to this constant angst. I could nap all the time, waking up only to spout prophetic one-liners and gobble down some canned fruit.

I put my hand on Tara's cold forehead. If I'd learned one thing from Alastaire, it was that the physical-touch stuff was unnecessary, just a crutch to help us psychics focus our powers; it's easier to harness the invisible flow of thought if there's some sense of corporeal action. Still, I wanted to touch her. It felt right that way.

With a death imprint, the broad details come first: what was important to the deceased, who they loved, those kinds of things. It was different with Tara. Even in death, her mind was filled with gaps and missed connections, like one of those redacted government documents with the black marker blotting out all the verbs. There weren't any cherished memories or passions to uncover, nor was there any insight into the NCD or the Deadzone. It had all been stripped out, only the barest foundations left, just enough for her mind to keep functioning.

Had Alastaire done this to her? Or had all the guilt made her do it to herself?

Bare feet. That's what left the biggest impression—Tara liked walking in bare feet, feeling textures on her toes. The simple pleasures of the lobotomized.

Before I could stop myself, I was trying on Tara's final memory. I looked through her eyes as

the blood spatters across the tops of my feet. Warm and sticky. This is wrong. I should run. Up the concrete steps, out of the shelter. Running, running, running. Feels good, even though the grass is sharp.

And then I saw myself through Tara's eyes, pinned underneath Amanda, this wild look of come-at-me-bitch anger stapled to my face. I didn't even know my facial muscles were capable of that; wouldn't ever want to duplicate that look in the mirror.

Oh, look, Cass and her friend are playing too. Is that why I'm running? Is this a ga—?

Oof! He grabs me from behind, too hard. Not fun.

"Hey."

I broke contact with Tara and retreated back behind my own eyes. I'd snapped out too quickly and had to keep centered against a tremor of vertigo, even though I was sitting down.

Cody stood over me looking, well, looking a lot of things.

Filthy and blood covered, for starters. Filthy because he'd been out in the field, digging three graves. Bloody on account of the others—Tara, Lucy, and Roy, the three we'd rescued from certain death.

The ones Cody had eaten when he first necrotized.

Really should've seen that one coming, Cass.

I'd missed the signs. His pallor this morning; the stomachache; the way that zombie didn't seem interested in biting him. Jeez, he even told me about his nonviolent run-in with his zombie ex-girlfriend a few weeks back. I really needed to learn how to read between the lines.

After Cody chased down and mauled Tara, Amanda had managed to get hold of him. I grabbed the guinea pigs from the car, which was probably the first time in recorded history fat rodents were someone's go-to in an emergency. I handed them to Amanda one by one while she held Cody down and shoved them into his gnashing blue-gray zombie mouth. The two of us watched in stunned silence as he went from thrashing corpse back to handsome farm boy. The teeth marks on his cheek even healed.

Then, the crying started.

He'd bawled out of control for like a half hour with Amanda rubbing his back and whispering gentle things to him, freaking guidance counselor for the newly undead. Whatever, I guess she had experience in this sort of situation. While all that was happening, I went back to the bunker. I thought about grabbing Truncheon's rifle and putting Cody down, but Lucy's severed hand was still clutching it and anyway I knew that I wouldn't pull the trigger.

Peeking in on the mess Cody had made of Roy and

Lucy reminded me of my days of analyzing zombie massacre scenes, and that's what put the death-imprint idea in my head. That and morbid curiosity, and shell shock, and maybe a general feeling that there was nothing in the world that could ever go right, so maybe let's find out what it's like to just turn off.

That's what put me in the grass next to Tara when Cody came to collect her body for its freshly dug grave.

"Hey," he said again, even though I was looking right at him. I must've looked glassy eyed and spaced out, my usual expression when I've detached from someone's brain. "You okay?"

He flinched when I laughed at him.

Cody crouched down opposite me, Tara's body in between us. I definitely wasn't giving off a hey-let's-have-a-heart-to-heart vibe, but that didn't stop the doofy zombie hick from trying.

"I didn't mean for this to happen," he said shakily, his watery gaze on Tara. "I was just trying to keep them safe. I didn't know that—that I'm a—I didn't know. It makes me sick, what I did. You understand that, right?"

I shrugged. "I hardly know you, man."

"But still," he said, turning his desperate gaze on me. "You saw what I was like, what I was doing. I was trying to *help*."

"Did you want a medal or something?"

"You know I'd never hurt her or—or—or any of them."

"All right, whatever." I sighed. "I absolve you. It doesn't matter."

Cody touched my shoulder, but I jerked away. Out of my peripheral vision, I noticed Amanda take a step toward us. She'd been hanging out over by the car ever since Cody—spouting some folksy crap about needing to do it himself—turned down her offer to help dig graves. She was keeping an eye out, in case he tried to eat me. After all, she still needed me to find Jake.

"It does matter," Cody insisted. "You—you know me best now. Out of everyone left, you know me best."

"That's sad," I said. "That's really, really sad."

Cody stared down at his hands, at the blood crusted under his fingernails.

"Can I take her?" he asked, motioning to Tara. "I've— I've already buried the others."

I stood up, dusting off the backs of my jeans. "Do what you need to do."

Cody stared up at me, as if he was puzzled by my coldness. Like he couldn't possibly understand why I wasn't sympathizing with him. I guess that's what made me want to twist the knife. I wanted to pound a little self-awareness into him.

"There's something I don't get," I said as he gathered Tara into his arms.

"Yeah?" he replied, almost hopeful.

"You've been fighting zombies for *a year*. You've got to

know how the disease spreads or, at the very least, what the symptoms are, right?"

Cody didn't respond, so at least he understood what rhetorical questions sounded like. He watched me, face scrunched up like he was getting ready to take a punch.

"So, I'm wondering, after you hooked up with your zombie ex or whatever—were you in denial about getting infected, or are you genuinely so mind-blowingly stupid that it didn't occur to you as a possibility?"

He actually seemed to consider my question, even though I'd mostly meant it as an insult.

"Mind-blowingly stupid, I guess," he said, hugging Tara's body to him. "My dad had just died and—"

I threw up my hands, and Cody finally shut up. Everyone had justifications for the crappy things they did. I was tired of hearing them.

I had a ticking clock and crappy things of my own to accomplish.

I left Cody hunched over and whispering quiet apologies into Tara's unhearing ear. I walked toward the house, ready to put some distance between me and these zombies.

Amanda cut me off.

"Where do you think you're going?" she asked, fists balled up in case we fought again. "We need to finish our talk."

Before she could get too close, I shot her in the chest

with the stun gun. She looked supremely mad as she collapsed, seizing, onto the ground. I glanced over my shoulder to see if Cody noticed and was relieved to find him too busy lowering Tara into her grave. I stood over Amanda; her teeth were gritted tight, eyes superwide, looking like she might pop a blood vessel.

"I really enjoyed that," I told her, twirling the stun gun around my index finger. "See you around."

I resumed my walk toward the house. For a few paces, Amanda tried to roll after me. Seeing that was almost as satisfying as shooting her had been. Eventually, the seizures too much, she gave up and lay there, jaggedly panting.

With a stick, I knocked the severed pig's head off the hood of the zombie's police car. Inside, the keys still dangled from the ignition.

Off I went. Alone.

It occurred to me as I drove down a deserted stretch of highway that I'd begun a pattern of running away whenever things got ugly and hard, which seemed like all the time lately. I tried to get out of the NCD when my feelings got complicated. Back at the farmhouse, when it seemed like everyone I cared about was getting killed or maimed, I'd wandered unprotected into a full-on zombie blood orgy rather than fight. Heck, if you really wanted to dig deep with the psychoanalysis, maybe part of the reason I'd joined the NCD in the first place was to get away from home after Dad died.

Here I was again—bailing, hitting the road, the lone driver on some of the most human-unfriendly roads in America.

Except that's not what this was. I wasn't running away from anything, not this time.

Like everyone else in this screwed-up world—particularly in this horrible, blood-drenched state—I'd decided to be selfish.

For once, I was going to get what I wanted.

I had a plan.

JAKE

THE THREE OF US WALKED THROUGH THE TREE-LINED plaza in front of Kope Brothers headquarters. I could almost picture the well-to-do business types out here, eating their brown-bag lunches on the ergonomic benches, daydreaming about mergers and acquisitions before the trio of marble fountains. Almost. Because, you know, there were piles of dead bodies in the fountains and someone had hung intestines like tinsel along the backs of the benches. Probably Red Bear.

"Who was she?" Reggie asked. "The one who turned you?"

"Just some girl," I answered. "Met her at a bar. I remember she had amazing hair."

"Damn, dude. That's literally one hundred percent more girls than I ever picked up at bars," Reggie replied, smirking.

"You can't even get into bars, liar," Red Bear sneered.

"I have my ways." I shrugged, brushing it off, but Reggie had stopped walking and started mean-mugging Red Bear.

"Walk ahead," Reggie said sternly.

Red Bear slumped his shoulders. "Aw, come on, boss. I was just messing with the little 'tard."

"Walk ahead," Reggie repeated, introducing some of that Lord of Des Moines bass to his voice.

Red Bear shot me a dirty look and then did as he was told. Reggie waited for him to be out of hearing distance before we continued through the plaza.

"You didn't have to do that," I said.

"Man, I'm sick of not being able to have a normal, civilized conversation," Reggie complained. He paused for a moment, took a deep breath, and then continued. "Anyway, this was some other zombie too, right? Not your girlfriend."

"Nah, it wasn't Amanda. She wasn't my girlfriend then," I said. I was pretty sure I'd spilled all these relationship details to Reggie that first night, but we were pretty stoned then and right now he wanted to talk about something besides drones. So, the topic was girls. "That started up after. We sort of, um, bonded because of the whole undead thing."

"That's beautiful, man," Reggie said, patting me on the back. "My heart is so swollen for you right now."

"Shut up."

"I'm serious, though," he replied. "You're in love. That's magical."

"It's only been like two weeks," I said, feeling embarrassed, like when Adam and Henry used to bust on my crushes around the lunch table. "It's early."

"That's a lifetime in undead years, man," Reggie said. "Enjoy it while it lasts. Treasure it."

"Uh-huh."

"I wasn't so lucky," Reggie said. "I didn't get a wild one-night stand with some bar skank."

I slowed down and then stopped entirely. This seemed important. I didn't want to walk and process information at the same time. Multitasking is not my strong suit.

"How did it happen to you?" I asked.

Reggie chuckled. "I feel like we're having the talk. The birds and the bees."

"Well, you can skip the STD part," I grumbled. "I already know that much."

Reggie clasped his hands behind his back, all professorial. "The infection presents in the blood," he recited, "but also in semen, vaginal secretions, and in some cases breast milk. Saliva and sweat have, so far, proven noninfectious."

"Huh," I said, mulling over his speech and also mentally patting my own back for not laughing at *semen*. "So . . . breast milk?"

Reggie patted the inside of his elbow. "I caught it from a blood transfusion. So did Red Bear. So did a ton of other people. If you were just regular sick thirteen months ago, you probably got some bad blood from the nice people at Des Moines General. Then us sickies, we leave the hospital while the virus is still incubating and spread it further. Pretty soon—chomp, chomp, chomp. That's how it all went down."

"How do you know all this?"

Reggie gestured at the skyscraper before us. "I haven't just been collecting video games over the last year, man. I've been doing research too."

We started walking again.

"I still don't get why bites don't spread it," I mused, brow furrowed.

"Didn't I say saliva was safe?" Reggie replied. "You know that means spit, right?"

"Yeah, uh, maybe you're a tidier zombie than me. When I turn, I'm usually oozing all kinds of funky stuff."

"Oh, it's gotta be *live* blood," Reggie explained. "That sludge in our veins when we turn, that's what's left behind when the virus burns out and retreats to the brain. Eat some live flesh, the virus gets stronger again, and our bodies are restored. We're only contagious when we're *alive*."

"Not like the movies," I said.

"Ugh, I know," Reggie replied. "I used to be a zombie purist too. I would've shredded this walking, talking, carefree-biting genre-hijacking on my blog."

As we drew closer to Kope Brothers headquarters, I noticed there were lights on in the lobby. We're not talking burning-furniture lights here either. It was the mellow mood lighting big buildings always leave on after hours. I didn't hear the telltale caterwauling of generator motors like back at Reggie's apartment.

"How does this place have power?" I asked.

"It isn't on the same grid as the rest of the city," he said, shaking his head. "It generates its own electricity. Not sure how much longer it'll last, but it's been going strong so far."

I gazed up at the Kope building—the newish, fancy-looking architecture stood out from the rest of Des Moines. In fact, it looked like it took significantly less damage than other buildings had during the undead uprising.

"That's, um . . ."

"Sinister?" Reggie finished for me. "Yeah, man. We're just getting started."

As we approached the front doors, Red Bear stepped into view along with a trio of serious-looking zombies. They were all older than us, probably in their thirties, and they lacked the sense of drama of the other Des Moines zombies—these guys didn't go in for leather or costume flair. Instead, they were dressed in body armor that looked hijacked from the NCD and carried machine guns. I faltered at the sight of the guns, but Reggie kept right on walking. Red Bear smirked at me.

"Sir," said one of the guards, snapping off a lazy salute.

"Any problems?" Reggie asked.

"No, sir," the guard replied.

"All right. We're on high alert until further notice," Reggie said. He turned to Red Bear. "Stay out here."

Red Bear frowned, but then turned to one of the guards to bum a cigarette. Reggie led me past them and into the lobby. It was totally posh, pretty much untouched by the madness outside, with the conspicuous exception of a huge pile of smashed computer hard drives.

I glanced over my shoulder. "So, who are *those* guys?"

"We don't eat every army boy the NCD throws at us," Reggie answered. "Some of them are open to changing sides. We convert them."

I'd kind of assumed zombiehood was an unhappy accident for everyone. The idea of some soldier choosing to be a zombie didn't surprise me—in Des Moines, the alternative was to get eaten. But the idea of infecting people on purpose gave me a chill.

"I keep this place under guard because it's where we keep our food," Reggie continued. "We have strict rules about who can eat what and when."

"And *who*," I added. "You *are* talking about people, right?"

Reggie shrugged like that was obvious. "We've got a doctor that sees to them. Keeps them healthy. I like to think of it as the first post-apocalypse occupation. Undead nutritionist. Our communist undead utopia serves only the finest grass-fed humans."

When I didn't laugh at his joke, Reggie's face fell. We'd reached the elevator, which was amazingly still working. He hit the DOWN button.

"I try to treat them decently," he said quietly.

"Dude, you call that crap yesterday *decent*?" I replied, a little stunned by his level of delusion.

"Those ones don't count," Reggie said. His voice had become stern, but he avoided looking me in the eye. "A little bloodletting is necessary to keep the real psychos in line. And trust me, the only humans we put through that are the ones who have it coming. NCD goons or Kope cronies, basically."

I thought about that huddled group of Kope employees in their stupid company-picnic T-shirts, looking terrified. The revulsion I'd felt for Reggie had faded when he'd lost his batshit Lord of Des Moines getup and reverted to normal-guy mode, but now it was back.

"What did those Kope people do? I mean, they were, like, secretaries and old dudes."

"They tried to profit from this shit," Reggie spat, and I heard some of that Lord of Des Moines passion in his voice. He gestured at the pile of busted computers. "Innocent people don't sledgehammer computers while a statewide epidemic is happening."

"Yeah, I'm sure the bosses were scumbags, but damn," I countered. "You planning to torture the people who, like, mopped the floors?"

"No," Reggie replied, serious. "I spared the janitors."

"Oh good."

The elevator doors hissed open. Inside, Reggie hit the button for a restricted subbasement, then keyed a four-digit pass code into a wall-mounted LCD display. With a sinking feeling in my guts not entirely due to gravity, we started to descend.

"These Kope people, man," Reggie continued, defending himself. "They probably let the infection loose as an experiment, all confident they'd be able to control it and corner the market on the undead-prevention industry. Snatch up a fat government contract from those dimbulbs in the NCD, retire to their mansions richer than God, with only a few thousand or so regular people dead. But it went tits up."

"You know that for sure?"

He shrugged. "It's a theory."

I started to call him paranoid but, thinking about everything I'd seen over the past couple weeks, decided against it.

The elevator doors slid open and we walked into a brightly lit hallway. The place was sterile and spotless, a bewildering change of pace from the chaos outside. It was like stepping onto a neat freak's spaceship. I was glad I hadn't called Reggie paranoid—there was definitely more going on here than baby aspirin and butt wipes.

"All this mad-scientist, secret-laboratory shit was already down here, by the way," Reggie said. "We don't even know how to use half of it."

I remembered the crazy old man from YouTube, the Grandfather, whose desperate broadcast about a cure was what brought us out here. That video could've been shot down here.

"Is this where the Grandfather works?" I asked.

Reggie gave me a funny look. "He doesn't really *work* anymore. But yeah, he was squirreled away down here when we first busted in. Everyone else'd abandoned the place except for him, working away on his *wonderful* cure."

Our footsteps echoed in the empty hallway. We turned left, through a heavy-duty steel door that looked like it was on loan from a prison.

"That's dedication," I said.

"Sure, the old crackpot has passion," Reggie snorted.

"I should write him a thank-you card."

"Come on, we can go see him."

We walked past holding cells. Crowded holding cells. In padded rooms behind bulletproof glass, hopeless-looking people stared listlessly out as we passed. I gulped.

Here were the uninfected of Iowa. I'd known they were down here, but it was still startling to see them in person. Some of them looked bruised and beaten up, probably from when they were captured, but most just looked pale and despondent. They slept four to a cell, some of them sharing cots. It didn't really look like they were malnourished or anything—I'm sure there was plenty of people food floating around—and they'd been provided with comfortable-looking prisoner pajamas, so at least they had that going for them.

Oh, who am I kidding? It was freaking horrible, like walking through one of those black-and-white POW camps they showed us in history class. I swallowed hard and tried not to make eye contact with any of them.

Reggie caught my expression and, with the same half-apologetic face I'd made when I spoiled Santa Claus for my little sister, reached out to pat my shoulder. I flinched away from him.

"This . . ." I waved my hands. "This is seriously wrong, dude."

Hearing me, one of the imprisoned humans slapped his palms against the glass and screamed. Others joined him, and others still recoiled or covered their ears or started rocking back and forth in panic. Seriously, I could've joined them in doing any of the above.

"Not in front of them," Reggie hissed, and dragged me down the hall. We veered into an area dedicated to complicated science labs.

"Get off me, man," I snapped, shaking loose from Reggie's grip.

He held up his hands. "All right, Jake. Relax. You're not ready to see how the sausage gets made. It's cool."

"Uh, yeah, I'll never be ready for that," I said.

"Right." Reggie nodded, humoring me. "If you say so. Have you taken that cure yet, by the way? You don't smell human."

I didn't reply. Reggie walked into one of the labs and, after taking a deep, cleansing breath, I followed.

"I bet you still have rules about which people to eat, huh?" Reggie asked over his shoulder.

I thought about my system with Amanda, our unanimous voting on bad guys and assholes. It wasn't perfect, but it was a code. I kept quiet, though, not wanting to give Reggie the satisfaction.

"It's cool," Reggie continued. "Everyone goes through

that shit. Eventually, though, they get hungry. Too hungry."

"It doesn't have to be that way," I argued. "Instead of, like, holing up in your zombie city, you could be handing out Kope Juice."

"Uh-huh." Reggie laughed, not maliciously, but in a condescending way that annoyed the shit out of me. "Tell me how I can make the world a better place, Disney Channel. I'm listening."

I folded my arms and shut up.

"The world's changed, man," Reggie said as he walked toward an observing window on the far side of the room. "The NCD, Kope, and probably dozens of other old, white dudes just like them are—right this second—having meetings on how to monetize the undead. We need to eat them before they eat us. You get that, right?"

I shrugged and walked over to join him. "Whatever, dude. I'm not really into politics."

"You're a cool guy, Jake, but you're fucking naive as hell." Reggie tapped on the glass. "Here's your pal."

There was a normal-looking hospital room set up on the other side of the window—heart monitors, IV drips, leather restraints. In bed, sound asleep or maybe comatose, drooling a river either way, was the Grandfather. His bushy white beard and wild head of hair had grown even more unkempt since the video. A big chunk of his face was covered in heavily bandaged gauze, and I got the feeling there were other bite wounds hidden from view. Bad ones.

"Jeez," I said.

"Yeah," Reggie replied, sounding almost sad for the old man. "Here's a guy that tried to change the world and got half eaten for his trouble. I keep him alive because . . . I don't know, exactly. Feels wrong to eat him, I guess."

"So, you draw your line at heroic-if-wackadoodle scientists?"

Reggie thought about it. "I don't eat dogs either. No dogs."

I nodded. We were quiet for a while, listening to the muffled beep of the Grandfather's heart monitor. I think we both had the feeling that things were about to change. I certainly did, probably due in no small part to my plans to inject myself with a less-than-stable wonder cure.

But the two injectors back at Reggie's apartment weren't enough.

"So . . . ," I said, breaking the silence. "You store all your Kope Juice down here?"

"Smooth," Reggie said, smirking at me. "You gonna try to steal from me, Jake?"

"Uh, no."

Reggie walked across the room and crouched down over one of the floor panels. He slid it aside, revealing a stainless-steel handle and a digital keypad.

"It's all down there," he told me. "Locked up tight."

I took a step forward, but what was I going to do? Try beating the combination out of him? It didn't seem like a sound plan.

I opted for pleading.

"Just give me one more, man," I whined. "You know she'll get killed if she comes here."

"Probably."

"She's harmless," I said. "Seriously. She's out of the NCD. They, like, kidnapped her mom and shit."

"Right," Reggie replied, his voice level. "So I give her the cure, she trades it for her mom, and then the NCD has it. Which means they've got no reason not to nuke Des Moines, right? You see my logic here, Jake?"

"They're not gonna nuke anybody," I said weakly. "Are they?"

"Naive, like I said," Reggie replied, standing up. "You know, I'm not stopping you from leaving, Jake. You can go cure yourself whenever. Or you can take that Kope Juice I gave you, turn it over to your NCD girl, and endanger the lives of all your zombie brothers and sisters here. But that shit is gonna be on you, not me."

I shifted from foot to foot. "I mean, it'd sort of still be on you since you gave it to me."

"Jake," Reggie said. "Come on."

I pictured the two vials of Kope Juice I had stashed back at Reggie's apartment, nestled in next to Amanda's perfume. Could I really give one of those to Cass? What would Amanda say? Which one of us would . . . No, I didn't want to think about that.

"You don't think I'll do it, do you?" I asked Reggie.

Reggie shook his head, smiling.

"Man, I don't think you're gonna take that cure at all. Your ass is having too much fun."

AMANDA

WHEN I WAS A STUPID LITTLE KID, LIKE TEN OR SO, I had this huge crush on Johnny Depp. Not regular Johnny Depp, because he's old and kinda douchey with the whole pretentious French thing. Captain Jack Sparrow. In fourth-grade art class I made a Captain Jack puppet out of a brown paper bag, those stick-on plastic eyes, and lots of felt scraps cut to look like his wild goatee and sexy/crusty hair. I used to sleep with this puppet and practice kissing on it and defend it from my brother, Kyle, who used to chase me around with scissors.

Aww.

So lame, right? Hold on. It gets worse.

I used to write Life Goals on scraps of paper and shove them inside puppet Jack Sparrow's paper-bag body. I actually wrote *Life Goal* on each one. I don't remember the specifics. Mostly, they were names of places I'd seen in magazines and wanted to travel to someday, possibly with the real Jack Sparrow because I was an idiot and thought that was a thing that could happen. They all had a basic unifying theme.

LIFE GOAL: get the fuck out of New Jersey.

Mission accomplished.

Eventually I got over Jack Sparrow, more interested in guys made out of flesh and blood, although in Captain Jack's defense, what he lacked in arms he made up for in not saying dumb shit all the time. Even grown-up, I couldn't throw him out. He was too important to me. I hid him underneath my mattress in a small box with Dad's postcards from the joint and pictures of Penelope (my mother, who I've referred to by her first name since I caught her drunkenly flirting with some of my friends at a party she'd "allowed" me to throw) when she was young/hot. He'd be safe there, I assumed.

After school one day, while I was downstairs listening to Penelope bitch about something, my so-called friend Cindy St. Clair discovered Captain Jack in his box while she was snooping under my bed, probably looking for dildos, the dumb slut. I came upstairs to find my secret Life Goals scattered on the floor and Jack Sparrow shoved onto an unfamiliar hand, making loud donkey noises because Cindy claimed I had big teeth. I vowed on that day to destroy her socially, and a couple years later she was the first person I ate when I turned into a zombie.

That might have been an overreaction.

You think?

Captain Jack went in the garbage after his defilement by Cindy. I didn't stop thinking up Life Goals, though. Considering how my desire to escape lame New Jersey had come true in a roundabout, messed-up way after marinating in the belly of Jack Sparrow, maybe it was time to make a new puppet. Because I was having trouble figuring out what to do next.

LIFE GOAL: find Jake.

LIFE GOAL: stop being a smelly/ugly zombie.

LIFE GOAL: start over.

I stood at the edge of the firelight, gazed out over the darkened farmland, and missed him. I know, right? Like I was one of those stupid lighthouse maidens gazing out to sea waiting for her ship-captain husband to return home. (Enough with the pirates already.) It'd only been a couple days and he talked way too much and was half-retarded and it shouldn't have felt like such a big deal. But it was. I'd felt different since we unzombied in that parking lot. Like I could finally be myself.

Turns out, the you that eats people is the truest version of yourself.

Since I'd been with Jake, I didn't worry so much about what Dad called *the angles*. I didn't care about how every little thing would reflect on me, what other people would see, how they'd use my actions against me. I didn't look at every interaction as a stepping stone to something better. Yeah, maybe a certain amount of social burdens had been stripped away when I'd eaten all my important peers. But something else had changed too. I liked who I was when I was around Jake and I wanted that back. I wanted our easy rhythm back. I wanted us to be all right. I wanted—

Okay, stop thinking about him.

Behind me, the campfire crackled as Cody poked it with a branch.

"I don't think she's coming back," he said, interpreting my distance gazing as keeping watch for that snotty psychic sucker-puncher.

"She better not," I said quietly.

Ooohhhh.

The smell of Cody's bonfire reminded me of the burnt odor my skin had been giving off earlier. The blistered, gray electrical burn on my chest had healed with the help of one of our last guinea pigs, yet the smell still lingered on in my brain. A shame stench. I wouldn't be letting that one go anytime soon. I'd let my guard slip and Cass had gotten away. She was my only surefire way of finding Jake and now she was gone, leaving me stranded here in shit creek with no clear course of action. I never trusted her; should've never let Jake guilt me into being civil. Who knows what nefarious shit that little government lackey was up to now. I hoped the ghouls got her.

Forget about Cass. You don't need her. Start thinking about the angles again. That's more you.

I sighed and joined Cody at his bonfire. It made sense he wouldn't want to stay in the bomb shelter after the mess he'd made in there, but if I had my way, we'd be spending the night in the adjoining house. Cody didn't want to do that either, spouting some shit about respect for the dead. He'd been brooding/sulking all day until he found out I had camping equipment in the car.

Even during his whole glum *woe is me, I'm a zombie* period, Cody's eyes had been on me pretty much non-stop. I was used to that. At least he was handsome and polite, qualities that in my experience very rarely went hand in hand, but maybe they did things different out in the country. He looked eager to talk, his eyes all moony with need, and I realized maybe I'd done too good a job comforting him after he first turned zombie. He looked all attached. Wasn't going to happen, duder.

But he is really, really good-looking. And strong. He'll make for a great zombie partner, don't you think? He'll be useful. He's your type.

I caught myself staring at him. Cody smiled at me

with his perfect white teeth. He'd changed out of his bloody clothes and into a clean pair of jeans and form-fitting blue T-shirt. He reminded me a little of Chazz, actually, but with all the rough edges sanded off. Here was a guy who wouldn't just park his Camaro on the curb and lay on the horn. My man would come in and introduce himself to Mom.

"I love the outdoors," Cody said. "It feels so natural out here."

"Cool," I replied. I mean, it was a nice night, but we didn't need to talk about it.

"You like camping?" he asked me.

"Um, no," I replied.

Too harsh. Be nicer.

"I mean, I've never really been before," I clarified.

"Gosh, I miss it," Cody said, shaking his head. "I used to go every other weekend before all this."

"Yeah, you really know your way around building a fire."

I hadn't really meant it as a compliment—who cares about building fires? We aren't cavepeople anymore—but Cody beamed from ear to ear like I'd just pinned a blue ribbon on his prize sow or whatever. Iowans.

He's sweet, though. And wouldn't it come in handy to have a partner who knows how to do things not involving video games? Practical, real-world skills that might keep you alive? Think about the possibilities. The angles.

"What else can you do?" I asked him suddenly, then immediately rephrased the question. "I mean, um, what else do you *like* to do?"

He thought about this. "I used to race cars," he replied.

"Like, street racing?"

"Lord, no." Cody laughed. "Amateur circuit. Stock cars." He looked at me, trying to gauge my interest. "Some figure eight, that's the most dangerous thing I've done. No street racing."

"Figure eight?"

"The track shape," Cody said, drawing an eight in the air with a flaming stick.

"Don't you crash?"

"Not if you're good," he replied, and shot me a wink that was more cheeseball than lecherous, yet still violated my strict prohibition on winking and/or eyebrow wiggling.

Oh, come on. He's charming.

And yet, I couldn't help laughing a little. I covered my mouth, surprised at myself.

Think about the possibilities. You hotwire cars. He drives them really fast. You'd make a good team. Probably have the cure locked up in no time. He's an upgrade, all around.

I felt strange. Maybe it was the smoke and heat from the fire. I stood up, walked around to the other side, and sat down next to Cody. It was better over here, I guess.

"Are you cold?" Cody asked.

"I'm sitting in front of, like, a raging fire," I replied.

But maybe you're a little cold. Just a chill.

"Okay," I admitted. "Kinda."

Cody stood up and unzipped one of the sleeping bags. Gently, he draped it around my shoulders, and then sat down even closer than before. One of his arms lingered around my shoulder, like he was making sure the sleeping bag would stay put. Sure. That old move.

"Uh—" I started to draw myself up, ready to unman this presumptuous hick.

Oh, stop. It's nice. Comforting. Feel those muscles.

"Is this okay?" he asked uncertainly.

"Yeah," I replied without much conviction.

We sat there in silence, watching the fire flicker and snap. It didn't feel right—being under this blanket, this random dude's arm around me. I couldn't quite figure how I'd gotten into this position. I kept meaning to stand up, to brush him off, but something stopped me.

It's insta-love. Just go with it.

Cody sighed contentedly.

"You know, I spent the last year running for my life," he mused. "Trying not to get eaten. Sleeping underground. Keeping quiet. Hiding. Watching everyone I know get eaten or . . . change."

"Uh-huh," I replied, only half listening.

"I would've never dreamed I could have something

like this again," he continued. "Jeez, something simple like making a fire, that would've been unthinkable. The ghouls would get us for sure."

He looked around. Nothing moved out there in the darkened fields.

"I don't know what I was running from all that time," he said, almost like he was trying to talk himself into this new life. "It's better, being one of you."

I tensed up. *I didn't even want to be one of me.*

Take it easy. He's new. He'll see it your way, eventually. They always do, right?

"It isn't always like this," I replied without any heat.

"No." He shot a surreptitious glance in the direction of the unmarked graves. "Guess it couldn't be."

"It can be all right, sometimes. . . ." I thought about the long stretches on the road with Jake, how we—

Nope. Forget him. He abandoned you. Screwed you over, just like Chazz.

Focus on Cody.

"If you've got someone with you." I finished my thought and pinched the bridge of my nose. My head hurt. The smoke again, probably.

Cody reached over and tucked a strand of hair behind my ear, even though it wasn't really in my face or anything. At some point, we'd inched even closer together.

"I can tell you've been through a lot," Cody said gravely, all overwrought with sympathy for me. Normally, I would've rolled my eyes at a come-on that half-assed.

Not this time. Dopey sincerity—that's exactly what I wanted.

I found myself nodding and staring down at the ground between our feet—like, Yes, I've been through so much and it's painful to even think about. Rescue me with your powerful arms and strongly felt feelings, handsome man.

Cody lifted my chin with his index finger.

"I hope this isn't forward," he started, peering into my eyes, "but I've been thinking a lot since I turned and I've decided, um, YOLO, you know."

YOLO. Isn't he dreamy?

"But, jeez, I like you, Amanda. I think we could make a go of it, being zombies. We could go to Des Moines and find the others. Try to make the best of it. If you'd want to do that. With me."

Me and my boyfriend were on our way to Des Moines, I almost said.

But you don't have a boyfriend.

So many things were wrong with this hick's proposal: We just met. This crush of his only blossomed because (1) I'm hot, and (2) he seems like the type to get easily attached. He's got some kind of savior/mother/girlfriend complex going on because I gave him that stupid pep talk after his first undead experience and told him that eating all those people wasn't his fault (which it wasn't, but get over it already, move on). He's used to having someone to protect and he's just stumbled into this new un-life and is flailing for direction and . . .

Don't think about it. You should just . . .

I kissed him. He seemed a little surprised. Hell, I seemed surprised. But it wasn't a bad kiss. Not too much tongue. A real gentleman, all the way. Then we were falling backward in the sleeping bag, his arms curling tightly around me. Kissing with more heat.

There. Isn't that better?

And part of me knew that I shouldn't be doing this—didn't even *want* to do it, actually—but I shut that part away. I couldn't quite grasp why this was wrong. I couldn't think of a reason why I shouldn't hook up with this beautiful new zombie, in front of this romantic fire he'd built with his own hands, under the stars.

It's perfect, isn't it?

Yes.

This way, everybody's happy.

JAKE

REGGIE PUNCHED HENRY ROBINSON HARD IN THE shoulder.

"I told you, man," Reggie said as he slammed his locker shut. "I don't eat dogs."

"Ow, sorry," Henry complained. He bent down to pick up a couple of the LOST DOG fliers that he'd dropped when Reggie hit him. "I just had to ask. You guys are unpredictable."

"You really are," Adam DeCarlo chimed in, rubbing the spot on his neck where I'd gnashed open his jugular. "Seriously."

I wasn't paying any attention to my friends. We were gathered around Reggie's locker like we always were before homeroom, in perfect position to watch the daily Procession of the Bobbleheads. I was locked in, of singular purpose. This was the day that I'd talk to her.

"Here they come," I whispered. The guys all groaned or rolled their eyes, but I didn't care.

The doors to the parking lot flew open and in walked the Bobbleheads, fresh from a prehomeroom session of cigarettes and car revving. They were beautiful and glowing, all of them, in their letterman jackets and cheerleading skirts, their gaping bite wounds all bandaged with branded Abercrombie gauze. All of them except for their leader—Amanda Blake—she was something else entirely.

Unlike her tanned and perfect-skinned brethren, Amanda possessed that ashen, newly dead look that really got me going. She flipped her blonde-and-black-streaked hair over her shoulder, plucked a licorice-colored piece of chewing gum out of her mouth, and smacked it onto the freshly polished glass of the RRHS trophy case. She kept her eyes straight ahead the whole time.

"Oh, to be that gum," I said longingly.

I started forward hesitantly, my planned opening gambit something about a geography assignment we could help each other with.

"Uh, hey, durrrrr—"

She didn't even glance in my direction. Maybe I wouldn't make my big move today after all. The vibe didn't seem right.

I shrank back to where my friends stood, but they were gone, off to class. The Bobbleheads passed in a stampede of polo shirts and jeggings, and then the hallway was empty except for me and some brown-haired girl digging through her locker across the way. The bell rang. We were late.

Vaguely, I became aware of a tickling sensation on my upper lip. At the same time, I realized this was a dream.

The brown-haired girl closed her locker and turned to face me. It was Cass, looking more normal and healthy than I'd ever seen her. No giant bags under her eyes, no doped-up space-cadet gaze, no crusty, bloody nose remnants. Her hair was brushed and pulled back in a cascade-y ponytail. She was dressed in a retro-looking button-down blouse thing and a funky skirt, way nicer than any of the crappy thrift-store stuff from the road. I shouldn't say that I realized how cute she was for the first time right then—obviously I'd noticed if she was manifesting in my dream this way—but whoa. Right on, Cass.

"Hey," she said, smiling. Her voice was clearer somehow than the voices of my friends had been, like she cut through dream static or something.

"Hey yourself," I replied. I was happy to see her.

I felt a strange sizzling sensation in my brain.

"Don't freak out," Cass said, as if reading my mind.

"You're in my dream," I said. "In my head."

"Sort of," she replied. "Technically, I've pulled your unconscious mind onto the astral plane with me and this is how you're processing it."

"You're like Freddy Krueger."

"It's actua—"

"Uh, hold up," I said, staring at her as something potentially disastrous occurred to me. "Can you see, like, all my thoughts?"

"Well, it doesn't work exactly like that, but—"

Suddenly, every dirty movie I'd ever watched began playing out simultaneously inside my old high school. It was like one of those dreams where you show up to class naked, except on ecstasy and in stereo. Loud moans and cheesy jazz music spilled out from every classroom. Cass grimaced.

"Try not thinking about that, please," Cass yelled over all the fake orgasms, some of which were still buffering even in my dream space.

I tried not to think about all my lurking sex memories, which involved putting both my fingers to my temples because that's how you control psychic powers. Just like that, RRHS was quiet again and we were alone.

"Sorry," I said, pushing a hand awkwardly through my curly, non-mohawked head of hair.

"It's okay," Cass replied, blushing. "The id can get a little gross sometimes, I guess."

I didn't know what the hell an id was, but I made a real, concerted effort to control my thoughts, which isn't actually something I have a whole ton of experience with. I focused on Cass.

"So, you can just pop into my brain whenever, huh?"

She looked away from me. "Um, yeah."

"And do you?"

Cass didn't answer right away. My mind spiraled away from me, matching what I felt now—I can only describe it as *itchy frying-pan brain*—with past incidents, like on the highway when I'd stopped Cass from collapsing in front of Truncheon. It was as if I'd just chugged a bottle of ADD pills. Connections were being made. The opposite of my id brain, the analytical, nonpervy part, was working overtime.

I blinked, uh, mentally, and Cass and I were no longer in RRHS. We were in a gas-station bathroom filthy with trucker viscera, and we were standing really close together. I was holding her face, actually, like we'd just finished kissing. She was covered in my barf.

"Ew," she said. "Come on."

"Whoa!" I yelped, letting go of her face and stepping back. "You were in my head *then*?"

Cass hesitated. I saw it flicker across her face because my signal-picking-up was way more finely attuned here.

She considered lying to me.

"It was my job, Jake," Cass said, trying to sound blasé about it, but I could tell recalling this moment, my first kiss with Amanda, really bugged her. "I was tracking you. I just happened to peek in and . . ."

Cass trailed off. She looked down at her puke-stained outfit, focused for a second, and was back in the new duds she'd been rocking at RRHS.

"For the record, I'm not really cool with that," I said. "The peeping, I mean."

"I know. You shouldn't be," Cass said quietly. "I'm really sorry. For what it's worth, I've stopped doing it."

"Well, all right," I said. Because what else could I say? I didn't have any precedent for how long to stay mad after psychic violations. Anyway, I had more important theories to test out.

I gazed down at myself and tried to picture my body in polished, blue-and-white Mega Man armor. *Bloop.* It appeared. And it wasn't even heavy!

"Also for the record," I added, "this lucid dreaming shit is amazing."

Cass smiled at me, looking relieved that I wasn't mad at her. I mean, maybe if I'd really chewed on it, I could've gotten myself worked up about the whole invasion-of-privacy thing. But she hadn't, like, done anything bad with my brain access. A little snooping, sure, but I'd be all up in everyone's business if I had psychic powers. And if she could sift through all my weird-ass thoughts and still want to hang out with me, well, that was kind of flattering, I guess.

It also occurred to me, now that the initial shock of dream chatting had passed, that maybe I should be serious. If Cass was dipping into my subconscious, something could be wrong. Just like that, my preposterous armor was gone and I found myself clad in my normal jeans and T-shirt.

"So, you guys are safe, right?" I asked. "You're not, like, a dream ghost?"

Cass shook her head. "There's no such thing as dream ghosts."

"Oh, that's where we're drawing the line on crazy things existing? Good to know."

Cass laughed and walked to the bathroom door. I followed her and we stepped onto the football field behind RRHS. Once upon a time, Amanda and I had sprinted across this field in a full-on zombie frenzy. That seemed like so long ago.

"We're fine. Safe," Cass said hurriedly, like she wanted to get off the subject. "How are you?"

The two syringes of the Kope Brothers' magical, slightly horrible mystery cure appeared in my hand. At first I tried to conceal them behind my back, but what was the point? I had to break the news sometime and considering the level of psychic oversharing I was prone to in here, I figured it'd be best to get on with it.

"I found the cure," I said, showing her the injectors, which in my dream space finally glowed. "Well, a sort of nice zombie warlord gave them to me. Except I didn't get enough and I don't know—"

Cass touched my arm, cutting me off. "Jake, it's okay. We'll figure something out. But right now we seriously need to get out of Iowa. Des Moines especially."

As we walked across the football field, I noticed storm clouds gathering over the end zone.

"Yeah, it sucks here," I replied, "but what's the hurry? I think I can still talk him into giving me another vial."

Cass shook her head. "No time. The NCD is coming. The army. It's going to be bad."

"Eh, Reggie said they've tried stuff before and—"

"It's not going to be like before," Cass insisted. "No more little squads running extractions. They're going to torch everyone and everything. Zombies, humans, probably anything with a heartbeat."

I smelled smoke. Barbecue smoke, like someone was cooking hamburgers and hot dogs, but the ominous kind!

"Okay, you're scaring me," I said.

"I'm back at Truncheon's garage," Cass replied. "Do you remember where that is? Can you make it to me?"

I blinked. "Wait. It's just you?"

"We have to get out," Cass said, ignoring me. "Like, right now."

I stopped in the middle of the field. "Uh, what aren't you telling me? What happened to Amanda?"

Cass stood in front of me and stared down at her feet. "I don't know how to tell you this."

"You said you guys were *safe*," I said, my voice rising with panic.

"She is safe," Cass replied. "She just, um, bailed."

"On you?"

"On *us*."

They appeared on the bleachers over Cass's shoulder. It was Amanda and that hunky head-wound guy we'd rescued from Truncheon's meat wagon. She had a blanket thrown over her shoulders and he had his arms around her and they were making out. I stared at this wide-eyed from the fifty-yard line until Cass tracked my gaze, turned around, and gasped. Immediately, Amanda and the Headwound Heartbreaker, as he'll one day be referred to in the death-metal song I write about him, blinked out of existence.

"Sorry, sorry," Cass said quickly. "You weren't supposed to see that. My subconscious must have—"

I cut her off. "That—that happened?"

Thunder pealed nearby.

Cass nodded solemnly. "That guy, Cody, he's a zombie now. They—I don't know, Jake—they hit it off, I guess."

"Oh," was about all I could muster.

"They drove off somewhere," Cass continued, even though I really wished she wouldn't. "I'm not sure where."

"We were in love," I said dumbly.

Cass gently patted me on the back. "I don't know what to say, Jake. I guess she changed her mind."

It felt like someone had pulled a chair out from under me and then broken that chair across my back. Part of me half suspected this would happen sooner or later—that Amanda would come to her senses, our whirlwind love affair written off as an unfortunate side effect of first turning undead. The other part of me—the apparently self-deluding part that believed it was possible to dig past superficialities and social statuses and get at something real—unfortunately, that's the part of my mind I'd been listening to.

"Did she say anything about me?" I asked Cass. "Did I—I don't know—do something wrong?"

"Um, I guess she just got tired of waiting," Cass replied, frowning. "You know how girls like that are."

The grass on the football field had turned brown and dead. A wintery wind carried in brittle leaves. From somewhere, the discordant electric-violin solo from Severed Lung's seminal breakup song "Sadness and Longing for the Rest of My Days (Until the Pavement Rushes Up to Meet Me)" jangled into my ears. So this is what happened in a lucid dream when you got really bummed out.

"Are you all right?" Cass asked, her head tilted, biting her lip.

"I'd like to wake up now," I said. "I don't want you in

my head right now."

"I know you're hurting," Cass said, touching my arm. "But will you still meet me at Truncheon's? We really do need to go, Jake."

I nodded. "Sure. What the hell."

Her smile was big and relieved, but she quickly toned it down.

"We can cure you," Cass said, trying to cheer me up. "And then, if you're still up for it, we can do the road-trip thing. I need to go to San Diego and you can come. Have you ever been to California?"

I shook my head. I kept glancing toward the bleachers, half expecting Amanda and Cody to reappear. Actually, if I focused on it, they did start to flicker back into existence. Except it was a slightly changed version: Cody was supermuscular, they made out with lots of tongue, and Amanda kept laughing cruelly in my direction.

Meanwhile, Cass started ticking off things on her fingers. "No more rotten smells. Fish tacos. Good music. Cowboy hats. I promise, Jake, I'll get you through this."

I glanced away from the bleachers. "Cass. I want to wake up."

My chest opened up like the trapdoor on a cuckoo clock and spit out my heart. It was all gray and shriveled and flopped around in the grass like a fish out of water. Cass and I both watched until it split open with a farting noise, the insides completely hollow.

"Wow," Cass said.

"Sorry," I replied. "Emo."

"No, I'm sorry," Cass said. "I shouldn't be, um, making plans right now. You need time."

I looked at her and tried for a casual shrug, but my shoulders were stuck in slouch mode. "It's okay. It's not your fault. Let's just get the hell out of this butthole state."

She stared at me for a second like she wanted to say something more, but whatever it was, she swallowed it. Instead, she went on her tippy-toes and kissed me on the cheek.

"Things will get better, I promise," she said.

I felt exhausted, which is a really incongruous feeling to have in the midst of a dream. I wanted to sink into that black, dreamless, nothingness part of sleep, turn my mind off, and not think about anything for a while.

I forced a smile for Cass, although being psychic I'm sure she could tell it wasn't the genuine article. "Yeah, so." I glanced down at my dead heart in the grass. "Let's, uh, forget the awkward parts of this happened and just say good-bye, okay?"

"Sure, Jake," Cass replied. "See you soon. And hurry."

The football field opened up beneath me and I plummeted into that deep sleep I'd yearned for.

CASS

GOOD EVENING, CLASS. TODAY AT THE DEADZONE
Academy for the Emotionally Stunted and Traumatized,
we'll be learning about fun concepts like *shades of gray*
and *the end justifies the means*.

After days of studying that road atlas looking for a
way into Iowa, I'd gotten a pretty firm grasp on which
rural routes and interstates led where. The roads were
mostly clear, and where they weren't, the cop car was
powerful enough to go over the shoulder and into the
fields, looping around the occasional overturned wreck.

I didn't see anyone else on my way. Well, I spotted some ghouls, staggering toward the noise of my engine, heads lolled miserably as they realized they'd never catch me. No real people, though.

I made it to Truncheon's in about two hours.

Since our last visit, a lone ghoul had stumbled into one of the bear traps that littered the parking lot outside the garage. He was dressed like a doctor: lab coat, stethoscope, the whole nine. The trap had sunk deep into his hamstring, tripped him, and left him sprawled on the pavement. A bunch of those cheap cherry lollipops pediatricians give you were scattered on the ground around him. When he caught sight of me, the ghoul started trying to army crawl in my direction. The trap was too heavy and his mostly decomposed limbs were too weak, so all he did was make a lot of scraping and gurgling sounds.

I stood next to the cop car and watched him for a few minutes. There was no human left in that ghoul. It was just an eating machine. It'd kill me or someone else if it got loose, or else it'd just struggle on miserably in the parking lot until whenever these things decomposed to dust.

Today was a day for personal improvement, I figured. I was done overthinking things, done grinding my teeth over the morality of every little decision, and done freezing up when something tried to eat me.

I found a cinder block around the corner of the

garage, carried it over to the ghoul, and dropped it on his head.

He was the first one I'd ever killed. I didn't feel any great change in me at the loss of my z-card. Putting down that ghoul seemed almost like a mercy. I wondered if all the hardened zombie killers, guys like Jamison and Truncheon, felt the same way with their first one and kept using that justification over and over. Whatever. I'd proved to myself that I could do it. That I could get my hands dirty.

All things considered, it wasn't even the worst thing I planned to do today.

All the entrances to Truncheon's lair were sealed with heavy-duty padlocks and the first-floor windows tightly boarded up. However, Truncheon hadn't bothered with the second floor over the garage. I guess ghouls couldn't jump that high, and if coherent zombies were on the prowl, you'd want the higher ground. If I could climb up onto the gas station's roof, I figured I could scout around for a door or, at worst, make it to one of the upstairs windows.

I parked the cop car right up against the front of the gas station and climbed on top of it. With a good jump, I was able to get hold of the gas station's sign and pull myself over to the building. I'd chosen the *E* in the creatively named GAS AND GARAGE because it made for a makeshift ladder. I tore open the knee of my jeans on the middle branch, but it didn't hurt so much.

After some pretty ungraceful climbing, I swung myself onto the building's roof. My sneakers stuck to the tarred surface. There were a ton of cigarette butts up here along with a rickety beach chair and an empty cooler. It looked like this was where Truncheon spent his free time. Across the roof, a door I was happy to find unlocked led inside the garage. I opened it cautiously, but to my surprise Truncheon hadn't booby-trapped the door with any bear traps or swinging axes or whatever. I guess he didn't expect anyone to make it this far.

Before going in, I paused to catch my breath. I felt a weird sense of pride at having climbed up on that roof; it felt good to do something purely physical. The sun had started going down and even though I didn't have much of a view, I took a moment to gaze out over the flatlands of Iowa.

Man, it sucked here. I couldn't wait to get the cure, save my mom, and get the hell out of Iowa. Kinda ironic, I guess, that I'd bailed on California to join the NCD, and now I was headed back there hoping to start a new life. One where zombie cheerleaders didn't make my life miserable; where the only guy I'd ever really liked wouldn't be obsessed with the most superficial human in existence. He wouldn't be undead anymore either, and I wouldn't be considered a weirdo freak by all who met me. Once I was in California, I could start over.

I touched my throat, where bruises had puffed up from when Amanda choked me. The ache reminded me of what I planned to do. I went inside.

I explored Truncheon's digs, but didn't find much of interest. He'd been living in the upstairs employee-break room, or at least that's where his flea-bitten and sweat-stained mattress sat. Loose ammunition and nudey magazines were pretty much the extent of his decoration. Down below, the garage itself stored his motorcycle and a Jeep. I found a hatch in the floor, which led down to a small basement, probably where the mechanics once stored spare parts. I didn't go down; just opening the hatch released a flood of pungent panic smells and I figured this was where Truncheon had been storing his "human currency." A different kind of spare parts, I guess.

"Hello?" I called down, and was relieved no one answered. Right then, I didn't want to be responsible for anyone but myself.

Truncheon had pretty thoroughly scavenged the adjoining gas station of anything edible. I poked around the dusty shelves, the day's dying light squeezing in between the narrow cracks in the windows' mismatched lumber barricades. Eventually, I found an unopened package of stale rice cakes. I picked away at them while exploring the little store's small back office. It was the cleanest place I'd found and seemed to carry the least amount of residual Truncheon, so I settled on it as my base of operations.

I thought about what Truncheon said before we'd gone into the Deadzone. He'd liked it in here; the lack of rules suited him. I wondered if maybe I was a person like that, just searching for an abandoned gas station in a derelict state to finally shuck off society's constraints and give in to my worst urges. Maybe that's how it was for everyone. Maybe that's why this whole zombie plague was allowed to get so out of control. Because we all wanted an excuse to eat one another.

I settled into the office's threadbare swivel chair and finished the rice cakes. Then, I closed my eyes and slipped out of my skin, onto the astral plane. It wouldn't be hard to find who I was looking for.

She was right where I'd left her.

It'd gotten dark when I finished rearranging things in Amanda's psyche. I'd felt such determination when I slipped into her mind, like with the ghoul in the parking lot. It was something that I had to do. It was impossible for me to turn back once I was in there, even if the content of her thoughts made me feel a little guilty, like I'd misjudged her.

But I had to save my mom. And if doing so meant prematurely ending what was obviously a doomed relationship, so be it. I'd crossed a line, but what choice did I have? She would have done the same thing to me.

Anyway, hadn't I gone easy on her? She'd eaten a lot of people. She ate Harlene and would've eaten Tom if I hadn't stopped her. They were the only family I'd had for the past few years. If I'd really wanted to, I probably could've made her forget how to walk. I could've blotted out the important parts from her memory just like Alastaire had done to my mom. But I didn't. Instead of some horrible fate, she got to fall in love with that beautiful, corn-fed mimbo. If only we were all so lucky.

Tactical Romantic Reassignment. That's what the NCD would call it.

Was I lying to myself by pretending this was a purely practical decision? Probably a little, but like I'd decided out in the parking lot, I was done agonizing over the ethics of the ex-NCD, blackmailed, fugitive, psychic, black-hat lifestyle. I wiped a trickle of blood from under my nose and shuddered at my own thoughts.

You've gone this far, might as well keep going.

"No, I'm sorry," I said, focusing hard so the guilt wouldn't leak through and spill like an oil slick all over the astral plane. "I shouldn't be, um, making plans right now. You need time."

Jake stared at me, looking like he might just fold in on himself.

"It's okay," he said. "It's not your fault."

I sunk down in the swivel chair beneath the weight

of a burgeoning migraine. My sinuses let loose a high-pitched, depressurizing whistle. I was going to feel like crap tomorrow morning. Even now, it was difficult to stay conscious.

I smiled.

Beyond the psychic fatigue, somehow, I felt loose and relaxed. How long had it been since I could picture a future for myself that wasn't entirely horrible?

As I began to drift off, I envisioned what was to come.

Tomorrow, Jake would bring me the cure. He'd use it on himself and never eat another person again.

We'd escape from Iowa and head west.

I wouldn't be alone anymore. We'd get to know each other for real.

If Alastaire wouldn't leave me alone after I brought him the cure, I'd find a way to kill him. I was stronger now and he had it coming.

I'd rescue my mom, no matter what. I loved her and didn't want to see her hurt, even if lately it felt like she belonged to a past life.

I wouldn't be staying home. Just visiting. I couldn't go back to life in San Diego, not after what I'd seen. Not when I was pretty sure the world was ending.

For however long we had left, Jake and I could go wherever.

We'd be free.

Here's where Tom would say something like, *You*

barely know each other, your relationship is imaginary, blah blah blah—but that wasn't so true anymore, and anyway it didn't matter. I'd seen into his mind and he'd seen into mine, admittedly to a lesser extent, and I knew it would work. We'd be good together.

And if you know something is good, what does it matter how it comes about? As long as the end result is worth it.

I was really knocked out. I didn't wake up when the Humvee pulled up outside. I didn't so much as stir while they set up a perimeter. The splintering wood as they smashed down Truncheon's barricade didn't even register.

I only became dimly aware that I wasn't alone when they shouldered through the office door. The flashlights mounted on the barrels of their assault rifles shone through my tightly closed eyes. I moaned and groped for a pillow to shove over my face, forgetting that I'd passed out sitting up. Forgetting, in fact, that I was in a very dangerous place.

"Point team, report," a demanding voice crackled over a walkie-talkie. "Is the asset secured?"

"Ten-four," replied the man standing in front of me. I hadn't opened my eyes yet. I didn't need to. "Asset secured."

The military had arrived in Iowa.

I didn't think they were going to shoot me. And

anyway, I was too telepathically spent to do anything about it. I decided the smart move was to play dead. It wasn't hard; I was slipping in and out of consciousness anyway. I drifted off to the stomping and jangling of men with guns coming and going.

It could've been minutes or it could've been hours, but eventually a cool hand came to gently rest on my forehead. A man's fingers brushed wild tangles of hair out of my face and started to carefully blot my nose and upper lip with a damp rag.

"Okay," a familiar voice whispered in my ear. "You're okay, Psychic Friend. I found you."

JAKE

"JAKE!" REGGIE SHOUTED RIGHT IN MY FACE. "JAKE! Wake up!"

It was just after dawn and Reggie was shaking my shoulders. I'd spent the night sprawled out on his couch, at first delightfully buzzed and then thunderously buzzkilled. I woke up with a giant knot in my stomach and an unmistakable urge to paint my nails black and listen to some of that '80s goth hate-yourself music. I wondered if Reggie had any The Cure records in his collection.

"Let me sleep," I groaned, squeezing my eyes shut. "Love is a lie."

"Huh?" Reggie replied, annoyed, and then punched me twice in the arm. "Get *up*, man. Jesus. Don't you hear that?"

I couldn't hear anything above Reggie's yelling in my face and/or the howling vortex where my heart used to be. I strained to listen.

Whup-whup-whup.

I opened my eyes. Oh, right. The army was coming.

Reggie stood over me wearing boxer shorts and a bulletproof vest. The Lord of Des Moines actually looked frightened.

"Helicopters," he said. "Like those Black Hawk joints from the movie."

I sat up, trying to figure out how to tell him I'd received advance warning of our impending strafing from a dream. "Yeah, uh, I think we're in trouble, dude—"

"No shit." Reggie stared at me. "The hell happened to you?"

I touched my nose and upper lip, both stiff with blood thanks to Cass's psychic visit. The couch was stained where I'd had my face too.

"My girlfriend dumped me via third-party telepathy," I explained. "Sorry about your couch."

Reggie looked at me like I'd gone crazy. "Fuck your girlfriend! Fuck the couch! I think we're under attack!"

"Yeah, she mentioned that too."

Reggie gaped at me for a moment, then charged toward the front door. I stumbled after him. He stopped to grab a second bulletproof vest out of a coat closet and shove it in my direction.

"Put that on," Reggie said.

I pulled it on over my head. It was a lot heavier than I expected.

"Don't you have anything that, like, shields our brains?" I asked.

"No," Reggie said. "Headshots are hard. They get you in center mass, though, you go all out-of-control wounded zombie, and pretty soon you're dead anyway."

"Oh," I replied. "I always go for headshots."

"*Call of Duty* isn't real life, bro."

We ran out the door and sprinted up the steps to the roof of Reggie's building.

This isn't a video game. I said that to myself a lot lately, especially since beginning my vacation in Des Moines, but it'd never been more appropriate than watching those insectoid-looking choppers crisscross the skyline. These weren't like the traffic copters I'd seen floating past my house at rush hour or even like the ominous black chopper that shadowed Amanda and me on that first day. (Agh! Memories! My heart!) They were like flying sharks, huge and fast, with missile teeth.

"They've been circling for fifteen minutes," Reggie

said. He'd produced a pair of binoculars and was peering through them. "They've never come at us like this before. I don't like it."

"Maybe they're just sightseeing," I suggested.

Above the constant *whup-whup-whup* came the sound of displaced air, a brief *shoom*, like a car whizzing by on the highway. A red flare broke off from one of the choppers, moving quickly, a shortly lived vapor trail like an accusing finger behind it.

And then a building downtown exploded. Even though we were a few miles off, the roof shook beneath us. The resounding *boom* rattled my back teeth.

"Or not," I said, my knees bent and ready to run.

Reggie didn't move except to lower the binoculars.

"They just hit the Ramada," he said. "Paradise lost."

Another missile from another helicopter. Another explosion. From our vantage point, I saw one of the skywalks crumble and collapse.

"Maybe we should get off the roof!" I yelled.

Reggie seemed dazed, so I grabbed him by the arm and dragged him toward the stairs.

"I always knew this day would come," Reggie said, pretty much forcing me to drag him along. "Well, I hoped maybe the government would collapse before they got around to wiping us out, but . . ."

I got us into the stairwell doorway because if it was safe in an earthquake, it should be safe during a missile strike, right? I grabbed Reggie's shoulders.

"So what's the plan?" I yelled to be heard over another *whoosh-boom*.

Reggie blinked. "Plan?"

"You're the Lord of Des Moines and your city is under attack!" I screamed. "You said you knew this was coming! Don't you have, like, a contingency plan?"

He seemed to come back to himself, the shock and awe wearing off.

"I do," Reggie said. "I have a plan."

I fist-pumped. "There we go! What is it?"

"Run like hell," he replied. "I'll go be the Lord of Denver or some shit."

"Good enough for me."

We booked it downstairs back into Reggie's apartment. The building shook with another nearby missile hit. Dust drifted down from the ceiling and a precarious stack of records toppled. They shouldn't have been piled up, anyway—bad for the vinyl. Reggie took the steps to the loft two at a time, disappeared for a moment, and then flung a backpack down to me.

"Grab whatever you want!" he yelled as he disappeared again. "What's mine is yours!"

I grabbed the bandana I'd wrapped around my two syringes of Kope Brothers Dezombifying Elixir and the dumb body spray I'd picked out for Amanda probably while she was erotically trampling our sacred bond with that Cro-Magnon hay-bale fetishist. I stuffed the little bundle of spurned good intentions into the pack. I scanned the room looking for other essentials. It was all crap, though. Nerd stuff. None of it useful in cases of aerial bombardment.

I wandered over to the capsized stack of records. Amid the swirl of colorful dust jackets and faded faces, something caught my eye. I felt a lurch in my stomach that was nonmissile related as I picked up the worn Frank Sinatra vinyl. The bony-faced old mobster dude stared up at me with his piercing blue eyes, reminding me of when Amanda and I had spun one of his records in a funeral home's basement.

I hoped she was all right and staying well clear of any missiles. And if she was out there, getting bombed in the less-fun sense, I wished it could have been me with her. It should've been, but I'd screwed up, stayed in Des Moines too long, blown it.

I sighed and shoved the album into my backpack because what the hell.

"Glad you've got your priorities straight," Reggie said, catching me in the act as he raced down from the loft. He had his own backpack pulled over his shoulders and held a heavy metallic carrying case that looked like something stolen from the army.

Reggie went to the fridge and grabbed his supply of drugged-out mice. I should've thought of that. He set down the case with a thud and emptied half of the mice into his backpack.

"Splitsies?" he asked, holding out the tray.

I held my backpack open so he could dump the rest in.

"What's that?" I asked, nudging the metal case with my foot.

"Bazooka."

"Get out."

Reggie grinned wildly at me. "I never realized how badly I wanted to shoot down a helicopter until right this second."

An explosion, this one closer than the others. Whatever strategy was dictating the choppers' bombardment targets, it was bringing them this way.

We ran for the door and blazed down the five flights of steps, leaping from landing to landing. Outside, the air smelled sharply of smoke and that poisonous dust that lurks in the bone marrow of buildings. I hadn't thought the air quality could get any worse, but the choppers proved me wrong. Towers of smoke from downtown explosions climbed into the early-morning sky. Luckily, Reggie's residential block was so far untouched.

"This way!" Reggie yelled.

We jogged instead of sprinted, not wanting to attract attention, ducking up against buildings whenever the ferocious *whup-whup-whup* got too close overhead. It didn't seem like they were targeting individuals—we passed plenty of ghouls wandering around unharmed when they would've made for easy prey. The choppers seemed intent on tearing down parts of the city where zombies had gathered en masse. They were stomping out anthills.

Reggie, in the lead, stopped suddenly. We ducked under the stone archway of a bank. Together, we watched a ghoul with his back consumed by flames wander through an intersection.

"I'm never playing another war game," I said.

"Were you serious before?" Reggie asked, setting down his bazooka case and flexing his sore hand. "About your girlfriend?"

I shrugged, not really wanting to get into my whole thing at that particular moment. It turned out death from above was a pretty good way to momentarily forget a broken heart. I wanted to keep running.

Reggie tried to look conciliatory, but did an altogether crappy job. He was actually smiling.

"You can come with me, Jake," he said. "We'll do it up road-gang style. Do you know how to ride a motorcycle?"

I shook my head. Reggie waved this complication away.

"You'll learn. It'll be some badass *Easy Rider*-bros-on-a-destructive-journey-across-the-country shit. You into that?"

"I'm . . ." I thought about Cass, waiting for me at Truncheon's auto shop. "I can't."

Reggie grimaced. "Still wanna do the whole human thing, huh?"

I shrugged and looked down at my soot-covered sneakers. I wasn't sure what I wanted to do anymore. I liked Reggie, but I didn't like Lord Wesley, and the two seemed pretty inseparable. It'd been fun getting sucked into an undead approximation of my old life. But those brief reprieves into normalcy were counterbalanced by some seriously out-of-control misanthropy. I didn't want to wear a leather vest, stage gladiator fights, or blow up helicopters. All of that would've seemed totally badass and amazing to me when I'd spent most of my time getting stoned and gaming in my basement, but something in me had changed during my time on the road with Amanda. I guess I'd grown up. Or something.

"I've gotta find my friend," I told him. "She's waiting for me out west. Off the interstate."

Reggie nodded and jerked his thumb left, around the corner. It was the opposite direction of all the destruction. "You want to go that way."

I squinted at him. "What about you?"

Reggie pointed in the other direction, toward the destroyed hotel.

"I'm gonna see if anyone's still alive," he said, seeming to come to this decision just now. "Maybe blow some shit up, in the spirit of the day. Then I'll head west too. Right behind you."

"All right," I said awkwardly.

"All right."

We slapped hands.

"Don't get killed," I told him.

"You either," he replied. "And I hope if I see you out there, I don't have to eat you."

I smirked. "Ditto."

And then the zombie warlord and I ran in opposite directions, both of us in pursuit of something we couldn't quite figure out, trying to escape this city before it crumbled for a second time.

I'd made it to a less-bombed part of Des Moines when destiny reared up before me in the shape of Kope Brothers Pharmaceuticals. I stopped the steady jog I'd kept up since leaving Reggie and stared up at the monolithic structure, this monument to corporate greed or capitalist neglect or free-market amorality or whatever the politics were. I didn't care about all that.

There were people inside that building. I'd felt hella lousy when I found out they were going to be zombie food and even worse now that it seemed like they'd eventually be buried alive by missile fire.

"Aww," I scolded myself. "No, Jake. Stupid idea."

I tried to just breeze on by, but I couldn't. Hadn't I

come to Des Moines with vague aspirations about heroic deeds and saving the world from a zombie plague? And yeah, it'd since boiled down to some bad decisions, horrific reality, and a small amount of chilling. Even so, wasn't I, like, morally responsible to save a bunch of people from certain death if it was within my power to do so? I mean, it seemed to me it was people shirking their responsibilities to one another that got us in this mess to begin with. That and unprotected sex.

I thought about Amanda and Cass. When we first got to Iowa, Amanda had almost gotten us killed because she disagreed with Truncheon's whole human-bartering plan. And Cass, she'd told a government agency to go screw because she didn't agree with their ethics. Maybe they were more alike than they realized.

I thought about my parents and sister. My dead friends. I tried to imagine anyone who wasn't a zombie despot yelling at me, *No, dude, don't run into that not-yet-but-probably-soon-to-be burning building.*

And I couldn't. So in I went.

Cass would understand if I was a little late getting out to Truncheon's garage.

The machine-gun-toting guards who'd greeted Reggie and me the day before had abandoned their posts, probably around the time the sky started falling. I ran across the lobby and then danced from foot to foot while waiting for the elevator, all keyed up with altruistic energy. Once inside, I punched in the key code to the subbasement I'd spied Reggie enter with my mad peeking skills.

Into the sterilized subbasement I went. I retraced my steps from last night—down a couple corridors, through a heavy-duty door—and quickly arrived in front of the cells packed with the dispirited people of Iowa.

They hardly noticed me. With the soundproofing down here, I doubted they even knew there were air strikes happening above us. I glanced over the panels of bulletproof glass that trapped them, looking for levers or switches or a PRESS HERE FOR FREEDOM button.

I didn't see any way to open the cells, so I knocked on the glass of the nearest one. The people trapped inside—mom, dad, and daughter by the way they shielded her—all fearfully shrank toward the cell's back wall.

"Uh, hey," I yelled through the little breathing holes in the glass. "Do you guys know how to open this thing?"

They stared at me.

"Oh, I'm not going to eat you," I clarified. "It's cool."

The parents exchanged a look. Shakily, the mother pointed down the hall.

I ran down the hallway in the direction she'd pointed. People were starting to gather at the front of their cells, sensing something was up. I tried to flash them reassuring smiles as I raced by, but then baring my teeth was probably ill advised.

I stopped in front of a door labeled CONTROL ROOM. Ah yeah, that made sense. Maybe I should've looked for that before scaring all those people.

Inside the control room was a bank of monitors, its cameras cycling through the dozens of cells, each feed ominously labeled with a number and CLINICAL TRIAL. Beneath the monitors were a whole shitload of buttons as well as a microphone for an intercom.

Without really thinking about it, I flipped the intercom's switch onto BROADCAST and pressed down the button.

"Um, hi, Iowans," I said, hearing my voice echo out in the hallway behind me. "So, I'm about to let you guys all go once I figure out which button to hit but, uh, it's pretty hairy outside, so fair warning. You might be in danger. Probably better than dying down here, though, huh? Although maybe you'll want to stay down here until they stop all the bombing? Anyway, the point is, you'll have the freedom to choose. Okay, here goes nothing. Oh, and if I, like, hit the sleeping-gas button or something by accident, which is totally possible considering my luck lately, uh, sorry in adva—"

I smelled cooked meat. That's the only thing that saved my hand from being chopped off because a second after I smelled him and spun around, Red Bear brought his tomahawk down on the intercom. Sparks flew out and a piercing shriek broadcast through the halls.

"Whoa!" I yelled, backing up along the control panel.

"What the fuck are you doing down here?" he snarled.

"What are *you* doing down here?" I countered.

He looked terrible. I mean, worse than usual. Red Bear had gotten scorched at some point. The burns on his shoulders and arms looked like the surface of a tar pit, pus bubbles oozing and cracking to expose mortified flesh. He had fresh blood around his snagglemouth, like he'd just eaten, but it still looked like he was just barely holding on from going full zombie.

"Safest place in the city," Red Bear said, waving his hatchet at the monitors. "And plenty of food."

Discreetly, I hit some random buttons on the control panel behind me. Nothing happened.

"Reggie down here with you?" Red Bear asked woozily, creeping closer to me.

"He left."

"Figures." He pounded the heel of his hand against his ear, like it was water-clogged. "Cheyenne's dead."

"Oh," I replied.

"I think she is anyhow," he continued, glaring at me. "You think we die when we get all blown apart? Or does the head just keep biting forever? Should I go find her head?"

"Uh. If you want. Yes. Go."

He ground the handle of his hatchet into the corner of his eye. "I loved her, man."

So, we'd both lost our ladies in the last twenty-four hours. I felt a sudden surge of sympathy for Red Bear. Stupid, yeah. But I unzipped my backpack and opened it for him.

"Taco mouse?" I offered.

Red Bear stared at me for a second. Then, he snatched the backpack away from me and whipped it against the wall. I heard something shatter.

"Dude, wha—ooof!"

He punched me hard in the stomach, right where the bulletproof vest stopped. As I doubled over, he brought his knee up hard into my forehead. I flopped onto my back, clutching my face.

He'd smashed the cure. I knew he'd smashed the cure.

"Why did *you* get to go upstairs?" Red Bear ranted. "I'd been running with him for a year and he never invited *me* up. I always had to use the fire escape. That shit hurt my feelings."

"Ugh," I groaned. I rolled over and crawled toward my backpack. My face hurt and I felt a distant bubbling in my stomach. Not good.

"You show up and ruin everyhurrrgghh—!" Red Bear convulsed behind me, the zombie in him shifting the balance against the raving sociopath.

I managed to reach my backpack and dig around inside. The bundle with the cure seemed to be intact. It was the Sinatra record that'd absorbed the impact, broken pieces shaking loose from the dust jacket.

I looked back at Red Bear. He was hunched over the control panel, gulping down deep, calming breaths. He caught me staring at him and kicked a desk chair over on top of me.

"I feel like killing you," he said, lisping through a buildup of saliva. "But I've got to eat first."

Red Bear hit a green button on the control panel—one button in a row of similar buttons—and, on the monitors, I saw one of the cells open up. The people inside looked too scared to leave, even after my totally chill announcement. Red Bear pushed off from the control panel and staggered toward the door.

"Hey, *Gene*," I said, getting his attention. I felt like if I could just distract him for a minute or two, he'd go full zombie and I could barricade him in an empty office without him trying to scalp me.

He spun toward me. "Red Bear. Not fu-fu-fu—not *Gene*."

"Were you always this nuts?" I asked him. "Or is it, like, a recent development? Did you dress up as an Indian for Halloween one year and the whole thing just stuck?"

Of course, my plan didn't account for any immediate scalping attempts.

With a feral scream, Red Bear dove on me. I managed to get my knees up and he landed on top of them, his hatchet scraping the ground next to my head. I grabbed his hatchet wrist and struggled to keep it from recoiling—he was strong, though, stronger than me. His foul-smelling spit dripped down through the open section of his cheek and onto my face.

"Kill you—!" he seethed, barely human.

With my free hand, I reached into my backpack, grabbed one of the broken record shards, and jammed it pointy end first into Red Bear's eye. He shrieked and rolled off me, grasping at his face.

"The way you look tonight, bitch!" I yelled, because one-liners.

Both of us got back to our feet at the same time. I was breathing heavily and Red Bear wasn't breathing at all. The triangle of record sticking out of his face was totally forgotten. He wasn't interested in me anymore, only in eating. He groaned and staggered toward the doorway.

Quickly, I ran my hand across the green door-open buttons like I was showing off on the piano. I could hear the cells outside hissing open simultaneously.

I managed to grab Red Bear around the waist just outside the control room. Down the hall, people had begun to nervously poke their heads out of cells. Seeing the fresh meat, Red Bear surged toward them, trying to shuck me off. I planted my feet and dug in, but he was a fighter.

"Run!" I yelled down the hall. "Run for your lives!"

From behind, powerful hands grabbed the scruff of

my neck and the seat of my pants, pulling me loose from Red Bear and tossing me easily aside. I hit the wall hard with my shoulder and slid down it.

"Oh shit," I said, staring up at Jamison, bandaged all up and down his arms and looking seriously cheesed off. When I'd released everyone down here, I'd kind of forgotten one of them was a hardened zombie slayer who bore a personal grudge against me. Oops.

For the moment, Jamison ignored me. He grabbed Red Bear by the back of his head. Red Bear flailed and twisted, trying to bite Jamison, but couldn't. With a grunt, Jamison slammed Red Bear face-first into the wall, driving the shard of vinyl the rest of the way through his eye and into his brain. Red Bear crumpled to the floor. For-real dead.

Jamison let loose a satisfied sigh. Then he turned to look down at me, the recognition plain on his face.

"You," he growled.

CASS

"HOW'D YOU FIND ME?"

Tom and I sat side by side on the sun-faded plastic chaise. If the day got just a little hotter, the rickety beach chair would start sticking to any exposed skin. For now, it was an altogether pleasant late morning here at the end of civilization, which I was enjoying from the roof of Truncheon's garage with the man who used to be my only friend in the world. I'd been properly awake for about fifteen minutes.

"I've been looking since last week," Tom replied, his

tone mildly scolding. "Thanks for knocking me out, by the way. That was a fun experience."

"Sorry."

"Mhm," Tom said, fussing with his shirt cuff. Somehow, he made a voyage into the Deadzone look fashionable; he wore a sleeveless quilted jacket over a plaid shirt that looked expensively rugged, perfectly broken-in blue jeans, and spotless hiking boots. I struggled to work a knot out of my tangled mop of long-unwashed hair.

From an army-issue rucksack, Tom produced a thermos and a pair of paper cups.

"You want?" he asked.

I nodded and Tom set about pouring us each a cup of coffee.

"Things got out of control back at that farmhouse," he said.

"I feel that way all the time now," I said. "Out of control."

Tom handed me a cup of coffee, and raised his own in my direction in a deadpan cheers.

"Welcome to adult life," he said.

I sipped the coffee and couldn't stop myself from a contented little rumble. It was the best thing I'd ingested in days. Even out here, Tom managed to make the best coffee. The pounding in my head eased back a smidgen.

"I don't blame you for doing what you had to do," Tom was saying. "Well, what you *thought* you had to do.

What you wanted to do. It was only slightly disconcerting waking up in the woods by myself, and the migraine went away eventually."

"Jeez, all right," I replied. "Easy on the guilt. I already feel like crap."

Tom reached over to squeeze the back of my neck, partly out of affection and partly like he wanted to strangle me. He sighed.

"So, how did I find you." He paused for a moment. "Well, I checked to see if you'd gone back home and—"

"Alastaire."

Tom nodded grimly.

"Is my mom all right?" I asked, feeling my grip tighten dangerously around my dainty coffee cup.

"Define *all right*," Tom replied. Realizing that maybe wasn't the most comforting answer, he revised. "She's fine, Cass. Unhurt. Just not totally with it."

Before I could ask a follow-up, the trio of NCD grunts who'd escorted Tom into the Deadzone came filing through the access door. Or were they army commandos? I couldn't really tell the difference anymore; the traditional NCD jumpsuit had a new camouflage print, their weapons looked lethal, and all of them had severe buzz cuts. Government boys, any way you sliced it. I recognized one of them as the young dope I'd ordered around when we crossed through the wall. He was very careful not to meet my eyes.

The soldiers all snapped off salutes. Tom stood up so he could awkwardly return them.

"We're needed elsewhere, sir," said the leader. "They're taking heavy losses in Cedar Rapids, and word is a chopper went down in Des Moines."

"Wow," Tom replied. "Okay?"

"Can you make it to the exfil point on your own?"

Tom glanced questioningly at me. I shrugged.

"I'll keep you safe," I told him with a forced smile.

"Don't forget to steer clear of other units," the leader added. "They haven't been briefed on your presence and mission parameters dictate—"

"Kill everything," I finished for him.

The soldier eyeballed me, but Tom jumped in quickly.

"We'll be fine," Tom said. "Be safe, guys."

The trio synchronized another set of hasty salutes, then hustled downstairs. Tom wandered over to the edge of the roof to watch the grunts pile into their Humvee. I joined him. One of the soldiers paused for a second to slap a corncob bumper sticker, found in large quantities downstairs, onto the back of the vehicle. Then he hooted excitedly and clamored in with his buddies.

"Did we just get ditched?" I asked him.

"I guess the chance to kill some actual zombies is more exciting than babysitting us," Tom replied.

I thought about Jake. It seemed so peaceful out here, but apparently there were aircraft crashing in Des

Moines. I hoped he was safe.

"Are they really . . . ?" I hesitated, watching the dust kicked up by the soldiers' squealing rear tires. "They're going to what? Gun down everything that moves?"

"Supposedly," Tom answered, shaking his head. "Seems like a disorganized mess to me. They had a bigger zombie-holocaust operation planned, but then Florida happened and—"

"Florida?"

"Oh right, you've been in here awhile." Tom tightened his lips and furrowed his eyebrows, his bad-news face. "There was a major outbreak there a couple days ago."

"How major?"

"All-over-the-news major. They're talking thousands."

"The news? What about Containment?"

Tom shook his head. "They're done with that."

I blinked. "Wow."

"Yeah," Tom said. "Anyway, forces are spread pretty thin. Between the army, the NCD, and every other government agency with initials, no one's really sure who's in charge. It's how Alastaire was able to get me hooked up with an army escort. Pulling strings while the world burns."

Pretty soon the Humvee was out of sight and a stillness settled around us. In the silence, I studied Tom's face. He hadn't been keeping up with his shaving, but otherwise looked unchanged. I felt comfortable around him, more centered, like the me of the last few days had just been a bad dream. Even so, I still wasn't sure I could trust him.

"So, you're working for *him* now?" I blurted.

Tom looked at me. "Aren't you?"

"Not by choice," I replied. "You know that."

"Yeah, well, me neither," Tom said, shooting me a meaningful look. "I'm still your guardian, Cass. That hasn't changed."

I smiled and leaned against him for a moment.

"So what? Did he come to you in a dream?"

Tom arched an eyebrow. "He can do that?"

I shrugged.

"Ew, no. We met in San Diego. He insisted on some cheapo Italian restaurant."

I shuddered. It was probably the same place I used to work. I hoped a roach crawled across Alastaire's spaghetti.

"You know he's missing half an arm?" Tom asked. When I nodded, he continued. "Anyhoo, he told me where I could find you. He said you'd be ready to leave today."

"He was right."

"And that your zombie boy would be bringing you a cure for the plague," Tom added, the skepticism rich in his voice.

I didn't say anything, just gazed off down the empty

road that led away from the motor garage.

"So it's true?" Tom persisted.

"Which part?"

"The cure?"

"Apparently."

"And your zombie boy?"

"He's not mine," I said, rolling my eyes. "We're just—it's complicated. Anyway, he won't be a zombie much longer."

"Huh," Tom said, that one syllable so laden with romantic judgment I almost dove off the roof. He still didn't approve, but I didn't care. He didn't know everything that'd happened. He didn't know Jake.

"Alastaire arranged an exit for us," Tom said. "They aren't letting anyone through that wall thing, obviously, but he'll have some of his people manning it tonight. We need to be on the road by sunset."

"Don't worry," I replied. "He'll be here by then."

Tom nodded, his smile shaky. "Can't wait to meet him. In a noncombat capacity."

We stood in silence for a while, watching the wind blow through the weeds and the sky stay blue and empty. I lay down on the chaise and Tom paced. After a while, we traded.

"So," Tom said. "What else have you been up to?"

I laughed; it was such a casual question. I tried to think of something I'd done over the last week that hadn't been awful. I thought of that hotel pool.

"I got drunk for the first time," I told him. "That was . . . different."

Tom clucked his tongue. "What a difference a week makes, Psychic Friend."

He was about to say something more when we heard the motorcycles. Both of us rushed back to the edge of the roof to squint down the road. They were still a ways off; we could only hear the jagged snarling of the engines and see a steadily advancing cloud of dust.

"Is that him?" Tom asked nervously.

I swallowed hard and leaned into my headache, the dull pain doubling into a murderous throb as I slipped my skin. I found Jake's mind easily enough, but could only manage to linger there for a moment—he was staring at a spotless expanse of bright, white tile and counting slowly backward from one thousand. What the hell did that mean?

Well, for starters, it meant he wasn't riding a motorcycle.

"Gah," I moaned, snapping back into my own body. Tom steadied me. I pinched the bridge of my nose. "Not him," I said.

"Crap," replied Tom.

The vehicles were in view now. Six motorcycles all mounted by gaunt shapes in various leather costumes, one with a flapping cape, another with huge football shoulder pads. They rode in ranks of three on either side of a Humvee. I couldn't see the Humvee's bumper, but I bet it bore a freshly applied corncob bumper sticker.

"The soldiers," Tom said hopefully.

"I don't think so," I said, touching his shoulder. "We should probably hide."

We ducked down behind the GAS AND GARAGE sign. From underneath his vest, Tom pulled out a shiny chrome handgun. I looked from the weapon to his face and he shrugged.

"After Illinois, I really started liking guns," he explained, frowning with embarrassment.

"Wow, things *have* changed," I replied.

Obviously, it was too much to hope for that whatever motorcycle gang had hijacked those soldiers' Humvee could just pass by without incident. They pulled into the gas station, cutting their engines in unison. I peeked over the edge of the building and watched as they started checking out the pumps. I couldn't hear what they were saying, but they sounded giddy and dangerous, like guys at my school used to sound in the lunchroom right before a fight broke out. Tom tugged at my sleeve.

"Stay down," he whispered urgently.

Too late for that.

"I see you up there," a youngish voice called from below. "You might as well come out and say hi."

My eyes widened. I looked at Tom.

"Damn," he whispered, and chambered a round.

"Heard that too," the voice called. "It's quiet as shit out here in the country."

Tom and I exchanged a look, then stood up together. He kept his gun low, next to his hip, ready to fire. Like an idiot, I'd left my stun gun downstairs somewhere. I'm not sure it would've even had the necessary range to hit the lanky guy with the unkempt Afro grinning up at us. I recognized him from Jake's head.

"Hiya," Reggie said, a malicious glint in his eye. "What you doing up there?"

"Leave us be," Tom said warningly.

The zombies behind Reggie snickered. They'd given up on the gas pumps and now made a loose half circle around their Lord, all of them glaring up at us. Some of them had guns of their own slung over their shoulders.

"Guy who used to live here would do me favors. He knew ways across the border," Reggie continued casually, like we were talking about the weather. "He around?"

"No," Tom said.

"Huh." Reggie folded his arms. "Can *you* do us any favors, man? Or should we just come up there and get on with it?"

I jumped in before Tom could reply or start shooting. "Cut it out, Reggie. We're waiting for Jake."

Reggie's eyes flicked to me. His smile changed into something a little less homicidally Cheshire.

"Get out," he said, more to himself than me. "So I get to meet the mutant after all. Small world!"

I bristled, but forced myself to wave. "Cass," I said.

"Yeah, cool," Reggie replied, appraising me. "You know, you should've come to Des Moines. I was going to convince you to be my psychic aide-de-camp. Would've even turned you to the good side. Could've been fun."

"Yeah," I replied dryly. "Sorry I missed that. Truly."

Reggie laughed. "I can see why he'd be into you. Sarcasm. The whole grunge thing. It's a good look."

I didn't have a *whole grunge thing* going, at least not purposely. I smoothed down my hair.

"He, um, said he was into me?"

Tom shot me a look like, *Really?* I shrugged. I was doing a lot better at not getting us eaten than he'd been.

"You, the hot one, I dunno," Reggie said, waving it all away. "You know, he left before I did. If he's not here yet, that doesn't bode well."

"He'll be here," I insisted.

Reggie smirked. "You better hope so. This friend-of-a-friend shit isn't going to fly with anyone else out on the roads today."

Reggie turned to his gang and made a spinning gesture with his finger. One by one, they begrudgingly stopped eyeballing me and Tom, and returned to their motorcycles. Reggie looked back at me.

"Hope it works out for you," he said. "If he's actually

alive, tell him I said what up."

As we watched the remnants of the Lord of Des Moines's zombie empire disappear over the horizon, Tom put a hand on my shoulder.

"That freak said . . ." He paused. "You're sure Jake's coming?"

"Yes," I replied. "I'm sure."

He didn't come.

The day wore on. Tom had packed sandwiches and individually wrapped servings of baby carrots. I ate my portion greedily, and perhaps fearing cannibalism of the more traditional stranded-somewhere-bad variety, Tom handed over half of his own.

"Do you still go into his head?" Tom asked me over lunch. "All the time?"

I shook my head. "I try not to. I want it to be real."

Tom nodded with the minimum amount of approval. "That's a step in the right direction, I guess."

Of course, I didn't tell him about what I'd done to Amanda. I'd felt so vindicated by it last night, like I was setting the world on its proper course. And yet today, I couldn't admit it to my closest confidant. What did that say about my decision making?

A little later, Tom nudged me. "Maybe it wouldn't hurt to check on him just this one time."

"My head hurts," I told him.

It did hurt, but not enough that I couldn't have checked in on Jake. The truth is, I didn't want to know. I didn't want to know for sure if he wasn't coming. I know I should've been worried about the cure—about saving the country, my mom, humanity—but I wasn't. In fact, I'd been totally at ease about that since I'd briefly jumped into Jake's mind before. I'd picked up something—an intuition, I guess—that made me sure the cure was going to be here.

I just wasn't sure about Jake.

It was late afternoon when the pair of school buses trundled down the road toward our gas station. It was such a strange sight, we forgot to even hide. If the zombies were using buses to escape from Iowa in large tour groups, well, they could just go right ahead and eat me, because the world was stupid.

The two buses pulled into the parking lot. They were packed with people. Not zombies. Real people. I'm not sure how I could tell—maybe the lack of crazy costumes—but more likely the ever-present fear on their faces, the tear streaks, the sticky, red cuts on their faces and hands.

The door of the lead bus opened and out stepped Jamison.

It was like a race between Tom and me to see who could make it to him first. I felt pretty lucky we didn't accidentally step in one of the bear traps scattered throughout the parking lot.

I won. I think I surprised the big brute with the force and velocity of my hug. I never thought that I'd see him again. I clung to his neck and squeezed, noticing too late the bandages all up his arms and shoulders. Jamison didn't seem to mind. He picked me up and squeezed back.

"It's all good," Jamison whispered, wiping tears off my face that I hadn't realized had shaken loose. "We're all good now."

"Wow," Tom said. "That's a much better reception than I got."

Tom and Jamison shook hands, then hugged awkwardly. At the buses, a few bedraggled folks were warily setting foot in the parking lot.

"He said you'd be here," Jamison said with a mix of admiration and surprise. "I didn't really believe him, but here you are."

"Who?" I asked, even though I already knew.

"The kid. Jake." Jamison nodded toward the buses. "He helped set these people free. Although I don't know where the hell we're gonna go next. Already had some bad run-ins with some soldiers—must've thought we were zombies." His look darkened. "I started out with three buses."

Tom patted Jamison's shoulder. "I've got us a way out," he said. "We can get them out of Iowa. After that, I think we're all pretty much on our own."

"What about Jake?" I butted in. "What happened to him?"

Jamison frowned, his face deeply lined, eyes cast down. I realized it was his sympathetic look. I'd never seen it before. My heart sank.

He walked back to the bus and retrieved a large metal safe from the space next to the driver's seat. Grunting as he lifted it, Jamison carried the box over to me.

"He helped me tear this out of the floor. Said to give it to you," Jamison said.

One corner of the safe had been sheared off during its removal, so I could see the contents within. Vials upon vials of Kope Juice, ready for injection, more than I could've hoped for.

"He also said to tell you he's sorry."

JAKE

I DIDN'T KNOW WHERE I WAS HEADED. I TRUDGED FOR-
ward, the toes of my sneakers darkening with dirt and
ash, one lace broken and untied, crusted with dried
blood.

Outside Des Moines, on one of the dusty rural routes
that twisted through emerald-green fields of corn, the
ghouls kept me company. I guess they still had enough
sense to flee the burning city. I came across one of the
bedraggled things every few miles, their wide, yellow
eyes always looking at me with disappointment. I'm sure

they would've appreciated me taking the cure. They were starving, and with just one quick injection I could've been fresh meat.

Plenty of practical reasons to remain a zombie. Plenty of moral reasons to turn back into a human.

I'd thought about my species conundrum a lot during my timeout in the Kope Brothers subbasement and hadn't come to any decision.

After I helped him pry Reggie's safe out of the floor (Red Bear's hatchet came in handy for leverage), Jamison told me to wait in the basement until he'd escorted the last Iowan topside, then to count backward from one thousand. After that, he said, I could do whatever I wanted, but if he saw me again, we'd have problems.

I listened. The counting was almost like meditating, except I kept losing my place whenever my brain skipped off on its own. I'm assuming that's what meditating is like anyway. I've never actually done it. I tried not to think about Amanda or Cass, but thinking about not thinking about them was basically the same as thinking about them. I tried to just clear my mind, but that made it really hard to count.

Anyway, I lingered in the deserted basement longer than a 1,000 count. It probably wasn't the worst idea to stay out of the carnage for a bit. Especially since I had no idea what to do next.

When I finally made it to zero, I left the emptied Kope

Brothers building behind and started walking. The helicopters were gone, but a sizable portion of Des Moines appeared to be on fire. The air stung to breathe and I kept getting flecks of ash in my eyes. I covered my mouth and nose with my T-shirt and kept downwind.

Besides getting the hell out of Des Moines, I didn't really have a destination in mind. That seemed okay.

I wasn't going to Truncheon's place. That much I knew for sure.

It wasn't fear of Jamison that stopped me from keeping my meeting with Cass. With his hand around my neck, I'd hurriedly explained to him how Cass and I were friends, how she was waiting for me, and how I knew where he could score a metric buttload of zombie cure. I guess that's when he decided not to bash my head in.

When I finished helping him with the safe and told Jamison *he* should be the one to go meet Cass, he gave me a look I'd only seen once before. It was at the grocery store when I ran into Mr. Tremens, father of my ex-girlfriend Sasha, approximately two weeks after we'd broken up. It was a look that managed to convey both *You're a dirtbag* and ask *What's wrong with my daughter?*

Point is, I think he would've been okay with taking me to meet Cass. I guess my recent Silver Star heroism outweighed his zombie prejudice. Temporarily, at least. Until I needed to eat again.

I conveniently left out that I possessed a couple vials

of Kope Brothers' No More Rotting Funtime Formula. I didn't want to answer any pesky questions from the zombie hunter about why I hadn't gone ahead and cured myself. He could go right on assuming I was Captain Altruism, saving edible prisoners and selflessly giving up my chance at restored humanity.

Hell, maybe I was Captain Altruism. I could be that guy, if I chose. The world—however much on fire it happened to be—was wide open. I wasn't sure what I wanted to do yet, but being Captain Altruism didn't seem so bad.

Except I'd need a cooler name. Something that could compete with whatever villainous alter ego Reggie settled on in his next city.

The King of Good Intentions and Broken Hearts. That could be me.

I had time to figure my alias out. It was a long walk out of Iowa.

At scattered intervals, big, canvas-covered military trucks and some blocky Humvees zipped up and down the road. I made sure to duck into the corn whenever I heard one coming. Once, I watched from between the stalks as they slowed down just long enough to blow the head off a ghoul greeting them with grasping arms. I knew I didn't want to be seen.

Other things I knew:

I couldn't be with Cass. Not right now anyway. I'd thought a lot about that dream we shared and admitted to myself that her whole plan sounded pretty incredible. Sunshine, fish tacos, all that shit. And she liked me. She gazed into my mess of a mind and still decided she wanted me.

But I knew hardly anything about her. The gap between us seemed unfair. I hadn't gone rummaging through the secret drawers of *her* mind and I didn't want to. Because weren't we more than the sum of our thoughts? Didn't action count for something? The me that she wanted, assembled by whatever notions and private thoughts of mine she'd spied on, he didn't really exist except in the space between our brains. Whatever thoughts of mine she'd gotten attached to, they were post-zombie thoughts. The guy she liked hadn't existed two weeks ago and he probably wouldn't exist two weeks from now.

No. It was too complicated. It made my head hurt.

I missed Amanda. That I knew for sure.

I missed the impossibly consistent fruity smell of her hair. I missed the mean way she talked, especially when I could tell it was just a put-on. I missed the way she smiled at me when she didn't think I was looking.

We knew each other, for real. We'd shared something. We'd grown together. It'd been special. Or at least I thought it had.

I pictured her making out with that cow-milking lothario—an image burned into my mind courtesy of Cass, I realized—and my stomach went into a tumble-dry motion that rivaled the quaking pangs of zombie hunger.

I decided that I'd walk until this feeling went away.

I heard a vehicle coming and ducked into the corn to hide. It wasn't soldiers, though. The brakes were way too squeaky and there wasn't any clanking of military-grade metal plating. I inched forward in time to make out the familiar dents in the passenger side as the Maroon Marauder slowly drove by, bound for Des Moines.

I hesitated. What was I going to do? Run into the road and wave my arms, make a big scene, and get dumped again in person? No thanks.

Before I could even successfully choose inactivity, the car stopped a few yards up the road and Amanda practically leapt out of the passenger seat. She cupped her hands around her mouth and yelled.

"JAKE! JAKE? ARE YOU OUT HERE?"

I stayed put and watched. She couldn't possibly have seen me while driving by. Did she sense me? Was our connection that deep? She looked exhausted with worry. I noticed some new dings in the back and sides of the car too. They looked like bullet holes.

I was about to show myself when Cody stood up from the driver's seat, nearly as broad-shouldered and good-looking as I'd built him up in my imagination.

"Mands," he said. "Come on. He's not out here and it isn't safe. I'm not sure how many times I can outdrive these soldier guys."

"Shut it, you," Amanda snapped, shading her eyes and looking around. "We need to find him."

"Okay, okay," Cody said pacifyingly. "Gosh, though, I guess I don't really understand why."

"Because I *want* to, okay?" Amanda hissed at him.

I'd eavesdropped enough. I stepped out of the corn. Cody saw me first and pointed.

"Hey, is it this guy?" he asked.

"Booya," I said, and immediately regretted not coming up with a better line while hiding in the corn.

Amanda didn't seem to care. She rushed toward me and wrapped me in a hug that was really difficult for me not to reciprocate.

"Jake! I knew you'd be here!" Amanda exclaimed against my ear. "I, like, felt it in my bones!"

"Uh-huh," I said.

She touched the front of my bulletproof vest with her fingers, eyebrows raised. "Um, this is pretty hot."

I stepped back from her. "Who's your friend?"

Amanda looked at me strangely, hurt that I'd kept my hands to myself. She lowered her voice so Cody couldn't hear. "Okay, we, um, have to talk, but—"

Cody raised his hand in greeting. "Hi, Jake. I'm Cody."

"I know who you are!" I screamed at him.

"Oh." He looked baffled by the hostility. "You asked."

"You looked better with a potato sack over your stupid face!" I yelled at him. "Dick! Fuckhead! Home-wrecker!"

"Oh my god," Amanda said, her eyes wide with a mixture of surprise and embarrassment. The embarrassment was for me, I realized. "Jake, calm down—"

I turned to her. "Why are you even out here looking for me? Aren't you hooking up with this guy now? You want to rub it in my face?"

"Hooking up? Ugh, it was, like, second base one time and I don't even know why—" Amanda rubbed her temples like she had a headache. "How do you even know?"

"Were we planning on keeping it from him?" Cody asked Amanda, confused. "Jeez, are you two an item?"

"Cass told me," I said to Amanda, ignoring Cody. "She *showed* me."

"Showed you?" Amanda looked mortified. "How the hell does that work? She'd already taken off."

My brow furrowed. I thought back to our astral-plane conversation the night before. In Cass's version, it was Amanda who did the taking off.

Meanwhile, it was Cody's turn to look hurt.

"I thought we had something special," he said to Amanda, taking a few steps toward us. "New, but special."

Amanda turned to him. "We *do*," she insisted. "Well, we did."

Whatever connection I'd been making about Cass was crushed beneath a new surge of wounded pride. "You *do*?"

"Yes, no, I don't know." Amanda ran both her hands through her hair and held them there, ready to pull out a couple handfuls. "It's weird and complicated and I don't know what I'm feeling."

"Do you still love me?" I asked her.

"Yes," Amanda answered without hesitation, teary eyes looking right into mine. "Although you are seriously pissing me off right now."

Cody cleared his throat. "What about us?"

Amanda stomped her foot. "Can we *please* just sort this out where there aren't soldiers shooting everything that moves?"

"Amanda's right," Cody said, giving me a look. "This is very high school."

"I'd like to duel you," I replied, staring him down. "I'd like to find some pistols and fucking duel you."

Cody started to laugh like I was goofing around, but cut it off abruptly when he noticed the intensity of my glare.

Or maybe because he noticed the Humvee careening down the road toward us. A soldier leaned out the window with an AK-47.

"Run!" Cody yelled, as if we weren't already.

The three of us took off for the corn. Amanda grabbed my hand and Cody grabbed hers and for a moment we made for a sprinting zombie chain. But then my grip slipped and Amanda stumbled toward Cody and the soldier started strafing the cornfield.

An ear exploded right next to my head, flecking my face with kernel shrapnel. Then it felt like an anvil hit me between the shoulder blades. I hurtled forward, onto my belly, and barely managed to cover my head. My body felt crushed.

The shooting kept on for a solid minute as the Humvee crawled slowly down the road. Once the bullets finally stopped, I lay on my face for another minute, unmoving, my ears ringing. I wheezed and coughed. It felt like a vise had been clamped around my chest. I covered my mouth with both hands, trying to stay quiet.

When no zombies came stumbling out of the cornfield with fresh bullet wounds and insatiable hunger, I guess the soldiers figured us for dead. They didn't bother to stop and check the cornfield for our bodies. They had other things to do, more citizens to gun down.

I listened to the Humvee pull away. When I was sure they were gone, I rolled over and quickly unbuckled the straps of my vest. I tore it off and could immediately breathe again. The two slugs that would've lodged in my spinal column gleamed in the sunlight.

Thanks, Reggie.

I stood up, shaking loose the cob chunks and sliced pieces of husk that were stuck to me.

"Amanda?" I called quietly. "You okay?"

A sob answered.

I shoved through the corn in the direction of the crying, not caring that the leaves were sharp and that the stalks liked to smack me right in the face. I didn't care because it wasn't Amanda crying. It was Cody.

I found them a few yards away. Cody kneeled over Amanda's body and practically convulsed with tears. He didn't look hurt. Not that I gave a shit. He heard me come crashing into his area and stared up at me.

"She—she didn't get down," he stammered. "She tried to run toward you."

The gunfire had cut Amanda almost in half. She was perforated. Organs the color and consistency of porridge spilled out into the dirt. She moaned wetly, like one of the worst ghouls back in Des Moines. Her empty eyes turned toward the road and she started trying to drag herself in that direction, her arms working but not her legs. When she did, her body made a slimy *shhhlick* sound and began to pull apart at the midsection.

"Fuck, dude!" I screamed at Cody. "Don't let her do that!"

Startled out of his tears, Cody threw himself on top

of Amanda. He pinned her down so that she couldn't split herself in half.

"What do we do?" he begged. "What do we do?"

I knelt down next to them and started—I don't know—shoving things back inside her. Once I'd gotten everything, my hands slick with the oily mess, I scrambled around to Amanda's feet and pushed her body up, trying to get the two halves of her as close together as possible. Maybe if I mushed her into one piece, she'd heal.

"Is this going to work?" Cody asked.

"I don't know," I growled. "Shut up and hold her."

I opened my pack and started scooping out the taco mice. One by one I lowered them into Amanda's snapping mouth. She crunched through them like they were nothing, thrashing continuously against Cody's arms, arching her torso in a grotesquely acrobatic way to swallow the meat.

I kept an eye on her abdomen. It definitely wasn't returning to perfect, smooth, and lightly tanned, but I got the sense that her flesh was becoming a little more solid. A little less likely to fall apart if we moved her.

But then I was out of mice.

"Is that it?" Cody asked.

I nodded. "Yeah."

"She's not much better."

I squeezed my eyes shut. "No."

"We've got some guinea pigs in the car," Cody

offered. "I can get them."

I nodded. "You should do that. I'll hold her."

We got close together in order to trade positions and that's when I jabbed the syringe of Kope Juice into Cody's neck.

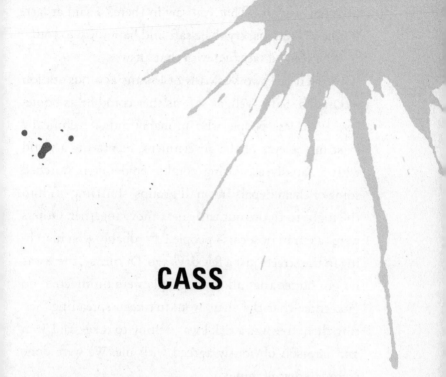

CASS

ON THE SCHOOL BUS, ONCE WE'D MADE IT THROUGH the wall and were able to stop holding our breath, a grandmotherly lady hugging a sleeping child who didn't resemble her in the least turned to me.

"What are we supposed to do now?" she asked.

I guess she assumed I was some kind of authority because I'd been hanging around with Jamison and Tom. I wasn't. None of us were. We were in the zombie-killing business, which rarely overlapped with the people-saving business. I thought about my answer for a full minute.

"Tell everyone what you saw in there," I said at last. "Or don't, and just try to be safe and happy. Up to you."

She seemed satisfied with that answer.

We left the two busloads of Iowans at a bus station in Omaha. Safe. Well, as safe as they could be as homeless, penniless people who probably didn't technically exist in the eyes of the government, reentering a world with a rapidly escalating zombie epidemic. I watched some of them depart in small groups, shuffling off into the night to figure out their next move together. Others were taken in by locals—people I'd probably seen marching in the streets just a few days ago. Of course, there was no guarantee that all these people were uninfected; no guarantee that the virus wouldn't keep spreading. Setting them free was a risk I was willing to take—and Tom and Jamison obviously agreed with me. We were done trying to *control* things.

Maybe I'd been wrong that everyone just wanted an excuse to metaphorically—and sometimes literally—eat one another. No, not maybe. I'd definitely been wrong. There were still people out there who cared about strangers, and not in that fake NCD way where protecting civilians was just a front for something ugly and wrong. For all the crap I'd been through in the last couple weeks, for all the less than virtuous and sort of selfish stuff I'd done, I'd finally accomplished something unequivocally good.

Well, anyway, I'd ridden on a bus with some people Jamison saved. So maybe it was a baby step. But there was still time to be one of the good guys, one of the people I'd thought I could be when I signed up for the NCD. There was still time to get myself together.

I wouldn't be buying a new black hat.

Back at the wall, Jamison had commandeered a black SUV, just like the ones we used to take on missions. The four of us drove west in that: me, Jamison, Tom, and the one refugee we didn't cut loose. Jamison said he'd found the bearded, crazy-haired old man in the Kope Brothers subbasement hooked up to life support. Jamison didn't expect for him to make it long, yet disconnected from his machines the stubborn old goat just refused to keel over. The old man wouldn't wake up, but his breathing seemed steady and he was completely capable of producing a consistent stream of drool. Of course I knew exactly who he was, even without the skateboarding bulldogs. When I told Tom and Jamison his identity, they decided we better keep him.

So, the Grandfather, aka Dr. Nelson Fair, rode in the backseat with me. That pungent hospital aroma wafted around him, but I didn't mind so much. It was a vast improvement over the stench of Iowa.

Jamison played with the SUV's radio, skipping quickly between stations. Reports were coming in from all over about undead attacks. There were frantic transmissions of widespread cannibalism in southern Florida and stories about similar violence in every corner of the country. The NCD had completely lost their grip.

Eventually, Tom reached over and turned off the news. Jamison glanced at him, frowning, but Tom gave him a look like, *Enough is enough,* and we drove on in silence.

Night had fallen and the prairie outside my tinted window looked deep blue and lonely. Out here, you couldn't tell that everything was falling apart. It was peaceful. I rested my head against the cool window and closed my eyes.

Selfishly, I wished that I was making this drive with Jake. I didn't blame him for not coming to find me, though. Those last couple days in Iowa, I'd turned into something I didn't like. I couldn't set right what I'd done to Amanda, but I could at least try to be better. For starters, I could stop living in other people's heads and spend more time working on my own.

With that in mind, I slipped out of my skin and onto the astral plane and . . .

Flopped down on my couch in San Diego.

Alastaire, or his psychic projection anyway, stood next to the fireplace, admiring the photographs on the mantel. He pretended to be surprised to see me, as if he hadn't felt me coming. With an approving smile, he broke into a slow clap.

"Well done, Cassandra," he said. "Well done."

I settled back into the couch. It was just as comfortable as I remembered it.

"Do you miss doing that in real life?" I asked him. "Clapping?"

Alastaire stopped. He pushed his glasses up with his forefinger, an unnecessary gesture in here, one that meant he was trying to control his temper.

"I'm on my way," I told him. "I've got a whole case of the cure and I've got Doctor Fair."

"I know," he replied.

"It's not too late, is it?"

He shook his head. "Of course not, dear. Your mother is fine."

"Well, that's good to hear and lucky for you, but I meant for the world," I clarified. "It isn't too late for us to fix things in the world, is it?"

Alastaire smiled at my bluster. "No. We're going to be *heroes*, Cassandra."

I rolled my eyes at him. "What's your definition of *hero*, Al? The weasel left standing when everyone else is dead?"

"And here I thought you were beginning to understand pragmatism," Alastaire replied. He picked up a picture from the mantel. In it, Cody and Amanda embraced under a sleeping bag. "I saw what you did to that girl, Cassandra. It was *impressive*."

I looked away. Alastaire's approval drove home just how badly I'd screwed up.

"Then did you see what I did after?" I asked. "How I showed her where to find Jake?"

Alastaire sat down on the couch next to me and patted my leg. "Such a conflicted young thing. One day, you'll understand. *We* know so much more than *them*. Therefore, why shouldn't we be the ones making the decisions? Even, as in your case, the silly, inconsequential ones."

I grimaced. What he said was dangerously close to my own justifications back in Iowa. I didn't want to think that way, not anymore.

"How's all that working for you?" I asked, gathering myself. "Making a lot of decisions while you hide at my mom's house?"

He rolled his shoulders. "Touché."

"Maybe ask the NCD how that whole *control* thing is working for them too," I continued. "Nah. I think we're done with trying to control things. I've got a cure for the undead and you're going to help me get it out there. We're going to heal people because it's right. Not because we want something in return or to better the standing of psychics or to turn a profit. And you're going to fix my mom too. Got it?"

Alastaire smiled at me indulgently. "What if we should have, shall we call them, philosophical differences?"

This time, I reached out and patted his leg.

"Then like any old, outdated idea," I said, smiling, "something new is going to come along and stamp you out."

JAKE

WE CLIMBED UP THE WATER TOWER'S LADDER IN THE
dark. Hand over hand, rung after rung, until we were
100 feet up over the darkened state of Iowa. We were in
some abandoned suburb in the southwest. We figured it
was better not to sleep in the car, just in case some trig-
ger-happy patrol should drive by. And anyway, I'd wanted
to climb a water tower ever since I saw those pothead kids
do it on that sitcom.

We sat next to each other with our legs dangling off
the catwalk. From up here, Iowa looked like a patchwork

blanket, farms and houses neatly sectioned off, divided up by those goddamn cornfields. On the horizon, we could see triangles of flickering orange light. Fires.

Amanda made a hiccupping sound like she was trying not to cry. She'd been making that sound a lot since she came back from the undead. She'd also been rubbing her stomach a lot, maybe imagining the horrible wounds she'd suffered and maybe imagining the dude I'd fed her to heal them.

"Do you want to talk about it?" I asked quietly.

She grasped the railing in front of us and squeezed tight. "I—I hardly even knew him," she whispered. "I don't know why I feel this way. . . ."

She trailed off. I didn't press her.

"Something came over me," she continued eventually. "Maybe I was lonely or scared or desperate. I don't know. I just needed him. It was like, um, love at first sight or something."

I cringed and rested my head against the railing. After a second, Amanda rubbed my back.

"I'm sorry," she said. "I never stopped—I mean, Jake, I still wanted to be with you the whole time. It didn't make sense."

"You loved us both," I said, my voice cracking stupidly with the effort I was putting in to keeping it level.

"I guess," Amanda said, "but, um, differently somehow. I hardly knew him."

"You hardly knew me when we started."

"I knew *of* you."

"We didn't have love at first sight."

"No, idiot," Amanda said, and I think she smiled in the dark. "You wore me down."

She rested her head on my shoulder. Carefully, I put my arm around her. It was the first time we'd really touched since I was shoving all her guts back into her body.

"I'm sorry I made you eat him," I said after a while.

"It's okay. You saved my life. Or, I guess my unlife. And I mean, I'm sad about him. But I'm glad it was him instead of you." Amanda knuckled her forehead. "God, my head is so messed up. What is wrong with me?"

I had a feeling I knew, but didn't say anything. For now, I'd keep that broken promise to myself.

"I still want to be with you," I said.

"Me too," Amanda replied. She smiled up at me. "I didn't know you were the jealous type, Stephens."

"Does it really count as jealousy if you actually make out with another guy?"

"Eh. Gray area. Maybe don't ditch me again."

"Sorry," I said. "It was really shitty without you, by the way."

"Good."

We kissed then. Slow and gentle, but when I tried to pull away, Amanda sucked on my bottom lip and wouldn't let me go, so we kissed some more. We kissed until she hiccupped again and broke away to wipe her eyes.

We sat quietly for a while and watched the horizon burn. Eventually, I opened up my backpack and unrolled the bandana. In the dark, I handed Amanda the little bottle of body spray I'd stolen from the mall.

"I got this for you," I said.

She laughed, easy and surprised, and sprayed a little bit in the air. It was a vast improvement over the heinous combination of fire and rot.

"Thanks," she replied, and squeezed me.

"I got you a record too," I continued. "But it broke and I had to use it to stab Red Bear in the eye."

"Wow. Crazy day."

"Yeah."

There was just one last thing left in my bag. I pulled out the remaining syringe of Kope Brothers Un-Undead Super Serum. It glistened with significance in the moonlight, or maybe that was just my imagination.

I tried to hand it to Amanda, but she shoved my hand away.

"No," she said, shaking her head. "You should."

"I won't," I replied. "Not without you."

"That's stupid," she said. "Stop being all fucking chivalrous and do what we came here for, Jake."

"You stop being all whatever girl-chivalrous is," I retorted.

She sighed. Both of us stared down at the syringe in

my hand. Amanda pushed a hand through her hair and looked me in the eye.

"If—if I hadn't gotten shot, if you hadn't—hadn't used that one on Cody to save me," she said shakily, "we could be human right now. It's my fault. You shouldn't have to save me twice in one day. It's ridiculous."

"No way," I said. "It's not your fault at all."

Because it wasn't. There were other forces at work here. Other reasons why everything had gotten so screwed up.

Sensing me tense up next to her, Amanda ran her hand across my mohawk. She touched her forehead to mine.

"I don't mind staying this way with you," she said. "It's not so bad."

I knew she was lying. I pictured her crying in that hotel room when I'd mistakenly yanked out a chunk of her hair. Amanda wanted to be human again more than I did. The last couple weeks had worn her down and today was the worst day yet. And she was lying to me, for my benefit, willing to keep living this miserable existence so that I didn't have to go it alone.

It made me furious, but not at her.

"There's another way," I said. "I know where we can find more."

Amanda leaned back, searching my face to make sure I wasn't joking.

"Where?"

I pictured it. Sunshine, fish tacos, psychic manipulation.

"Out there," I said through gritted teeth, keeping it vague. "Back over the wall. West."

Amanda was quiet for a moment. "You gave some to *her*, didn't you?"

I nodded. On the horizon, something huge exploded, a rippling ball of fire rising into the night sky. The force of the blast reached us a second later, the rusty struts of the water tower creaking.

"World's ending," I observed.

"I'm not sure we could make it back to the wall," Amanda said. "Not sure we could make it over."

"We could hunt down some of those soldiers," I suggested. "Figure out how to dodge machine-gun fire this time."

Amanda smiled sadly. "Let's just sit awhile longer."

We both fell silent, the reality sinking in that this night on the water tower might be it. That we were just two rumbling stomachs away from not being us anymore. We didn't move, though. I think both of us realized that maybe enough was enough—there was only so much highway you could travel, so many people you could eat, before it was time to call it quits.

Amanda reached across me for the backpack and for a moment I thought maybe she'd had a change of heart, that maybe she wanted to take the cure after all. Instead of the Kope Juice, she took out the T-shirt it'd been wrapped in and tore off a strip from the bottom.

"Give me your arm," she ordered.

I did as I was told and Amanda carefully looped the strip of fabric around our wrists, binding us together.

"In case we turn, this will keep us together," she explained. "Those ghouls seem so lonely. I don't want to be like that."

I smiled and squeezed her hand.

"Okay, but it's going to make it really hard for us to climb down the ladder."

Amanda snorted. "If that's what we decide to do."

"Yeah," I replied. "If."

Amanda put her head on my shoulder, and together we watched the fires gutter and wink in the distance. Pretty soon we'd have to definitively decide the great zombie debate of the modern era: Which is better? Fast zombies that charge relentlessly toward their next meal, or slow, shambling hordes that stick together in undeath because it'd be too unbearable not to?

Pretty soon, but not just yet. For a little while longer, we could just be ourselves. The living dead, living it up.

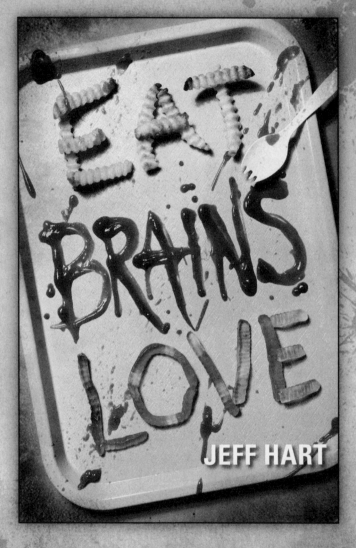

n love. On the run. Undead.

JEFF HART

See where Jake and Amanda's zombie road trip began.